Praise for the novels of
SHARON SALA

"Veteran romance writer Sala lives up to her
reputation with this well-crafted thriller."
—*Publishers Weekly* on *Remember Me*

"Chilling and relentless..."
—*Romantic Times BOOKreviews* on *The Chosen*

"Wear a corset, because your sides will hurt from
laughing! This is Sharon Sala at top form. You're going
to love this touching and memorable book."
—*New York Times* bestselling author
Debbie Macomber on *Whippoorwill*

"[A] rare ability to bring powerful and emotionally
wrenching stories to life."
—*Romantic Times BOOKreviews*

"Perfect entertainment for those looking for a
suspense novel with emotional intensity."
—*Publishers Weekly* on *Out of the Dark*

"...knows just how to steep the fires of romance
to the gratification of her readers."
—*Romantic Times BOOKreviews*

"Sharon Sala masterfully manages to get
deeply into her characters."
—*Romantic Times BOOKreviews*

SHARON
SALA

NINE
LIVES

MIRA®

ISBN-13: 978-0-7783-2352-5
ISBN-10:   0-7783-2352-8

NINE LIVES

Copyright © 2006 by Sharon Sala.

www.MIRABooks.com

Printed in U.S.A.

For Bobby

You taught me how to enjoy life to the fullest.
Now I'm having to learn how to live it without you.

One

It was December in Dallas, Texas.

Cat Dupree hated winter and all that came with it. The weather made for miserable stakeouts, although stakeouts were a part of a bounty hunter's life. The time of year only added to the chip she carried on her shoulder and reminded her of all she'd lost.

When she was six, she and her mother had been shopping for groceries when they'd been hit by a drunk driver. It had killed her mother instantly and put Cat in the hospital for days. When she was finally dismissed, her mother's funeral was over, and she and her father were on their own.

Over the years, she learned to adjust, and she and her father grew closer. Then, just before her thirteenth birthday, and only days before she and her father were planning to leave on vacation, a man with a tattooed face broke into their house, stabbed her father and cut her throat, leaving her unable to scream as she watched him die.

After that, the Texas Social Services system finished the raising of Catherine Dupree, during which time she'd acquired the nickname Cat.

Being a bounty hunter had been a job she'd thought about during those long years. What better way to find her father's killer than to work in his world? At eighteen, she'd aged out of the system, then, two months later, gone to work for a bail-bondsman named Art Ball.

Art had been taken with the dark-haired, leggy teenager, and hired her to file and deliver papers to the courthouse, even though he hadn't needed the extra help. But, he would say later, it was the smartest thing he'd ever done. By the time she turned twenty-one, she had a black belt in Karate, was licensed to carry a firearm and had gone through several kinds of schooling to learn private investigation techniques, as well as the ins and outs of bringing home bail jumpers.

Also during that time, she began accumulating mug shots of perps with tattoos on their faces in hopes of finding her father's killer. She'd been looking for him ever since, and often thought it strange that a man with such markings was so difficult to find. Logically, one would have assumed that a man with the equivalent of a road map on his face should stand out in any crowd.

Every time she left to go after someone who'd jumped bail, Art would tell her to be careful. He would add to that by reminding her that she didn't have nine lives left like the cats who hung out in the alley behind the bail bond office, because she'd already used up two.

The ensuing years and her cold-blooded determination had given her a hard-nosed and enviable reputation. The fact that she was tall and, in many men's eyes, very beautiful didn't matter to her. She'd grown up fast, with a whiskey-rough voice and a bad attitude. She had a fine set of boobs, which she didn't consider an asset. They were, however, nicely distracting to the men she went after. Most of the time they were looking elsewhere when she threw the first punch.

Such, she was certain, was going to be the case today for bail jumper Nelson Brownlee. Following up on a tip, Cat had located Brownlee at an old apartment building in Fort Worth. Now all she had to do was take him down and bring him in.

Nelson Brownlee was a four-time loser with a penchant for armed robbery. He'd promised himself the last time he'd been released that he was going to move back to Michigan, but Nelson had never been good at keeping promises, even to himself. All the way to the Quick Stop, he'd been thinking something didn't feel right. Still, he'd ignored his instincts, robbed the store and then gotten himself caught on his way out the door by an off-duty cop. He figured it had served him right and never dreamed he would be able to bond out. But he had. He'd taken it as a sign from God to change his ways.

However, he and God had never been on very good speaking terms, and instead of making an appearance in court on his due date, he'd jumped bail. For the past week he'd been in hiding without money, hanging out at an old girlfriend's apartment in Fort Worth.

He'd been here six days, and was sick and tired of the scent of boiled cabbage and bratwurst. Even the free sex from the old girlfriend was losing appeal. So when the knock sounded on the door, he ignored his better judgment and went to answer it.

Cat's fingertips were numb from the cold, but persistence had paid off. Frostbite was a minor hazard of the job compared to the satisfaction of having a healthy bank account. Her badge was in plain sight, so there would be no mistaking her purpose when she confronted her perp. She checked for the set of handcuffs she tucked under the waistband in the back of her jeans, felt to make sure her handgun was in the holster beneath her coat, then ran her fingers along the taser in her coat pocket as she started up the stairs. Brownlee's woman had an apartment on the sixth floor, and in a building this old, an elevator did not come with the deal.

Cat's nose wrinkled as she moved from floor to floor. The compilation of scents coming from beneath the doors was staggering. She could smell everything from a backed-up toilet to boiled cabbage—a disgusting combination. It didn't, however, deter her from her goal, which was bringing Art's bail jumper back.

She wasn't even breathing hard when she reached the sixth floor. Her steps were sure as she strode down the hall, pausing only briefly before doubling her fist and pounding on the door of apartment 609. She re-checked the location of her gun and taser, then braced herself.

Nelson Brownlee opened the door.

"Well hell," he muttered, and tried to slam it shut.

The door caught on Cat's boot as she shoved her foot in the doorway, then swung inward as she pushed her way in.

"Now, Nelson," Cat drawled, as she grabbed him by the collar and slammed him belly first up against the wall. "That's no way to say hello. It's cold outside. The least you could do was offer me a hot cup of coffee."

"Like hell!" Nelson yelled, and bowed himself backward, then spun and took a swing at her.

She took a quick step sideways, dodging his fist. As she did, she came off one foot and kicked upward, landing a neat but lethal blow to his chin. He went down like a felled ox. She quickly handcuffed him, then grabbed him under the arms and was about to drag him out the door when she heard someone scream.

She dropped Nelson's arms and ran out of the apartment. Smoke was filling the stairwell from above, drifting downward in thick deadly fingers.

"Oh, Lord," she muttered, and glanced back inside the apartment. Brownlee was still out.

She couldn't leave without him, but he weighed a good hundred pounds more than she did. This wasn't good. She glanced down the hall again, grabbed her cell phone and quickly dialed 911. After giving the dispatcher the address of the building, she ran back to Brownlee. Already the smoke was so thick on the sixth floor that it was becoming difficult to breathe. Cat raced into the kitchen, grabbed a dish towel from the cabinet, doused it with water, then tied it around her face. The scent clinging to the towel was not enhanced by getting it wet, and sucking it up her nostrils came close to making her gag. Still, it was better to gag than burn.

Smoke was filling the apartment as Cat ran back to the living room and pulled Nelson into the hall. His head bumped hard as she dragged him over the threshold, but it couldn't be helped. Better a headache than dying.

"Come on, Brownlee, wake up!" Cat cried, but Brownlee wasn't talking.

Cursing beneath her breath, she got him as far as

the landing, then bent over, and with what she would later consider a burst of adrenaline spurred by an overwhelming fear, pulled him up and over her shoulder in a fireman's carry and started down the stairs, staggering slightly under the weight.

Cat hadn't counted on the difficulty of balancing dead weight on a decline. Every time she took a step down, Brownlee's head bumped against her back, keeping her slightly off balance. But the heat behind them and the smoke swirling around their heads was all the reminder she needed to keep moving. They'd cleared the fifth floor and were just past the fourth floor landing when Cat sensed someone on the stairs in front of her. Her instincts proved right as she stepped down onto the heel of a boot.

Staggering to keep from losing her load, she grabbed the railing with one hand and the back pocket of Brownlee's jeans with the other.

"Move faster or get over! I'm coming through!" she yelled.

Wilson McKay was, what the waitress at his favorite diner called, "a looker." He was four inches over six feet, with a linebacker's build. His hair style wasn't a style at all, but a buzz-cut that was always in the process of growing out. He wore one small gold hoop in his ear, and denim or leather with equal distinction. His nose had been broken twice, and there was a small scar beneath his right eye. Every scar, bump and line on his face was a testament to the hard knocks of his life.

He had turned forty yesterday, and a bunch of his friends had thrown a big party for him down at the bar across the street from his bail bond office. The beer had been flowing freely. They'd even sprung for a day-old cake from the deli section of one of the big grocery stores across town. Their gift to Wilson had been Wanelle, the prettiest hooker on their side of the city, which was a title Wanelle held proudly, even if her claim to fame came from a real long stretch of the truth.

Still, Wanelle had all her own teeth and clear skin, and she was almost pretty when she laughed. Wilson knew her slightly. He'd seen her around Ft. Worth from time to time, but buying a woman had never been his style. He'd felt trapped when Wanelle had been presented to him, especially since his buddies had tied a big red bow around her neck. Turning her down would have been a serious social faux pas to his friends *and* to Wanelle. So, rather than hurt everyone's feelings, Wilson had graciously accepted, and they'd spent the night in her fifth floor apartment, only to be awakened by the scent of smoke.

Wilson was just coming out of the bathroom when he saw tiny gray fingers of smoke coming from under the front door and curling upward.

"Oh, shit," he muttered, and ran to the door. He

put a hand on the wood to check for heat, and when it still felt cool, took a chance and opened it.

Smoke was pouring down the stairwell from above. The moment he saw it, he slammed the door shut and spun away, grabbing his shirt from the back of a chair as he ran toward the bedroom.

"Wanelle! Wanelle! Wake up, honey. The building is on fire! We've got to get out of here."

Wanelle rolled over. Her hair was smashed to her head on one side, and her makeup was smeared beneath her eyes. She looked a bit like raccoon road kill.

"Wha'sa matter? What did you say?"

He grabbed the clothes she'd taken off last night and threw them on the bed.

"Get dressed. Fast! The building is on fire."

"Oh Jesus! Oh Lord!" she screamed, and began to cry.

"Save the prayers for later," Wilson said, as he pulled her out of bed. "Here. Put these on."

She looked at the panties and bra as if she'd never seen them before.

"Uh… I need to pee before—"

"Make it fast," Wilson said.

Wanelle ran for the bathroom. He gave her less than thirty seconds before he was knocking on the door.

"Come on. You've got to come now."

Wanelle opened the door, wild-eyed and muttering beneath her breath. Wilson began dressing her as if she were a child, then handed her the boots she'd been wearing and grabbed her coat.

"Now, honey! We've got to go now!" he said, as she thrust her arms into her coat.

She was right behind him when he opened the door. The smoke that had been in the hall began filling her apartment. As soon as she saw it, she started to scream. If Wilson hadn't grabbed her arm, she would have bolted back into the apartment and closed the door.

"No you don't," he said.

She fought back, stronger than he would have believed her capable of being. The smoke was getting thicker, which meant their time-line to safety was getting shorter.

"Sorry, honey, but you leave me no choice."

Without hesitation, he doubled up his fist and popped her on the chin. She went out like a light. He caught her before she fell and threw her over his shoulder, then ran out into the hall. Seconds later, he was descending the stairs with the dead weight of her body swinging behind his back, the smoke continuing to thicken, seriously dimming his view.

Wilson pulled the collar of his turtle-neck sweater up over his nose like a mask, while every now and then, Wanelle would moan. Wilson knew she was inhaling too much smoke, but there was nothing he could do.

They were just past the fourth floor landing when someone stepped on the heel of his boot. Before he could react, he heard a woman yelling at him. From the panic in her voice, he had no doubt that she meant what she said. He turned abruptly, saw little more than her shadow through the smoke, then hefted Wanelle to a more secure position.

"Right in front of you and going down!" he yelled, and started taking the stairs two at a time.

Even though the muscles in Cat's neck and shoulders were trembling from Nelson Brownlee's weight, she never gave in or slowed. A few steps more and she began hearing footsteps coming down the stairs behind her. Fearing someone would run into her and send both her and Brownlee tumbling, she yelled out a warning.

"Traffic on the stairs! Traffic on the stairs!"

The footsteps faltered, then kept on coming, but with less speed. They all passed the third floor landing, then the second, and when they finally hit the first floor and ran out into the street, firemen were running past them into the building.

Wanelle was beginning to come to as Wilson handed her off to some EMTs. He mentioned smoke inhalation and that he'd knocked her out when she'd started to panic.

The medics nodded their understanding as they transferred her to a stretcher and carried her toward a waiting ambulance.

Wilson's legs were shaking as he watched them take Wanelle away, knowing she would be all right. Then curiosity made him look for the woman who'd been behind him on the stairs.

At first he thought she was already lost in the gathering crowd, and then he caught a glimpse of a tall, dark-haired woman carrying a man over her shoulder. He'd had no idea she'd been carrying someone. Added to that was the fact that she had not handed the man she was carrying over to the medics scattered around. For whatever reason, she was headed toward an SUV parked on the opposite side of the street. What surprised him most was that the man she was carrying appeared to be twice her weight.

"Damn, a real superwoman," he muttered, then decided to follow her.

He started across the street at a jog, dodging hoses and firemen, coughing a couple of times as fresh air slowly cycled through his smoke-filled lungs. She had already reached her vehicle and was in the process of stuffing the man in the back seat when he arrived.

"Hey, lady, do you—?"

Cat's hand flew beneath her coat, shoving it back as she reached for her handgun.

"Back off," she said.

Wilson stopped, his eyes narrowing as he caught a glimpse of her weapon, as well as some kind of badge fastened to her belt. He held up his hands in a gesture of submission.

"Easy…"

"I'm never easy," she snapped.

Wilson stifled a smile. He would have bet money on that.

It was all he could do not to stare, but she was truly a sight. There were sooty streaks on her cheeks, her eyes were red-rimmed; and from the number of times she was blinking, they were probably burning. But her legs were long, her hips almost boy-slim, and she looked ready to fight. Black hair hung way below her shoulders, and there was a small drop of blood on the curve of her lower lip. If it wasn't for the muscles she quite obviously had, and the impressive size of her breasts, he would have called her skinny.

"Was it you who called out to me on the stairs?" he asked.

"I yelled at somebody," she said. "Sorry if I hurt your feelings."

He grinned. "I just wanted to make sure you're okay," he said, then reached out and wiped away the blood drop with the pad of his thumb.

Cat swatted at his hand. "I'm fine," she snapped, then swiped the back of her hand across her mouth, as if to wipe away his touch.

Wilson stifled a second smile. Pure hellcat. He eyed the handcuffs on Brownlee's wrists, then pointed.

"What happened…lost the key in the middle of your game?"

Cat's eyes narrowed angrily. He was accusing her of sex games with the piece of shit in the back seat of her car. She kept telling herself to ignore him all the while she was opening her mouth.

"He's a bail jumper," she said. "I'm taking him in. You want to make something of it?"

Wilson eyed her closer. The only female skip tracer he knew of in Texas was Cat Dupree, but he'd never met her.

"Okay, okay, lady. Don't get all hot and bothered. It looks like we're in the same business." He pulled out a badge and ID.

"My name is Wilson McKay."

"Of McKay's Bail Bonds," Cat said, well aware of her boss's competition. "Good for you," she said, then heard noise in the back seat of her car and realized Brownlee was beginning to come to.

Nelson opened his eyes, felt the cold steel around his wrists and kicked. The car door hit Cat on the backside before she could turn and sent her flying forward, right into Wilson McKay's arms.

It was an automatic reaction that made Wilson grab her to keep her from falling, but he turned her loose on purpose when she came up swinging and lit into the man in the back seat of her car.

"You sorry bastard! I should have let you fry," she growled, then tasered Brownlee as he was trying to get out.

He screamed with pain as he fell backward in the back seat.

"No more! No more!" he begged.

Cat was still glaring as she yanked him upright and shoved his legs inside the car. She fastened his seat belt and then slammed the door shut so hard that it rattled the glass. Before she got inside the SUV, she pulled a baton from beneath her seat and whacked it on the top of the seat about six inches from where Nelson was sitting.

"Do you see this, Brownlee?"

"Yes, oh God, yes, I see it, I see it. Just don't hit me no more."

"Then stay where you're put," she snapped. "I'm not the one who robbed a Quick Stop, and I'm not the one who jumped bail, so being mad at me isn't going to solve your damn problem. You screwed up and walked out on a man who did you a favor. He bonded you out, and this is how you repay him?"

Brownlee shuddered as he rode the wave of electric shock continuing to ripple through his body.

"I know. I know. I didn't mean to hurt you none. I just woke up disoriented and all. I'd never—"

"Shut up, Nelson. You're lying, and we both know it. You already tried to cold-cock me. Now sit back and relax. We're going for a ride."

Cat got into her car, locked the door and buckled up without giving Wilson McKay a second look.

But Wilson *was* looking. He knew his suspicions

had been right. He'd just met the infamous Cat Dupree. This was the first time he'd seen her up close and personal, and he was surprised by how truly beautiful she was. He was, however, more than a little bit put out that she hadn't even given him a second look.

It took him a few moments to realize that the fine spray of water from the fire hoses was drifting down on him, and that it was freezing to the outer surface of his leather coat.

"Well, damn," he muttered, and started to walk away when he saw something glittering in a growing puddle.

He bent down and picked it up, then realized it was a small silver charm in the shape of a cat. He glanced back up at Cat Dupree's disappearing vehicle and grinned as he dropped the charm in his pocket. Now he had an excuse to see her again.

He shivered, watching the firemen as they continued to spray water into the building and thinking how close they'd all come to dying. Finally he stuffed his hands in his pockets and headed down the street to where he'd parked his car the night before. As much as he wanted to go home, take a hot shower and crawl into bed, good manners meant he should go to the hospital and make sure Wanelle was okay.

Cat's lungs were still burning when she turned Brownlee over to the authorities.

The ride from Fort Worth to Dallas had given

him plenty of time to consider what had just happened. Granted, Cat Dupree had tracked him down to take him in. That had been inevitable. But she'd also saved his life. How was he supposed to stay pissed when she'd gone and done something like that? He went back to lockup without comment, unwilling to look Cat in the face.

Cat couldn't have cared less what life-changing behaviors Brownlee might be considering. He'd been nothing but a job to her, and now it was over. She just wanted a bath and about twelve straight hours of sleep.

The traffic from police headquarters to her apartment was worse than usual, thanks to the freezing rain that had started to fall. By the time she unlocked the door, her hands were shaking and her stomach was doing somersaults, reminding her that she had yet to eat a decent meal today.

She tossed her car keys in a bowl on the hall table and started to hang her coat up in the closet, then wrinkled her nose when she realized it smelled of smoke. She tossed it on the floor near the door as a reminder to take it to the cleaners when she next went out, then began undressing on her way to the bath. She stopped in the kitchen to get a bottle of water and noticed that the message light was blinking on her answering machine. She took a big drink of water and put off the task of checking the messages in favor of a hot shower.

She was standing in front of the mirror over the

sink when she realized something was missing. The tiny links on the silver chain around her neck were familiar enough, but the small cat charm that had been on it was gone.

"Oh no," Cat said, and then quickly traced the length of the chain, praying that the charm had somehow shifted to the back of her neck. It was the only thing she had left from her life before Social Services, and now it was gone. She thought back over the past few hours. The stakeout, the fire, the altercation with Nelson Brownlee. Even if she could retrace her steps, a good portion of them had gone up in smoke. She had to accept that the charm was gone.

A hard, burning knot filled the back of her throat as she swiftly turned away from the mirror. The pain was so sharp she couldn't bring herself to look at the wound it surely left on her face.

She turned on the shower and then stepped beneath the spray, not waiting for the water to heat. The cold water was like a slap in the face. Shivering slightly, she reached down for the soap and lathered her washcloth.

Soap burned her eyes as she began to scrub at her face, then washed herself all over. When the soot and smoke were gone from her skin, she shampooed and rinsed her hair until it felt clean, as well. Then she turned her face up to the water and closed her eyes.

Most of the time, her world sucked. Today was no exception.

Two

It was almost dark by the time Wilson left the hospital, satisfied that Wanelle was going to be all right. The fire at the apartment building had left Wanelle homeless, but her cousin, Shirley, had come to collect her. Shirley had a good heart and an extra bed, which left her better off than most. Wilson had given Wanelle a couple of hundred dollars to go toward replacing her lost clothing, which was all the cash he had on him.

"You're a doll," she said, as she pocketed the cash. "Any time you want a freebie, just give me a call."

Wilson stifled a grin as he gave her a hug.

"You are, without doubt, the most memorable birthday present I've ever had." He brushed a finger along the side of her jaw, where a noticeable bruise was forming. "Sorry about having to whack you like that."

"No biggie," she said. "It was my fault for freaking out."

"You had a reason to freak," he said. "So...take care of yourself, okay?"

She smirked and rolled her eyes at Shirley.

"He's the best, I tell you. The best."

"See you around," Wilson said, and watched as they drove away.

Then he got into his car. For a few moments he just sat, thinking back over the events of the day. He'd been watching the evening news in the lobby of the E.R. while waiting for Wanelle to be released and had seen footage on television. It was daunting to learn that seven people had died in the fire they had escaped. Were it not for the grace of God, they could have been included in that statistic. Even now, as a cough bubbled up from deep in his chest, he was reminded of how close they'd come and wondered how Cat Dupree had fared.

Lights from a passing ambulance swept across his line of vision and broke his musing. His belly growled from hunger as a cold gust of wind rocked the truck. He shivered slightly and quickly started the engine. As soon the motor warmed up, he put the truck in gear and drove to work.

He put in several hours at his office, then sent his receptionist home when the weather began to worsen. He set the phones in the office so that they would ring at his apartment, then locked up and went home.

Due to the freezing rain, traffic was heavier than normal. There appeared to be some kind of pile-up on the freeway he normally drove, so he took the closest exit and wound through a small business district before driving into a residential area.

He couldn't help but notice the colorful Christmas lights decorating the outsides of the homes. He tried to imagine what it would be like to drive up one of the driveways and be met at the front door by a loving family. There would be kids—maybe three, two boys and a girl—and a wife who, after fifteen years of marriage, still rocked his world.

In the middle of the fantasy, a car sped out of a side street and cut in front of him without caution. If it hadn't been for Wilson's quick reflexes, he would have broadsided the other vehicle.

"Dumb ass," Wilson muttered, as he watched the man drive away. He had everything Wilson wanted and didn't have the good sense to take care of it by even looking where he was going.

A muscle ticked at the edge of Wilson's mouth as he shifted mental gears. Obviously he didn't want that kind of life bad enough, either, or he would have done something in the last ten years toward making it happen. His parents would be ecstatic if he ever committed himself to a woman. Of all their children, he was the only hold-out. His brothers and sisters had married years ago, making him an uncle many times over.

A short while later, he drove into the parking lot

of his apartment complex. His steps were dragging as he entered the building. When he got inside his apartment, he dropped his smokey clothes in the floor of the utility room, turned up the thermostat and headed for the shower. As soon as he was clean, he dressed in an old pair of sweat pants and a long-sleeved T-shirt, then moved to the kitchen. He hadn't eaten all day, except for a Coke and a package of cheese crackers he'd gotten from vending machines in the hospital, and he was hungry for real food.

The contents of his refrigerator were slim, but there was enough to make a decent-sized cheese omelet—one of his favorite quick meals. He finished it off in front of the TV, watching an old Chuck Norris movie and washing it down with the last of the Coke.

Remembering the pile of dirty clothes he'd left in the utility room, he went to put them in the washer. As he was going through the pockets, he found the cat charm again. Fingering it lightly, he set it on a shelf, poured in the soap and started the machine.

The phone rang as he was going to the bedroom. He could tell by the ring that it was a call being forwarded from the office. It wouldn't have been the first time he'd been called back to some jail to bond someone out, and he frowned as he answered.

"McKay Bail Bonds."

"Um…hey, Wilson, old buddy. It's me, Shooter."

Wilson's frown deepened. "Well, old buddy, you

better not be in jail again, 'cause if you are, then you've just wasted your free call."

Shooter Green shifted to whining.

"Aw…now, Wilson…it ain't like you think. They've got me on a bad rap and—"

"I'm serious," Wilson said. "You and I aren't doing any more business. The last two times I bonded you out, you let me down. The first, you were a no-show. If your public defender hadn't sweet-talked the judge on your behalf and gotten you a second appearance date, you would have cost me my money. Then, the second time I bond you out of jail, I have to go after your ass…remember?"

"Yeah, but—"

"No buts, Shooter. Sleep tight, and don't let the bed bugs bite."

Shooter was still begging as Wilson hung up the phone.

Cat slept fitfully through the night, reliving the trip down the stairs with Brownlee over her shoulder so many times that her legs were actually aching when she woke up. She rolled over on her side and opened one eye just enough to see that it was after ten in the morning. With a sigh, she sat up in bed and ran her fingers through her hair. The urge to lie back down and sleep away the day was strong, but there were a couple of things she'd been planning to do, and one of them was taking her best friend, Marsha, out to lunch.

There weren't many people that Cat Dupree called friend, but Marsha Benton was one of them. She and Marsha had been fostered to the same family just before their seventeenth birthdays and had become fast friends. Their bond had lasted, even after they'd been processed out of the system.

Cat and Marsha often laughed at how different their lives had become once they'd been on their own. For the past eight years, Marsha had been a private secretary for Mark Presley, CEO of a company with worldwide distribution rights for farm implements, while Cat chased down bad guys with a taser and a gun.

Marsha was a little over five feet tall.

Cat was almost six feet in height.

Marsha was a curvy redhead who loved to eat.

Cat often forgot to eat, which accounted for her lanky build.

But they spoke the same language, laughed at the same jokes, and were the only family each other had.

Cat stretched languidly and then reached for the phone, punching in the number for Marsha's office from memory. She was already smiling to herself as she waited for Marsha to answer.

"Presley Implements."

"Hey, Mimi, it's me, Cat. Are we still on for lunch today?"

There was a moment of silence, something Cat hadn't expected.

"Hey, girlfriend…are you there?"

Cat heard what sounded like a stifled sob; then Marsha answered.

"Yes, I'm here, and lunch sounds great. Where do you want me to meet you?"

"Um…how about Billy Bob's?"

"Good," Marsha said. "One o'clock?"

"Yeah," Cat said, and then added, "Are you okay?"

"Absolutely," Marsha said. "See you later. I've got to go."

"Okay," Cat said, and disconnected, but she was still frowning as she got out of bed.

She knew Marsha well enough to know that something *was* wrong. She'd heard it in her friend's voice. Then she shrugged off her concern, knowing that once they got together, Marsha would talk. She never could keep secrets.

Cat got some clean underwear and headed for the bathroom. Even though she'd washed her hair last night before going to bed, she imagined it still smelled of smoke.

A short while later she was blow drying her hair and trying not to think about the missing cat charm. The loss was something she wasn't going to get over any time soon, but dwelling on it wasn't going to bring it back. Sick at heart, she hoped seeing Marsha would help. Maybe a reminder of what they'd overcome in their young lives would put the loss of a simple charm into perspective.

As she was going through her closet for something to wear, she abandoned what would have been a normal choice. Marsha would be dressed to the nines, so the least Cat could do was leave her gun at home and wear something besides leather. A cold blast of wind rattled the bedroom windows, which reminded her that whatever she chose, it needed to be warm.

A short while later she was dressed, unaware of how her choices had softened her appearance. Instead of denim and leather, she wore a soft white cable-knit sweater and a pair of brown wool slacks. Her brown alligator shoes looked great, although they were a pair she'd owned for several years. Today she chose them for comfort, rather than style. She pulled her hair away from the sides of her face and fastened it at the nape of her neck with a tortoise shell clip.

She glanced down at her fingernails and frowned. The nails were short and unpolished, with one broken to the quick thanks to Nelson Brownlee, but they were clean. In her line of work, polished fingernails were the last thing she was concerned with.

After swiping her lips with a pale, glossy lipstick, she flipped off the light as she exited the dressing area, grabbed her coat and headed out the door.

Considering the number of holiday shoppers out on the streets, the drive to Billy Bob's went smoothly. When Cat pulled into the parking lot, she quickly spotted Marsha's silver Lexus with her personalized license plate, ALLMINE. It never failed to make Cat smile.

As she got out, she caught a whiff of the faint scent of burning hickory, a tempting hint of meat grilling inside. She was already pulling off her coat as she entered the restaurant and threw it over her arm as she scanned the room for her friend. When she saw Marsha stand up and wave, she began weaving her way between the tables.

"Hey, you," Cat said.

Marsha kissed Cat and gave her a brief hug as Cat draped her coat over an empty chair.

The tension in Marsha's body was unusual. Warning bells went off as Cat returned Marsha's embrace.

"Sit, sit," Marsha said, and waved toward a free chair. "I've already ordered some chips and queso. They'll be here shortly, and that margarita is yours."

"Yum," Cat said as she sat, then took a quick sip of her drink.

Marsha's smile was genuine. Impulsively, she reached out for Cat's hand and gave it a quick squeeze.

"You look great, as always. So what's new with you?"

Wilson McKay's face immediately came to mind, but Cat ignored it. They hadn't even had what would amount to a real conversation, so there was nothing to report.

"Nothing," Cat said, then leaned closer and lowered her voice. "Spit it out, Mimi, and don't lie. I'll know if you do."

Marsha blinked, then looked away as tears immediately pooled. The sound of her old nickname from her best friend's lips was a painful reminder of a happier time.

"You are too smart for your own good," she mumbled.

Cat felt sad. Seeing Marsha in such distress broke her heart.

"And you're too gentle-hearted for yours. Who hurt you? Tell me and I'll make him sorry."

Marsha tried to smile through the tears. "Why would you assume it's a man?"

Cat rolled her eyes. "Because they're always trouble. Am I right?"

Marsha sighed, then nodded.

"Who is he?" Cat asked.

"It doesn't matter. Besides, you can't keep fighting my battles."

Cat frowned. "I can and I will. Come on, Mimi… I don't like to see you this way."

Marsha shrugged. "It's my own fault. I knew better, but I did it anyway."

Cat knew there was more. Suddenly it dawned.

"He's married, isn't he?"

Marsha hesitated, then dropped her head without answering.

It was answer enough for Cat, although Marsha stayed silent.

Cat stared at her for a few moments, waiting for

details. When they weren't forthcoming, she began to think back over the past few weeks to the times when Marsha couldn't meet her for dinner because she had to work late. As she did, suspicion grew.

"Is it your boss?"

Marsha didn't answer, but she didn't have to. Cat could see the truth in her eyes.

"It is, isn't it? It's that damned snake Mark Presley."

Marsha covered her face with her hands.

Cat stifled another curse and lowered her voice even more.

"Mimi… I'm sorry. Talk to me, honey."

Marsha dabbed at her eyes with a tissue, trying not to smear her makeup as she considered what to say, even though she knew she could never keep secrets from Cat.

"Oh, Cat, just let it—"

"No. I'm not letting it go. Talk. Now."

Marsha leaned back, took a sip of her iced tea, then shoved it aside. "He fed me a big line that I fell for. There's nothing else I can say."

"Did the line have anything to do with, 'I'm getting a divorce and I love you madly'?"

Marsha's expression crumpled.

"Pretty much."

Cat slumped. She couldn't believe Marsha had fallen for that. Then it occurred to her that there was a reason why Marsha would even give that line consideration.

"Oh, Mimi…you were already in love with him, weren't you?"

Marsha's chin trembled. "Yes."

"The pig. So he got in your pants. How's he treating you now?"

"Like I've stolen the company secrets and he's looking for a reason to fire me."

Cat's eyes narrowed angrily. "He can't do that."

"Well, yes, he can," Marsha countered. "He owns the company, so he can do whatever he pleases."

Cat's instincts to protect were on point.

"Let me talk to him," she said. "I'll make sure he sees the light."

Marsha's eyes widened in panic. "No. No. No way are you getting in the middle of this. He didn't hold a knife to my throat. I slept with him, and it's too late to change what—"

Suddenly Marsha stopped talking, and the look on her face was no longer just sad. She looked scared.

Cat's frown deepened. "There's more to this mess than you've told me, isn't there?"

Marsha nodded nervously, as she chewed on her bottom lip.

Cat grabbed Marsha's wrist, her fingers curling into the flesh.

"Mimi…it's me. We don't lie to each other. Ever. Remember?"

"I'm pregnant."

Cat reeled backwards as if she'd been slapped.

"Oh man. Does he know?"

"Yes."

"Don't tell me. Let me guess. He's pissed, right?"

"He wants me to get rid of it."

"What did you tell him?" Cat asked.

Marsha rolled her eyes. "What do you think? You know how we grew up. I told him no."

"And that made him mad?"

Marsha tried to smile, but it didn't quite work.

"That's an understatement. He thinks I'm trying to work some kind of scam. I tried to assure him that I didn't want anything from him except my job, which I already had, but he doesn't believe me. And…he's been making threats."

Now Cat was really on alert. "What kind of threats?"

"The kind that leave you six feet under," Marsha said, then pressed her fingers against her lips, as if she couldn't believe those words had come out of her mouth.

"That does it," Cat said, and would have gotten up, but Marsha stopped her.

"You can't get involved in this," Marsha said. "You don't know what he's like. Please. As a favor to me. Stay out of it."

Cat's face was flushed with anger as she tried to make Marsha see sense.

"But, Mimi, you—"

Marsha's expression darkened. Even though there were still tears in her eyes, her chin jutted stubbornly.

"I'm telling you…stay out of it!"

Cat straightened, staring at her friend in disbelief.

Marsha persisted, unwilling to quit until Cat had given her promise.

"I'm waiting," Marsha said.

Finally Cat could do nothing but agree.

"All right," she said reluctantly. "But I'm telling you, if he so much as puts a bruise on your body, he's mine."

Marsha hesitated for a moment, then nodded.

"Deal."

"Deal," Cat echoed, then grabbed her margarita and downed it like medicine. "Crap," she muttered, as she sat the empty glass back on the table.

Marsha laughed through her pain, and for a moment Cat laughed with her.

But later, as their food came and they ate, talking about everything except the problem at hand, Cat felt a sense of impending doom. She didn't know what was going to happen, but none of it could be good.

The next morning dawned cold, gray and wet, adding a wind chill factor to the miserable day. Cat hadn't slept well, and what sleep she'd had, had been filled with nightmares about Marsha. She winced as her bare feet hit the cold floor, and stepped into slippers as she went about her morning routine. As she moved through the hall, she turned up the thermostat. She strode into the kitchen and turned on the coffee maker, waiting impatiently for the first cup of coffee to brew.

She downed the caffeine, hoping it would settle her rumbling stomach, and checked her machine for messages. There were none. In a way, she was glad. Her bank account was healthy enough to get her through a dry spell. Christmas was only a couple of weeks away, and she had yet to go shopping for gifts. That was what she needed to do, and it wouldn't take long. A good bottle of whiskey for Art and a gift for Mimi. After that, she might drop by the gym. It had been more than a week since she'd had time to work out, and after the conversation she'd had with Mimi about Mark Presley, she felt the need to set something on fire. It might as well be her muscles.

Wilson was on his way to the gym when he began to hear sirens. He pulled over to the side of the street just in time to let a trio of police cars go racing past. The thought that someone was in trouble crossed his mind, followed by selfish gratitude that it wasn't him.

As traffic resumed, he drove to the next stoplight, then turned right. He had a membership at Body Builders, Inc., but his visits were sporadic. Most of the time he was either on a job or home trying to catch up on lost sleep. When he'd awakened to the cold, overcast day, a hard workout had seemed like a good way to pass some time.

Then, less than four blocks away from his destination, he ran into a roadblock and recognized the three police cars that had passed him earlier. Besides those, there were close to a dozen more. Spying a cop he knew, he rolled down the window.

"Hey, Daughtry, what's up?"

The officer turned, recognized him and moved closer. "Bank robbery with hostages involved," he said.

"Which bank?" Wilson asked.

"First Federal Credit Union," Daughtry said.

Wilson frowned. That was right across from his gym, which meant his workout wasn't happening—at least not there.

"Good luck, buddy, and watch your back," Wilson said, and waved goodbye as he turned right at the blocked off intersection. There were a couple of other gyms in the area that didn't require memberships to work out. He would try one of them.

A short while later he was at Bab's Abs, stripped down to his gym clothes and on a stationary bike, working up a good sweat, when Cat Dupree walked in. She was wearing a pair of bright red sweat pants and some well-worn tennis shoes. When she shed her coat and began twisting her hair up into a ponytail, her breasts tightened the fabric of her old gray T-shirt.

Wilson was a man who believed that lives were dictated by fate, and he was giving his good luck a mental thank-you when she strode past him without looking.

He started to speak, but the jut of her chin seemed

more like a warning than a welcome, so he remained silent as she walked by. She moved to a Stair Master and began to warm up before stepping on board. Within seconds, she was in motion.

It took Wilson a few seconds to realize he was staring, so he shook off his moment of lust and resumed his workout. He pedaled for another fifteen minutes without looking up, telling himself that if it was meant to be, she would see him and speak. If it wasn't, then he would keep to himself. He didn't understand what he was doing, playing mental games with himself about her, but there was a part of him that believed no matter what he asked, she would say no. And, being a man who didn't like to be thwarted in any way, he was thinking that the best way not to be turned down was not to ask in the first place.

When he finished his bike time and looked up, he saw that she'd moved on to free weights and was impressed by the amount she was lifting. This time he watched with guilt, admiring her form and strength.

About the time he'd decided to call it a morning, he realized she was in trouble. She was lifting without a spotter and had pushed herself about two lifts too far. On her last lift, she'd barely gotten the bar up and locked her elbows, but it was obvious that she didn't have enough strength to lower the weights safely to the rests. He knew that when she let go, she was going to drop the bar right across her chest.

Six long strides from one side of the gym to the

other and he had the bar in hand and was easing it onto the rests. Once it was safely in place, he looked down. She was still flat on her back on the weight bench, looking up at him.

Cat knew she'd pushed herself too far, too fast, but she'd taken her worry and anger at Mark Presley out on the weights. By the time she realized she was in trouble, she was too focused on not killing herself to shout for help. Then, when the weights were miraculously taken from her hands, she groaned with relief. When she looked up to see who'd come to her aid, she was looking at him upside down. It wasn't until she sat up and turned around that she realized who'd come to her rescue.

"You," Cat muttered.

Wilson's face was expressionless. "You're welcome," he said briefly, and then turned his back on her and walked away.

For whatever reason, Wilson had to face the fact that he did not ring her bells. It was something of a disappointment to accept that, since she was the first woman since he'd turned sixteen who was obviously not interested in him.

The moment he walked away, Cat realized how rude she'd been. She dismounted the weight bench and hurried after him, catching him midway across the floor.

"Hey! Wait! I didn't mean to take my mood out on you. Thank you for saving my butt back there."

Wilson felt a surge of pleasure. So she wasn't as cold and standoffish as she appeared.

"Yeah…sure, and you're welcome."

Cat eyed his cropped haircut as well as the tiny gold hoop in his ear and told herself he wasn't all that. But she was lying.

"Thanks again."

"Next time, take it easy on the weights."

"Definitely."

Then Wilson remembered the charm.

"Say…you didn't happen to lose something the day of the fire, did you?"

Cat's heart skipped a beat.

"Yes, actually I did."

"Like what?" Wilson asked.

"A charm. It was a small silver cat. The only thing I had left of my childhood before…" She hesitated, then shrugged. "It was sentimental. Please tell me you found it."

"I found it."

Cat's eyes rounded in disbelief.

"Oh my God…you're serious, aren't you?"

Wilson was surprised by her sudden burst of emotion. It was, after all, just a charm. A small grin tilted the left corner of his mouth.

"Yes, ma'am, serious as a heart attack."

Cat threw her arms around his neck, and kissed him hard and fast.

Before he could react, she'd pulled away and high-fived him so vigorously that the palm of his hand actually burned.

"I can't believe it," Cat kept saying. "I was so certain it was gone forever. Thank you! You don't know what it means to me."

"I'm beginning to get an idea," He said, rubbing his burning hand on the backside of his gym shorts.

She glanced at her watch, then back at him.

"Where do you live? I'll come get it. Or, if you'd rather, you can drop it off at my place. Here... I'll give you my address."

She tore a piece of paper from a little notebook in her gym bag and quickly wrote out her address.

"That's my phone number, too," she said.

Wilson stifled a grin. It wouldn't do to let her know that he was as excited about the number and address as she was about the charm. He was still holding her address when Cat's cell phone rang.

She reached into her gym bag, saw the caller ID, recognized Marsha's number and frowned.

"Look. I'm sorry, but I need to take this. Call me. We'll set up a time to meet later."

"Absolutely," Wilson said, but Cat was already walking away.

"That was weird," he muttered. She'd been ecstatic to know he had the charm, then had turned all businesslike and cold.

Still, he had her number and he had the charm. It was only a matter of time before they got together.

He packed up his things and left the gym, much happier than when he'd gone in.

Cat, on the other hand, had just had her joy reduced to a large knot in the middle of her belly.

"Mimi, what's wrong?"

Marsha was sobbing. It was all Cat could do to make out what she was trying to say.

"He fired you? Is that what you said? The sorry bastard actually fired you?"

"Yes," Marsha said, and then drew a deep, shaky breath. "I was escorted from the building as if I'd try to steal company secrets."

"Are you okay to drive home? Do you want me to—"

"I'm fine," Marsha said. "My feelings are just hurt. Even though I knew he was angry, I never really thought he was capable of something like this."

"I'm coming over," Cat said. "I'll be there by—"

"No, no, I'm not even home," Marsha said. "I have a doctor's appointment in an hour. I'll come over later."

"What time?" Cat asked.

"I don't know. I'll call you, okay?"

"If you're sure," Cat said. She didn't like it, but Marsha was a grown woman. She had to give her some room to grieve.

"I'm sure," Marsha said. "Talk to you later."

"I'll be waiting," Cat said.

Three

Cat went home, showered quickly and dressed, then began an anxious vigil, waiting for Mimi to call. If she'd had the good sense to ask who her doctor was, she would have met her there, but she hadn't asked, and Marsha wasn't answering her cell phone.

Noon came and went, and just when she was getting really worried, her telephone rang. She picked it up on the first ring.

"Mimi?"

"No, it's me," Wilson said.

Cat's heart dropped. "I'm sorry. I'm waiting for a call from a friend who's in trouble. Can I call you back?"

Wilson didn't know whether he was getting the runaround or she was telling the truth, then decided it didn't matter. He would find out soon enough, one way or the other.

"No problem. I'm working at home today, but I'll be back in the office tomorrow." He rattled off his phone number. "Good luck to your friend," he said lightly, and hung up.

Cat was a little surprised by the abruptness, then decided she'd given him no choice.

"Rats," she muttered, and hung up. "Come on, Mimi, call me. Call me. You know I don't like to wait."

But the call didn't come. Cat tried her friend's cell phone again, but all she got was voice mail. Finally she left messages on both Mimi's cell and her home phone, then settled in for the day. She ordered Chinese from a restaurant around the block, picked at the sesame chicken when it came, tore her spring roll apart without eating it, then tossed the lot down the garbage disposal and called it quits.

Before she could talk herself out of it, she grabbed her coat and keys, and headed out the door. Mimi had to be home by now and was probably ignoring her calls. She knew Cat would be ready to take Mark Presley apart, and she probably didn't want to deal with it. She had a habit of ignoring what she couldn't face, and they both knew it.

Cat fed the fuel of her anger all the way to Mimi's townhouse, but when she got there, the silver Lexus was nowhere to be seen. Cat circled the entire complex twice, looking for that car and its telltale license tag, but to no avail. Then she decided Mimi could have had car trouble; maybe the car was in the shop and she'd taken a cab home.

She parked and got out. When she got to Mimi's door, she rang the bell. Still no answer. She knocked several times, then called out her name. When that got no response, she picked the lock. It wasn't exactly legal, but these were extenuating circumstances.

After a quick check of the rooms, she confirmed what she'd already suspected. Mimi wasn't here. Still, the fact that she wasn't home yet didn't really worry her. She could be doing any number of things, from shopping to having her nails done, to being detained at the doctor's office for some reason. Cat was still irked with herself for not asking who she'd chosen as her obstetrician, but she resisted the urge to dig through Marsha's personal papers in hopes of finding the doctor's name and address. All she could do was go home and wait for the call, and when it came, read Mimi the riot act for causing her so much worry.

Mark Presley was a self-made man. He'd grown up in a rural community in southwest Texas, the only child of a blue collar family. His father had been a mechanic, his mother a beautician. He'd had a normal childhood up until his senior year of high school.

The end of phase one of his life began on homecoming day at the local high school. Besides a parade and a pep rally before the big game that night, the chamber of commerce had sponsored a city-wide barbecue. Mark, being the starting quarterback for the local football team, was one of the honorees who would be riding the school float in the parade. Two hours before the parade, his daddy had dropped dead at work from a heart attack.

Mark missed the parade. He missed the big homecoming game. He missed graduation. He missed the athletic scholarship he'd been counting on. And the day he realized all his dreams were as out of reach as his father, he made a promise to himself that he would never miss out on anything again.

When his girlfriend realized his status wasn't as shiny as it had been, she slowly drifted away. After that, it was anger and disappointment that fueled his drive to succeed.

He'd gone to work at the local auto parts store, sweeping up and making deliveries. By the age of twenty-one, he was head of the parts department. By twenty-five, he'd married the daughter of his boss, who also owned a large farm implement company. When his father-in-law passed away six years later, Mark was named president of the company. He'd taken it from a profitable business to one with worldwide recognition.

He cheated on his wife on a regular basis, as did most of the men in his social circle. Power was a big turn-on for pretty girls wanting a free ride, but he made sure his wife never wanted for a thing, including his attention. That was his safety net, because he had vowed he was never getting caught.

He'd known Marsha, his personal assistant, had a thing for him. He'd known it for years, but he'd never made a practice of playing where he worked. Then, about four months ago, in a moment of weakness, he'd broken his own rule and, for a while, thought it would all work out. Marsha was a beautiful woman and smart as they came. It had been a refreshing change to be with someone who was his mental equal, only she'd gotten all crazy, talking about love and babies. He'd tried to give her money for an abortion. She threw it in his face and made an appointment with an obstetrician instead.

He'd had her followed. He knew she was seeing an OBGYN on a regular basis. It was at that point that he'd known he would have to take a different tack with her. He couldn't have her showing up nine months later with a kid bearing his DNA. In spite of the aggravation, he wasn't all that concerned. It was just another hitch in his world that needed to be smoothed out.

Presley was in the middle of a transatlantic conference call when his cell phone rang. He glanced at the caller ID and silently cursed. As soon as he could, he ended his call and called Marsha.

The fact that Mark hadn't answered had been upsetting for Marsha, but not unexpected. She was leaving the parking lot of the doctor's building when her cell phone rang. When she realized it was Mark, she was elated. He'd been so cold when he'd fired her, but now he was calling her back. Surely this was a good sign. She parked in the first empty space she could find and reached for her phone.

"Mark! I knew you would call."

Mark was so angry he was shaking, but he wasn't going to alert her that all was not right in his world.

"What did you want?" he asked.

"To talk to you...but not to make any demands. Please, you have to believe me."

"I'm not leaving my wife."

"I don't want you to. I've accepted what I meant to you, but I was hoping you'd take our child into consideration. You know my background. You know how hard it is for a child to grow up without parents."

"The kid will have you."

"Every child deserves both parents," Marsha said. "Won't you at least meet with me to talk? Just to talk? I'm not making demands. I just want you to think of the child."

"I'll meet with you," Mark said. "But no promises."

Marsha's joy surged. "Oh, Mark...darling...thank you, thank you. I promise you won't be sorry."

"Penny and I are leaving in a couple of days for Christmas vacation. If you want to talk, it will have to be today."

It was all Marsha could do not to giggle. He was going to see it her way after all.

"That's fine. Just name the time and place," she said.

Mark smiled to himself. She was playing into his hands, just as he'd planned.

"I'm on my way to the airport, so my time is short."

"Are you going to the company airport?"

"Yes."

"I'll be there within the hour."

"I'll be waiting," Mark said. He'd already given the airport employees their Christmas bonuses, and they'd scattered to the four winds. He would have the place to himself.

He walked out of his office, told his secretary he wouldn't be back until morning and left. It was nothing he hadn't done a thousand times before. Within thirty minutes he was at his private airport.

He put on an old pair of coveralls he got out of an employee locker, took a baseball cap from a hook inside the office and gave the company helicopter a flight check, then sat down to wait for Marsha.

He didn't have to wait long.

When he saw her car turn off the main road and onto the property, a knot formed in his belly. Then he reminded himself that he could do this—he had to. She'd given him no choice.

When she pulled up beside his car and parked, he swallowed once, then stood up and put on the work gloves that had been in the pocket of the coveralls.

Through a dusty window, he saw her get out and pause beside the car door. It was cold but sunny, and he noticed how pretty she looked. How odd that he would notice that today, when he was about to end her life. Marsha was stunning, but she was also a death sentence for him. If one of them had to go, it wasn't going to be him.

Marsha's heart was thumping erratically as she got out of the car, but she was filled with hope as she wrapped her red coat more tightly around herself to cut the cold. She'd been out to the company hangar plenty of times over the last few years, so even though the place appeared deserted except for his car, she felt no hesitation in going inside.

Once inside, she paused, allowing time for her eyes to adjust to the dimness. When she saw the office door open and a man in coveralls step out, she assumed it was one of the employees.

"Hi, it's me, Marsha. I'm meeting Mr. Presley. Is he in the office?"

The man just raised his arm and waved as he continued toward her.

It took a few moments for Marsha to realize that the man in the coveralls was Mark.

"Mark?"

"Yes, it's me."

She thought no more of the odd clothing as she started to talk.

"Thank you for meeting me like this," she said.

"Don't mention it," Mark said, and pulled a large wrench out of the carpenter's loop on the side of the coveralls. Without hesitation, he drew his arm back and hit her.

It was so unexpected and so fast that Marsha never realized what was happening until it was too late.

She went down like a rock.

Mark saw the deep indentation in the side of her head, as well as the blood beginning to seep from the wound. He grabbed a greasy rag from his pocket and clamped it on top of the blood as he picked her up in his arms. Without looking at her face, he carried her to the open door of the helicopter. There was a large sheet of blue plastic on the floor behind the pilot's seat. He laid her on it and then rolled her up.

He drove her car inside the hangar to hide it, then got in the chopper, checked to make sure that he'd loaded what he would need for later and revved up the engine. There was no flight plan to where he was going, but it didn't matter. He knew the way by heart.

Marsha floated in and out of consciousness several times, and each time she came to, she found it difficult to breathe and impossible to move. She tried to call out, but her lips wouldn't open. There was something wet and sticky on her face and an indescribable pain in her head. She could hear a loud roar, and she could feel a sense of motion.

Fear was swallowing her so fast that she couldn't keep herself focused. She knew she was hurt. She knew Mark had done it. She also knew that he meant to kill her.

Anger swept through her, knowing he was going to get away with it. She'd been so damned vague about her personal business with Cat. If only she'd called her and told her where she was going. At least Cat would have had a starting place from which to find her body.

At last Marsha's focus began to waver. She knew she was going to pass out again—this time, maybe for good—and she couldn't let Mark Presley get away with her murder.

But what could she do? Surely there was something....

Suddenly she remembered her cell phone. It was in her coat pocket. If only she could reach it.

Her fingers felt numb as she tried to move her arms. Whatever Mark had rolled her up in was so tight she could barely breathe, let alone move. Still, she had to try.

Slowly she managed to ease onto one side just enough to give herself room to maneuver. As she did, her arm slid downward, almost of its own accord. She tried not to panic and focused on the baby she was carrying, knowing that the child deserved justice, even if she did not. It was her own foolishness that had gotten her into this mess. It broke her heart to know that her baby's life was going to be over before it had a chance to begin.

Again and again, she tried to find the opening of her coat pocket, but with no success. Just as she was on the point of giving up, her fingers slid into the void. The contours of the phone were so familiar. She slid her fingernail between the flip-top and bottom, then pushed upward, revealing the tiny buttons beneath.

Her hands were shaking horribly as she tried to picture the numbers on the keys. Finally she punched in the numbers to Cat's home phone, knowing that, as long as the line was open, the answering machine would record everything.

She tried to count off the time it would take for the call to go through, then for the phone to ring a certain number of times before the answering machine would come on, then the time it would take for Cat's message to play before it would pick up her call.

She was still counting when she passed out.

Time was a word without meaning, but when she next came to, the sound of the roar had changed, as had the sense of motion. It was then she knew they'd been flying and now they were descending.

When the motion stopped, she tried to call out, but intent never got past thought. She felt herself being dragged for what seemed like forever, and then, abruptly, everything was still.

Before she could think, she was being unrolled. Her arms and legs were like rubber as her body was ejected into a blistering cold. The drastic change in temperature was a metaphoric slap in the face, the push she needed to open her eyes. She did, only to see someone leaning over her. In a last desperate attempt, she reached up.

"Help me," she whispered.

Mark Presley had flown all the way from the airport to an oil lease he owned in East Texas without a thought in his head beyond what he still had to do. When he dragged Marsha's body from the chopper and then started pulling it through the woods, he made himself think of what he was going to buy Penny for Christmas instead of what he had yet to do.

He'd never killed anyone before or even imagined being in a predicament where it might be necessary. But there was no way he could have gone through with what Marsha had asked. He was too afraid of what Penny would do, should he be found out.

By the time he got to the edge of the gully, his legs were shaking from the effort of dragging the body. He started to just toss her over, then stopped. The bright blue plastic sheeting in which she was wrapped would be too visible, especially from the air.

Determined to do this right, he began to unroll her. She flopped out face down onto the cold, wet ground.

When he gave the sheeting a last hard yank to get it out from under her, it rolled her over onto her back.

When she suddenly opened her eyes and looked at him, reached for him, he was so shocked she was still alive that he staggered and fell backward.

"God damn, why aren't you dead?"

For a few seconds they were on their backs and lying side by side. Her hair and face were soaked with blood, and yet he saw his own reflection in her eyes, saw her lips move. When he realized she was asking for help, he panicked.

With a spurt of adrenaline born of nothing but fear, he picked her up and threw her over the rim into the tree-lined gully below. The pop and crack of the breaking limbs echoed loudly as they gave from the weight and momentum of her falling body. He was sick to his stomach and shaking in every muscle as he waited for the sound to cease.

Finally it was over. He leaned forward and finally saw a tiny blotch of red through the trees.

"Damn. Her coat. I should have taken it off," he muttered, but it was too late.

Suddenly, the enormity of what he'd done swept through him. Desperate to be gone, he turned, grabbed the blue plastic sheet and ran through the trees, back to where he'd set down. The still spinning rotors were stirring up a tornado of dust and leaves as he reached the chopper. Frantic now to get away, he ripped off his coveralls, as well as the baseball cap he'd been wearing, wrapped the clothes and the wrench, which was now a murder weapon, in the plastic sheeting, and tied them up along with a couple of nearby rocks he would need for ballast.

When he took off, he went straight up, then headed for a nearby abandoned rock quarry holding more than forty feet of dark, murky water. He circled it once, then dropped the entire package into the middle of the quarry, circling overhead as he watched it sink. Once it was gone, he took off like a bat out of hell, bound for Dallas. He'd only gone about a half mile when he saw a small plane and recognized it as one belonging to a pipeline company in the area. They often flew the path of the buried pipelines searching for leaks, and that was obviously what they were doing today. Too late to take another course, he could do nothing but fly on, knowing full well they'd seen him.

He'd intended to fly straight back to Dallas, but now that he'd been spotted, the only thing he could do was what he did every time he came out to his leases. He turned the chopper toward Tyler, a small town not too far away, then landed on a heli-pad often used by oil and gas companies, and started walking.

There was a barbeque joint a couple of blocks away that he visited each time he was in the area. If this was going to be his alibi, then he didn't dare alter his habits. Eventually someone would discover that Marsha Benton was missing, but it wasn't going to be on his head.

By the time he got to the restaurant, his step was lighter. This was going to work out perfectly. He had been seen flying over his own oil leases, which he did on a regular basis. And he was eating at his favorite restaurant, as he did with every visit. Nothing out of the ordinary. No one to blame.

The owner greeted him jovially as he walked in the door, then led him straight to his favorite table. Mark ordered a slab of baby back ribs, a side order of fries and coleslaw, and cleaned his plate. He left a big tip on his credit card as he paid, then walked out. A short while later he was on his way home. The night was overcast, and the weather was already beginning to change for the worse as he landed the chopper back at the company hangar. He was home, but still not done.

He put on another pair of gloves, got into Marsha's car and headed for what he called the projects. Within the hour, he was circling an old housing complex. When he found a likely spot, he called a cab, asking to be picked up at The Bump and Grind, a busy, well-known nightclub with a reputation for drugs and whores, which was a few blocks over.

He parked the car on a corner beneath a broken street light, and left the keys in the ignition and the car unlocked. He got out without looking back and jogged to the club. Once there, and without making eye contact with the crowd around the front door, he waited for the cab to arrive.

Luck was with him.

Within five minutes he was being driven away. As they left the bad streets of Dallas behind him, he began to relax. He knew that Marsha's car would be gone before morning, most likely stripped or on its way to Mexico. Even if it showed up somewhere down the road, they would never be able to link it to him.

He rode the cab to within a half mile of the company airport, paid the driver off, then walked the rest of the way back. When he finally reached the hangar and crawled into his own car, it was close to four in the morning. His hands were shaking as he reached for his seat belt.

It was ten minutes to five when he entered the house. He reset the security alarm before it sounded, then removed his shoes and hurried upstairs, side-stepping the family cat, who, as always, was roaming the rooms in the dark. When he finally made it into the bedroom, he was relieved to find Penny sound asleep.

As badly as he wanted to crawl into bed beside her, he needed to maintain his alibi. When he saw how she'd curled up in a ball, he put an extra blanket over the bottom half of the bed, then hung up his clothes. Then, conscious of the continued need for an alibi, he wadded up his pajamas and messed up the sheets and his pillow as if he'd been in them all night, before hurrying into the bathroom.

His face was drawn, his eyes red-rimmed and

bloodshot as he looked at himself in the mirror. He stared at himself until he started to smile, and then he did a little jump-hop and turned the water on in the shower.

He'd done it! His troubles were over, and no one was the wiser.

By the time he came out of the shower, Penny was sitting up in bed and combing her hair out of her face.

"Darling…what on earth are you doing?" she asked.

Mark bent down and kissed her as he tossed his wet towel toward the bathroom.

"Got to get to the office early," he said. "I have some overseas phone calls to make."

Penny made a face.

"What time did you come home? I never even knew when you came to bed."

"Lord, honey, I'm not sure. It was late." Then he leaned down and kissed her again, this time lingering on her pouty lips. "You looked so cute. You know how you get when you're cold, all rolled up in that little ball? I put extra covers on your feet and you relaxed."

Penny blew kisses at him. "Poor baby, working so hard, and it's almost Christmas."

"I know," he said. "But we'll be leaving for Tahoe in a day or so, with plenty of time to enjoy ourselves there."

She got up and went to the bathroom. Mark was

dressed and ready to head downstairs by the time she came out. She made a face because she'd missed a morning quickie, then crawled back into bed and closed her eyes.

Mark was riding an adrenalin high as he arrived at his office. He felt no guilt for what he'd done. Marsha Benton had been a threat to everything he'd accomplished. The only downside was that he was going to have to find another personal assistant.

A few hours passed before he got tired of answering his own calls. He was reaching for the phone book to call the employment agency when the door to his office opened. Frowning, he looked up. It was Penny.

"Darling, where on earth is Marsha?"

Mark quickly shifted gears mentally as he strode across the room to greet her, then ignored her question by taking her in his arms.

"Penny, darling, I didn't know you were coming into the city. Please tell me you have time to let me take you to an early dinner."

Penny Presley giggled and fluffed her freshly done hair as she threw her arms around her husband's neck.

"Oh, darling, you can take me anywhere you want."

Mark made a low growling sound in the back of his throat and nuzzled the spot behind her ear. She moaned as she rubbed herself against his groin.

Mark's reaction was just as she'd expected. She smiled slowly as she looked up at him.

"You want me, don't you, honey? I can tell you do. Even after all these years, I still turn you on, don't I?"

"Lord, yes," Mark said, and cupped her hips, pulling her closer. "Feel me, honey? You're the best there is, and you're mine."

He grinned at her, locked the door to his office, and for a short while the business of hiring and firing—and killing—was put aside as he gave Penny Presley everything she wanted.

Four

Cat had been home for three hours before her patience wore thin. Despite the cold and rain, she'd driven back over to Mimi's townhouse again and had staked out the building, intent on confronting her the moment she arrived. But when sunset came and then went, and the street lights came on, she got a knot in her belly. She left message after message on Mimi's cell phone but never got an answer. All night, she sat outside the building, growing more fearful by the hour. When sunrise was only a heartbeat away, she picked the lock on Mimi's apartment one more time. This time, she was going to go through the place like she owned it.

Two hours passed as she went through everything there was to see. She found note pads where Mimi had been doodling Mark Presley's name. There were notes to herself to pick up her dry cleaning, a grocery list that had yet to be filled and a note to call the doctor. Still Cat could find nothing identifying which obstetrician Mimi might have chosen out of the hundreds in the city. All her suitcases were in the extra bedroom where she always kept them, and the closets were full. She should have been there, but she wasn't. Sick with a growing panic, Cat went back to her car and drove away.

Wilson had been wondering why he hadn't heard from Cat Dupree. She'd seemed so excited that he'd found her charm; then, when he'd called her, she'd all but brushed him off. He'd gone about his business, telling himself that if it was meant to be, they would run into each other again.

He'd been in court for part of the day, testifying at a trial, and had gone from there to the police station to drop off some papers. It was one of the few times he hadn't been thinking of her, and then she walked into the building.

He saw her pause and speak to a uniformed officer who was going out the door. The officer spoke to her briefly, then pointed up. At that point she walked toward an elevator. Curious, Wilson watched her get in; then, against his better judgment, he followed, taking the stairs in a run.

He caught a glimpse of her backside as he exited

the stairwell. She was going toward Homicide. He frowned and continued to follow.

He had a couple of good friends in the department and was ready to use them for an excuse when he walked in. Almost immediately, he saw the back of her head. He grinned to himself. Luck was holding. She was sitting at his buddy Joe Flannery's desk.

Cat was worried sick, but even more, she was certain this visit was going to be a bust. It had occurred to her that she should report first to Missing Persons, but she knew they wouldn't take her seriously until a certain length of time had passed. Too scared to wait and with no evidence to back up her fears, she was going to go out on a limb. She would happily take some hard knocks from the cops if they would just listen and believe.

She'd been directed to the desk at which she was now sitting with the information that a Detective Flannery would be right with her. The longer she sat, the more certain she was that this had been a mistake. She should have gathered more evidence before coming here.

She had started to get up and walk out when she heard someone say her name.

"Cat? Is that you?"

She looked over her shoulder. Wilson McKay was walking toward her.

"It is you," he said, smiling as he reached her chair.

"If I'd known I was going to see you here, I would have brought your charm."

"I was…uh, I came to—"

Before she could stammer out an answer, the detective arrived.

Joe Flannery grinned when he saw Wilson, then slapped him on the back and shook his hand.

"Hey, you. You've been dodging me for weeks. What's wrong? Scared I'll beat you at handball again?"

"You didn't beat me the first time," Wilson drawled. "I got a phone call and had to leave, remember?"

Flannery laughed and cuffed Wilson again, and, believing that Cat was with Wilson, included her in the moment.

"You're taking a big chance hanging out with such a lowlife," he teased.

Cat didn't smile back.

"I'm not with him," she said. "I think something's happened to a friend of mine. I think she's dead."

Both Flannery and Wilson shifted mental gears so suddenly that the effort was visible on their faces.

"I'm sorry. I misunderstood," Flannery said, and quickly sat down.

Wilson frowned. Suddenly all of the brush-offs she'd been giving him began to make sense. Without waiting for an invitation, he pulled up another chair and sat down beside Cat. When she gave him a questioning look, he put his elbows on his knees and leaned forward.

"Moral support," he said.

Cat was past caring who listened to her story. The more people who believed her, the better it would be. Still, she clenched her hands into fists to keep them from trembling as she turned her attention to the detective.

Flannery glanced at Wilson. "You know her?"

Wilson nodded.

Flannery looked at the woman. She wasn't objecting, so he let it slide.

"Ma'am, would you please tell me your name?"

"Catherine Dupree."

Flannery noticed the odd, husky quality to her voice as he flipped open a page in his notebook and jotted down her name. It wasn't until he'd written *Dupree* that he frowned and looked up.

"Don't I know you?"

She held her gaze firm. "I don't know you."

"What's your occupation?" he asked.

"I work for Art Ball."

Flannery shifted in his chair as he looked at the woman with new interest. As he did, he noticed a thick, ugly scar extending halfway around her neck and then quickly looked away, ashamed to be caught staring.

"The bounty hunter...you're his bounty hunter, aren't you?"

"My occupation isn't the issue here," she said.

He made a note by her name, just the same.

"You're claiming a friend of yours is dead…is that right?"

"Yes."

"So tell me what happened?"

"She's gone."

"Have you reported her to Missing Persons?"

Cat sighed. This wasn't going to go well. "No."

"Why not?" Flannery asked.

"Because I don't believe she's missing. I believe she's dead."

"Why do you think that?"

A muscle jerked in Cat's jaw, but her voice remained calm. "Because she told me she'd been threatened."

"By whom?"

"Her boss."

At that point Wilson interrupted. "How long has she been missing?" he asked.

Flannery frowned. "I'm asking the questions here," he said.

"Sorry," Wilson said, but he still waited for Cat's answer. He watched her face, expecting a mirror of her emotions, but she gave nothing away.

"I last talked to her yesterday morning. She had been crying," Cat said.

"Why?" Flannery asked.

"Because she'd just been fired."

"By the same boss who threatened her?" Flannery asked.

"Yes."

"And this boss's name is…?"

"Mark Presley."

Flannery's pen ran off the end of his notebook onto his desk, making a slight scratching sound as it dug through years of old varnish.

"Mark Presley of the Presley Corporation?" he asked.

"Yes. She's been his personal assistant for years."

"Did she say why she'd been fired?"

"They were having an affair. She got pregnant. He wanted her to have an abortion. She wouldn't. He fired her."

A muscle jerked in Flannery's jaw as he laid his pen down beside the notebook and then raised his head. He didn't bother to hide the sarcasm in his voice.

"What makes you think she isn't complying with his request? Maybe she's at some clinic now and just not up to answering your calls."

Cat answered his sarcasm with anger.

"They broke up because she wouldn't have an abortion. I had lunch with her just the other day. She was scared."

"Of Presley?"

"Yes. She said he'd threatened her."

He picked the pen up again. "Did she say how?"

"What she said was that he'd made threats to her, and she used the words, 'six feet under.' Then, yesterday, after she told me that he'd fired her, I wanted to get together with her, but she said she was going to go to a doctor's appointment first and then she'd come over to my place. I didn't think to ask which doctor, but she did tell me that as soon as she got out, she would give me a call. I waited all day. She didn't call."

"Maybe she's just not in the mood to talk to—"

"She's not home. I staked out her apartment last night. I searched it this morning. She never showed. Something has happened to her."

"What's the make and model of her car?"

"She drives a silver Lexus. New this year. The license is one of those vanity tags. Hers says ALLMINE."

Wilson frowned as he listened to Cat's story. None of this sounded good, but he wasn't a cop.

Flannery rubbed at a mole behind his right ear. It was something he did when he was frustrated.

"Look, Miss Dupree, I understand your concern. But this isn't a case for Homicide. In fact, it's not yet a case for Missing Persons. Your friend is an adult. She has the right to come and go without notifying anyone. She could be anywhere. Maybe she re-thought her decision not to have the abortion and has gone somewhere to recuperate."

Cat's anger was evident by the fact that her fists tightened until her knuckles went white. It was Flannery's good fortune that she still had her hands in her lap.

"We grew up in the system. We knew what it was like to be unwanted kids. The last thing she would *ever* do is reject a child of her own. Don't argue with me about that, because you don't know a fucking thing about our lives."

"I don't appreciate your language," Flannery said.

"And I don't appreciate your piss-poor attitude," Cat fired back.

Flannery knew he wasn't handling this well and wished Wilson was somewhere else. Fortunately Wilson interrupted by putting a hand on Cat's shoulder.

"Anger isn't going to find your friend," he said.

Cat stood abruptly.

"Doesn't look like the police are going to make an effort, either. I knew I was wasting my time when I came here, but I didn't do this for myself. I'm doing it for Marsha. I don't think she's missing. I think she's dead. Presley threatened her, and I think he made good on the threat."

"Look, Cat…murder is a big accusation," Wilson said.

Her eyes were flashing, but her voice was clipped and steady.

"I know you two don't know me, and you also don't know Mimi. But trust me when I tell you…she would never kill her own child, and she would not leave town without telling me. Never."

Wilson heard more than anger in Cat's voice. She was scared—as scared as a person could be and not be screaming.

"Cat…"

She turned on him, directing her fury with one succinct word. "What?"

"Maybe when you turn in a missing person's report tomorrow and—"

"Tomorrow?" She threw her arms over her head and then slapped her hands hard against her thighs. "Tomorrow. And what about tonight? She didn't sleep in her bed last night. She won't be sleeping in it tonight. She's pregnant. Her life was threatened. She's missing." She pointed angrily at Wilson. "You report her missing tomorrow." Then she jabbed a finger in Flannery's chest. "Or maybe you do it. Oh, wait. I know! Let's just wait until there's no hope in hell of finding her before she rots, and then we can identify her from dental records and the broken arm from when she was seven. How's that?"

Then she turned angrily, grabbed her coat from the back of the chair, and strode out of the office with her head up and her jaw clenched. She hit the door with the flat of her hand and slammed it shut behind her so hard that a coffee mug someone had left on a nearby file cabinet vibrated off the edge and shattered when it hit the floor.

Wilson looked at Joe. "I think that went well."

Joe grimaced. "What do you think?"

"I think she's pissed."

"What do you think she's going to do?"

Wilson shrugged. "Hard to say, but I would bet money that whatever happens next, you'll have to hear it from someone besides her."

'What do you mean?"

"She won't come back and ask for help a second time," Wilson said. "You saw her face. She doesn't trust the system, and from the little she just said about her background, you can't blame her."

There was a message from Art on Cat's cell phone. She called him back on her way to her car.

The message was the same old thing. He had bonded out a woman who'd been picked up for writing hot checks, but she'd been a no-show in court earlier that day.

He needed her brought in.

Cat needed something to do to keep herself from going crazy.

She picked up the phone and punched in the numbers. Art answered on the third ring, and, as always, coughed into the phone as he answered. Cat immediately lit into him.

"Damn it, Art, you need to quit smoking. One day that cough is going to be the last thing to come out of your mouth."

Art coughed again, took a quick drag of his cigar, then put it out in an ashtray already overflowing with ashes and butts.

"Yeah, yeah, that's what you always say," he said.

"So fax me the particulars on Charity Ann Kingman."

"You sound all pissy and fierce. I want her back in one piece," Art growled.

Fear she wouldn't admit to was making her sick to her stomach. Here she was, going about her business as if nothing was different in her world, when in truth, she knew it was crumbling about her ears. She just couldn't make anyone believe.

"That's because I *am* all pissy and fierce," she muttered. "I won't break your bail jumper. In fact, I won't even bend her. Now fax the info. I need to be busy."

"You needin' money, hon?"

Cat looked down at her shoes, trying hard not to scream. Art thought of himself as her father. Most of the time she appreciated his concern, but not today.

"No. I just need something to do."

"What's wrong?" he asked. "And don't give me no runaround. We've known each other too long for that."

Cat swallowed past the knot in her throat.

"Mimi is missing. I think something bad has happened to her."

"Oh hell, honey. I'm sure sorry to hear that. You go to the cops with it?"

"Yeah."

"Well, that's good. That's good. Still, I'll bet she shows soon, and you'll see that you was all worried for nothin'."

Cat shoved a hand through her hair as she unlocked the door to her SUV and got in. The cops were as useless to her as a third tit, and Art's "it'll be all right" attitude was no better.

"Yeah, sure," she mumbled.

"So, I'll be faxin' that info to you now. Call me if you run into trouble."

"Okay," Cat said, and hung up, then headed home.

She was moving fast when she got back to her apartment. She hurried to her office, grabbing the fax that had already come through. She picked up a couple of other pages that had obviously been faxed earlier and walked to the window for a better look.

As always, they were of men with tattoos. She had a network of people all over the United States who, on a regular basis, faxed her mug shots with rap sheets. She was determined to find the man who'd killed her father. So far, she had yet to get a hit, but she wasn't going to give up.

She tossed the two sheets into a box on the floor that was already overflowing with similar papers, made a file from the papers Art had faxed her regarding Charity Kingman and walked out of the room. She hurried to her bedroom, packed the bag she normally took on a stakeout and left without thinking to check the answering machine in the kitchen. It was a quarter to eleven in the morning. Even though her world felt as if it was coming to an end, the day wasn't even half over.

* * *

Charity Kingman considered herself streetwise and sharp, although she was facing a second stay in lockup for bad paper, which even she knew didn't really back up her opinion of herself. However, she knew she was looking good. Her skirt was short; her legs were long. She had rock-hard abs, and what nature had shorted her on, she hid with what she called "personality."

She knew Art Ball would be mad about yesterday, but she'd never intended to show up for court. She didn't have any defense. She'd written the hot checks, and she'd gotten caught. But what else was a girl to do when she needed to look good and was a little short on cash? Besides, she had a plan. All it was going to take was a quick make-over at a cushy day spa and she would be set to go.

Cat read the particulars on Charity Kingman while eating most of a breakfast burrito in her car. She passed a lot of time and had a lot of meals in there, and was finishing her coffee as she finished the file Art had sent her. As the last swallow went down, she reached for her cell phone. Her first call was to the nail salon Charity normally frequented, the second was to her landlord. When she found out that Charity was behind on her rent, Cat knew she wouldn't be hiding out in her apartment. The call she made to the salon where Charity had her nails done was revealing as well. Charity had a standing appointment, but she'd called in and canceled yesterday. After a couple of follow-up questions, though, her nail tech had let it slip that Charity was planning a trip.

The timing added up. Charity Kingman needed to make herself scarce. All Cat could hope for was to catch her before she ran.

But where had she gone?

She went back to the file again and began to study it. Charity was from the Midwest, a little town outside of Cleveland. Since coming to Dallas six years earlier, she had never held a job for more than six months. She'd been arrested for soliciting, for bad checks, and for busting the windshield of a boyfriend who'd dumped her for another woman. She wasn't what Art called a "bad ass," but she was constantly in trouble and dumb enough to keep getting caught. The way Cat looked at it, finding Charity had to happen within the next twenty-four hours or it was probably going to be too late to find her easily. She didn't strike Cat as the kind of woman who would go running home, so she mentally crossed off Ohio as a place she would go.

Halfway through the file, she ran across a notation regarding a former roommate named Danni Chester, and an old address on the south side of the city. It was the only thing in the file that could be construed as a permanent link to another person. It was almost a year old, but it was a place to start.

She checked her cell phone for messages, but there were none. As she was gathering up her trash, it occurred to her that she hadn't checked the answering machine at her apartment. She got out of her car, dumped her trash, and was just about to call home to check it when her cell phone rang. When she saw who was calling, she decided not to answer it, but then changed her mind.

"Hello."

Wilson winced. The clipped tone of her voice didn't bode well for this becoming any kind of a pleasant conversation.

"Cat, it's me, Wilson."

"What do you want?"

He winced again.

"I thought maybe I could come by with your charm."

"I'm not home. I'm working. Call me later."

She hung up in his ear.

He disconnected. Then, disgusted with her and also with himself for still trying to connect with what appeared to be a certified bitch, he threw his cell phone on the bed and kicked a throw pillow that had fallen on the floor.

Wilson's call distracted Cat enough that when she hung up, she forgot she'd been going to call home. Instead, she got back in her vehicle, slammed the door and drove out of the parking lot in a huff, leaving rubber behind as she went.

* * *

Charity considered her new look a sure cure for the warrant that was bound to be out for her arrest. Her long blond hair was now short and red. She'd had her eyebrows dyed to match, and was wearing five earrings on each ear, the fake kind that looked pierced but really weren't. She'd traded her designer clothes for an off-the-rack mini-skirt and little-bit-of-nothing top covered by a white fake fur coat that barely cupped the bottom of her backside. She'd found a pair of high-topped black boots in a thrift store that went over her knees, and for a last bit of flash, wrapped a thin red scarf around her neck.

Finally she was ready to split. All she needed to do was pick up her stuff from Danni's apartment and get to the bus station. After that, her troubles would be over.

Cat hadn't been outside Danni Chester's apartment building for more than fifteen minutes when she saw a cab pull up to the curb. She tensed, leaning forward as she watched the door open, but when she saw the female getting out, she leaned back. Wrong woman. She noted that the cab didn't leave, then went back to watching for Charity.

A few minutes passed, and then the same red-headed woman came back out, this time carrying a small suitcase. Another woman walked out with her,

her arm over the redhead's shoulder. When they hugged, Cat's focus moved from the redhead to the other woman.

She grabbed the file on the seat beside her and thumbed through the pages until she found a mug shot of Danni Chester, who'd been arrested more than once for prostitution. After a couple of glances, she recognized the woman standing by the cab as Danni Chester, which told Cat she needed to check out the redhead, if for no other reason than to exclude her from the hunt.

She checked the mug shot of Charity one more time, then tossed the file onto the seat beside her and got out of her car. She patted the outside of her coat, making sure her gun and handcuffs were still in the waistband of her pants, and then started across the street.

The closer she got, the faster she went. By the time the redhead was opening the door to get into the cab, Cat was at the back rear fender.

"Hey, Charity...love your new do," she called out.

Charity Kingman was smiling as she turned. It wasn't until she saw that Cat was a stranger that she realized she'd just given herself away. Then she saw Cat's badge and the handcuffs in her hand.

"Well, shit," she muttered.

Danni Chester started to shove Charity into the cab when Cat pointed at her.

"What? You in a big hurry to go to lock up with her?"

Charity sighed. Danni was a friend. She didn't want to get her in trouble, too.

"Don't, Danni. You don't want to fight Cat Dupree."

"Never heard of her," Danni said, giving Cat a rude lookover.

"She's Art Ball's bounty hunter. Everyone knows her," Charity said.

"Never heard of you, either," Cat said and pointed at Danni. "Get out of my way."

Danni blinked rapidly and took a couple of steps backward. On closer inspection, the Dupree woman looked a little too scary to mess with.

Charity spat out the gum she'd been chewing as Cat calmly handcuffed her.

"Hey, honey, button up my coat for me, will ya? I'm freezing here."

Cat eyed the long stretch of bare legs between the hem of the mini-skirt and the top of the black boots, then the size of the breasts pushing at the low-cut sweater, and snorted lightly.

"Cold boobs are the least of your worries," she stated, and then took Charity by the arm.

"Wait!" she cried. "My bag. Danni, get my bag out of the cab!"

Danni took the bag and sent the cab driver on his way.

"Please," she asked, as she held the bag out to Cat. "Can't she even have her things?"

Cat kept on walking, pushing Charity along in front of her.

"The state of Texas is about to provide all she's going to need for the next year or so."

"Danni, keep my things for me," Charity asked.

"Let me know where you're going!" Danni called after her.

Cat opened the back door to her SUV and gave Charity a little push as she got her inside. Then she leaned in and buckled the seat belt.

"Thanks so much," Charity snapped.

Cat eyed her without answering.

Charity opened her mouth to say something else, then Cat leaned in.

"I didn't put you in this position, you put yourself in it. So don't give me any crap. I'm not in the mood."

Charity's nostrils flared in anger, but she stayed quiet. She didn't have to like the bitch, even if she was right.

Five

By the time Cat got to the precinct to turn Charity in, she felt feverish. She started getting shaky and weak down in booking. A drunk had thrown up in a waste basket by the door, and two homeless men were trying to report the theft of their shopping cart from outside the alley near a Chinese restaurant. Along with the heat being pumped through the overhead vents, the mingled odors were appalling. She could feel her stomach starting to roll.

The desk sergeant was asking her something about Charity Kingman. She could see his mouth moving, but his words were all running together. When she looked away, the wall behind the desk started to melt. That was when she knew something was wrong.

"I don't feel so good," Cat muttered, and slipped her

arms into the sleeves of her coat. "If you have any more questions, call Art's Bail Bonds. She's one of his."

She walked away without looking back, telling herself that she would feel better once she got some fresh air. But it didn't work. The cold blast of air just made her shiver.

She started across the parking lot toward her car, thinking that if she just got inside, she would be okay. But the more she walked, the farther it appeared to be. There was a part of her that knew she shouldn't drive, but she wanted to go home—needed to go home. There might be word about Mimi. There had to be word. You couldn't just "lose" a friend like you lost a wallet. She had to be somewhere.

Wilson's day had been just as productive as Cat's. He had turned in a bail jumper over an hour ago and was walking through the parking lot to his truck when Joe Flannery hailed him.

"Hey, Wilson. Heard anything more from your girlfriend?"

Wilson frowned. "She's not my girlfriend, and you know it. At the moment, she's as pissed off at me as she is at you."

"She didn't turn in a missing person's report," Joe said.

"Are you waiting for me to say, 'I told you so'? Fine, I told you so," Wilson said.

"Yeah, I figure her friend showed up and she's too embarrassed to let us know."

Wilson thought about it a minute, then shook his head.

"That doesn't sound like something she would do. She appears pretty forthright to me."

Joe grinned.

"She's pretty, all right."

But Wilson couldn't play easy about what he felt for her. He didn't even know why he kept thinking about her, other than he had that damned charm. Maybe when he got rid of it he would be rid of her, too.

"She's tough as hell," Joe said. "'Course, she had to be, to survive what she did."

"What do you mean?" Wilson asked.

"You saw that scar on her neck?"

Wilson nodded.

"The man who killed her dad, some tattooed guy, also cut her throat. She was just a kid, but his death put her in the system. Eventually she aged out. Word is, she's in this business because she's always looking for the killer."

Wilson felt a little sick to his stomach, imagining what a trauma like that would do to a child.

"Jesus…they never caught him?" he asked

"No."

"What about her mother?"

"She and Cat were in a car wreck when Cat was six. The mother died. Cat didn't."

It was suddenly becoming clearer to Wilson why Cat Dupree kept an impenetrable wall between her and the world. It was too damned painful when she didn't.

"So...you going home for Christmas?" Joe asked.

"Probably," Wilson said. "I always do."

"Tell your folks I said hello."

"Yeah, sure," Wilson said, and then Joe's cell phone rang, and they parted company.

Wilson was on his way to his truck when he caught a glimpse of a tall, dark-haired woman staggering through the parking lot. Almost immediately, he recognized Cat, and when he saw her stumble, he began to run.

Cat was going to fall, and she knew it. She could see the dark wet surface of the parking lot coming at her and tried to brace herself, but her reactions were too slow.

Then, just as suddenly as she was falling, the motion stopped. There were hands on her arms, then around her torso. She could hear a voice that sounded vaguely familiar, but she couldn't focus enough to see who it was.

Wilson was nervous. Cat was almost unconscious. That alone was unsettling. When he turned her in his arms, he realized she was hot—far too hot for the winter chill in the air.

"Miss Dupree... Cat! It's Wilson McKay."

Cat moaned and tried to hold on to him, but her

fingers seemed disconnected from the rest of her body, and she couldn't make them grip.

"I need to go home," she muttered.

"You're sick. You need to see a doctor," he said, and started to pick her up.

She took a swing at him.

"No doctor."

As sick as she was, the message came loud and clear. He braced her to keep her from falling, then picked her up in his arms.

"Don't feel good," she mumbled, and kept pushing him away.

At that moment a police cruiser drove into the parking lot. The headlights swept over them where they stood. Wilson caught a brief glance of her pale face and the scar at her throat, thought about what Joe had told him and weakened.

"Damn it, Catherine…quit fighting me and I will take you home."

Her lips twisted as her hands went to her throat.

"Daddy calls me Catherine."

The admission was telling in its simplicity. God only knew what her nightmares were like. As much as he hated to admit it, he was beginning to feel sorry for her.

Her head fell forward. He could smell the lemon scent of the shampoo she used. It was no fuss, just like her, but from the feel of her in his arms, she was too damned thin.

"Home… I want to go home."

He stood her up against her SUV, then took her car keys out of her hand, opened the door and slid her into the passenger seat, carefully buckling her in. He could always take a cab back to the precinct to pick up his car. This way, her vehicle would be at her home when she was well enough to drive.

"Hey, McKay, need some help?" someone yelled.

He turned around. The man who'd called out was a detective going off duty.

"I got it," he yelled back, then shut the door and ran around to the driver's side.

"What's wrong with her?" the detective asked, as he stopped on his way to his own car.

"Not sure, but she's got a heck of a fever. She's too sick to drive."

"Want me to follow you and bring you back for your car?"

Wilson thought about it, then shook his head.

"No, but thanks. I might need to take her to an E.R., and if I do, I'll use her car."

"Yeah, okay. See you around," he said, and walked on.

Wilson jumped into the car and started it up, quickly turning on the heater and then re-checking her seatbelt. Once he was satisfied that she was as safe as he could make her, he drove out of the parking lot with a mental map of the route to her apartment in his head.

Twenty minutes later and with only one missed turn, he pulled into the parking lot of her housing complex, found the building her apartment was in and parked.

Before he got out, he checked her key ring, making sure that her front door key was on it. He saw one that looked right, then slipped the keys into his coat pocket and opened the door. The cold air cut straight to the bone. He buttoned the top button of his coat as he circled the SUV.

Cat roused up as he lifted her from the seat. A few feet from the apartment building, she knew she was going to be sick.

"Throw up," she muttered.

She didn't have to say it twice. He set her down on her feet and then braced her just as the nausea struck. By the time she was through, she was even weaker than before.

"Sorry."

Wilson was staggering, trying not to let her fall.

"It's okay. Just be still. I'm trying to help you."

Even though she was sick out of her mind, Cat wasn't the kind to give up or give in. Her legs wouldn't work, but she kept trying to walk and ended up stepping all over Wilson's feet.

A couple who happened to be Cat's neighbors were coming into the building as Wilson was struggling with her and the door. When they saw she was ill, they quickly offered to help. The man held the door for Wilson as the woman ran ahead to get an elevator. They rode up to the sixth floor together, chattering rapidly about their concern for their neighbor while admitting that they hardly knew her.

The man took the key from Wilson's pocket and opened Cat's door. Wilson walked in with Cat braced against him, still weaving and moaning. The man leaned in, shook his head at Cat's condition, then laid the key on the hall table and left.

Wilson sighed with relief. They were home. Now all he had to do was get her into bed. He picked her up, eyed the layout of the rooms, then headed for the hallway to the left. The first door he came to was closed, but the second one on the right was ajar. He toed it open, grunting with satisfaction when he saw a bed.

Cat began to rouse as he laid her down, and when she recognized her surroundings, began unzipping her pants, clearly forgetting she wasn't alone.

Wilson didn't know whether to help her or get the hell out of the room before she got naked, but the decision was taken out of his hands when she tried to get up, staggered and almost fell.

"Here," he said, and guided her back to the bed. "Sit down and let me help."

She didn't bother to argue when her boots came off, and when he pulled her sweater off over her head, she lifted her arms like a baby.

"Oh, God," she moaned. "Am I going to die?"

He started to smile, but she'd already faced that question twice in her life and survived, so he supposed, from her standpoint, it was a fair question.

"You're not going to die. You're just sick, but I don't think it's food poisoning, because you have a hell of a fever."

He opened the closet and took a flannel nightgown off a hook as Cat motioned toward the bathroom.

"Pills in the medicine cabinet."

"I'll get them in a minute," he said, and then pulled the nightgown over her head, letting it fall loosely down to her waist. "Can you get the rest of your clothes off by yourself?"

Cat looked down, confused by the nightgown bunched around her lap.

"What clothes?"

"Never mind," he said gently. "I'll help."

He slid his hands beneath the gown, undid the clasp on her bra and then pulled it off without touching her. As soon as he had it off, he held out the sleeves of the gown.

"Slide your arms inside," he said.

She did as he asked, then fell backwards onto the bed with a groan. Her voice was so weak Wilson barely heard her whisper.

"Oh Lord, oh Lord…make this go away."

Wilson felt sorry for her. Being this helpless was probably twice as difficult to accept for a woman as strong and independent as Cat Dupree.

"Scoot up a little," he said, and then maneuvered Cat's head onto her pillow. As soon as he had the covers down and her settled in the middle of the bed, he pulled the hem of the nightgown down, then reached up beneath it and pulled off her jeans and panties.

"Hey," Cat murmured, and took another helpless swing at him when she felt the panties coming off.

"It's all right. You're still decent," Wilson said as he dodged the blow and quickly pulled the covers over her.

She exhaled on a shaky sigh as he tucked her in.

She was trembling and feverish. It worried him that he hadn't taken her to the hospital. What if she was desperately ill and he was only making it worse?

He didn't know what to do next, then remembered the pills she'd mentioned. He ran into the bathroom, got a bottle of pain and fever relief tablets and a glass of water, then hurried back. Once she'd downed the pills, he got a wet washcloth, folded it lengthwise and laid it across her forehead.

Cat sighed. "Feels good."

He breathed a little easier as she closed her eyes, and while he was watching, she fell asleep.

Wilson sat at her bedside until he was confident that her breathing had evened out. When she finally broke into a faint sweat, he knew the fever had broken and the pills were working.

He thought about calling a cab and going home, but he was afraid that when the pills wore off, her fever would come back and she would be in worse shape than before. Sometime after midnight, he decided he wasn't going anywhere until he was sure she could cope and began to make himself at home.

He kicked off his shoes in the living room and hung his coat on a tree in the hall. After a quick look into her bedroom to assure himself she was all right, he went to the kitchen and began digging through the refrigerator for something to eat.

To his surprise, there was plenty of food, mostly leftovers, but still intact. Nothing looked moldy or on the verge of turning green, which wasn't always the case in his own kitchen. He shuffled through the drawers and cabinets until he found what he needed, then dished up some food onto a plate and popped it into the microwave. While he was waiting, he gathered her mail and newspapers, which had accumulated under the slot in the door, and brought them to the kitchen. He tossed everything on the counter, ignoring the fact that several envelopes fell across her answering machine. He did, however, notice the red blinking light, which reminded him to check his own messages. Later, as he was eating, he decided to check his calls.

He pulled his cell phone out of his pocket and listened to the messages, none of which were pressing. When he finished eating, he rinsed the dishes and put them in the dishwasher, then went back to check on her.

She had twisted and turned from the fever, until one side of her nightgown was rolled up above her waist and the covers were off. He couldn't help but notice the length of her legs and the slender curve of her hip. And, while he wasn't going to mess with her gown and take the chance of waking her up, he could pull the covers back over her.

It wasn't until he bent down to grab the blankets that he saw the small tattoo on her hip.

His eyes widened. He looked at her profile. Even asleep, she appeared daunting. But this little tattoo was proof that there might be a softer side to Catherine Dupree.

The tattoo was a butterfly—and it was pink.

Who would ever have believed that Cat Dupree would be the kind of woman to have a girly thing like that?

Barbed wire? Yes.

A skull and crossbones? Sure.

A snake with fangs exposed? Plausible.

But a tattoo of a small pink butterfly on her butt? Priceless.

Still grinning, he straightened the covers and left her alone. Another facet of this woman had been revealed. It was definitely something to consider, which set him to wondering what else she might be concealing.

As she slept, he prowled. It wasn't the gentlemanly thing to do, but no one had ever called him a gentleman. He was curious about her and, despite his better judgment, a little intrigued. It wasn't until he got to her office and saw the boxes stacked against one wall, saw that they were filled with the same things that adorned the walls and the top of her desk, that he got a slow chill.

Every page was of a different man—all criminals with rap sheets—all with varying numbers of tattoos. It was then that he remembered what Flannery had told him—that she and her father had been killed by a tattooed man. The case had long since gone cold, but she, obviously, had not given up the hunt.

Wind was whipping the branches of the lilac bush against Catherine's window. The sound was familiar, and it barely registered as she turned over and pulled the covers a little closer beneath her chin.

In seventeen days school would be out for Christmas vacation, and she could hardly wait. Daddy had promised to take her to New Mexico to go skiing. It would be their first trip to a skiing resort, but hopefully not their last.

Suddenly the sound of breaking glass filtered through her dreams of hot chocolate, roaring fires at the ski lodge and flying down the slopes so fast that she would outrun the sound of her own laughter.

She opened her eyes, then rolled over and sat up just as a loud thud sounded in the hallway.

"What the—"

It was her daddy's voice, but it was cut short by the thud. She jumped out of bed and bolted toward the door.

What if Daddy had fallen and hurt himself? They couldn't go skiing if Daddy was hurt.

When she ran out into the hallway, she saw her father crumpled on the floor.

"Daddy! Daddy!" she screamed, and was running toward him when someone came out of the bathroom and grabbed her around the waist.

She started to scream as she fought, kicking and swinging her arms in an effort to get free. Then she heard a rough, ugly voice cursing in her ear and someone telling her to shut up. She answered by kicking backward and knew that she'd hurt the assailant when he suddenly shrieked with pain.

"Bitch!" he screamed.

Catherine saw the glitter of lamplight on metal; then she saw the hand and arm swinging toward her, like an extension of the knife that was going to end her life.

At that moment her father got up from the floor, staggering toward them and cursing the man who held her, begging him to turn her loose.

Suddenly she was falling.

At first she felt no pain, but within seconds of hitting the floor, the coppery scent of blood was in her nose and her throat was on fire. She grabbed at her neck, thinking she'd been burned, only to find her hands covered in blood.

She looked up just as the assailant grabbed her father and began stabbing him repeatedly in the chest.

She tried to scream, but when she inhaled, she choked.

Her father fell lifelessly to the floor as the assailant

jumped over him and ran to the front door. Catherine watched him disappear into the night as she waited to die.

Over and over, she struggled to breathe, then finally, blessedly, everything went dark.

Cat sat straight up in bed, choking and coughing and grabbing her throat, certain that her hands would come away covered in blood. Instead, all she felt was the hard ridge of scar, followed by the certainty that, although she was in her bedroom, she was not alone.

She rolled toward the bedside table, pulling a handgun from the drawer as she turned on the lamp.

Wilson had been dozing in a small, overstuffed chair, but the sudden brightness, coupled with the fact that he was now staring down the barrel of a gun, was better than any alarm clock he'd ever owned.

"Don't shoot," he said quickly. "It's me, Wilson McKay."

Cat was breathing hard and shaking as she leaned back against the headboard and let the gun fall in her lap.

"What the hell are you doing here? How did you get in?"

He frowned as he eyed the gun lying in her lap.

"Put that thing away," he muttered, waiting for her to do as he'd asked. When the gun was back in the drawer, he answered. "You nearly passed out in the parking lot of the police department. Good Samaritan that I am, I brought you home, then held you in the parking lot while you threw up on my shoes."

"Oh Lord," Cat muttered, but Wilson seemed bothered that she'd pulled a gun on him and wouldn't stop talking. If he only knew how badly her head was pounding, he would shut the hell up. Trouble was, she couldn't focus enough to tell him.

"Your neighbors in 6E helped me get you inside the apartment. I put you to bed and gave you some pills—which have obviously broken your fever, because you're back to your normal bitchy self."

Cat fell back against the pillows, staring at him in disbelief.

Wilson's tirade ended as quickly as it had begun. He took a deep breath then stood, walked to the bed and felt her forehead. It was damp, but cooler. The fever was gone.

"Do you need anything?" he asked. "Water? Something for pain?"

She shook her head no, then groaned when the motion made her feel as if the bed was spinning.

"Are you going to be sick to your stomach again?"

"No."

"Can I get you anything?"

"Water?" Her voice sounded weak.

"Not a problem," he said and took the glass from the table and filled it with cool, fresh water, then carried it back to her bed.

He steadied her as she sipped it, then watched her give in to weakness as she fell back onto the pillow with a thump.

"I feel like shit. What happened?"

Wilson eyed the dark circles beneath her eyes and then laid the back of his hand against her forehead just to make sure the fever had abated.

"I'd guess you picked up some kind of flu bug."

Cat closed her eyes.

"Not a bug. Nothing that small could possibly be causing this much agony."

Wilson grinned. Her sense of humor was unexpected. He watched her hand go to her throat, then trace the scar on her neck. His grin died as he remembered how abruptly she'd awakened.

"Did you have a bad dream?" he asked.

He heard her snort. At least it sounded like a snort, but he'd never heard a woman really snort before. It was somewhat surprising, as was most everything else about Catherine Dupree.

"Are there any other kinds?" she asked.

He frowned.

She scrubbed her hands across her face in an effort to wipe away the memory. When she lowered her hands, he realized she was staring straight at him.

"Sorry about the gun. Sometimes my dreams get mixed up with reality."

"Remind me never to sleep with you," he said, and when her mouth dropped open, he realized what he'd said. "Well...that's not exactly what I meant. I just meant that I need to be the one sleeping on this side of the bed, so that when you go for the gun, you have to crawl over me to do it."

Cat's cheeks burned.

"Not in this lifetime," she muttered.

He grinned again, then winked.

"I think you're well enough to be left on your own now." He stood up, then dug in his pants pocket and pulled out the little silver charm. "Hold out your hand,"

Cat did so, palm upward. When she saw the glint of silver as he dropped the charm into her hand, her vision blurred.

"I've been carrying it with me for days," he said.

A muscle jerked at the side of Cat's mouth.

"I didn't think I'd ever see this again," she said, and then closed it within her fist.

"I can see it means a lot to you. Glad I found it."

Cat looked up at him, shivering slightly as she realized it was the first time a man had ever been in her bedroom. Not that she was a virgin. Far from it. But she'd never allowed anyone into the world that was hers alone. Now here he was, mopping up her puke and wiping her brow as if she were nothing but some helpless baby.

"I owe you," she said.

He grinned again. "Yeah, I know."

His grin was aggravating. She glared.

"Lock the front door behind you when you leave."

"No problem. I just need to call a cab first."

She frowned again. "Where is your car?"

"Back in the precinct parking lot."

"Then how did you get here?"

"We got here in your car. The keys are in the drawer there." He pointed to the small table beside her bed. "You're welcome, and I'll be seeing you soon, so get well, okay?"

"Uh…yes, but—"

Wilson put his hand on the drawer where she kept the gun, then leaned down and kissed her on the cheek.

"I would much rather have kissed your lips, but I was afraid you might be catching. However, on second thought…" He readjusted his aim and brushed his mouth across her lips. "It can't really matter."

Cat was ill-prepared for Wilson's onslaught. She pulled back in anger.

"Get your pushy ass out of my bedroom."

He straightened up, then shoved his hands in his pockets and stared down at her without speaking.

"You heard me," she said. "If I owe you something, I'll pay up in money, not with my ass."

Wilson glared back. "I didn't hear anyone mention your ass except you, and just for the record, it's too damn skinny for my liking."

He walked to the door, then turned around, as if memorizing the way she looked with her hair tumbling down about her face and her eyes glittering with anger. Finally he shook his head, as much at himself as at her.

"Call me if you need me. I left my card by the phone."

Before she could gather her wits enough to speak, he was gone.

Six

By morning Cat was lucid enough to remember that Wilson McKay had spent the night in her apartment and that Mimi was still missing. There was a knot of pure fear in the pit of her stomach. No matter what anyone said—no matter how logical they made Mimi's disappearance seem—she knew her friend was gone. She would never hear her voice again.

Still feeling miserable from whatever she'd caught, she ignored her frustration and anger with Detective Flannery and gave him a call.

Flannery had been at work all of fifteen minutes and was stirring sugar in his coffee when his phone rang.

"Homicide—Flannery."

"Detective, this is Cat Dupree."

Flannery resisted the urge to duck as he reached for a pad of paper and wrote down her name.

"Yes, ma'am, how can I help you?"

Cat frowned. He wasn't going to make this easy for her, and she wasn't going to apologize for her outburst.

"I'm calling to ask if you've discovered anything regarding the disappearance of my friend Marsha Benton."

Flannery frowned. So the woman was still missing. That was news to him.

"Miss Dupree, I told you when you were here that, at this point, this isn't a case for Homicide."

Cat closed her eyes.

Flannery didn't defend his stance. He just kept talking.

"I *will* tell you that I made a couple of calls. A call to Presley Machines verified your belief she'd been fired, and there was no answer at her apartment. I did this purely on my own. It's not an active case and won't be unless there's further reason to investigate. I'm sorry. Again, if you're still convinced there's been foul play, you need to file a Missing—"

Cat hung up while he was still talking.

When Flannery heard the click and realized she'd disconnected, he cursed beneath his breath. He didn't like being accused of shirking his duties, because he took them very seriously. But he didn't know how to deal with someone as single-minded and hard-headed as Cat Dupree. There were ways to proceed with a situation, and she was ignoring them all.

Meanwhile, Cat was sitting on the side of the bed

with her head reeling. She thought about going into the kitchen and making some coffee, but she feared her stomach was still too upset to tolerate anything but water.

She thought about what Flannery had said. She knew, if she intended to get anyone in the police department interested in what she had to say about Marsha's disappearance, she would have to go through Missing Persons, even though it seemed all wrong to her. Still, being pissed wasn't going to help find Mimi.

She picked up the receiver and called the police again, and this time she asked to be connected to Missing Persons.

Adam Bradley was a nineteen-year veteran of the department and was known for his bulldog attitude toward closing cases. Nothing bugged him more than a case going cold without a resolution.

He'd come to work this morning nursing his bum knee and a toothache. He had an appointment with the dentist later in the day, but for now, he was going through the motions. When his phone rang, he answered with his usual gruff bark.

"Missing Persons…Bradley."

"I need to report a missing person," Cat said.

Bradley reached for his pen and pulled a pad of paper closer to the phone.

"What's the name?"

"Marsha Benton."

"Address?"

Cat rattled it off.

"What does she drive?"

"A new Silver Lexus. It has a vanity plate that says ALLMINE."

"Okay…got it. And what's your name?" Bradley asked.

"Cat Dupree."

Bradley made a note, trying to figure out why the name was familiar.

"Why do you think she's missing? It's December. Maybe she just went home early for the holidays."

Cat felt nauseated and lay back on the mattress to keep from falling out of bed. She didn't like the sound of this man's voice any better than she had Flannery's attitude and almost hung up. But then she thought better of the notion and kept talking.

"She's missing because I'm convinced her boss killed her, and she didn't go anywhere for the holidays because I'm all the family she has."

Bradley's heart thumped, and his pen shifted on the paper.

"You know for a fact she's dead?"

"I haven't seen the body, if that's what you're asking," she said. "But I had lunch with her the day before she disappeared. She'd been crying. She told me she'd been having an affair with her boss, and she was pregnant. He wanted her to get rid of the baby. She wouldn't…couldn't. She said—and these were her words—he'd said something to her about 'six feet under.' I spoke to her the next day. He'd fired her. She was on her way to an appointment with an obstetrician, then she was coming to my house. She never showed up. She never called."

Bradley was writing as fast as Cat was talking.

"Where did she work?" he asked.

"Presley Implement and Machines."

"Who is this boss she's having the affair with?"

"Mark Presley."

Bradley voice rose an octave.

"The owner?"

"Yes."

There was a long moment of silence. Cat could hear the sound of pen scratching on paper.

"Detective…are you still there?"

"Yeah. I'm here. Just finishing up some notes. Here's the deal. I have to verify your statements regarding her firing and the relationship she supposedly had with her boss."

"But you're going to take this seriously…right?"

Bradley frowned. "I take everything seriously, ma'am. You need to come down to headquarters and sign the complaint."

"I'm in bed. I have a fever, and I've been throwing up."

Bradley didn't want the exposure.

"I'll be in touch."

Cat rolled over, replaced the receiver on the cradle and then staggered into the bathroom. She managed to stay upright long enough to shower. She came out later, weak and shaking. Whatever bug she had was still lingering, so she popped a couple of pills for fever and crawled back in bed. Within minutes she was asleep again. She dreamed, but not about Mimi or the attack that killed her father. This time she dreamed about a pirate with a gold hoop in his ear and a devilish smile, who stole kisses when no one was looking.

After a half dozen phone calls, Bradley knew that Marsha Benton, who'd once been Mark Presley's personal secretary, had, indeed, been fired. He also knew that the manager at her apartment hadn't seen her in several days, which was unusual because her apartment was directly above his, and he always knew when she was home.

He'd run a make on her car and found a report that a car matching the description of hers had been found abandoned on a Fort Worth bypass. It had been stripped of everything, including the tag, but he was running the VIN number he'd gotten from the DMV to see if it matched the one on the wrecked vehicle. It changed nothing other than adding a new supposition to why Marsha Benton wasn't where she belonged. Maybe the car had quit on her and she'd been abducted, and her troubles with Mark Presley were nothing more than coincidence.

Still, Bradley wasn't a man who jumped to easy

conclusions just to close a case, and he had taken Cat Dupree's claim of an affair and pregnancy just as seriously as the discovery of Benton's car. In his experience, people had killed for less.

He'd tried to get in touch with Mark Presley at the company, only to be told that Mr. Presley was not at the office and was, in fact, planning to leave the state for the holidays.

No big deal. If Presley wasn't available at the office, he would just have to be available at home. He got his notebook, his overcoat, a to-go cup of coffee, and headed for the parking lot. It was time to pay a visit to Mr. Presley.

Mark Presley was packing when the maid came to tell him there were detectives from the Dallas police department downstairs.

Penny came racing out of the bathroom, naked except for a pair of bikini panties. Her hair was wrapped up in a towel, and her face was covered with a mint facial mask. When she saw the maid was still in the room, she shrieked.

"Get out! Get out!"

The maid dashed out as Penny turned on Mark and nailed him with a look.

"Detectives! Why would detectives want to talk to you?"

Mark stifled a curse. Penny had a tendency to scream at the least little thing.

"Honey… I have no idea. Go ahead with your facial. I'll be right back."

"But what if—"

He walked out before Penny went ballistic.

His stride was unhurried, his shoulders back, his chin up. He showed no fear because he had no fear. Whatever the police had to say, he was ready for them.

Detective Bradley and his partner, Ed Frost, were waiting in the foyer of the Presley mansion. There were empty chairs visible through the door that led into the library, but they hadn't been invited in any farther than where they were standing. The opulence of the place was obvious. Amber-veined marble formed the newel posts of the winding staircase that led to the upper stories, while matching tiles of the same marble covered the floor in the entryway.

A massive chandelier hung from a large gilded chain about halfway down from the eighteen foot ceiling. The scent of warm spices wafted through the air, giving visitors the impression that fresh cookies and warm wassail awaited. From where Bradley and Frost were standing, they could see into three large rooms and in each room stood a fully decorated Christmas tree, each with its own theme.

Ed pointed to the tree in the far corner of the room on their right.

"Would you look at that?" he muttered. "That's a ten-footer if it's an inch."

Bradley nodded. "Yeah, and look at those gold-colored ornaments."

Ed snorted softly. "In this house, they're most likely real."

Bradley eyed them curiously, then elbowed Ed as Presley appeared at the top of the stairs.

Ed straightened up and resumed his business face, as did Bradley, and waited for Presley to grace them with his presence.

Mark Presley had not had his decisions questioned for years, and his demeanor showed it. He descended the stairs with the behavior of a royal. He was a long way from the mechanic's kid who missed out on his childhood dreams. He'd set new goals for himself and surpassed them a dozen times over, and still it wasn't enough. It would never be enough. And these detectives were crazy if they thought they were going to take him away from all he'd created.

As soon as his foot hit the last stair and not before, he acknowledged their presence with a nod.

"Gentlemen, please come with me. We'll have our conversation in the library. There's a nice fire in the fireplace that will offset the discomfort of the weather today."

Bradley and Frost followed.

Mark walked all the way to the fireplace, then turned abruptly, placing one hand on the mantel and gesturing toward the sofa with the other.

"Please. Have a seat. Can I get you something to drink? Coffee? Tea?"

"No, thank you," Bradley said, and pulled a notebook from an inside pocket of his coat as he sat. "Mr. Presley, we'll get straight to the point. We're investigating the disappearance of Marsha Benton. We understand she—"

Mark interrupted quickly, letting surprise color his expression.

"Marsha is missing? That's terrible! I hadn't heard."

Bradley frowned.

"As I was saying…we understand she'd been working for you for several years and that you'd recently fired her. Is this true?"

Mark never broke eye contact.

"Yes. She'd been with me for years. I hated to lose her."

Frost spoke up next.

"Then why is she no longer working for you? We've been told she was fired."

Mark took his hand from the mantel and moved to a large easy chair opposite the sofa. When he sat down, he leaned forward, elbows on his knees. The gesture was open and inviting, as he meant it to be.

"That's true. I did fire her." Then he glanced up at the doorway, as if making sure they were still alone, and slightly lowered his voice, making their conversation even more intimate. "It was a shock, to say the least. She'd been with me for…oh…I don't know…going on nine years, I think. Absolutely priceless when it came to organization. Always on top of everything concerning my work and travel. She's going to be hard to replace."

"So if she's so great, why replace her?" Bradley asked.

Mark's voice softened yet again.

"It was a shock, and embarrassing, I tell you. Completely blindsided me."

"What did?" Bradley asked.

Mark grimaced slightly. "We were working late last week, and out of the blue she began coming on to me. At first I thought she was kidding, although that kind of humor was definitely out of place, but she persisted."

"I told her I was flattered, but that my wife and my marriage meant everything to me, and that I wasn't interested."

Bradley stifled a snort. He'd already researched enough of Presley's background to know he was anything but faithful to his wife. Still, that wasn't proof of any kind of crime.

"How did she take that?" Bradley asked.

Mark shook his head, as if in concern.

"She was upset…started crying and saying that she'd loved me for years and couldn't stay quiet about it any longer. At that point I suggested that perhaps she would be happier working at one of the other corporate offices."

"And…?"

Mark acknowledged Frost's interruption.

"And she would have none of it. She began to disrobe, which shocked me. I told her to get her things and get out, that she was no longer needed in my company."

"So she offered you a freebie and you fired her?"

Mark frowned. The detective was doing little to disguise his sarcasm. He stood up. "I don't like your tone."

Bradley stood up as well. "Yeah, and it's been years since I believed in fairy tales. All fantasies aside, when was the last time you saw Miss Benton?"

"Three days ago, when I let her go," Mark said.

"What do you have to say about the fact that there are claims she was pregnant with your child?"

It was to Mark's credit that the shaft of panic he felt didn't show. How in the hell had they come by that bit of information?

He stood his ground and tempered his urge to scream at them.

"I am not even going to give that gossip the dignity of an answer."

Bradley pressed the issue by rephrasing it. "So your answer is…it's not true?"

Mark lifted his chin and glared at both men.

"I think we're finished here. If you have any other questions about this unfortunate matter, you will ask them through my lawyers, Walters, Walters and Hale."

Frost arched an eyebrow as he made a note. It figured that Presley would have the biggest law firm in the state on retainer.

Bradley was a big man in every way. Tall, heavy-set, and with a big mouth, to boot. He shut his notebook and dropped it back into his pocket, then moved until he was standing about a foot away from Presley, well aware that he towered over the man.

"If we have any other questions for you, you have the freedom to have your attorney present, but if need be, you will be the one answering."

At that moment Bradley could tell he had made an enemy. If there was ever a way that Presley could bring him down, he would do it.

Mark tilted his head sideways, as if deflecting the warning.

"See yourselves out. I have no more time for this. My wife and I are spending Christmas in Tahoe, and I need to finish packing."

"Leave a number with your lawyer as to where you can be reached…just in case," Bradley ordered, then turned his back on Presley and nodded to his partner, and they both walked out without a backward look.

Mark was furious. This wasn't happening. Not to him.

He grabbed the telephone and called Ken Walters, his lawyer, who was, to Mark's dismay, in court and unavailable.

"You tell him to call me the moment he gets out,"

he said, then hung up just as Penny entered the library.

"What's been happening? Why were the police here? What did they want to talk to you about?"

He figured the more truth he told, the less likely it would come back and bite him in the ass.

"Marsha Benton is missing. They wanted to know when I'd seen her last."

Penny's mouth dropped. She liked Marsha.

"Oh no! How awful! Why didn't you tell me she was missing?"

"Because I didn't know it," he said.

"But…wasn't she at work today?"

"No."

"And you didn't think that was strange?" Penny said.

"No."

"Why on earth not? I can't remember her ever missing a day."

"I didn't think it was strange because, a couple of days ago, I fired her."

Penny actually paled. "Why on earth? She was invaluable to the company and a—"

"She acted inappropriately toward me. I offered her a chance to work at one of the corporate offices in another state. She declined. I fired her. End of story."

A dark flush swept up Penny's neck and onto her face. "I don't believe it!"

"Believe it or not, it's what happened," Mark said,

then folded his arms and glared at his wife. "I have to say, I am more than a little shocked that you have so little faith in my word. I would hardly make something like this up. It was embarrassing enough without you calling me a liar. What on earth would I gain by admitting that an employee was infatuated with me?"

Penny saw the anger in Mark's eyes and knew she'd stepped over a line. Still, there was a part of her that found it difficult to believe Marsha Benton would do something so outrageous. She'd always been the epitome of professional. And, while Mark didn't know it, she was well aware of his indiscretions.

"Yes, well… I'm sorry to hear she's missing. I sincerely hope she's all right and hasn't met with some kind of accident."

Mark shrugged. "Accidents happen every day. Now, are we going to Tahoe or not?"

"Yes, we're going," Penny said.

"Are you finished packing?"

"No."

"Then I suggest you get to it. I have the corporate jet scheduled for early afternoon take-off. I want to get there before dark."

"All right. I won't be long," Penny said, and started for the stairs. Then she paused in the doorway and looked back. "Are you coming?"

Mark stuffed his hands in his pockets, jingled his change in frustration, then followed his wife up the stairs.

* * *

Unaware of Mark Presley's plans, Cat was making plans of her own, but first, she had to get well. It was another day before she could get out of bed or tolerate anything in her stomach that wasn't liquid. When she woke up the next morning and the bed wasn't spinning, she showered, then headed for the kitchen.

She made coffee without conscious thought, going through the motions and hoping she could hold it down. She got cream from the fridge, sniffing it cautiously to make sure it hadn't gone bad, then set it on the table and reached for a spoon.

She stirred her coffee, then began picking up some of the clutter that had accumulated during the time she'd been sick. She added to the pile of the newspapers on the counter, along with several days' worth of mail, which scattered, completely covered her answering machine. It wasn't until she began sorting through the mail that she saw the red blinking light indicating waiting messages.

Frowning, she punched the button. There was one from her dentist, reminding her of an appointment that she'd missed while she was sick. There was someone who'd hung up without leaving a message, and one from Art, then silence. She was about to delete them all when she realized there was one more, someone taking his own sweet time before talking.

She reached for her coffee and took a slow sip, waiting for it to hit her stomach. When it didn't come up, she tried another sip, then another, and finally she began to feel human, alert enough to realize the message *was* playing, and she was hearing noise, but no voice.

She set the coffee cup aside and moved closer to the machine. Frowning, she stopped it and then hit replay.

The noise was loud and repetitive—and familiar, but she couldn't put her finger on what it was. She hit Caller ID to check the number. Her heart stopped.

"God…oh God."

She listened again, trying to hear something within the noise.

For three minutes there was nothing but the wash of an engine. No voice. No precious sound of Marsha's presence in any way, and yet the call had come from her cell phone.

When the call clicked off, she staggered backward to the table and fell into the chair with a solid thump. The air in the room around her felt wrong— like it was thick, too solid to breathe. All these days. The call from Marsha that she'd been waiting for…it had been there all these days, and she hadn't known.

She didn't know what it was that she'd heard, but she knew without being told that it was, most likely, the last thing Marsha heard, as well.

She pushed herself up, then staggered to the

bedroom and began to get dressed. Twice she had to stop and sit down to keep from falling. She couldn't find her car keys and then remembered Wilson McKay had driven her home in her car. She began looking for the second set and couldn't find them, either.

Angry and trembling, she tore through the phone book until she found his number. The phone rang four times before an answering machine came on, giving the caller the option of leaving a message or calling his cell. She scribbled down that number, then called it.

Wilson answered on the second ring.

"McKay's Bail Bonds."

"Where are my car keys?"

Wilson frowned. "Good morning to you, too, Miss Dupree."

"I can't find my keys," she repeated.

She sounded strange—at least, stranger than usual.

"What's wrong with you? Are you still sick? If you are, the last damn thing you need are your keys."

"I can't find my car keys! I need my keys!" She didn't know she was screaming. "For God's sake, what did you do with my keys?"

Wilson frowned. "They're in the—"

"Damn you, McKay! I don't need this crap! If you took them just to have a reason to come back, it sucks. I need my keys! I need my keys!"

She was so out of her head, he couldn't help but think something bad was wrong. Maybe she was feverish again. If he told her where the keys were and then she got in her car and caused an accident, he would feel guilty as hell. The only way to alleviate his conscience was to make sure she was physically okay.

"Look, chill out. I'll be right over."

Cat hung up the phone, then staggered to the kitchen and replayed the message over and over again. As she was listening to it for the fourth time, the phone rang.

She grabbed for it.

"Hello? Marsha…is that you?"

Art Ball frowned. "It's me, Art. Where you been, girl?"

Cat closed her eyes and took a deep breath, willing herself not to scream.

"Art…it's you. Uh, I've been sick."

"Yeah, you don't sound so good. You want me to come over and take you to the doctor? All you have to do is ask. You know that."

"Yes, I know. No, I don't need the doctor."

"Okay…so, how's things with Marsha? She showed up, right?"

Cat sighed. She didn't want to talk about it, but Art had been her friend for a long time and had known Marsha almost as long as he'd known her.

"No. She's still missing."

"The hell you say? For how long?"

"Three…no, four days now."

"What do the cops say?"

She rolled her eyes. "The cops? Get real."

Art frowned. "You better call them or I will," he said.

She sighed. "I already did."

"All right then. You know that's the way to go." Then he changed the subject. "What are you thinking?"

"I think she's dead."

"No way. You been to her place? Maybe she just went on a trip. Did you check her clothes, her luggage, stuff like that?"

"Yes."

"Well, dang it, honey…I don't know what to say. Maybe she just took off."

Cat glanced up at the clock, wondering what the hell was keeping Wilson McKay, then made herself focus on Art's question.

"Look, Art… Mimi would *never* drop off the face of the earth without telling me what was up. You should know us better than that."

Art sighed as he scratched at a dried drop of gravy on the edge of his tie.

"Yeah, I know, I know. But she's got to be somewhere. People don't just up and disappear."

"I can't believe that came out of your mouth. You, of all people, should know that people *do* up and disappear, as you put it. That's where my job comes in."

"Well, I didn't mean it like—"

"It's all right," Cat said. "I know this all sounds

dramatic, but I know Mimi. Something happened to her. If the situation was reversed, she would be looking for me."

Art cleared his throat.

"I'm not about to butt into your personal business. I just want you to be careful and stay safe, okay? If we're talkin' murder, here, then remember…they say it's easier to kill the second time around."

Cat snorted lightly.

"What *they* said that?"

"Specs Charleston, that's who, Cat."

She shivered. Specs Charleston had been the first really dangerous bail jumper she'd ever brought in. He was a serial killer who targeted women who wore glasses, hence the name Specs. The trophies from the crimes had been as brutally taken as the man himself. He'd cut out the eyes, then taken them and the victims' eyeglasses. Cat still had an occasional nightmare about the authorities finally nailing Specs and his gory keepsakes in the root cellar of his grandmother's home outside Austin. She'd bad-mouthed Art for months afterward for ever bonding the man out.

"Specs Charleston was a creep. For God's sake, Art, do not even speak my name and his in the same breath."

"I didn't mean nothin' by it. I'm just trying to—"

"I'm taking some time off," she said.

Art sighed. It didn't surprise him. Cat and Marsha were as tight as two friends could be.

"Just keep yourself safe, you hear me?"

Cat eased back on her anger. Art wasn't the one she was mad at. He meant well, and she knew it.

"I'm sorry. I hear you."

"All right, then," Art said.

"Talk to you soon," Cat said, and disconnected.

She stared at the phone, then at the answering machine. She was about to listen to the message again when the doorbell rang.

"Finally," she muttered, and strode out of the kitchen.

It was Wilson. She didn't ask him in; she just held out her hand.

Wilson eyed it as if she were carrying the plague, then stepped past her and walked in without an invitation.

"Hey! My keys are all I need from you, okay?"

He stalked past her, heading for her bedroom. Cat followed, arguing all the way.

Wilson paused in the doorway, then moved to the bedside table. He opened the drawer, took out the keys and put them in her hand.

Cat's fingers closed over them.

"You could have told me this much over the phone."

Wilson glared. The woman was driving him nuts.

"I should have," he muttered, as he grabbed her

by the shoulder, then laid a hand on her forehead, checking for a fever. Her skin was cool.

"Don't touch me," Cat said.

"Shut up, woman. I'm only checking to make sure you're not feverish before I go off and leave you on your own. If you self-destruct after I'm gone, then it's on your head, not mine."

Cat stomped out of the bedroom.

Wilson followed.

She opened the front door and then stood back, waiting for him to exit. She wouldn't look at him. She didn't want to see the concern in his eyes. She didn't want to know that he'd cared enough to come all the way over just to make sure she was lucid.

He was all the way across the threshold when she suddenly cursed herself, then called him back.

"Hey, Wilson."

He turned around. "What?"

He thought he saw her chin trembling, but when he looked again, decided he'd been mistaken.

"If you have time…there's something I want you to hear."

Wilson didn't know what it was, but he knew what it cost her to ask. He walked back into the apartment, closed the door behind him and followed her into the kitchen.

"Sit down," she said, pointing to the kitchen table.

He sat.

She punched a button on the answering machine.

He waited. All he could hear was noise.

"What am I supposed to be hearing?" he asked when the machine clicked off at the end of the message.

Cat played it again.

Wilson stood up and walked closer until he was standing right beside the machine—and her.

"What? Tell me what I'm hearing," he asked.

Cat glanced up at him. She heard the kindness in his voice and saw the concern on his face. She shifted her gaze from the gold loop in his ear to the shape of his mouth, then looked away.

"You tell me," she said. "What does that sound like to you?"

He frowned.

"Play it again, please."

She did.

He closed his eyes and let go of everything but the sound. It was familiar, something he'd heard before, but he couldn't quite put his finger on what it—

"A chopper. It sounds like what a chopper sounds like from inside."

Cat shuddered.

"You mean…when you're riding in one?"

"Yeah. Why?"

"The call is from Marsha's cell phone. It's been on my answering machine for days. I didn't know."

Wilson's heart skipped a beat. It seemed as if Cat might have been right all along.

"Have you told the police?"

"No."

"Jesus, Cat. You can't do this by yourself. You need to call Missing Persons and—"

"I called them. Talked to a man named Bradley. Haven't heard from him since."

"Then we call him. Now."

"But I need to—"

He took the keys out of her hand, then dropped them on the table and turned her around.

"You're shaking like a leaf. What you *need* is to sit down." He took his cell phone out of his pocket. "I'll give Bradley a call and—"

Cat took away his phone.

"I don't need to be taken care of. All I needed were my keys. *I* will call Bradley. Thank you."

Wilson stared at her a moment, then took a deep breath and held out his hand for his phone. As he waited, he saw the silver chain disappearing underneath her shirt and knew she was wearing the charm again.

Cat dropped the phone in his hand. For some reason she chose not to examine, she couldn't bring herself to look into his face.

He put the phone in his pocket and let the silence lengthen between them.

Cat fidgeted. It wasn't often that someone made her uneasy, but this man did. Finally she lifted her head, only to find him watching her intently. Before she could speak, he shoved his hand beneath her hair. She felt his fingers curling around her neck, holding firm, but without hurting. When he leaned down, she guessed he was going to kiss her—again.

His breath was on her face, along with the faint scent of mint, most likely from his toothpaste. She felt his fingers shift.

"Look at me," he said.

Her eyes narrowed defensively.

"I see you."

"Then listen carefully. I don't like being told what to do, either. I don't know why our paths keep crossing, but so far, none of it has been my doing. I'm sorry as hell that your friend is missing. I hope, with every fiber of my being, that you're wrong about her fate. I also know that you don't trust a goddamn person except yourself. In the words of a famous Texan with his own talk show, who shall still remain nameless… 'How's that workin' for you?'"

Cat flinched.

She wished he'd just kissed her. It would have been far less painful than this.

Seven

"I'm in over my head."

Wilson exhaled softly. The admission was surprising. He'd never thought he would hear that admission coming from Cat Dupree's lips.

"It's because you're too close to the pain."

She dropped her gaze.

He turned her loose, then jammed his hands in his pockets to keep them off her and fiddled with his phone instead.

"Call Bradley."

"Okay."

She dialed as he watched.

"Missing Persons. Bradley speaking."

"Detective Bradley, this is Cat Dupree. I discovered a message from Marsha on my answering machine. At least…it's a call…no words…just some sounds."

"I'll be there within the hour."

"Thank you."

She hung up.

"See, that wasn't so hard."

She laid down the phone, then covered her face.

"Mimi was all I had."

Wilson sighed. "For what it's worth, I'm offering my services…but only as a friend."

Cat turned away, then shoved her fingers through her hair in quick frustration.

"I don't deserve it," she said.

Wilson grinned wryly. "You're right about that."

She glared.

He grinned.

"I'm still offering, if you're interested."

Cat looked at him then, as if really seeing him for the first time. He was big and tough, and, even if he did have a gold earring in his right ear, he looked like he could fight his way through a roomful of bears. It might be a good thing to have him on her side—but only because of Mimi.

"Yes," she finally said, and offered her hand.

He took it.

She waited, curious to see what would happen next.

He held it for a moment, as if testing the weight in his hands, then solemnly shook it.

"So, how can I help?" Wilson asked.

Cat thought about it for a while.

"How good are you on research?" she asked.

"What kind of research?"

"Stuff you can get off a computer if you know where to look...personal things about someone's life."

He arched an eyebrow.

"Publicly, I only do what's legal."

"How about personally?"

"Let's just say, in another life, I think I was a bloodhound."

Her jaw set as her eyes narrowed.

"That's good. If you really want to help me, I need information."

"About who?"

"Mark Presley. I need to know where he was, what he did, how he spent his money, where he spent it, and especially everything that would clock his whereabouts from the day before Marsha went missing to the day after. Oh...and I need to know what he owns and where it's located."

He arched an eyebrow.

"Anything else?"

"If I give you Marsha's phone numbers, social security number and address, can you do the same thing with her?"

"Yes."

"Follow me," she said, and headed to her office.

As she rifled through a notebook, he fingered the stacks of mug shots.

"Hell of a collection you have here."

She glanced up, then looked away.

"I guess."

"You're looking for the man who killed your father, right?"

Cat didn't bother to ask how he knew about her past. It wasn't a secret, and people gossiped. She'd heard the question plenty of times before.

When she didn't comment, Wilson pressed her.

"Do you know his name?"

Cat looked up, then frowned.

"No."

Wilson thought about that for a minute, uncertain as to what to say next.

Cat took the decision out of his hands by adding, "But I'll find him, and when I do, then he'll know mine."

Wilson was still absorbing the threat she'd just made when she handed him a list. He eyed it quickly, then folded it up and put it in his pocket.

"I'll be in touch," he said.

Cat walked him to the door.

"You're still pale," Wilson said. "Go back to bed after Bradley leaves."

"I can't. I need to—"

"No, you don't. Right now, all we know is that your friend isn't where she's supposed to be. We need a place to start looking. Give me some time to see what comes up."

"Maybe…"

"Call me if anything changes," Wilson said.

"I will...and thank you."

"You're welcome," he said, then left.

Wilson drove home without stopping at the office. He called his receptionist to let her know where he would be, then called Red Brickman, the bondsman he'd bought the business from, and talked him into subbing for him for a while.

Brickman welcomed the chance to get back into the thick of things and quickly agreed, leaving Wilson to concentrate entirely on Cat's situation.

By the time he got home, he had a mental list of what was ahead of him. The door locked automatically as he shut it behind him. The click was loud and distinct, as distinct as the scent of cold coffee and an old pizza box that had missed being tossed out with the trash.

Wilson wrinkled his nose as he took off his jacket and gun, hanging one up in the closet and carrying the other to his bedroom. The scent of the place wasn't particularly appealing, but it was familiar, and for Wilson, it was enough. He laid the gun on top of the dresser, changed into a pair of sweat pants and a T-shirt, then retraced his steps through the living room, this time heading for the kitchen.

His stomach was growling, but after a quick prowl through the cabinets and the fridge, he settled for what was left of a package of Oreo cookies and a

Pepsi that had gone flat. The "meal" settled his belly but not his soul.

He felt lost, even aimless, which made no sense. He thought about what he'd agreed to do for Cat Dupree. He didn't regret it, but he couldn't help but wonder why he kept involving himself in her business. She was sexy, aggravating, hard as nails and not prone to being friendly. He couldn't figure out why he even cared what she thought about him. He knew plenty of pretty women. But, he had to admit, none of them were Cat Dupree.

He thought of Cat again, alone in her apartment and waiting for Bradley to arrive. He knew she was scared. He also knew she would never admit it.

Problem was, he wouldn't put it past her to play detective alone, which was a foolhardy thing to do, but that scar on her neck was visible proof that she'd been in danger before. He didn't know what she wanted of him, but he knew he was going to have a hard time telling her no.

Finally he headed for his office, booted up his computer and began going over the list she'd given him. Hours later he looked up, realized how long he'd been at this, and then glanced down at his notes and the pages he'd downloaded. He'd made some headway into Mark Presley's private life, but whether it led them to Marsha Benton remained to be seen.

He looked toward the phone. He'd half-expected

Cat to call after Bradley's visit, but she hadn't, which meant there was probably nothing to tell. All Bradley could have done was take the machine in and have their experts analyze it to see if they could separate anything specific from the noise. It was a long shot, but all they had.

He thought of his family, trying to imagine losing track of one of them, and felt guilt at how long it had been since he'd called them. Despite the hour, he picked up the phone. His dad wouldn't go to bed before the *Tonight Show* with Jay Leno was over, no matter what.

The phone rang twice and was in the middle of the third ring when someone picked up. He heard his dad's gruff voice and smiled.

"Hello?"

"Hey, Dad, it's me. Wilson."

The gruffness shifted to one of delight.

"Hey, son! How have you been?"

"I'm good, Dad. How about you guys?"

"Oh, I'm fine. Having a little trouble with arthritis in my hip and knee, like always. Your Mom's chin deep in Christmas. The house looks like Santa's damn workshop, if you know what I mean…but don't tell her I said so."

Wilson laughed. He could imagine the sight. His mom was big on setting up what she called "scenes" all over the place. One room had the Christmas tree with the wrapped presents underneath. For the past twelve years or so, she'd also been collecting pieces of what she called her "village," adding to it each year, which also meant that the setting for the village continued to get larger. Last year, he remembered, she'd set up her village on the sideboard in the dining room. His dad had complained all Christmas Day that there were so many doodads in the house that there was no place left to put the pies. She'd set up a card table in the kitchen for all the holiday desserts, which had been eaten anyway, regardless of where she'd put them.

"You comin' home for Christmas?"

"Don't I always?" Wilson asked.

His dad chuckled. "If you know what's good for you."

"Is Mom asleep?" Wilson asked.

"Yeah, but I can wake her up. You know she'll want to—"

"No, don't do that," Wilson said. "I'll call again when it's a more decent time of day. Just tell her I said hi and that I love her."

"I'll do that. Take care of yourself, son."

"You, too, Dad. I'll call again soon."

Wilson was still holding the receiver long after the line had gone silent, thinking about his parents, and what a good life they'd given to him and his brothers and sisters. He couldn't imagine what Cat Dupree's life had been like after her father's murder, but from her 'don't trust, don't touch' attitude, he knew it couldn't have been good. Still, he would do what he could to help her and, in the meantime, keep his emotional distance.

Finally he left the office and moved back through the rooms. It was dark outside now. He thought of getting dressed and going to get something to eat, then decided against it and ordered in.

He called his favorite Chinese restaurant, knowing it stayed open until eleven, ordered two entrees and three egg rolls, as well as a side order of vegetable fried rice. While he was waiting for it to arrive, he made some fresh coffee and drank it at the window while watching the busy traffic on the streets below.

It was raining hard—what his daddy called a toad strangler. Thankful he wasn't in his truck on some stakeout, he poured himself a second cup of coffee.

When the food finally arrived, he gave the delivery boy a generous tip for having to come out in this weather, then sat down and ate his way through sesame chicken, and beef and vegetable stir fry, as well as the rice and egg rolls.

As he started to throw the empty boxes in the trash, he noticed the fortune cookie in the bottom of the sack and opened it. He grinned when he read it.

Be ready for great changes.

In his business, that was a given on any day. He tossed the fortune, ate the cookie, then turned out the lights on his way to bed.

The bedroom was quiet, and the bed was cold. The wind was coming up outside, and it sounded to him as if the rain blowing against the windows was turning to sleet. Thankful that he was home, he pulled the covers up over his shoulders and settled in.

The sheets were chilly, but his body heat and the extra blankets on the bed soon warmed them up. He rolled over onto his side, relaxing with every breath that followed. Outside, the icy pellets quickly covered the roadways, making travel deadly while Wilson slept.

Detective Bradley hadn't stayed long at Cat's apartment. He'd heard the message, agreed with Wilson McKay that it sounded like a helicopter, and packed up the machine.

"Here's what I'm going to do," he said. "I'll take it in and let our techs examine it more closely. They can filter and separate all kinds of sounds from a recording."

Cat watched him bagging up the machine in frustration. Her first instinct, after hearing it, had been to charge out the door and start searching, but she didn't have a notion in hell of the first place to start. She thought of what she'd asked Wilson to do. If he was successful, it would help. At least then she would know where to start looking and what to ignore.

"Have you talked to Presley?" she asked.

Bradley shook his head. "I'm sorry, but I don't share information about an ongoing case."

Cat frowned. "But the case is my business."

"Not at this point, ma'am," Bradley said.

Cat glared.

"So there's nothing you can tell me?"

He hesitated, then remembered the car.

"I can tell you that Ms. Benton's Lexus showed up on one of the exits off the freeway. It had been stripped clean but was identified by the VIN number. We're looking at the possibility that it might have quit on her and she took out on her own to get help. Maybe met with foul play from that angle."

Cat rolled her eyes.

"Did you check the calls on her cell phone?"

Bradley frowned.

"We've requested the list."

"I can tell you one thing. Marsha wouldn't have walked across the street when she could have ridden. If she had car trouble, she would have called immediately for help."

Bradley fired back. "Not if her cell phone was dead. They do go dead, you know."

"Her car was equipped with all kinds of high-tech stuff. I know there was a built-in phone, as well as a GPS mapping system with a built-in phone. If one thing quit, she had a half-dozen other gadgets at her fingertips. She called me. Remember?"

He glanced down at the answering machine and sighed.

Cat continued to hammer him with questions.

"Had the car been wrecked?"

"No, but—"

"Then it was dumped," Cat said.

At that point Bradley thanked her for calling and left.

Frustrated, Cat paced from room to room until her stomach growled. She went to the kitchen, opened a can of soup, ate it straight out of the pan in which she'd heated it, then went to bed.

She fell asleep within minutes, unaware that the rain that had been falling since evening had turned to sleet, or that the roads were becoming impassable.

As she slept, she began to dream, but instead of a continuous scene, it consisted of images flashing through her mind, like looking at old pictures in an album.

Cat was sitting at the kitchen table. Her mother was standing beside her, laughing as she set a birthday cake in front of her. There were four candles on her cake, and her daddy was taking a picture.

"Smile," he'd said.

She looked up just as the flash went off.

She was still blinking from the flash when the image shifted. It was cold. The blowing wind burned her skin. She was at a cemetery, staring down at a small, flat marker. Cat couldn't read, but somehow she knew it bore her mother's name. She could hear her father crying. It scared her worse than the fact that her mother had gone away.

"Daddy...where did she go?"

"Heaven."

"Is it far?"

"Yes."

"Can we go, too?"

She never heard his answer, because the image shifted again. This time, she was being led through a long series of hallways. The smell of orange oil from wood polish burned her nose. The sound of her footsteps echoed on the tiled floors. Yesterday she'd been in the hospital. She'd asked to go home. But someone had told her she couldn't go home because there was no one left to take care of her. The horror of that knowledge had frightened her so much that she'd been afraid to ask what came next.

She walked through an open door as a woman said her name. The woman took her by the hand, and they walked away. She couldn't see the woman's face. She never remembered the faces, and it didn't matter, because they never stayed the same.

When the image shifted again, she was with Marsha. They were standing in front of a mirror, putting on makeup. Marsha was laughing at the blob of mascara on Cat's eyelid. Cat stuck out her tongue.

It was the night of their high school prom and they'd gone without dates. They were seventeen.

When the image shifted again, Cat and Marsha were putting icicles on a Christmas tree. It was their first tree, in their first apartment. It had a single strand of lights and a gold-foil star. Marsha was bending down, hanging the last of her icicles on the bottom of the tree. As she did, Cat hung the last of her icicles on Marsha's butt.

Marsha stood up, laughing, then flung hers at Cat.

A siren sounded, sweeping past Cat's apartment in a blaze of lights and noise. She woke up with her heart pounding, her cheeks covered with tears. The dream had been so real. Even though the rational part of her knew it was nothing but an old memory, she still had to get up and see if there was a Christmas tree in the living room.

Her heart was pounding as she walked down the hall and checked. Disappointment was shattering. The reality of her life was far different from her dreams. There was no tree. There was no Marsha. Not here. Not anywhere—ever again.

The siren that had awakened her was fading in the distance. The silence in her apartment should have been comforting—like a promise that all was well— but it made everything seem empty, instead. Only after she started walking back to her bedroom did she realize that her feet were freezing. She hurried down the hall, then, once in her room, got a clean pair of socks before jumping back into bed. She put the socks on beneath the covers, taking comfort in their softness and extra warmth, and tried to go back to sleep, but she couldn't.

She rolled over onto her back, then pulled the covers up beneath her chin and stared at the shadows her night light was making on the ceiling. There was a huge weight in the middle of her chest, and she kept repressing the urge to wail.

She couldn't prove it—but she knew it. Mimi was dead.

Three simple words that, used together, became something obscene.

Morning came in a blast of cold wind, with the roads dangerously slick, coated in a good inch of sleet and ice. Even though she'd been willing to brave the weather, everything she'd planned to do had to be delayed. Cat was still willing, but the rest of the city had come to a halt.

After a half-dozen phone calls, it became apparent that the businesses that were open were operating on half staff, while the rest of them hadn't bothered to open at all. It left her with renewed frustration as she was forced, once again, to delay her search.

Being a bounty hunter, she knew how to find bail jumpers. For the most part, they weren't very smart, and most of them had a tendency to hide out in their old neighborhoods, either with an old girlfriend or some family member. It was just a matter of checking out the addresses, then running them down.

But Mimi's disappearance was different. Whatever had happened to her had been beyond her choice or control. Cat was firmly convinced that Mark Presley had done it, but with the resources he had at his fingertips, he could make anyone disappear.

Then there was the phone message she'd left on Cat's machine. If the last place Mimi had been with him had been in a helicopter, that meant her body could be anywhere—even out of state.

Frustrated, Cat stood at the windows overlooking the highway, watching the traffic. Very few cars were on the roads, but the few that were, were sliding all over the place. Even as she was standing there, she witnessed a three-car pile-up. When the drivers got out to survey the damage, two of them wound up falling, and only one got up. She winced at the pain on the fallen driver's face. From the way everyone was behaving, he'd most likely broken a bone.

She thought about going down to help, then realized that she wouldn't be able to do anything more than what the others were already trying to do. One of them was on a cell phone, obviously calling for help, while the other was kneeling beside the fallen driver.

When she finally saw a police cruiser and an ambulance approaching, she walked back to the sofa, picked up the remote and then sank down onto the cushions. She'd never been any good at mindlessly watching television, but there wasn't a lot left to do. She glanced at the phone, thinking about calling Wilson McKay, and then changed her mind.

But the longer she sat there, the more antsy she became. Whether it was his go-to-hell attitude or his less than proper buzz-cut and earring, he was hard to ignore. He'd promised to help. She could at least call and see how his investigation was going. As she was going to get the phone, it rang.

"Hello?"

"Cat, it's me, Wilson."

The sound of his voice eased her sense of isolation.

"Everything's a mess outside," she said.

"Yeah, I know, but I have some info. I just don't know if it's going to help our situation," he said, as he stretched lazily, then strode toward the windows.

Ice was layered on everything. If it hadn't been so dangerous, it would have been beautiful. He remembered then that Detective Bradley had been going to her place yesterday.

"Did Bradley show up?"

"Yes. He took the machine. Said he'd put their techs on it and see if they could sort any kind of background noise from what we heard."

"They'll do their best," he said. "Did he mention anything about Presley?"

"No. If he's talked to him, he didn't share what he knew."

"That's probably because there's nothing to tell," Wilson reminded her.

"He did say they found Mimi's car."

"The hell you say? Where?"

"Somewhere on the freeway."

"Wrecked?"

"No. Just stripped and abandoned."

"Damn. That doesn't help much."

"I know," Cat said, and then added, "What about the stuff you found on line?"

"I printed off a bunch of information."

"Good."

"Let me ask you something," Wilson said.

"Anything."

"Did you ever think about him hiring someone to do her in and dump her?"

"No. What was between them was personal. I don't think he would have wanted to advertise the problem to anyone."

"Yeah, you're probably right."

"So, Wilson, you said you printed out the stuff you found on Presley and Mimi, right?"

"Yes."

"Fax it to me."

"Yeah, I can do that. Give me your number."

She rattled it off, then hung up without saying goodbye.

Wilson stared at the phone, wondering if this was how a woman felt who'd just been fucked and dumped without comment. While he hadn't had sex with her, he was being used. Trouble was, he'd offered, so he could hardly be pissed that she wasn't being as appreciative as he would have liked.

He tore off the page from his notepad where he'd scribbled her fax number and headed for his office.

Eight

Mark Presley handed his credit card to the jeweler, then smiled benevolently as the sales clerk wrapped the Christmas gift he'd just purchased for his wife. Tahoe was a place that catered to wealth, and this jewelry store was no exception. The necklace Mark had chosen was elegant, the teardrop diamond a perfect shade of yellow. He knew the exact moment when he was going to present it to her, too. It would be on the pillow beside her when she woke up Christmas morning. She would squeal, open the gift, then cry. She would throw her arms around his neck and shower him with kisses, after which he would strip her naked and make mad, passionate love, or what passed for it.

Penny wasn't exactly the type of woman who was willing to branch out and try something new. She wanted it missionary style, three times a week, and usually in the dark. Only once in a while did she get frisky, but whenever it happened, Mark was happy to oblige. After all, she was directly responsible for his current lifestyle, and he wasn't going to do anything to mess that up. There was always a time later for Mark's predilection for erotica, and plenty of women who were willing to participate.

Only now and again did Marsha Benton cross his mind, and when she did, it was without guilt. What had occurred between them was unfortunate, but he felt as if he'd handled a sticky situation successfully. He had no fears that he would be connected to her disappearance, or that she would be found. He believed that, as surely as he knew his name. He believed it because he knew how the system worked. She was an orphan, unmarried, unattached. He was Mark Presley, a mover and shaker.

Satisfied that his world was back in order, he pocketed the gift and strutted out of the jewelry store. The sun was bright, and the reflection coming off the snow-packed streets was almost blinding. But the weather was clear and the skiing perfect. The evenings at the lodge were successful from a professional perspective, too. He'd already acquired two new customers over hot buttered rum, as well as met a half-dozen men whose only jobs in life were investing their inherited millions as they saw fit.

He strode down the sidewalks, admiring the

elegant window decorations and the holiday music being piped out into the streets. Tahoe was a haven for those who had, rather than the have nots. Fitting in gave him a great sense of pride.

"Hello there, Mr. Presley," someone called.

Mark turned and waved at the middle-aged woman in après ski gear sweeping off the steps at the front of her store.

"Hello yourself," he called back, and moved with a jauntier step.

Being recognized was as important to Mark as being in charge. By the time he got to the hotel, he was positively beaming.

Penny had left him a message that she'd gone to the spa for a massage, then a shampoo and styling. He glanced at his watch. Plenty of time for a drink down at the bar. He took the little package from the jewelry store and hid it in his sock drawer, then headed for the lobby.

Cat had been going through the info Wilson had sent. She'd made lists upon lists, separating information, then sorting it together, trying to make it fit—wishing for a neon sign with an "x marks the spot" to show where Mimi might be. She'd looked at the stuff for so long that, in her mind, it was all running together.

She wondered if this was the way caged animals felt—able to see freedom but unable to attain it. Between getting sick, then being iced in, she'd been stuck in her apartment for almost a week. Tomorrow was Christmas Eve, but she'd never felt less like celebrating.

She was something of a cynic, although she knew what the holidays were supposed to be all about. Mimi, however, had been over the moon about doing all the right things—helping to serve Christmas dinner at the Salvation Army, going to the neighborhood church to see the children's Christmas pageant—everything she thought "real" families did.

But she and Mimi had always been the outsiders. They didn't have family to go home to, so there were no family dinners. They didn't have husbands or children, so Cat found no reason or joy in putting up decorations. But Mimi did. She read the Christmas story from the Bible every year, then insisted they open their presents to each other at the same time. Cat freely admitted that if Mimi hadn't insisted on the tradition, she never would have bothered with the holiday at all.

Yet now Cat was so despondent that she wished she could sleep through the entire holiday. Being iced in and knowing Mimi was out there somewhere was like being in a never-ending horror story. Cat's need for revenge was at the point of making her sick. She needed to see justice done. Someone needed to pay for what they'd done, but the weather wasn't cooperating, and while she was fuming, Christmas arrived.

* * *

Cat woke up in tears on Christmas Day. She was so despondent that it hurt to draw breath, and her head had been aching for hours. Still, it was nothing to the ache in her heart. She had been pacing the floor since daybreak and was on the verge of screaming when her doorbell rang.

She was so startled by the sound that she stumbled and almost fell on her way to answer. With most of her neighbors also iced in, she was guessing it was someone coming to borrow something. She was willing to share anything she had except toilet paper. If the weather didn't let up, that was going to become a precious commodity.

She opened the door.

It was Wilson, wearing a red and white fuzzy Santa Claus hat.

"Well? Aren't you going to ask me in?"

Cat felt her face turn red, and then she heard herself stuttering.

"Yes, well… I didn't expect—"

He held a piece of mistletoe over her head, kissed her square on the mouth, then took himself inside and closed the door.

She was still frowning when he handed her the mistletoe.

"Want to reciprocate?"

She tossed it in the trash.

He grinned.

"There's coffee," she said.

"Is that an invitation to drink a cup, or were you just giving me the lowdown on what you've accomplished today?"

Cat glared. "You're a smart ass, aren't you, McKay?"

His smile spread. "I've been accused of it now and then."

She wasn't buying into the frivolity. "So do you want some coffee or not?"

"Yes, please," he said, took off his hat and coat, and hung them on the hall tree, then followed her to the kitchen.

He felt a little awkward about being here. He wanted to help her. He'd offered to help her. But there was a part of him that wondered if he was doing it for the right reasons. Somewhere around three o'clock this morning, he'd realized he'd been thinking about sex—with Catherine Dupree.

He'd tried to shame himself out of the notion, aware that she tolerated him only because she needed help. Trouble was, she was driving him crazy. He thought that if they just did it, then he could get it off his mind. But at the same time, it made him feel like a heel, knowing that, if given the chance, he would take it without a conscious thought that he might be catching her at a weak moment.

However, he'd consoled himself with the fact that even though he'd decided to spend the day with her so she wouldn't be alone, instead of braving the weather and driving home for Christmas, he wouldn't make a pass. Even he couldn't stoop so low as to catch her when she was at a weak moment.

"How do you take your coffee?" she asked.

"Black."

She reached for a cup. He reached over her head and got the cup down himself.

"Don't fuss. I've been here before, remember?"

Cat looked startled; then, slowly, understanding dawned.

"Barely. That's the sickest I've been in years, so I don't remember a lot of those three days."

"Pity," Wilson said. "It was a memorable time for me."

Cat glanced back at him, uncertain what he meant by that comment, then saw his eyes glittering. He was teasing her.

"You lie," she said shortly.

Wilson grinned. As much as he would like to tease her about it, this was not the time to bring up the pink butterfly tattoo.

"I never lie. Now, about that coffee," he said, and filled the cup, sniffing the aroma with appreciation as he let the coffee cool. As he did, he glanced around the kitchen, then back at her. "I don't smell the traditional turkey or ham cooking. What were you planning to do for Christmas?"

"Nothing," she said shortly.

"Why not?" Wilson asked.

Cat's vision suddenly blurred. "Because I always spent Christmas with Mimi...ever since we were teenagers...always with—"

She caught her breath and then looked away.

Wilson gave himself a mental kick in the butt.

"I'm sorry."

"Why did you come here?"

"Because I like emotional torture."

"What?"

He sighed. "Nothing. I was just muttering," he said.

She frowned. "Why are you really here, Wilson?"

"Beats the hell out of me," he said softly, and resisted the urge to kiss her again, this time without the excuse of mistletoe. "What have you learned from the stuff I faxed over?"

"It's hard to say," she said. "I've looked at it so many times that...sorry for the lame analogy, but I think my problem is that I can't see the forest for the trees."

"I can imagine," Wilson said. "You do know that everything I'm gave you was obtained without a search warrant, which means that a lot of the information is a violation of his privacy. If your friend is indeed dead, and if you find her body through information you got here, it's not going to be admissible in court."

"I know that," Cat said. "But if I use this information to find her body and it's proven that the baby she was carrying is indeed Mark Presley's child, then doesn't that give the district attorney enough information to start looking seriously at Presley as the possible killer?"

"Exactly," Wilson said. "And it would be in your best interests not to go into detail about how you went about finding her, if or when you do."

"I won't give you up, if that's what you're worrying about," Cat said, and then, to her horror, she choked on a sob. "Damn it," she muttered, and swiped away tears. "I can't believe I'm talking about Mimi's murder as if I was debating the pros and cons of a pair of shoes."

She slammed her hand against the wall, then ran from the room. He reached for her and missed, then followed, catching up with her in the hall. He grabbed her by the shoulders first, then turned her around.

Cat wouldn't look at him as she struggled to pull free. Wilson didn't let go.

"Let me go!" she cried, then covered her face with her hands.

Wilson cupped the back of her head as he held her close. The more Cat struggled, the firmer he held her, until, finally, he felt her resistance fade.

"It's okay to cry."

All the fight in her stopped. He felt her shoulders beginning to shake. He eased his grip on her arms and then wrapped his own around her.

Her voice was angry and shaking. "Why is it that the people I love most keep dying?"

"I don't know," he said softly. "But I'm so sorry it's happening."

His empathy was the final straw.

Wilson felt her body give way as she started to sob. He pulled her close, then tightened his grip. Her pain was almost more than he could bear. She clung to him as a drowning person might cling to a life preserver, and he let her, wishing he could make everything okay.

Cat cried until she was sick. She felt out of control, even lost. What if she never found Mimi? What if Mark Presley got away with murder?

Cat's breakdown was tearing Wilson apart. Finally he picked her up in his arms and carried her into her bedroom, then laid her on the bed.

Cat curled up like a baby, covering her head with her arms.

Wilson sat down beside her, then laid a hand on her shoulder.

"Cat... Catherine...we'll find her. I'll help all I can, okay? You don't have to do this alone."

"I can't believe this is happening. How can this be happening?"

"I don't know," he said. "Bad things happen to good people all the time. That's what our jobs are all about."

She shuddered on a sob, then closed her eyes. All the past days of losing sleep were catching up with her.

"I'm so tired."

"Then sleep," Wilson said.

"I need to find Mimi."

"Honey…we can't do anything until this weather clears. I nearly broke my fool neck just getting here. Sleep while you can."

"Are you going to stay?" Cat asked.

Wilson felt a kick in the pit of his stomach.

"Maybe…if it's okay with you."

There was a brief moment of silence, then she answered. "It's okay."

"Then I'll stay if you'll sleep."

She didn't answer, but he watched her stretch out, then roll over onto her stomach.

Wilson sat until he saw that she'd finally passed out. Reluctant to leave her, he covered her up with a blanket from the foot of the bed, then sat down in a chair near the window.

Time passed, but he never looked away. By the time she began to stir, he'd memorized ever curve of her face and hair on her head. He knew the pattern of her breathing and the way she slept with her lips slightly apart. When she turned from one side to the other, the scar on her neck was revealed. He couldn't imagine how frightened she must have been as a child, to experience what she had and live through it. It was a wonder she trusted anyone at all. And he suspected that because of all that was happening, the tough facade she kept between herself and the world was crumbling, and it was scaring her to death.

He couldn't imagine what it must be like to be alone in the world, without family or close friends. His own family had been disappointed when he'd called them this morning, but he'd used the weather as an excuse. His parents had been understanding and adamant that he not try to drive home and risk an accident. He hated lying to them, but his heart went out to Catherine Dupree. All he knew was that he couldn't bear to be the next person in her life to let her down.

Cat moaned in her sleep. In her dream, she was reaching toward a door, trying to get to it—knowing that Mimi was inside the room. But the harder she stretched, the farther away the door became.

"No, no," Cat mumbled. "Wait. Come back."

Wilson roused just as Cat reached out and rolled off the bed.

"Damn it." He jumped up from the chair and ran to her.

Cat looked up at Wilson, confused as to where she was and why he was there, and then she remembered she'd let him in.

"Lord," she said, as she struggled to her feet.

"Are you hurt?"

"Just my ego. I can't remember the last time I fell out of bed."

"You were dreaming," he said.

Cat shoved her hair back from her face and changed the subject as she got up.

"Is it still sleeting?" she asked.

"Yes."

She walked to the windows and looked out. The world was covered in inches of ice, with more coming down.

"You know you can't go home."

Wilson shrugged. "I got here all right."

"I don't want your death on my conscience, too," Cat said. "Besides, my sofa makes into a bed."

Wilson watched her fidgeting. The idea of spending Christmas night with her didn't sound so bad. Finally he relented.

"Go wash your face. I'll be in the kitchen making a fresh pot of coffee and putting that turkey in to cook."

"I don't have a turkey," she said.

He grinned. "I know that, but we still have to eat, right?"

"I guess."

"So…do you mind if I look through your pantry?"

"Knock yourself out," she said. "Just don't expect miracles."

He traced the curve of her cheek with his fingertip.

"But, Catherine, it's Christmas. That's what it's all about."

She turned away from his touch.

"I don't buy all that crap, so don't go getting all mushy on me."

Wilson frowned. Life really had done a number on her.

"I don't do mush," he said shortly. "I'll be in the kitchen."

By the time she joined him, Wilson had the coffee made and, out of curiosity, was glancing through the papers she'd been working on. He looked up as she entered.

"Quite an investigator, aren't you?" he said.

She'd made lists of everything, from what Presley owned to what he spent to where he went. She had checked off phone calls that corresponded with calls Marsha had made and vice versa, and checked times when Marsha had begged off dinner plans that she and Cat had made, as well as the credit card purchases that Mark Presley had made at restaurants and motels. The list was telling.

She also had a printout of the phone calls made from the private number at the Presley home, as well as Mark's personal cell phone number. Calls going in. Calls going out.

A quick count had revealed that Mark Presley had called Marsha at least five times during the week before her disappearance, but there was only one call made to her on the day she disappeared, and none afterward.

When Cat went through Marsha's calls, she had made note of the last call made on her cell. It had been to Cat's home phone.

Another hour passed, during which time Wilson found a package of chicken legs in her freezer and a package of dry uncooked noodles in her pantry. As he cooked, she kept digging through pages, but she couldn't help noticing that the kitchen was beginning to smell good, which in itself was a miracle.

The stewing chicken would soon be done, and when it was, Wilson planned to cook the dry noodles in the broth. He'd also found a can of green beans and a can of peaches. Within another hour, he was going to be able to serve up an entree, a vegetable side dish and dessert.

Catherine was impressed.

Wilson was just hungry.

Cat had been staring at the printouts without success for so long that her eyes were burning. She laid down the last set of papers she'd been studying and rolled her head, then stretched. Wilson was adding salt to the boiling noodles when she leaned her elbows on the table and rested her chin in her hands.

"So, McKay, when did you learn to cook?"

"College. Couldn't afford to eat out. It was cook or starve." He patted his belly. "I obviously didn't starve."

Cat eyed his physique carefully. "You look just fine to me," she said, and then flushed when she realized what she'd said.

He grinned. "Why thank you, ma'am. I didn't think you'd noticed."

She glared, and it reminded him of the look she'd

given him the day they'd met, when she thought he was trying to help her bail jumper get away.

"I didn't notice a damn thing," Cat muttered, then pointed to the stove. "Your noodles are about to boil over."

Wilson turned abruptly and slid the pan from the burner.

"Good call," he said, as he stirred down the boil and adjusted the flame. "Won't be long now," he said, as he set the pan of green beans on the burner and added some salt and pepper.

"It smells good," Cat said.

He decided not to push his luck with her and just accepted the compliment without any more teasing.

"So what's the verdict on all the stuff I sent you? Have you come up with anything interesting?"

"Maybe."

"Let me see," he said as he turned the fire off under the cooked pasta; then he dumped the cooked and deboned chicken back into the noodles and broth. He gave the mixture a quick stir, then set it aside before joining her at the table.

"Show me," he said.

She pushed some papers in front of him.

"Marsha went missing on the fifteenth."

"Yeah?"

"So I made three lists. One of everything he did on the day before, one on the day she disappeared and one on the day after."

"Did you find something?"

"Maybe."

Wilson measured the food on the stove against his hungry belly.

"What say we eat first, since everything's ready? Then you can fill me in on details as we eat."

"Works for me," Cat said, and got up to get glasses and silverware as he got down some plates.

Wilson pretended not to notice that her hands were shaking, or that there were tears in her eyes when she set matching Santa and Mrs. Santa salt and pepper shakers on the table. He didn't know that Mimi had given them to Cat years ago, and that, despite the fact that the holes were so small in Santa's head that the pepper would never shake out, they still used them every year.

By the time they sat down, Cat had her emotions back under control.

"This is really good," she said. "Thank you for cooking."

Wilson saw the tears in her eyes and tried to make light of the situation.

"Seeing as how I invited myself here with the full knowledge that I was probably going to be stranded, I considered it the least I could do."

"Yeah…well…thanks anyway."

"You're welcome."

The meal passed without much conversation. Cat didn't have any fond memories to reminisce about, and Wilson didn't think it was a good idea to offer any of his own, so they kept the talk geared toward the weather and the Dallas Cowboys football team.

By the time they'd gone through the chicken and noodles and the green beans, Cat was satisfied. Still, she couldn't bring herself to refuse the peaches, since Wilson had gone to all the trouble of opening the can.

"Um, these are really tasty," she said, as she swallowed the first bite.

He arched an eyebrow. "Not exactly pecan pie, though."

"Is that what you like?" she asked.

He nodded. "Mom always makes at least four, to make sure we all get enough."

Cat's expression stilled.

Wilson could have kicked himself the moment the words had come out of his mouth, but it was too late to take back.

"So…why aren't you with your family having dinner?"

He pointed out the window. "Well, Sleeping Beauty, I don't know where you've been the last few days, but I've been stuck in my damned apartment because of all this sleet and ice."

"You got *here*," she said accusingly.

"They're outside of Austin, which, as you know, is nowhere close. It would have meant hours driving on dangerous roads. I talked to my parents this morning. Mom would have had a fit if she'd thought I was trying to drive home today."

"Oh."

There was a long moment of silence; then Wilson reached across the table and laid his hand on top of Cat's.

"You're right. The peaches are really good."

She rolled her eyes, then slid her hand out from under his.

"Oh, for Pete's sake, you don't have to baby me. I'm a big girl, remember? I'm sorry about the weather."

"And I'm sorry about your friend," he shot back. "Now can we stop this aimless conversation and get back to the damned peaches?"

"Fine by me," she said, and ate until her bowl was empty.

They both stacked dishes in the sink, put up the leftovers and, as if by a prior agreement, sat right back down at the table and began to go through the papers again. This time, though, Wilson began to really read what she'd done.

At first nothing jumped out at him. An hour passed, then half of another, as they went through the pages together—offering comments about one thing, then vetoing it for another. Despite how badly Cat wanted to find the so-called smoking gun, she hadn't been able to sort much out except names of restaurants or purchases that were most likely Christmas gifts.

"East," Wilson said, suddenly.

Cat looked up.

"East what?"

"There's a credit card bill for a meal he ate at a barbecue place in East Texas."

"So?"

Wilson shoved a paper toward her, then pointed at a print-out line about halfway down the page. There was a large listing of oil and gas leases that belonged to the Presley drilling company, and some of them were in the eastern part of the state. Then Wilson pointed to another list and an expenditure made on the day Marsha went missing. Wilson found it difficult to believe that a man as smart as Presley would charge anything that might link him to a place and time that could get him in trouble. However, it could be something as simple as habit. A man like Presley would file an itemized tax return and wouldn't think twice about saving receipts— even the ones he should have thrown away. A habit was a hard thing to break.

"Okay. I see the lease list. But what about The Fire Pit?" Cat asked. "It's just a restaurant, right?"

"Yes, but it's in East Texas—close to this listing of oil and gas leases. That part of the country is pretty heavily wooded. It appears from these records that when he goes up there, he usually travels by helicopter, and he seems to always eat at the same place."

Cat grabbed the paper. "The date. What's the date on the credit slip?"

Wilson pointed again.

Cat grunted as if she'd just been punched in the gut. It was the fifteenth of December, the day of Marsha's disappearance.

Cat was so tense she was shaking. "Dinner? He killed her, then went and ate barbecue?"

Wilson frowned. "You're jumping the gun again. You still don't know that Presley killed her. You just think it. Remember what the man does for a living. He could have any number of reasons for being in that area."

"But we know her cell phone was in a helicopter. I'm saying it was on her when the call was made. And if he was in a helicopter that same day, flying over the leases, and ate at his usual place, that says to me that she was with him. Did he stay in a motel out there that night?" she asked.

Wilson quickly scanned the credit card receipts.

"If he did, he didn't pay with a credit card."

"Does he have a pilot's license?" Cat asked.

"He has plenty of people he could hire to fly it for him," Wilson said.

Cat frowned. "If you had killed someone and were trying to hide the body, would you let another person in on the secret?"

"No."

"So we need to know if he can fly his own planes," Cat said.

Wilson took out his cell phone and made a quick

call. His voice was terse as he requested the information. Despite the fact that it was a holiday, the man he called had a quick answer. It took less than two minutes for him to get an affirmative.

"He does," Wilson said, as he dropped his cell phone back in his pocket.

Cat's eyes widened with admiration. She didn't know how he did it, but she was going to have to learn some of the tricks.

"Okay, say he flew out to East Texas, which is hundreds of thousands of acres. So let's assume it was to go to his land, where the wells are being pumped."

"That's a real big assumption that might put you on a false trail," Wilson said, then went back to the credit card listings. "Look and see if he rented a car while he was there."

Cat scanned the list. "No. No rental. Nothing like that." She moaned in frustration, then covered her face with her hands. "What if we're missing the point? What if—"

"We're just following clues. You and I both know how deceptive that can be, especially if you're trying to make information fit a specific time or event."

Cat stood up, then paced a few moments. "Okay. You're right. I'm getting ahead of myself."

"Okay, there's no rental car," Wilson said. "So what? He has a pilot's license, remember?"

"Are there any landing strips on his oil leases?"

Wilson shuffled through the list.

"None that are apparent," he said, then added, "However, you don't need a landing strip when you're in a chopper, and we think Marsha's call was made from inside a chopper."

"You're right," Cat said, as she reached for another list. "He owns a property just shy of seven hundred acres in the Tyler, Texas, area. Looks like there are a dozen or so wells pumping on that land."

She got up from the table and strode to the windows. The weather was no better than it had been when she'd looked out hours earlier.

"I think I need to go there," she said.

Wilson shook his head as he stood up and followed her.

"Catherine…do you hear yourself? We're talking about seven hundred acres, some of it swampland. I don't know what the weather's like in East Texas, but something has to change here first before you can make a move. Besides that, you can't just drive up to Presley's land and expect to find your friend's body— and that's if she's really dead, and if Presley really did it, and if he really hid her there. God, with his money and connections, she could be anywhere."

Cat turned, her expression stern, her chin up as if bracing herself for a fight.

"She's lost, damn it. If the situation was reversed, she would be looking for me."

Wilson took her by the shoulders. The tension in

her body was strong as she tried to withdraw. He tightened his grip.

"You're running wild on this, which means you're not thinking things through. What you're doing could get you hurt." Then he sighed. "I don't want this to be the last thing you ever do."

Cat tried to get free, but he wouldn't let go.

"Damn it, Wilson, let me be. I don't need anyone's concern. I take care of myself."

He frowned as he ran his thumb across the curve of her chin.

"Don't ask me why, Dupree, because you sure haven't given me any green lights, but you're beginning to grow on me. I can't explain the attraction, but I'd damn sure like to take you to bed."

Cat felt as if she'd been sucker-punched.

Wilson loosened his hands from her shoulders, and slid them beneath her hair and up the back of her neck. Her pulse was pounding beneath the pads of his thumbs as he encircled her neck with his hands, then gently pulled her closer.

"I know you're a woman who doesn't like surprises," he said softly. "So I thought I'd better let you know that I'm going to kiss you now. And if that pleases you as much as it pleases me, there's a real good chance that we're going to make love."

Cat shivered at the promise in his voice, then surprised herself as well as him when she locked her hands around his neck and lifted her lips for his kiss.

Nine

Cat's heart was in her throat. Life and her job had made her tough, but right now she was as vulnerable as a woman could be. She wasn't naive, and she'd long ago lost her virginity, but she also wasn't in the habit of crawling in and out of the sack with just anybody.

She had never had a long-term relationship. She didn't *want* a long-term relationship. Having sex with Wilson McKay wouldn't bind her to anything, yet she had a feeling that if they did this, her life was never going to be the same. Still, she could no more have turned away from this moment than she could have stopped breathing.

Wilson knew this was going to change his life. He was already more than interested in Catherine Dupree. Taking her to bed seemed an appropriate step in the right direction. He wasn't leery. He was excited.

When she kissed him back, his excitement peaked. He deepened the kiss, feeling her lips part automatically as his mouth centered on hers.

There was a brief moment of discovery before every ounce of control he had took flight.

Cat moaned as Wilson arms tightened around her waist; then, when his hands slid lower and pulled her close against his groin, she shuddered.

Wilson felt the tremors in her body as he swept her up into his arms and carried her to the bedroom. A short time earlier, he'd watched her sleep in this bed, and now sleep was the last thing on their minds.

Cat began to undress. He stopped her with a look and a touch, then finished the job for her. By the time he was pulling off her panties, she was shaking all over. He tossed the tiny scrap of pale blue silk aside, then laid his hand in the middle of her belly and pushed her backward onto the mattress.

She felt a jolt of electricity, which only increased her need. She had made love many times before, but she was taken aback by how badly she wanted this to happen.

His dark eyes were unreadable as he quickly shed his own clothes. When she saw the powerful jut of his erection, she automatically reached down and touched herself, trying to ease the ache between her legs.

"Oh no," Wilson whispered, as he crawled onto the bed and slid between her legs. "Save that for me, darlin'."

Cat reached for him eagerly, locking her legs around his waist as he settled between her thighs.

Wilson momentarily braced himself above her with a hand on either side of her head. He was only vaguely aware of a faucet dripping in the adjoining bathroom, and never heard the squeals and laughter of the kids playing in the parking lot outside. All he could feel was the heat coming off her body and a growing ache to be inside her.

There was a brief moment of lucidity when Cat thought about how selfish she was to be letting her personal wants and needs supersede finding Mimi, and then a tiny part of her mind could almost hear Mimi laughing and telling her to go for it.

So she did.

From the first kiss to the shock of Wilson McKay sliding into her, she felt as if she were being washed in fire. Her heart was pounding, her breath coming in short, anxious gasps. The rhythm of their bodies was in perfect sync, as if they'd done this a thousand times before. She felt the thunder of his heartbeat beneath the palms of her hands, and could tell from the growing tension in his muscles that, whether he knew it or not, he was already out of control.

Wilson had lost all cognizance of anything but Catherine. He was caught up in the power of being one with this woman. Cat was a drug he couldn't quit. He kept going back for it time and time again, until the inevitable happened.

Overdose.

One second they were still in motion, and the next, Cat's fingernails were digging into his shoulders and she was moaning in his ear. He came so fast that he lost his breath. In the moment when he was spilling himself into her, he was convinced he was dying. Even more surprising was the fact that he wasn't willing to stop to save his life.

Cat stretched.

Wilson murmured beneath his breath, slid his fingers around her waist and then pulled her closer against his belly. She went willingly as he spooned himself against her back. When he straightened the covers up over her shoulders, every muscle in her body went limp.

Cat was no novice, but the term "sexual satisfaction" didn't even come close to what Wilson McKay had done to her.

It was magnificent.

It was mind-bending.

It was addictive.

Wilson was almost blind with exhaustion, but he'd never felt better in his life. Just at the point of falling asleep, he felt Cat's backside snuggling closer into his lap.

"Uh…Wilson?"

"Hmmm?"

"Could we do that again?"

He laughed out loud.

It started like a rumble down deep in his belly and came up his throat in husky ripples, until the sound, like a blowout, burst behind Cat's head.

His laughter was infectious.

A little embarrassed, she frowned, but when he buried his face against the back of her neck and kept laughing, she rolled out from beneath his grasp and punched him on the shoulder.

Wilson had never, in his entire life as an adult, experienced this much passion and fun at the same time. He laughed until his belly hurt, and when he tried to pull her back down to him, she wouldn't relent.

"It wasn't that funny," Cat muttered.

"On the contrary," Wilson said. "You just weren't looking at the request from my point of view. I was just lying there thinking that I'd never felt so used up and satisfied in my life, and then you're asking about a repeat performance."

Cat lifted her chin in the air, then arched an eyebrow.

"If the request was beyond your abilities, all you had to do was say so."

Wilson reached up and pulled her back down in his arms, then rolled until she was beneath him. When she looked up, her breath caught in the back of her throat.

A bit of light was reflecting off the gold hoop in his ear, and there was a sheen of moisture on his lips, as if he'd just licked them. Without thinking, she ran the tip of her tongue along her bottom lip, and as she did, Wilson kissed her, hard and fast.

Cat groaned.

Wilson paused, then looked down at her.

"Still interested?" he drawled.

Cat's nostrils flared as she locked her legs around his waist.

Wilson's eyes widened, then closed in disbelief.

It was the last thing Cat saw before she pulled him under.

Mark Presley stepped out of the shower with a smug expression on his face. He'd called Penny's reaction right down to the squeal when she'd seen the yellow teardrop diamond on the gold chain and the scream when he made her come. He loved to be right, but he hated to be late, which was why he began to dry himself quickly. He'd made a reservation at the restaurant downstairs for a special brunch he had planned for a couple dozen of his new acquaintances. Even though it was Christmas Day, it was never a bad time to do business.

He was just about to reach for the shaving cream when he heard the distinct ring of his cell phone in the other room.

He grabbed a towel as he left the bathroom, wiping his hands on the way to answer. Penny was at the vanity, drinking champagne and preening. He gave her an absent smile as he answered.

"Presley."

"Mark, this is Wyatt Beech. Merry Christmas and sorry to disturb you during your vacation, but I thought you needed to know this."

Wyatt Beech was the pumper on the oil wells on the lease near Tyler, and Mark couldn't imagine why he would be calling him at all, let alone on Christmas Day.

"Merry Christmas to you, too," Mark said. "So what is it you think I should know?"

"There was an explosion on Presley number nine. The well is burning out of control. We've got media all over the place. I'm trying to locate Dan Rimes and his crew. They're the ones who put out that fire for you down in Louisiana last year, right?"

Mark's belly flopped. Explosion? Fire? Media? The number nine well was less than two miles, as the crow flew, from where he'd dumped Marsha's body.

"How the hell did this happen?" he snapped, then shoved a hand through his hair in frustration. "Yes, Rimes is the one to call, but I heard he's in South America. Check with his answering service and tell them it's a fucking emergency, you hear?"

"The authorities aren't sure how it happened, but it's looking like it might be a car accident. The remains of a pickup truck are in the middle of the blaze, and they're guessing somebody might have driven up to the well site and accidentally ran into the pump in the dark. The fire's too big to tell how many people might have been in the truck, but one thing's for sure, they won't be talking about it."

"God damn it!" Mark yelled. "I thought there were locks on those gates leading in to the wells."

"There are. That one's been cut," Dan said. "Right sorry to give you bad news like this. Hope I didn't completely ruin your holiday. Oh…they're pumping water out of that old rock quarry to fill their trucks. I told them it was okay."

Mark's good mood was gone. "Keep me posted," he said, then, when they'd disconnected, turned around and threw his cell phone in a chair in frustration.

Penny was used to Mark's occasional outbursts of profanity, especially when something hadn't gone his way. She thought nothing of it as she got up from the dresser and sashayed toward him, naked as the day she was born.

"Markie…look at me," she said, dressed only in the yellow diamond dangling from the chain around her neck.

Mark was struggling to get past a growing panic. It couldn't be good for that much activity to be happening so close to where he'd dumped Marsha's body. And the fact that they were using water out of the quarry was dangerous. He didn't think that they'd find the stuff he'd thrown in, but he hadn't counted on the water being siphoned out. He glanced at Penny and tried to smile as he patted her on the butt.

"Yes, darling...you look fabulous."

Penny sidled closer, then cupped him suggestively with one hand while she rolled the tip of her nipple between her fingers.

"Mark...Markie...honey...I want to feel good again. Can you make me feel good again?"

Mark frowned. That meant getting it up. He wasn't in the mood to get anything up.

"Come on, Penny. You know we—"

"Markie...honey. I want to do it again."

Suddenly the pout on her face and the whine in her voice set his teeth on edge.

"Not now," he muttered.

She wrapped her arms around his neck and pushed herself against his groin.

"Yes. Yes. Now. I want it now."

Mark grabbed her arms and removed them from around his neck.

"We're not doing it again, so don't ask. Just get yourself dressed. The brunch is in less than an hour, and I still have to shave, okay?"

Penny pouted. "No. It's not okay. I want—"

Mark snapped. Before he knew it, he had his hands around her neck and was shoving her backward onto the bed. He jammed his knee between her legs, then shoved it upward—hard and fast. He heard the pop as his kneecap hit her pelvic bone.

Penny cried out in shock and pain.

"Markie, Markie…you're hurting me."

"Shut up," Mark growled. "You wanted this, remember?"

Penny screamed.

Mark's pulse accelerated. He liked causing pain, but he'd never revealed this side of himself to Penny before. His erection was instantaneous. He entered her, dry and hard, taking pleasure in her pitiful cry of disbelief.

Stunned by what she could only view as a rape, Penny clutched at the bed sheets in silent misery as Mark rode her. Less than a minute passed before he grabbed her by the hair and came in a final thrust so hard that her head bounced against the headboard.

He crawled off her without looking at her face and walked into the bathroom as if she wasn't even there. It wasn't until the door closed behind him that she reacted by bursting into tears.

Mark heard the wailing and opened the door long enough to curse, then informed her that she wasn't welcome downstairs.

"Don't bother getting dressed. I'll relay your excuses to our guests."

Penny was stunned by Mark's behavior, but not to the point of letting him tell her what to do.

"You'll do no such thing!" she screamed, then swung her legs off the bed and strode to the dresser. "I'll be downstairs welcoming our guests before you get your sorry-ass self shaved. I will smile, and I will nod, and I will play sweet little hostess to all your guests, but you and I aren't through. Not by a long shot!"

Then she slammed the door shut in Mark's face, leaving him inside the bathroom to simmer on that.

And simmer he did. He couldn't believe what was happening. Less than two weeks ago, his life had been perfect. He'd taken care of business as usual. Everything had gone as planned until today.

He grabbed a clean washcloth and some shaving cream, took a new disposable razor out of the packet and set it on the sink. He wasn't going to think about the fire, or the water they were taking out of the rock quarry, or of Penny. Not right now. She was pissed, but she would get over it, and the rest would take care of itself.

It was late in the afternoon when Cat woke up again. This time, Wilson was the one still asleep. She watched him for a few moments, remembering the pleasure they'd shared. But remembering also made her feel out of control, and that was a luxury she couldn't afford.

She rolled out of bed, grabbed her sweats and dressed in the hallway before moving into the kitchen, anxious to get back to her investigation. They'd been in the midst of discovering their first real clue as to where Presley might have taken Mimi when lust had gotten the best of them.

Cat had to call it lust, because the only other name for what they'd just done had rules and consequences tied to the act, and Cat wasn't into all that.

She poured out the coffee that had gone cold and made a fresh pot, then rifled through the kitchen for something sweet. Not wanting a replay of the peaches they'd had for Christmas dinner, she finally settled on a jar of peanut butter and some honey on the verge of turning to sugar. She took a spoon from a drawer, set the peanut butter and honey on the table, then reached for the lists. Before she started, she opened the peanut butter, dipped the spoon into the thick, nutty spread, pulled it out, swirled it through the sugared honey once, and popped it in her mouth, leaving the spoon sticking out from between her lips like a lollipop stick. Within a few minutes she was deeply engrossed in compiling facts that might fit her murder theory.

And that was how Wilson found her.

She looked up at him as he walked into the kitchen. Even though there was a part of her that remembered she wasn't alone, she was still a little startled by the sight of the half-naked man.

He smiled at her—a slow, secretive smile that sent shivers up her spine. Then she watched as he moved to the cabinet and poured himself a cup of coffee. He started toward the table, then paused, eyed the peanut butter, backtracked to the cabinet and got himself a spoon, then sat down at the table across from her.

Without comment, he dug into the peanut butter and popped it into his mouth.

"There's honey," she said, pointing to the jar.

"No thanks," he said. "I'm a purist."

She filed the information away for future reference and handed him her list.

"This might be where he dumped Marsha, and this is why I think it."

Wilson scanned the page quickly; then his eyes widened. He took a deep breath and started at the top of the list again, this time going slower—much slower.

Seven hundred acres of East Texas land, densely forested, with fourteen active well sites.

A *cash* receipt for the meal at the barbeque joint in Tyler, which was near the leases, from the evening of the same day Marsha disappeared.

One phone call to Marsha on the day she disappeared.

One phone call from Marsha's phone during the time Cat hadn't been able to contact her.

The knowledge that the last call from Marsha's phone had been from the inside of a helicopter.

The fact that Presley owned a helicopter, as well as a couple of small planes.

The knowledge that he had a pilot's license.

Then there were motel bills, receipts for personal gifts sent to his office, rather than his home, which meant that Marsha, not his wife, would have been the recipient.

The lists went on and on, giving proof to the personal connection between Mark and his secretary.

Wilson finished reading her findings, then looked up.

"So what do you think?" Cat asked.

"I think you'd make one hell of a detective," he said.

She sat up a little straighter. "Really? You think I'm on the right track?"

"Yes."

"Enough to put Mark Presley behind bars?"

"Not without a body," Wilson said.

"If I could only find out which obstetrician Mimi was going to, then we could confirm the motive."

Wilson leaned back in his chair. "No, you couldn't. The doctor isn't going to tell you squat about his patient, remember? And even if he did tell you she was pregnant, it doesn't prove it was Presley's child. You need DNA for that, and you're not getting that without her."

Cat slapped the table with the flat of her hand. "Damn it! This is making me crazy. It's like being caught on a merry-go-round that never stops."

She jumped up from her chair and strode out of the room.

Wilson sighed, then got up and followed her.

Cat was standing at the windows overlooking the parking lot. He walked up behind her, slid his arms around her and pulled her close against his chest, then rested his chin on the top of her head.

"I'm sorry," he said softly.

She shrugged but didn't pull away. It wasn't enough, but it was all he was going to get.

They stood there without talking, each lost in their own set of thoughts.

"Have you listened to the weather today?" Cat finally asked.

"Not since this morning. They said it was supposed to warm up."

"Good."

He chose not to take that personally as he added, "They're saying this front should move out around midnight. After that, it's anyone's guess. Why? Already trying to get rid of me?"

"No, I just can't stand waiting like this without doing anything."

"Okay. Because I'm beginning to like it here."

Cat tensed when he pulled her into his arms. A few seconds later, when he lifted her hair away from her neck and kissed her there, she flinched. She didn't think of the scar on her neck often unless someone was giving her one of those looks, or touching it, and he was definitely doing more than touching.

"Easy," Wilson said softly. "It's just me, remember?"

Cat tried to laugh it off, but she still felt the need to get back into her own space as she stepped out of his arms.

Wilson sighed. "I'm sorry," he said. "I didn't mean to overstep my bounds."

Cat looked at him, then looked away. This was Wilson. She knew he wasn't going to hurt her, and yet the moment he'd lifted her hair and touched her neck, it had flashed her back to the night of her father's death.

"Just bad memories," she said, and ran a finger lightly along the length of the scar.

Wilson wanted to hold her, but it was obvious he'd already done too much touching.

"Yeah. I understand. Sorry," he said, and then purposefully put some space between them by sitting down on the sofa.

Cat frowned. She knew she sounded whiney and ungrateful, and hated herself for feeling both.

"Stop apologizing," she said. "I'm the one with the hangup."

He shook his head. "I wouldn't call having my throat cut a hangup."

Cat shuddered in spite of herself.

Wilson leaned forward, resting his elbows on his knees as he watched her sit down in the chair opposite him. Her hands were trembling as she touched the scar once more, then waved them in the air as if trying to throw away the scar with the memory.

"It happened a long time ago. I shouldn't be so touchy," she said. "You know the story. A man broke into our house when I was thirteen, cut my throat and killed my father."

"And they never caught him, right?"

"Right."

"Did you see him?"

"I had a glimpse." She frowned. "It was weird. He had a lot of tattoos."

"Yeah, I saw the mug shots earlier, remember?"

"Oh. Yes."

"I heard that you got into this business as a way of looking for him. Is that true?" Wilson asked.

"Maybe. To this day, every time I hear of a perp with geometric tattoos on his arms and face, I make a point of checking him out."

To Wilson, this was something new. "Geometric?"

She nodded. "They were all over him in an odd, decorative pattern, like designs rather than pictures. His skin was dark, but they were darker."

Wilson frowned. "Black tattoos in a geometric pattern?"

"Yeah, weird, huh?"

Wilson's frown deepened. "Do you know what Maori warriors looked like?"

"Who?"

"Maori…once a very war-like race of people that inhabited New Zealand, I think. They've given up the warrior part of their lives, but I've read that some still adhere to the ceremonial scarring and tattooing."

Cat's heart skipped a beat. "Really?"

He nodded. "It might be worth your time to get

someone to run that info through the system. See what turns up."

"I will, but you have to remember that I didn't see much of his face, and every third perp I've picked up has been tattooed to one degree or another."

"Yeah, I guess, but the ethnicity is a facet you might want to check up on."

"Right now, what happened to me is immaterial," she said. "I need to find Mimi. One way or another, I have a promise to keep."

"I know. I'll help all I can."

"You've already done enough," Cat said.

Wilson felt as if he were being dismissed, which made him a little nervous. He knew Cat well enough now to know that she was by no means going to sit back and wait for someone else to find her friend.

"What are you planning to do?" he asked.

She hesitated, then shrugged, unwilling to give herself away.

"I'm not sure."

"You're going to check out that oil lease in East Texas, aren't you?"

Cat lifted her chin. "Wouldn't you?"

He didn't answer, only challenged her with another question. "You think you can drive onto seven hundred acres and find a body...just like that?"

"No. I don't think it's going to be easy, and I'm not even certain that's where he dumped her. But she's missing, she called me from a chopper, he took a chopper to his oil leases on the day she disappeared—and it's a place to start."

"You could give your info to Missing Persons."

"They're doing their own investigation. This is mine."

"How are you going to get there?"

"Drive, I guess."

"If you're following the theory that he took her somewhere in a chopper, then you need to look at it from the same view."

"What do you mean?" Cat asked.

"Say he flew Marsha's body out of Dallas and dumped it somewhere on that seven hundred acres."

"Okay, for argument's sake, say he did."

"All right," Wilson said. "Then if it was me, I'd be flying over that seven hundred acres just like you're theorizing Presley did. You've got to search from that perspective, and the view from a car is a far different sight than from in the air."

Cat's eyes widened. "Oh. Yes. I see what you mean. Like I need to be looking at places large enough to land a chopper…stuff like that."

Wilson nodded.

"All right. That can be dealt with," she said. "Anything else?"

"Wait until I can go with you?"

"Don't ask me that," Cat said.

Wilson frowned. That was exactly what he *had* asked. Obviously, her answer was no.

Ten

The thaw began around midnight, although neither Cat or Wilson knew it at the time. But what they saw when they woke up ended their self-imposed isolation.

"I have to go in to work today," Wilson said, as he stepped out of the shower. "There was a call on my cell phone. Had a pusher that was a no-show. I'm out twenty-thousand unless I bring him back, and Brickman isn't up to the chase."

Cat knew who Red Brickman was. Art played poker with him every Saturday. She didn't stop to think what a small world it was that the man who employed her was best friends with the man who'd first owned Wilson McKay's business.

Instead, she nodded in understanding as she spat toothpaste into the sink, then rinsed her mouth before turning around. She felt his fingers tracing the pink butterfly on her hip, but by the time she looked up, all she saw was his bare backside.

He strode past her into the bedroom to get dressed. Cat made a face at herself. If he was ready to get back to business, then she was, too.

She'd gone over and over the lists that she'd made until she'd convinced herself that Presley's trip to East Texas and Mimi's disappearance on the same day were connected. Now she had to either prove, or disprove it, in case she had to move on to another location, but to do that, she needed to get to Presley's lease. Seven hundred acres of dense forest would be a dandy place to get rid of a body without being seen.

However, if she took Wilson's suggestion to view it from the air as Presley had done on that day, she had to charter a chopper.

She began brushing her hair in long, steady strokes and tried not to think of the available hunk in the adjoining room, or the fact that she'd selfishly indulged herself when Mimi was lying dead somewhere. It didn't occur to her that she might be wrong about Mimi's fate. She knew what she knew.

As she glanced up in the mirror, she caught Wilson looking at her from the other room. His expression was a cross between worry and want. She didn't like the possessive look on his face. She wasn't available unless she said so—and for now, the answer was no. She'd taken care of herself without anyone's help for far too long to suddenly go all feminine and helpless. Wilson McKay was a great person to have sex with, but no one told her what to do or how to do it.

She dropped her gaze, tossed the hairbrush aside, and grabbed a band and fastened her hair at the nape of her neck. Today she'd chosen a blue turtleneck sweater to go with her jeans and boots, and, as usual, was opting out of wearing makeup. It wasn't part of the uniform she needed.

"You look beautiful," Wilson said, as she came out of the bathroom.

She eyed his half-naked state and then grinned wryly.

"So do you."

He laughed again, just like he'd laughed when she'd asked for a repeat of their marathon lovemaking session, only this time it didn't embarrass her. She just stood there, letting the look on his face wash over her.

A half hour later he was gone. She'd promised to let him know how the day went. That much she could do. It didn't interfere with any of her independence. It was, after all, only a phone call.

She'd chartered the chopper in Dallas. It was definitely an easier, quicker, more efficient use of daylight. With an aerial map of East Texas and the coordinates to the seven hundred acres that belonged to Mark Presley, Cat was on the move.

Fifteen minutes after ten in the morning, and she was already half-way there.

The pilot, a man who called himself Skippy, had been given instructions as to the area over which they would be flying. He'd given her a wild-eyed look when she'd told him she was looking for someone, at which point he had tried to explain to her that, because of the dense vegetation, it was highly unlikely anyone would be found from the air. When she didn't counter that remark, he moved on to the next and fairly obvious question. If someone was lost, then why weren't the police in on this?

Cat had listened politely, ignored his question about the cops and waited for him to get in the chopper.

"Okay, fine. It's your dollar," Skippy finally said.

"Yes, it is," she said shortly.

But he wouldn't let it go. "You won't find a lost camper from the air…not in that part of the country. Besides, I can't imagine why anyone with a brain would go camping at this time of year."

Cat poked her finger against his chest.

"Listen, Skippy, we're not looking for a lost camper, so quit worrying. All you have to do is fly that chopper and follow my orders."

Skippy shifted his weight from one foot to the other as he pointed back at her. "Now here's where you and me might be partin' company. I will fly this bird, but when I'm in the air, I'm in charge."

Cat's eyes narrowed and her voice lowered.

"Listen, mister, someone murdered my friend Mimi and hid her body. You are going to help me find her."

Skippy's mouth dropped. "Uh…you didn't say anything about—"

"Maybe this was a mistake," Cat said, and started back into the office.

"Wait! Wait! Where are you going?" Skippy yelled.

"To get my money back."

The little man huffed and then puffed and then spat.

"Well, there's no call to go and do all that," he muttered.

"Are we on the same page?" Cat asked.

"Hell, yeah. Get in."

"Thank you," she said, and climbed into the chopper. "By the way, what's your name?" she asked.

"Skippy. You been using it just fine for the past half hour."

Cat arched an eyebrow as she gave the short, stocky man a long look. "No one is named Skippy. What's your name?"

He sighed. "Melvin."

Cat nodded. "That's better."

Neither one of them spoke again for the entire trip. It wasn't until Melvin began to circle that Cat realized they'd reached their destination.

"Is this it?" she asked.

He pointed to the map and nodded, then pointed to a large, blackened area far to the east of them.

"Something been goin' on down there. Big burn area… see it?"

Cat leaned forward. "Yes, I see it. What do you think it means?"

"Something caught on fire, that's all."

"Well, that's obvious," Cat muttered.

Melvin leaned toward her. "What did you say?" he yelled.

"Nothing," she said, and then pointed to the map. "Can we start at the outer circle of the area and then work our way in?"

"Sure."

"How low can you fly this thing?" she asked.

Melvin glanced at her, then pushed the stick forward. The chopper dipped drastically.

Cat's stomach rolled. She grabbed the edge of her seat with both hands and willed herself not to throw up. The sensation passed once they leveled off, but she glared at the little man just the same.

He grinned.

She glared again, then moved her coat aside just enough for him to see the gun and shoulder holster she was wearing.

The grin slid off his face faster than cold butter on a hot plate.

"Hellfire, woman! You wanted to fly low, didn't you?"

"I'm looking for clearings large enough for a chopper to land in that do not have access to roads."

The way she figured it, if the location could be reached by car, Presley wouldn't have used a chopper.

Melvin swallowed nervously, then nodded his understanding.

And so the search began.

They flew into the sun, then headed north in a counter-clockwise motion, circling the area in a contracting spiral. The roads that had been cut through the timber led straight to pump jacks, some of which were still pumping, some of which were not. The ones that were inactive were overgrown, and it was easy to see that they were unfit for land travel and that no one had been there in ages.

As they neared the charred area, they soon realized that what had burned here had been a well. She didn't know when it had happened, but it could explain why Presley had flown up here. If that was the case, then it didn't help her cause.

"What do you think?" Melvin asked, as he eyed the fuel gauge against the slant of sun sliding toward the western horizon.

"I don't know what to think," Cat said.

"If you don't have any more ideas, I'm for headin' back."

Cat turned on him. "That's too damned bad, because we aren't going back. That's quitting. I don't quit."

Melvin's face turned red, but he put a clamp on his comments.

Cat was so mad she was shaking. Her hands were doubled into fists, and her stomach was rolling. This was a bad dream that kept getting worse. Her entire adult life had been dedicated to finding bail jumpers, and she was damned good at it. But she would never have imagined she would be looking for Mimi—not like this.

She buried her face in her hands, trying to regain some composure, but the rage kept pushing its way out. She lifted her head abruptly, unaware of the tears streaming down her face, and began hitting her knees with her fists.

"Damn it, Mimi…I can't do this. I can't fucking do this."

Melvin was startled by Cat's outburst, but when he saw that she was crying, he groaned. All his life he'd been a sucker for a crying woman. Didn't matter why they were crying, he just couldn't stand to see it.

"Now, now," he said, and patted her roughly on the shoulder. "Don't give up yet. I tell you what we're gonna do. We're fixin' to unwind this flight pattern we've been on. We might see somethin' different then."

Cat inhaled on a sob, then swiped her hands across her face with angry jerks.

"What do you mean?"

Melvin pointed to the map in Cat's lap. "We flew from outside to in. Now we're gonna fly the other way, from inside to out. We'll be lookin' at the same stuff, but from a different angle."

Cat nodded slowly. "You know what, Melvin? You're all right."

He beamed.

"So let's see what we can see. Tighten that seat belt. We're gonna do a little tree skating."

Cat thought it was a figure of speech until the little man pushed the stick forward again. By the time he leveled off, they were only yards above the trees.

"Lord," Cat murmured, as she saw a deer burst out of the trees and dash across a small clearing.

"We're fine," Melvin said. "I've never lost a bird or a passenger."

Cat tried to smile, but she was too rattled to do anything but hang on.

Soon the shock of being so low passed, and she realized she was able to see far more than they'd seen on their first sweep across. They'd been flying for fifteen minutes when Melvin suddenly swerved and did what Cat could only call a U turn.

"What is it?" she asked, as she leaned over, trying to see what had caught his eye.

"On your right!" he yelled, and pointed down. "Someone set a whirlybird down in there."

Cat stared but couldn't see it. She could see a break in the trees, but it seemed so small.

"Are you sure?" she yelled back.

He made a circular motion with his hand.

"Look at them trees. The limbs have been clipped some. See the bare ends of those branches?"

Cat's heart skipped a beat. "Yes!" she cried. "I do see."

"Reckon you wanna set down and look the place over some?"

"I need to, but can we do it?"

Melvin puffed out his chest. "Trust me, woman. If another man did it, then so can I."

"Oh Lord," Cat said, as Melvin turned back to the east, then began to set the chopper down.

The treetops were so close she could have reached out and touched them, and when they began their descent, she resisted the urge to close her eyes. The lower they went, the more real the sensation became of being swallowed up by the trees.

Tiny bits of leaves began to fly through the air like green confetti, along with small bits of wood from the limbs. The debris flew in every direction, some pieces even ricocheting against the body of the chopper. Just when she thought they would surely crash, the sensation of movement ceased, and she realized they were down. The rotors slowed, then finally stopped.

Cat opened the door and all but fell out. She steadied herself, then eyed the pilot.

"Way to go, Melvin," she said slowly, then gave him a thumbs up. Shivering from the cold, she pulled the collar of her coat a little closer around her neck as he came around the front of the chopper.

"I'll just run a little check on the bird while you

look around. If this doesn't feel right, we'll take her right back up and look some more, okay?"

"Okay," Cat said, and took her gloves out of her pockets as she walked away.

At first she circled the clearing slowly, hoping to find signs that would tell her they were in the right place. As she walked, she began widening the circle in the same way that they'd searched from the air. Within minutes, she found tracks.

In themselves, they meant little. Tracks were tracks. They could have been left by anyone. She paused, then knelt.

"What did you find?" the pilot asked.

"Skid marks from another chopper and some boot tracks," she said.

Melvin grinned. "I told you a whirlybird had been here." He turned around to check the oil gauge as Cat stood up.

Cat stood there for a moment without moving, looking for the next sign that would tell her which way to go. Wind suddenly gusted through the trees and blew wisps of hair into her eyes. As she turned away, her gaze landed directly on what appeared to be drag marks.

Breath caught in the back of her throat. She hesitated, then moved toward them, and as she did, she saw the occasional footprint off to the side, as if someone had been staggering while dragging a load.

A slight panic set in. This was what she'd come for, but she suddenly wasn't so sure she was ready for the truth. Bracing herself for failure, she took a deep breath and started to walk, taking care not to step into the tracks in case this place proved to be a crime scene.

She walked until she was almost out of sight of the chopper, then turned and looked back. Melvin was standing beside the bird, intently watching her. When he saw her turn, he waved to indicate he was paying attention.

She waved back.

The thought that she was not alone in these woods was suddenly comforting.

Something rustled in the underbrush, and she jumped as a rabbit bounded out from beneath a thicket.

"Easy now," she told herself, and continued to move, only it was becoming more and more difficult to see where the tracks were going.

The leaves were thicker here and had blown around enough that it was difficult to follow the trail. Just when she thought she'd gone the wrong way, she walked up on one of Mimi's shoes. As she did, it felt as if someone had kicked her square in the belly. Breath ceased, and spots swam before her eyes. She had to grab onto a tree to steady herself, then, finally, bend over and put her head between her knees to keep from passing out.

Seeing the shoe in a place like this was like being run over. She felt empty and all at once hopeless, but she couldn't give up. She owed it to Mimi to see this through.

Gritting her teeth, she stood up. Knowing the shoe would be evidence, she left it where it was and kept moving forward.

Within twenty yards, she walked up on a steep drop-off.

It was a ravine about thirty yards across and at least a hundred yards deep, maybe more—the sides sheer and the bottom completely covered in pine trees and brush. With all the undergrowth, depth perception would have been non-existent from the air. It would have appeared as green and flat as the rest of the conifer-covered land.

By the time she reached the rim, she was shaking. She had to look. It was the reason she'd come. But knowing that and doing it were two different things. She was still struggling with herself when she finally looked down.

The rim marked a drop-off with no slope. She stared down into it until her vision blurred, and still she saw nothing to indicate that a body had been thrown over the edge. Blinking away angry tears, she turned her back on the ravine and began searching beneath the trees, looking for signs of digging that would signify something had recently been buried.

Ten minutes passed, then fifteen; then thirty minutes came and went as she continued to search.

Twice she thought she'd found something suspicious, only to realize what she'd been seeing was nothing more than an accumulation of rotting leaves.

Frustrated, she walked back to the edge of the ravine and looked down again. She was convinced that no one could have gone down there, but she had to be sure. She walked back and forth along the rim, looking for a path. She saw nothing, and after a few more minutes, she convinced herself there was no way anyone could have been in there on foot, let alone walked in with a body, then walked back out.

She didn't know how long she'd been standing there when she realized she was looking at a path after all. But it wasn't a path and footprints—it was a line of broken limbs that had been made through the brush, something that might have occurred if something heavy had rolled through.

Her throat tightened as she sank to her knees. Then she leaned farther forward, her fingernails digging into the mud and leaves as she clung to the edge. The sensation of falling made her stomach roll. She looked quickly at first, then rocked back on her heels until her head quit spinning.

She needed to look again, only this time, she told herself, she wasn't pulling back until she was convinced there was nothing there. She lay down on her belly and then leaned out over the rim, hanging on to a young sapling for added balance.

At first, all she could see were the trees—green

cedar and pines, and blue spruce, as far down as the eye could see—but there was still the faint path of broken limbs angling a little to the right of where she was lying.

She leaned a little bit farther out, and that was when she saw it—a flash of red, deep beneath a pile of dead wood and pines. Even though it was what she'd been looking for, her heart sank.

Mimi's new coat had been red.

"God…oh God."

Tears burned her throat as she scooted away from the edge. She wiped her nose with the back of her hand and then tried to stand, but her legs wouldn't work. Instead of going for help, she fell backward. As she did, the trees around her turned into long green fingers, pointing upward toward heaven. At that point Cat realized she was seeing what Mimi must have seen—her last glimpse of the world into which she'd been born.

She rolled over on her belly and looked back down into the crevasse. From this angle, she could see more of the coat and what appeared to be a sleeve draped over a dead limb.

Even as she was looking, she wasn't processing the truth. She scooted back from the rim and began crawling away, as if something was after her. She was on her hands and knees when she started to scream.

She was still screaming when Melvin emerged

from the trees. He'd been scared shitless a few times in his life, but never quite as abruptly as this.

The moment he'd heard her first scream, he'd started running. Somewhere along the way he'd lost his cap, and the sparse hair left on his head was swirled in every direction.

Shaking in every limb, he dropped down beside her.

"Miss Dupree…uh…lady…oh hell…honey, honey, what happened? What in hell happened? Did you fall? Are you hurt?"

Still sobbing, Cat rocked back on her heels. For a second she couldn't remember who he was or why he was there. And then he touched her.

She looked up.

"Melvin?"

"Yeah, honey, it's me. Did you fall?"

"No."

"Then what's wrong?" he asked.

"She's down there. My friend…my Mimi…she's in the ravine."

Melvin grunted as if he'd been punched, then stood quickly, pulling Cat up as he went.

She was taller than him and at least twenty years younger, but she was as weak as a baby. He steadied her with an arm around her waist and then walked with her back to the rim.

"Are you sure?" he asked.

She nodded.

He hesitated to look over, but like a witness to a

bad wreck, he found that he couldn't look away. He followed the line of her finger as she pointed downward. At first he saw nothing; then, like Cat, he saw the spot of red in the midst of all that green.

"Is that her…the red color?"

Cat nodded. "It's her coat. She was wearing it when I saw her last."

"I'll be damned," Melvin mumbled, then became the voice of reason. "Come on, now. We got to get back to the chopper and notify the authorities. If we hurry, maybe they can get her up before dark."

"I'll just wait here and—"

Skippy frowned. "No. You're coming with me."

Cat slumped. He was right. She didn't need to be here. She'd found Mimi. Now she had to make sure the cops arrested the right man.

Wilson was signing off on the return of the drug pusher who'd jumped bail when his cell phone rang. He glanced at it briefly, but when he realized it was Cat, he quickly shifted gears. He tossed the pen back to the desk sergeant.

"He's all yours," he said, and answered his phone. "Hey, you." When she didn't immediately answer, he thought they had a bad connection. Then she said his name, and he heard tears in her voice.

"Cat! Catherine! What's wrong?"

"I found her," Cat said.

Wilson felt disoriented. Despite the fact that he'd

known Cat was serious about a search, he'd had a hard time believing she could just take off and find her friend the first time out. It took a few moments for him to realize how much information they'd sifted through before she'd started looking. Obviously her suspicions had been right on target. It was hard to believe, and yet…

"Dead?"

Cat choked on a sob. "Yes."

"Where?"

"In a ravine on an oil lease belonging to Mark Presley."

"Have you called the sheriff's department?"

"Not yet. I called you."

Wilson didn't stop to think about what that meant. "Jesus. Can you tell me exactly where you are?"

"No, but Melvin can."

"Who's Melvin?" Wilson asked.

"My pilot."

Wilson was trying to absorb the fact that since he'd seen Cat this morning, she had not only chartered a chopper, but had gone out and confirmed her worst fears. It all seemed too easy.

"Let me talk to him."

Melvin took the phone. "Hello?"

"Melvin…my name is Wilson McKay. I'm in the Dallas police station right now. If you'll give me the flight coordinates, I'll relay them to the proper authorities."

Melvin rattled them off, then okayed them as Wilson read them back.

"Yeah, that's right," Melvin said, then added, "So…when do you think the sheriff's gonna be able to get here? It'll be dark before too long, harder for them to find this place."

"I'll get the cops there. You just take care of Cat."

"Don't worry none about her. I won't leave her alone for a minute, but she's tough, I tell you. Tough as they come."

Wilson's heart went out to Catherine. He knew how tough she could be, but something told him that this was going to take her way down. Half the time they weren't even on speaking terms, but at the same time, it made him sick to think of her going through this alone.

Eleven

Wilson dropped his phone in his pocket, then headed for Missing Persons.

"Bradley in?" he asked.

"In the john. Have a seat. He should be right back."

Wilson sat down in the chair beside Bradley's desk. Within a couple of minutes, Bradley was back, somewhat surprised to see Wilson sitting at his desk.

"McKay, what's up with you?"

"Just got a call from Cat Dupree. She found Marsha Benton."

Bradley stared at Wilson as if he was nuts.

"You're shitting me," he said.

"No."

"Where?" Bradley asked.

"At the bottom of a ravine on an oil lease in East Texas that belongs to Mark Presley."

Bradley sat down in his chair with a thump.

"How the hell did she come to look in a place like that?"

"All I'll say is, she'd make a damn good detective," Wilson said. "I told her I'd contact the local authorities for her, then decided the call might be better coming from you guys, since you've been working the case."

"What's the closest town out there?"

"Tyler. Here are the coordinates to the location of her chopper."

"She found the body from the air?"

"I don't think so, at least, not exactly. Don't ask me details. I've already told you all I know."

Bradley wrote furiously, then finally looked up.

"Sam Lohman's the sheriff down there. I'll give him a call right now."

Wilson got up and started to walk away.

"Hey, where are you going?" Bradley asked.

"To help Catherine bring Marsha home."

Melvin tried to get Cat to come back to the chopper and get out of the cold, but she wasn't budging. All she could think of was how many days Mimi had been down there alone.

"Come on now, Missy, when the authorities arrive, we're gonna have to leave so they'll have a place to land."

Cat heard him talking but stood her ground.

"You go. I'm not leaving her here alone."

Melvin frowned. "If you don't come with me, you don't have a way to get home."

"I'll rent a car."

He threw up his hands in defeat.

"Damn hard-headed woman."

"You're not the first to call me that," she said, then shoved her hands in her pockets and hunched her shoulders against the cold. "Look, Melvin… Marsha Benton was my best friend…the only family I had. Whoever killed her also killed the baby she was carrying and then threw them away like garbage. You helped me find her, and I will be forever grateful, but my job isn't over. In fact, it's just begun. It's not that I won't leave. I just *can't*."

The bitterness in her voice punctuated her determination.

"Okay. I guess I understand. I was just worrying about your welfare, that's all. What happened to your friend is terrible. To be honest, I never thought we'd find her. We just got in the bird and flew right to her. Stuff like that just doesn't happen."

"I had help," Cat said, thinking of all the research she and Wilson had done.

"So you think you know who killed her?" he asked.

"Yes."

"Reckon you'll be able to prove it?"

"He's going to be hard-pressed to deny involvement once the DNA test comes back on the baby she was carrying."

Melvin nodded, then glanced at his watch before judging the level of the setting sun. It was almost at the edge of the treetops, which meant there weren't more than three hours of daylight left.

"It's been about an hour since you called your friend in Dallas. I'm guessing it won't be long before the cops arrive. I reckon I'll get on back to the chopper and check the radio. They may be trying to reach me."

Cat swallowed nervously. Now that the time was upon her, she was beginning to feel anxious. She couldn't bear to think about Mimi being left out here another night, even though she'd been located.

"Yes, sure," Cat said, and then eyed the little pilot. "Melvin…"

"Yeah?"

"Thank you."

He blushed. "I was glad to be of service. If you ever need another flight, give me a call. Just make sure there's no more dead bodies at the end of it."

"Count on it," Cat said, and then watched as he headed back to the helicopter.

Within minutes, she heard the distant sound of another copter. Seconds later, she heard Melvin firing up the engine. Even though she was at least a hundred yards away, she felt the wind gusts and saw the bits of leaves swirling through the air as he lifted off.

Anxious to be there when the authorities arrived, she began running toward the clearing.

Sheriff Sam Lohman had eighteen years of experience in law enforcement, fifteen of which he'd spent in this part of the country, and he'd worked his share of murder cases. But getting the word from Dallas P.D that there was a body in his county let him know that there was a back story to this murder that had already been in motion before the body wound up here.

From what he'd been told, this might turn out to be nothing more than the dumping ground. Still, it was a scene he didn't relish, especially when he'd learned that the body was that of a young pregnant woman.

It wasn't until he found out that the only way to get to the site was by chopper that he began to curse. He was one of those people who believed that if God had meant for man to fly, He would have given him wings. He'd taken the ride with tight-lipped concentration and an eye to the swiftly fading daylight, all the while trying not to think about how high he was off the ground.

He heard the pilot talking on the radio but was unaware that they were almost at the landing site until, seemingly out of nowhere, another chopper suddenly rose up from the trees in front of them, hovered for a moment, then flew away.

"Christ Almighty!" Lohman yelled, as Melvin sailed past, and grabbed hold of his seat. "Where did he come from?"

The pilot pointed down. Lohman leaned over, spied the small opening in the trees and swallowed nervously.

"Reckon you can set this thing down there?"

The pilot nodded, and down they went.

Sam was swallowing hard by the time the chopper landed. Everyone already knew he disliked flying, but he damn sure wasn't going to advertise it by puking in front of anyone. He and his deputy got out, and as soon as they were clear, their pilot took off so that the other chopper accompanying them could land.

Two crime scene investigators got out of it, followed by a couple of members of the Rescue Squad from the Tyler Fire Department. Their chopper was larger than the one Sam and his deputy had come in, so when it landed, they sheared another foot or so of limbs and leaves from the surrounding trees.

The crime scene investigators were grumbling about the leaves messing up the scene when Sam saw a woman running out of the trees. Her stride was long, her posture straight, the expression on her face unreadable. Remembering Wilson McKay's message, he decided this must be the woman who'd found the body.

"Ma'am… I'm Sheriff Sam Lohman."

"Cat Dupree."

Her husky voice was a surprise. It didn't seem to go with the rest of her. Then the name suddenly registered

"Dupree? I used to know a Marcus Dupree. Don't suppose you'd be any kin?"

"He was my father," Cat said.

Sam grinned as he clasped her hand, shaking it forcefully.

"Well, I'll be damned. It's real good to meet you," he said. "How's old Marcus doing, anyway?"

"He's dead," Cat said. "Murdered years ago."

Sam reeled as if she'd just slapped him. "I didn't know. Lord, I'm sorry."

Cat shrugged off the sympathy. "You didn't do it. No apology needed. Now…about my friend."

Sam got the message. The moment of reunion was over.

"Where is the body?" he asked.

"I'll show you," she said.

Sam waved to the others. They fell in line, walking single-file through the trees and underbrush as Cat pointed out the drag marks and tracks she'd originally followed. When they came to Marsha's shoe, Cat pointed it out to the forensic team.

One of the investigators stayed behind and began to take pictures of the shoe and the surrounding area before bagging the evidence. The rest of them continued to follow Cat.

"This is practically impenetrable," Sam muttered, as he pushed past some low-hanging vines. "Say,

Miss Dupree… Detective Bradley, who called me, said the missing woman is from Dallas."

"Yes. So am I," Cat said.

"How did you know where to look for the body? Were you tipped off?"

"No, I didn't get a tip. The land and the wells that are on it belong to Mark Presley."

Sam frowned. "What's one got to do with the other?"

Cat paused, then turned around and fixed Sam with an unflinching gaze.

"He's the father of the baby she was carrying. He told her to get rid of it. She wouldn't, so he got rid of her."

Sam didn't know what to say. Was Cat Dupree telling him facts, or was this just anger and grief talking? He would question her more later, after they finished the business of bagging and tagging, hopefully before dark.

They walked a short distance further; then she suddenly stopped. Sam didn't see the ravine until he stepped up beside her.

"This could be dangerous," he muttered, more to himself than to her, as he gazed down into the rift.

"Obviously," she said. Her hand was trembling as she pointed downward, but her voice was firm.

Sam peered over the side. "Where's the body?"

"Down there…a little to the left of those dead kudzu vines…beneath those pine branches. See the spot of red?"

220   *Sharon Sala*

Suddenly his gaze focused on the color.

"Yeah. I see it." He looked at her then. "Are you claiming that's a body?"

"Yes."

"Did you go down there to confirm?"

"No. Didn't have to."

Sam cursed softly. "Lady…Miss Dupree…that little bit of color could be anything."

Cat exhaled slowly, as if making herself stay calm. Her warm breath became a tiny cloud in the chilled air as she turned on the sheriff.

"That's my friend Marsha Benton, wearing the same red coat she was wearing the day before she disappeared. The shoe back there on the trail is hers, too. I was with her when she bought them." Then her voice broke. "Are you going to go down there and get her, or are you going to stand here and argue with me until it's too late to get to her and she has to spend another night down there alone?"

Sam wasn't in the habit of being called down—especially by a female and in front of his own men—but he was willing to give her a little leeway, considering her state of mind.

He turned without answering her and waved to the crew that had followed him.

"Suit up and get down there. If that's a body, do your thing and get it up here ASAP. It's getting dark, and it's too damned cold to stay out here any longer than we have to."

All the nerves and tension that Cat had been feeling slowly dissipated. She closed her eyes briefly, then looked down into the deep green maw cut through the earth.

I found you, Mimi, just like I promised.

Sam could tell she was overcome with emotion but refrained from comment and turned his attention to the men being lowered by ropes down to the bottom.

It was after ten p.m. when the chopper carrying Sheriff Sam Lohman, his deputy, Cat Dupree and the body of Marsha Benton landed at the heli-pad outside the local hospital. An ambulance was waiting to take the body to the morgue, and the driver was standing beside the ambulance.

Sam nodded to him. "Hey, Charlie. Sorry to get you out at this time of night. Did you have a good Christmas?"

Charlie Conroy rolled his eyes. "Forgot to buy batteries for the damned toys."

Sam chuckled. "Oh man, and everything in town was closed, right? What did you rob?"

"The remote controls…all three of them."

Sam grinned, but then they pulled the body bag out of the chopper, and he got down to business and introduced Cat.

"This here is Cat Dupree, friend of the deceased. She made a positive identification of the body when we got to her. The deceased's name is Marsha Benton, from Dallas."

Conroy eyed the steely-eyed woman who was walking beside the body bag. He watched her step back as they loaded it in the ambulance, and when they closed the doors, she laid her hand on the latch and bowed her head.

Sam sighed. "She's had a rough day. Reckon we can question her tomorrow. For now, I'm gonna see about getting her a room."

Charlie nodded, then got in his car and followed the ambulance to the morgue, while Sam and his deputy escorted Cat into a patrol car.

"If you wouldn't mind, I'd appreciate a ride to the nearest motel," Cat said, then leaned back and closed her eyes.

"Yes, ma'am," the deputy said.

Sam glanced back at Cat once, then started the car. They were backing up when his cell phone rang.

"This is Lohman," he said, then listened to his caller. "Yeah, sure…no problem," he said, and when the line went dead, dropped the phone back into his pocket and took a quick right turn.

Cat looked up just as they passed a well-lit motel.

"Hey, that one has vacancies." she said.

"I've got to go by the office first," he said.

"But, I…oh, never mind," Cat said. She didn't have it in her to argue.

Sam started to explain, but when he looked up

into the rearview mirror, he saw that she'd closed her eyes. She would know soon enough, anyway.

A few minutes later, the patrol car turned off the street into the parking lot of the sheriff's office. As soon as the car stopped moving, Cat sat up.

"Come inside," Sam said. "You're going to the motel in another vehicle."

Assuming that one of his deputies was going to take her, she got out without comment and followed them inside. They went through the outer office and down a small hallway before coming to the sheriff's office. As they walked through the doorway, she saw Wilson McKay stand up from a chair beside the desk.

Breath caught in the back of her throat as her eyes filled with tears. She tried to speak, but nothing came out.

"Hey, you," Wilson said softly, and enfolded her in his arms, then held her close.

Every emotion that Cat had been holding in came undone. The moment his arms went around her, she began to shake.

"As God is my witness, I will kill him with my bare hands," she mumbled.

"You've done your part," he said. "Let the police finish this."

"They have to make him pay."

Wilson didn't have to ask who she was talking about and was past doubting she knew what had happened.

"If he's their man, it will happen," he said, then looked at the sheriff. "I suppose you'll be wanting to question her?"

Sam nodded. "Tomorrow's soon enough. Just bring her by before you both leave town. That'll do for me."

"You got it, and thanks."

"No problem," Sam said, watching the way Wilson seemed to be putting himself between Cat and the rest of the world. Then he looked back at Cat. "Miss Dupree, I know it doesn't matter to you now, considering all you've been through, but I wasn't kidding about your dad. He was one of my best friends."

Cat nodded, but talking about the past was nothing but a heartache for her.

Wilson glanced at Cat. "Are you okay to leave?"

"Yes."

"Then we'll see you in the morning," Wilson said, and they left the office through a back door.

As soon as Cat stepped out of the building, a gust of cold air slapped her in the face. She shivered and pulled her coat a little closer.

Wilson noticed and hurried her to the car.

"I got here about thirty minutes ago, so it's still warm," he said, as he helped her inside.

Cat glanced around as she settled into the seat. There was an empty throw-away coffee cup in the cup holder and a partial pack of gum on the dash. It was warm inside, as he'd promised, but it also smelled like him—a mixture of the cologne he wore, and the soap and shampoo he favored. It was familiar and oddly comforting. Cat leaned back against the seat, took off her gloves, stuffed them in her pockets and closed her eyes as Wilson slid behind the wheel.

He gave her a quick glance, then started the car.

"We'll be at the motel in just a few minutes."

She didn't say anything at first; then he heard her sigh.

"You came."

The pain in her voice was his undoing. He took her hand and pulled it to his lips, then kissed the knuckles, pretending he didn't see the old bruises and healing scrapes.

"Of course I came," he said softly.

Cat looked at him then—searching the familiarity of his features before absently glancing at the small gold hoop in his ear.

"Thank you."

"You're welcome. Now let's get you to the motel. You look like you're about to fall over."

"I may never sleep again," she said.

He didn't comment, just changed the subject. "When did you eat last?"

Cat blinked. "Uh…this morning, I guess."

"Not good enough," Wilson said. "Do you want to eat out, or get something to go and take it to the room?"

Cat swallowed while trying not to think of what Marsha's body had looked like.

"I'm not very hungry," she said.

"You need to eat."

She closed her eyes and then pinched the bridge of her nose to keep from crying.

"I don't think I can...uh...I can't get the image of her..."

"Shit," Wilson said softly. "I'm sorry. I wasn't thinking."

"It's all right. I just don't want—"

"I understand. Completely. Just sit back and relax."

Cat took a couple of slow, deep breaths and went limp. Despite her vow of sleeplessness, she was asleep when he drove through the take-out lane at a local drive-in. She was still asleep when he parked in front of the room he'd rented at a local motel.

He left her in the car as he carried the take-out sack into the room. Then, leaving the motel door open, he returned to the car for her. She roused slightly as he opened the door.

"Are we there?"

"Yes."

She swung her legs out and stood up, then staggered slightly. He steadied her, then shut and locked the car door before guiding her inside.

The room was warm and quiet. Cat began to relax as soon as she crossed the threshold. When Wilson shut the door, she turned toward him.

"Thank you...for all this," she said, and began taking off her coat.

He frowned. "Knowing what you went through today, I couldn't have stayed in Dallas."

"Did you find your bail jumper?"

"Yes," Wilson said, then took her coat and tossed it on a chair before easing her backward onto the bed.

"Give me a foot," he said, and pulled off one of her boots. "Now the other," he said, and dropped that boot beside the first one.

"That feels so good," Cat muttered, as she wiggled her toes inside her socks.

Wilson tilted her chin up with the tip of his finger, then gently kissed her square on the mouth.

"That feels good, too," she said, when he pulled back.

He opened the sack he'd carried in, took out a paper cup with a straw, and handed it to her.

"Vanilla malt. No thought needed to drink or swallow. Trust me, it will be okay."

Cat swallowed past the knot in her throat. He'd understood and still been able to see to her needs. And he'd been right. The malt was perfect—cold and sweet, without the need to chew.

"It's good," she said, and continued to sip until it was gone.

Wilson opened his bag, took out a new toothbrush, a new hairbrush and one of his old t-shirts, and laid them at the foot of the bed.

"For you, too," he said.

Cat was overwhelmed by his thoughtfulness, and at the same time a little panicked. He kept doing all the right things, which sucked her farther and farther under his spell. She didn't want to like him—not like that.

In her experience, men didn't stay. They hit and ran and left the woman bleeding—or, in Mimi's case, dead. And while she knew Wilson might never physically hurt her, she didn't trust him not to break her heart.

"Thank you again," she said. "I think I'll shower first."

"Sure thing," Wilson said. "You go clean up. I'm going to call Bradley and tell him you made a positive identification."

Cat hesitated. "Is this case going to Dallas Homicide now?"

"Yes, although they'll need to wait for the coroner's report. And even if this wasn't the scene of the crime, the sheriff still has some precedence in the case."

"I reported her missing to the Dallas police, and she turned up dead." Cat said. "Why isn't it Homicide's case now?"

Wilson cupped the side of her face with his hand, then traced the frown lines away with his thumb.

"Stop worrying. We'll get it sorted out. Besides, you've already proved your point to Missing Persons, and when you give your statement, they'll know everything you know about Mark Presley."

"Yeah…okay."

"Trust the process. Give them time to get what they need to nail him the right way."

Cat understood what he meant, and whether she liked it or not, she knew he was right.

"Okay," he said when she nodded. "Now, you go get that shower while I make my call."

Cat undressed beside the bed and walked naked into the bathroom without looking at Wilson again. But he wasn't quite as removed. Even after she'd closed the door, he was still bemused by her tall, slim figure and the pink butterfly on her butt. It was several moments before he remembered he'd been going to use the phone.

Twelve

Tahoe was to snow skiing what the island of Oahu was to surfers—both claimed to be paradise if you were tough enough and skilled enough to enjoy it. Mark had been coming to Tahoe for Christmas for as long as he could remember, even before he'd met and married Penny. He was on a first-name basis with the manager and staff at the lodge, and liked the attention they gave him.

He'd felt their admiration in the looks they'd given him as he was leaving for the slopes that morning. It was like always being Big Man On Campus. He was one of those "men to go to" when the need for financial advice arose, a far cry from the high school boy who'd missed his chance at athletic fame.

He'd left Penny still sleeping in their suite and

enjoyed his solitary trip to the ski lift. After his loss of control the other day, the mood was still cool between them. He knew that he'd crossed a line when he'd touched her in anger, but she would come around. He would make sure of it.

And since the fire had been put out at the number nine oil well without any repercussions from getting water from the rock quarry, he felt secure in his self-satisfaction.

According to the pumper, Wyatt Beech, the driver of the truck that had hit the pump jack had turned up a day later, walking down the road with a hangover the size of Dallas and no earthly idea how his truck wound up in the midst of the fire.

When Presley reached the ski lift, he nodded to the attendant as he hopped on, then tightened his grip on his ski poles. The ride up was bliss, and once at the top, he jumped off, then skied off to the side before stopping. The cold air filled his lungs to the point of actual pain, and yet he smiled. It was good to be alive.

The bright sun made the snow-coated landscape pristine in its beauty. The sky was crystal clear, the slope in front of him all but empty. He picked up his poles, using them to steady himself as he checked the locks on his skis. Even though they felt fine, he stomped them sharply, making sure they wouldn't come loose on the way down.

He inhaled deeply, feeling the omnipotent thump of his own heartbeat as it moved the blood through his body, strengthening his muscles as he moved toward the lip of the slope. He was anticipating the adrenaline rush that would carry him down the hill to the hot breakfast of sausage and blueberry pancakes he was going to order, imagining the taste of French roast coffee as he shifted his goggles, making sure they were comfortable on his face.

He crouched slightly, his knees bent, his toes curled inside his ski boots as he started to push off. In the midst of his moment of Zen, his cell phone rang. The sound was as out of place in the moment as a thing could be, and he had only himself to blame. He dropped his ski poles and pulled the phone out of his fanny pack to check Caller ID. When he realized it was his lawyer, he answered it without a second thought.

"This is Presley."

"Mark…it's Ken. You need to come home."

"And a hello to you, too," he snapped.

"Sorry," Ken Walters said. "Please let me start over. Did you have a merry Christmas?"

"Yes, thank you, we did. And you?"

"Of course," Ken said. "Now that we've passed the niceties, you need to come home."

Mark sighed. "Why? Surely whatever it is can wait until Saturday. That's when we're due back. Our annual New Year's Eve party. You know."

Ken frowned. He was well aware of the Presleys' annual bash. It was one of *the* parties to go to in

Dallas during the holidays, but in Ken's opinion, a party was the least of Mark Presley's concerns right now.

"The Dallas police want to talk to you."

Mark's heart skipped a beat, then settled. "About what?"

"Your secretary. Marsha Benton."

Mark had a sudden urge to urinate, but he maintained a tone of firm control.

"They've already spoken to me about her. I told them I had no idea where she was."

"Yes, well, it's more complicated than that now."

"She's no longer my secretary, nor does she even work for the company anymore, so I can't really speak to what she's doing these days." Mark said.

"That's not the issue," Walters said.

Mark frowned. "Damn it, Ken, quit beating around the bush and say what you've got to say."

"Marsha Benton is dead. They found her body on that oil property you own up near Tyler. She was murdered."

Ken Walters heard Mark gasp, he assumed in shock at the news.

But that wasn't what had taken Presley aback. It was the fact that they'd already found her. How the hell had that happened?

"Mark? Mark? Are you still there?"

Presley shuddered. "Uh…yes…I, uh, oh my God, I just can't wrap my mind around this."

"I'm sorry to be the one to break the news. I

knew you'd be upset. So what do you want me to tell the police?"

"Why do you need to tell them anything?" Mark asked, then realized that he'd just snapped. He needed to maintain his cool.

"Sorry. I'm just upset by the news, that's all."

"I understand," Ken said. "However, I told the police I'd contact you myself and pass along their message."

Mark frowned. "Message? They sent me a message?"

"It's not exactly a message so much as a request. They want to talk to you. She worked for you for years."

"Yes, of course," Mark said. "I just wasn't thinking."

"So when can I tell them you're coming?"

Mark was getting more nervous by the minute. Ken was pinning him down to something he didn't want to do, and his attitude showed.

"As sorry as I am to hear about what happened to Marsha, I see no need to cut my vacation short."

"Even when the employee was found murdered on property you own? Property, I might add, that is about as isolated as it gets in the state of Texas. It's not like she just wandered onto the place and was assaulted by a stranger."

Mark inhaled sharply. "What the fuck are you getting at?"

Ken bristled. He knew Mark Presley inside and out. He knew about all the women with whom he'd had affairs. He couldn't imagine Presley as a killer, but this didn't look good.

"As your lawyer, I am strongly advising you to cooperate. Now...do you intend to do as I suggest and come home promptly, or do you want to piss off the Dallas Police Department and make yourself look guilty?"

Mark stifled a curse. "Of course not, and of course I'll cooperate. It's not like I have anything to hide, for God's sake."

"So can I give them a time line?"

"Tell them we'll be home this afternoon. I can talk to them at the office in the morning. You'll be there, of course."

Ken's frown deepened as he considered why Presley would want or need him there. "Is there anything you want to tell me?"

"No. Of course not," Mark said.

"Okay, good. I'll be there. Sorry to be the bearer of bad news."

"It's certainly not your fault," Mark said. "Besides, quit worrying. I'm not the kind to shoot the messenger."

The line went dead in Ken's ear while he was still trying to figure out exactly what Presley meant by that last remark.

Presley, however, wasn't confused about anything. He had a problem. If Marsha's body had been found this soon and as cold as it had been, decomposition would be far less advanced than he would have hoped. During the autopsy they would find out she'd been pregnant and would certainly want DNA from every male she worked with to eliminate suspects. He wouldn't pass.

He picked up the ski poles and stabbed them into the snow.

"I should have buried her. Why the fuck didn't I bury her?"

But he already knew the answer. He hadn't expected her to be alive when he'd unrolled her from that tarp. She'd looked at him, recognized him for what he was, and he'd panicked. It was stupid. It wasn't like she was going to identify him later.

His problem had been lack of experience. She was the first person he'd ever killed. He'd expected her to be his last. Now he wasn't so sure. Still, one thing was certain: he would do what it took to stay out of prison.

The motel room that Wilson had taken was clean and comfortable, but Cat had been afraid to close her eyes. If it hadn't been for his presence, she would have lost her mind. Even though she thought she'd been prepared for the horror of Mimi's murder to become a fact, she'd been wrong. She kept reliving the memories of their lives together—from the foster family and the room they'd shared there through the many years afterward.

Their first attempts at cooking had been a mess, but they'd laughed and learned together. And then there were the times they'd nursed each other through heartbreaks and illnesses, the birthdays and holidays that had come and gone—always together. She couldn't believe that life was over, that she would never hear Mimi's voice or share a holiday with her again.

Wilson was at a loss as to how to console her, especially because she wouldn't even let him touch her.

It was nearing midnight when Cat finally sat up in bed. Wilson was stretched out on the other bed but wasn't asleep.

"Wilson…"

He turned on the lamp, then stuffed the second pillow beneath his head. Her eyes were red-rimmed and swollen, and she was clutching a handful of tissues.

"Yeah?"

"I need to think of something besides Mimi. I don't know anything about your family. Tell me about them."

"We're just your average redneck Texas family."

She closed her eyes and sighed. "I don't know what that means."

He winced. He kept forgetting that "average" was a word that could never describe her childhood.

"Okay…so…first things first. My mom is a retired school teacher. My dad farmed a couple of sections and ran some cows. They still live on the place, although my youngest brother and one of my brothers-in-law do the farming now."

"Where do they live?" Cat asked.

"Near Austin…about fifteen miles outside of town. It's where I grew up. I have two brothers and three sisters who've made me an uncle several times over."

Cat eyed him curiously, trying to imagine him as a kid in the middle of that kind of life.

He rolled over, then got up and crawled onto her bed with her.

"Hey," she said, as he grabbed one of her feet and started giving it a massage.

"It's called TLC. Don't knock it," he muttered.

She rolled her eyes and tried to pretend that tender loving care was commonplace in her life. It wasn't easy to lie.

"Are you the oldest?" she asked.

"Yeah. How did you know?"

"You're bossy."

Light caught on the earring as he tilted his head sideways and grinned. It made her think of a pirate.

"I'm not bossy. It's called being right."

"I'll bet you were insufferable," Cat muttered.

"What makes you think I grew out of it?"

The verbal sparring was becoming just a little too friendly. She decided to cut to the chase.

"So why aren't you married?"

There was a long moment of silence, and when he spoke, the laughter was gone from his voice. "I was engaged once, a long time ago."

"What happened?" Cat asked.

"She married someone else."

He felt Cat stiffen, then start to withdraw, so he held her feet tighter, and kept on rubbing and talking.

"I'm thirty-eight, so that was almost fifteen years ago."

"Tough," Cat said.

Wilson moved his hand to the arch in her foot and began rubbing it in a slow, circular motion.

"It's history. My broken heart healed." Then his voice softened. "Yours will, too."

"It's not quite the same thing," Cat said. "I mean…Mimi was a sister to me, not a mate."

"When it comes to losing a loved one, everything is the same. Loss is loss. Pain is pain. Dead is dead."

"I guess," Cat said.

Wilson frowned as he watched her struggling to hide her emotions. She was so beautiful and so lonely—and so tough.

"So…are you completely turned off now, or do you want to hear more?"

"More."

"The three boys in the family came first. The girls were last, so as the older brothers, we took the job of protecting our sisters very seriously and gave their boyfriends all kinds of hell. There was never any danger of them being mistreated by their dates." Then he chuckled. "I guess it's a small miracle in itself that they all three managed to get married. We weren't nice to any of them."

Cat thought about the turmoil they must have caused, trying to imagine what it would have been like to be loved and cared for like that.

"It must be nice to belong to a big family," she said.

"They'd have a different story to tell," Wilson said. "Next holiday, you'll have to come home with me and see for yourself."

Next holiday? This was beginning to sound like a relationship with substance. Not just a meeting of two healthy people who enjoyed each other—and sex.

"Maybe," Cat said.

Wilson felt her pulling away again and kept quiet, letting her direct the conversation.

"Tell me your best memory," she said finally.

"There are so many," Wilson said. "Why don't you tell me yours, instead?"

Cat went still—so still that Wilson feared he'd said the wrong thing by bringing up any part of her past. Just when he was about to change the subject, she answered.

"I think I was about four or five, although I'm not sure. I do know that Mother was still alive, and it was summer. A carnival had come to town, and I wanted to ride on the merry-go-round, but I was afraid to do it by myself. So Daddy bought three tickets instead of just the one for me, then Mother lifted me onto the horse, and she and Daddy got on either side of me. When the music began to play and the horse started going up and down, I squealed. I remember the smell of cotton candy, the sound of their laughter and the wind blowing through my hair. It was the best day."

Wilson nodded, but there was a big knot in the back of his throat as he thought about Catherine Dupree's life. Most of it had been one kick in the teeth after another.

"That's a good one. What was your mother's name?"

"Catherine…like mine."

"Do you look like her?"

"No. Like Daddy. Mother was small, with light brown hair and green eyes. I get my height and coloring from him."

"You're beautiful, you know," Wilson said.

Cat frowned. "I'm too thin."

"You're beautiful."

Cat pushed at Wilson's hands with her foot. He turned it loose and picked up her other one without missing a beat.

"You don't have to say that," she said.

He rubbed at her toes, then began rubbing between them. It felt so good to Cat, she was mentally comparing the sensation to an orgasm when he answered.

"It's called a compliment, and don't tell me you've never had them," he said.

"Not one that came without something else attached."

He frowned, then dropped her foot and stood up.

"Just for the record, you're the most aggravating female I've ever known. You'd think by that look on your face that I'd just said a bad word. For God's sake, don't get yourself all in a twist. It's not like I'm fishing around on the off chance we might make love."

"We have sex," she said.

His eyes narrowed angrily. "I'm a liberal. You call it what you want to."

For some reason his defiance was making her nervous. She wasn't afraid of him. She just wasn't sure what she'd said that was pushing his buttons.

"Thank you again for today," she said.

A muscle jerked at the side of his jaw, but he didn't react.

"You're welcome," he said. "Now try to get some sleep."

The next morning was hectic. They overslept and then rushed to get ready. Breakfast was fast food on the way to the sheriff's office. Cat got through the interview dry-eyed and stone-jawed, leaving Sheriff Sam Lohman with the opinion that she pursued her beliefs with a passion that was close to dangerous.

She'd begun by explaining her suspicions about Mark Presley with regard to what Marsha had told her, then lightly brushed over the accumulation of information she'd gathered through Wilson's expertise before going on to the strange message from Marsha's cell phone that had been left on her machine. She tied it all up with the comment that the sum total had led her to this area.

It was after eleven a.m. when they left the sheriff's office and started the trip back to Dallas. Wilson made sure she had everything she might need—a bottle of water, something to read and a couple of snacks, should she get hungry again.

Cat smiled in all the right places, and said please and thank you when the need arose, but she was already mentally withdrawing from the closeness they had shared. It was nothing more complicated than an instinctive need to protect herself.

They hadn't cleared the city limits of Tyler before Wilson felt the distance between them. He didn't like it, but he didn't know how to get her back. Within an hour, she was asleep, and she stayed that way most of the way back to Dallas.

They were on the outskirts of the city before she woke up. Wilson heard her stirring and glanced over. Her breasts pushed at the fabric of her sweater as she stretched. Remembering the weight of them in his hands made him ache, so he turned his attention back to the road and shifted his emotions to neutral.

"You got a good sleep. Do you feel better?"

The lack of expression in his voice made his words sound cold. She knew she was responsible for the wall between them, but it was the way it had to be.

"Yes, I feel fine."

"Good," he said.

"Wilson?"

"Yeah?"

"I need to tell you something."

A knot tied itself into his stomach. "No, you don't."

Cat frowned. "Yes, I do. You have to understand that when it comes to relationships, I don't know how to have them or keep them, and most of the time I don't even want them."

Wilson felt well and truly put in his place. What was strange was, he could remember a good half-dozen times in his past when he'd said almost the same thing to women he'd known. It felt a bit strange being on the other end of the situation. He cleared his throat.

"I'll keep that in mind."

Cat fisted her hands in her lap.

"I didn't expect to see you yesterday, but you will never know what it meant to me that you came. Last night was hell. You helped me get through it."

Wilson nodded.

Cat turned slightly toward him, noting the firm grip he had on the steering wheel and the long, muscular length of him, then looked away. It was time to put the distance back between them.

He got the vibe and responded in kind. "I'm

taking you to your apartment, then I'll check in at work. You'll probably get a visit or a call from someone in Homicide."

"When are they going to arrest Presley?"

"Cat, we've talked about this, remember? Right now, there isn't any physical evidence to prove he has a connection to Marsha's death."

"But he—"

"None of what we know for sure is proof of a murder, and you know it."

Cat frowned. In her heart, she knew he was right, but she didn't have to like it.

"Well, hell. Aren't they at least going to talk to him?" she asked.

"Detective Bradley said Presley is in Tahoe but is coming back to Dallas today, and they're going to interview him tomorrow."

Cat's stomach began to knot all over again.

"Tahoe. He killed Mimi, then went skiing?"

There was a thin thread of mania in her voice. Wilson feared it was only a matter of time before she came undone.

"He and his wife did go to Tahoe for Christmas. Beyond that, I don't know what to tell you."

"Nothing," she said, and then leaned back, folded her arms across her chest and closed her eyes. "There's nothing to be said."

Wilson's frown deepened. She had gone too quiet too quickly.

"Just promise me that you won't do anything to get yourself in trouble, okay?"

Cat thought about what he'd said for a moment, then nodded. She could promise that easily. She wasn't in trouble, but Mark Presley was. He just didn't know it yet.

Thirteen

Cat was home. It felt as if she'd been gone for years. When she'd left yesterday, she'd been on a mission. But completing the mission and finding that her worst fears had been realized had changed her world.

Nothing would ever be the same.

There was no one left with whom she could laugh over remembering old times.

If she died tomorrow, as abruptly as Marsha's life had ended, it would hardly be noted.

Then she ventured a glance at Wilson, who had said very little to her since she'd walked into her apartment, and knew that wasn't exactly true.

Wilson would care—at least a little. He'd used the L-making word in context with sex.

Wilson was conscious of her gaze as he stood at the windows overlooking the parking lot. He had jammed his hands in his pockets to keep from putting them around Cat's neck and was trying to think of something to say that wouldn't be misconstrued again. It was then that he noticed her SUV wasn't in its usual parking space. That was when he remembered she must have driven to an airport to take the chopper, which meant her vehicle was in a parking lot somewhere. He turned around with a frown on his face.

"I just now realized your car must be in some airport parking lot. Do you want me to drive you there?"

"Don't worry about it. I'll take a cab out to get it."

He frowned. "Why didn't you say something sooner? I could have taken you to—"

"It was too far out of your way, and besides, the cab is easier. There are some things I need to do anyway. It's not like I came home to go to bed."

She was trying to get rid of him, and he knew it. God only knew what she was going to do next.

"Okay…uh…you can call me if you need me."

"I will, and thanks again."

Pissed at himself for getting attached to a woman who wore No Trespassing signs the way other women wore earrings, he knew he had no one to blame but himself.

"No problem," he said shortly, and left her standing at the door, watching him go.

Cat felt guilt and regret and other emotions she chose not to name as she watched him leave. He was sexy beyond words, and attracted to her, but she chose not to focus on anything other than watching Mark Presley die.

As soon as Wilson was gone, she began to regroup. The first thing on her list was a change of clothes. When she'd left Dallas yesterday morning, she hadn't planned on spending the night away from home.

She started toward her bedroom, then stopped and retraced her steps to her office. There were a half-dozen new faxes of criminals with tattoos, which she promptly grabbed. She stared at the faces long and hard, studying the tattoos and the men's features until she was satisfied none of them was the man for whom she kept looking.

"Some day, Daddy," she said softly, and laid the faxes aside.

She sat down long enough to scan through the Dallas phone book for a residence address for Mark Presley and soon found out he had an unlisted number. Undaunted, she got the number for his office and made the call.

"Presley Implements," a woman answered.

Cat lifted the tenor of her voice as best she could, hoping she sounded like a teenager.

"This is Benny's Floral. Ummm…uh…we have an FTD delivery for Mr. and Mrs. Mark Presley, but no home address. Can you help me?"

The receptionist, ticked because she had to work today even though most of the building was still empty because of the holidays, didn't even hesitate as she rattled off the address.

Cat wrote it down and hung up without a goodbye; then she called a cab and hurried into the bedroom to change. She'd found Mimi. Now she needed to look at the man who'd killed her. By the time the cab arrived, she had showered and changed and was outside, waiting for its arrival.

The day was clear but still cold, although the ice on the streets was gone. It seemed like another lifetime since she and Melvin had lifted off from the little airport where his chopper service was housed.

The cab arrived without a long wait, and when they finally arrived at the private airport, she had devised a plan. She paid off the cab driver, then got out and headed toward the back parking lot, where she'd left her SUV.

Melvin was servicing a chopper when Cat walked up.

"Hey, Melvin…I see you made it back okay."

He recognized that husky drawl and was grinning before he turned around.

"Hey back at you, Missy." Then his smile slipped as he looked at her face. As his old man used to say, she looked like she'd been rode hard and put up wet. "You okay?"

Cat shrugged. "Okay" wasn't the word, but he didn't need to know the miserable details.

"It was a long night. I came to pick up my car."

"Yeah...I figured as much."

"So I guess I'll be seeing you," she said, and walked away, then stopped and turned around again. "I should probably warn you that the sheriff who worked the crime scene might be calling you just to get your side of the story. His name is Sam Lohman."

"No problem," he said.

"And I'm not sure, but homicide detectives from the Dallas P.D. might want to talk to you, too."

He shrugged. "Don't have all that much to tell anyone, but I'll do my part."

"Thank you," Cat said, and then got in her SUV and left.

She drove straight to a shop specializing in high-tech surveillance equipment and spent two hours choosing and learning how to use what she bought before heading home.

Her steps were slow as she turned the deadbolt to the front door. The distinct click was supposed to be a sound of reassurance that she was safe inside her home. So why, she wondered, did it make her feel like a prisoner, instead? Why was she always on the outside of life, looking in?

There were a couple of messages on her answering machine. One was from Al, telling her to call him. She wasn't ready to discuss Mimi again, and she wasn't working any of his cases until there was justice for Mimi, so she deleted the call. The other was from Joe Flannery, the homicide detective who'd first rejected her story. His message was as cool and formal as the tone of his voice, asking her to come down to headquarters tomorrow to give a statement, and to please call him to verify the time.

She frowned, thinking of going down there and explaining herself all over again, reliving the horror of finding Mimi's body and trying not to think of how she'd looked when they'd dragged her up and out of the ravine. No sooner had she thought it than she heard Mimi's voice, chastising her over a year ago.

"You hide from life, Catherine. Even when you're in the middle of it, standing toe to toe with all the bad guys you bring in, you manage to keep an emotional distance. I understand why you do it, but ultimately, you're the one who will suffer. You're the one who's going to grow old alone."

Cat blinked back tears, remembering what she'd told her.

I won't be alone, Mimi. I'll always have you.

Obviously she had been wrong.

Wilson went through the motions at work, but he felt as if he'd been broadsided. He'd let a woman get under his skin and had been rejected as easily as a used grocery list. He felt a little like a green high school kid who'd been suckered by a pro. He'd mistaken the great sex they shared for something more.

As he was filing reports, the phone rang, giving him something else to think about besides Cat

Dupree. Since his receptionist was out to lunch, he answered on his own.

"McKay Bail and Bond."

"Wilson, it's Flannery."

"Hey, Joe. What's up?"

"I understand Cat Dupree found Marsha Benton's body yesterday?"

Now they were interested, Wilson thought, and felt a sense of righteous indignation on Cat's part, even though he knew it was misplaced.

"Why are you asking me? You should be talking to her."

Joe rubbed at an ache in the middle of his forehead and tried not to sound as miserable as he felt.

"I've called her. She hasn't called me back yet."

"Again…why are you calling me?"

Joe leaned back in his chair and closed his eyes.

"I'm curious. How did she do it? The way I heard it, she just rented a chopper, flew to some oil lease in East Texas and found her…all in one day."

"Yeah, that's what I heard, too."

"Did she get a tip that the body was there?"

"It's my understanding that between the time she spoke to you and yesterday morning, she's been gathering every bit of information she could on Mark Presley's business and whereabouts. I helped her with some of the research, but she put it all together."

"Helped how?" Flannery asked.

"Let's just say that I have ways of accessing personal info. She was looking for a break in the man's pattern of business, both personal and professional. And you know about the phone call she found on her answering machine, right?"

"No."

"You need to talk to Bradley down in Missing Persons. He can fill you in on that."

"What was on the message?" Joe asked.

"I don't know if Bradley found anything more on it than what we heard. It was made from Marsha's cell phone just after she went missing, but there were no words on it. All you could hear was what it sounds like from the inside of a helicopter—three minutes' worth before the answering machine clicked off."

"A helicopter?"

"Yeah. As if you were riding in one."

"But how does that get you to—"

"I told you, talk to Cat."

"Yeah, right," Joe said, and knew he was going to have to backpedal his former attitude to get cooperation from her.

"What do you know about Mark Presley?" Flannery asked.

"Other than what I read about him from Cat's research, next to nothing."

"We got a call from his wife this morning," Flannery said.

"About what?"

"She's offered to cooperate in any way needed to find Marsha Benton's killer."

Wilson frowned. "That's probably because she has no idea you're going to be pointing a finger at her husband."

"On the contrary," Flannery said. "I don't know what's been going on at the Presley mansion, but it couldn't have been all good."

"What do you mean?"

"It's a well-known fact in some circles that Presley has been having affairs behind his wife's back for years. It appears now that she knew all along about his indiscretions. Missing Persons interviewed Presley a few days ago, then left a card. According to Bradley, Mrs. Presley called this morning. Bradley told her that since Ms. Benton's body has been discovered, technically she's no longer missing and the case will go to homicide. She told Bradley to let us know she's available to help in any way."

"Think you've got a 'woman scorned' thing going on?"

"Don't know about that so much, but what we do have is access to Presley's DNA. Hair from his hairbrush, saliva from drinking glasses, toothbrushes. She offered it all in case he refused."

"And she's willing to hand it over? Just like that?" Wilson asked.

"So it seems."

Wilson flipped the pen he was holding, then laid it down on the desk.

"Maybe Cat will get some justice for her friend after all," he said, then hung up.

He thought about Flannery's phone call. As ticked off as he was at himself for letting her get under his skin, he couldn't get her out of his mind. Even after he went home for the day, the urge to call Cat was strong. But there had to be a starting point for regaining his dignity, and he'd made up his mind that today would be it.

So while Cat holed up in her apartment, gaining strength for what was to come, Wilson went home to lick his wounds.

As for the Presleys, they arrived home from Tahoe a few hours before nightfall. The trip had been virtually without conversation. Once back in familiar territory, Penny seemed to have gained backbone, while Mark appeared to withdraw. When the time drew near for their dinner hour, they met in the library for an aperitif.

Once the drinks had been served, they'd each moved to a separate part of the room to be alone with their thoughts.

Penny pretended great interest in a new magazine, while Mark scanned through a stack of newspapers, but the tension between them was strong.

Back in Tahoe, when he had broken the news to her that they had to go home, he had been put on the defensive by the fact that he was the one who'd had personal contact with a murdered woman.

He had the feeling now that she was never going to forgive him for what she viewed as rape, and this latest incident had only fueled her fire. For the first time in their married lives, she'd stood up to him and rejected his excuses. He was beginning to think she'd known about his dalliances for years but for her own reasons had chosen to play dumb. But when she'd learned that the police wanted to question him regarding Marsha Benton's murder, her days of playing dumb seemed to have ended.

Penny feigned interest in her magazine, but inside, her thoughts were tumbling wildly.

Last night while Mark was in the shower, she'd called Ken Walters, their lawyer. Ken had started off by claiming he couldn't divulge his conversations with Mark, at which point she promptly reminded him that the money in their house was hers first, not Mark's, and if he wanted to stay on retainer for the Presley Corporation, he'd better start talking.

So he did.

Learning that Marsha had been pregnant when she was murdered had nearly sent her to her knees. Knowing that her body had been found on their oil lease outside Tyler only made what she was thinking worse. She'd known Mark was devious, but she'd never believed him capable of murder. Now she wasn't so sure. What she *was* certain of was that she wasn't going to be dragged down with him if he fell. Tonight they were back in Dallas in what had been her father's home first and was now hers. This was her territory, and she wasn't leaving anything to chance.

Mark glanced up from the chair where he'd been reading, watching the casual attitude with which Penny was sipping her drink. She was flipping through the pages of the magazine in her lap and humming beneath her breath as if nothing was wrong.

It was unnerving.

As he watched, he began to realize Penny wasn't her father's daughter by birth alone. There seemed to be more of the old man in her than he would have believed. Ever since he'd put his hands around her neck back in Tahoe, she had been cold and unyielding, even when he'd apologized profusely.

Then, when he'd had to tell her that the police demanded his presence back in Dallas for questioning regarding Marsha Benton's death, she'd been livid. He'd tried to explain, but she wasn't having any of it. He didn't want to lose her. He *couldn't* lose her. Even though the world assumed that Mark Presley was the reigning power behind the Presley Corporation, it was really Penny. Mark had the authority simply because Penny was his wife. If she kicked his ass to the curb, the only thing he would be taking with him were the bruises.

* * *

Mark never got drunk. It was against everything he practiced, because being drunk meant being out of control, and losing control was not an option. Still, on this night, he'd had too much to drink, feeling sorrier and sorrier for himself with every swallow.

Penny had glared at him all during dinner and cut him off sharply every time he tried to start a conversation. The only advice she had for him was issued during dessert, when she warned him that if he was as smart as he pretended to be, then he'd better have a lawyer with him when he went to the police station the next day.

"What are you getting at?" he asked.

She didn't bother to hide her disgust.

"We'll be the talk of the country club as it is," she muttered. "This is all so common…being interrogated by the police like some criminal."

A dark red flush spread up Mark's neck and onto his cheeks as his fingers curled angrily around his glass.

"A lot of people work for me," he said. "It's not my fault if they become embroiled in something unsavory in their own time. The only reason they want to talk to me is because she was an employee."

Penny laid down her dessert fork and leaned forward, her gaze fixed upon her husband's face. All of a sudden, she felt as if she was talking to a stranger.

"I made a couple of calls on my own," she said. "It's not just because she was an employee, and you know it."

There was a faint ringing in Mark's ears now. "I don't know what you're getting at."

Penny slapped the table with the flat of her hand. "They found her body on our land east of Tyler. In a very desolate area that is approachable only by air. It's a big stretch to believe that a total stranger killed her and used a helicopter to dump her on our land."

Mark fidgeted nervously with his glass as Penny kept pushing.

"These are little details you neglected to tell me. Why, Mark? Why did you lie? Is it true? Do you know more about this than you're admitting?"

He slammed his glass back down on the table, and as he did, liquor slopped out and over the sides. An ugly stain quickly appeared and began to spread over the handmade Irish lace tablecloth.

"I can't believe you said that!" he yelled. "I can't believe you'd even insinuate I would do such a horrendous thing."

Penny leaned back and crossed her arms over her breasts.

"Before Tahoe, I might have been as indignant as you. I would have been horrified and thoroughly convinced that you could never be involved in something so shoddy. But that was before you put your hands around my neck and raped me!"

"Raped you? A husband can't rape his wife. It's called sex, Penny. Nothing more. Nothing less. Besides, I did no such thing, and you know it. I just lost my temper. I've already said I'm sorry."

Penny's eyes narrowed angrily. "Yes, I believe you are. Sorry, I mean. You're sorry that you let a piece of your true self shine through. That's what I believe you're sorry for."

Panic hit Mark deep in his gut. This was worse than he'd believed. Penny wasn't ranting—she was cold and far too collected to be accused of hysteria.

He sat there, too shocked to defend himself. Then, to his dismay, when he reached for his drink again, he began to cry.

Instead of sympathy, Penny cursed him beneath her breath and left the table.

Mark's hopes fell even farther. He stood up in anger, then swayed unsteadily on his feet as he gazed about the room. When he realized there were still a couple of inches of liquor in his glass, he downed it angrily, then stumbled out of the dining room and headed up the stairs.

His head was spinning by the time he got to their bedroom. To his continued dismay, Penny and her nightclothes were noticeably absent. He sat down on the side of the bed and kicked off his shoes. He was out before his head hit the pillow.

* * *

It was snowing. Mark could feel the bitter kiss of snowflakes on his face as he turned to face the wind. Yet even though he knew it to be cold, his skin was on fire.

And, to his shame, he was crying. His throat was tightening, and there was a pain born of guilt that was so far down in his belly he couldn't catch his breath.

He turned in a full circle, trying to find the path that had brought him to this place, but there was nothing to show where he'd come from—no tracks, no vehicle, nothing.

And then he saw the blood.

It was splattered in a haphazard pattern across the snow. He stared at it and then the spatters on his pants, trying to remember why the sight brought him such fear. Why did he feel the urge to pee from nothing more than a few red droplets?

The snow began to fall in earnest now, but to his horror, the blood was still there. No matter how much snow fell, it couldn't cover the trail. The sight sent him into a mental free fall.

He needed the blood to go away. He wanted to go home. He didn't want to be lost like this, but there was a part of him that knew he could never go back.

"Help!" he cried, and heard the wind swallow the sound of his voice.

"Help! Help!" he shouted, and tasted snowflakes on his tongue.

"Oh God...please. Help me."

Suddenly the blood on the snow began to get brighter

and thicker. The spots became tiny pools, and the pools became puddles, and the trail from the forest became a wide ribbon of red that curled around his feet and stained the hem of his pants.

He tried to run, but his feet wouldn't move. He looked toward the forest, and through the snowfall he saw movement. Was this the help he sought? Was he about to be rescued?

His heart started pounding in earnest as the shadows in the forest continued to sway. Snow was falling so thickly that he had to blink constantly to clear his vision. When the shadows began to take form, his heart leaped—then momentarily stopped. Even with the distance and the snow and the sweat running in his eyes, he recognized her.

She came closer, and it soon became apparent she was the source of the red path. Blood poured from her belly like water from a natural spring, bubbling and flowing in thick rivulets down her legs and onto the ground. It ran toward him like water from open floodgates, encircling his feet and then rising.

The thick, coppery scent of it was in his nostrils and warm on his skin as the puddle in which he was standing began to rise. The closer she came, the higher the puddle rose, until he was knee deep in her blood and his own urine.

"Get away from me!" he screamed, and covered his face with both hands. "You're not real. You're not real!"

When he dared another look, the blood was up to his

chin. He couldn't understand how this was happening. He could see her as plainly as the nose on his face. She was less than a yard away and still her blood pooled only around him. Without a reason. Without a container. And if it didn't stop, he would drown.

He stared in disbelief as it continued to spill from her belly. The horror of what he'd done was there, right in front of him. There was no denying its existence, no pretending to himself that Marsha Benton wasn't dead. He opened his mouth to scream, and as he did, he tasted her blood as it flowed into his mouth and down his throat.

He heard his own screams turning into gurgles, and in a moment of clarity, knew that he'd drowned.

Mark was convulsing on the floor when Penny, roused by his screaming from her bed in the guest-room, ran into the room. She screamed in horror, then fell to her knees beside him and grabbed his shoulders.

"Mark! Mark!"

Before she could dodge, one of his arms flailed up and hit her across the face. She screamed out in pain and fell backward, grabbing her nose as she fell.

Blood began to drip through her fingers and onto her nightgown as she struggled to her feet and ran to the phone.

Even as she was calling 911, she thought he was dying. There was a part of her brain that accepted the fact that this would certainly take care of whatever embarrassment his involvement with Marsha Benton might have caused her. She could play the grieving widow and bury her problem, instead of following him through the court system.

Then the 911 dispatcher answered, and she began to scream.

"Please! I need help! My husband is having a seizure."

"Ma'am, please slow down. Is this the Presley residence?"

"Yes!" Penny cried, as the dispatcher rattled off their address.

"Mrs. Presley, I'm dispatching an ambulance to your address as we speak. Is your husband breathing?"

"I don't know. I can't tell," Penny sobbed. "Foam is coming out of his mouth, and he's on his back, banging his head on the floor. I tried to help him and got a broken nose for my trouble."

"You're injured, as well?" the dispatcher asked.

"He hit me in the nose. It was an accident," Penny said. "Please. You have to hurry."

"Did you hit him back? Was that the first time he's hit you?" the dispatcher asked.

Penny gasped, and as she did, nearly blacked out from the pain. She lowered her head between her knees and tried to focus.

"Lady, we weren't having a fight. This isn't a case of abuse. I was asleep in another room and heard him screaming. When I got here, he was convulsing in the floor. When I tried to help him, I got whacked in the nose. He didn't do it on purpose. He doesn't even know what's happening."

"Do you know how to do CPR?" the dispatcher asked.

Penny felt like screaming. "No, but it doesn't matter. I couldn't get close enough to him to try it, so I guess the answer to your first question is, yes, he's still breathing. If he wasn't, he couldn't be flopping all over our bedroom floor like he is."

"Help is on the way," the dispatcher said.

"Thank you, thank you," Penny mumbled, and then grabbed the hem of her nightgown and used it like a handkerchief, trying to stem the flow of blood from her nose. "Oh, wait! I hear sirens. They're here! They're here! I have to let them in."

She hung up, despite the dispatcher's voice urging her not to, and headed downstairs on the run. For once in her life, she wasn't waiting for the servants.

She was at the door before the paramedics could ring the bell.

"He's upstairs!" she cried as she opened the door. "Second door on your right. Hurry! Please hurry."

"Lady, are you in need of—"

"No, no, it's just a nosebleed," she said, and then started up the stairs ahead of them. "Follow me."

Fourteen

Cat heard the doorbell as she was getting out of the shower. She grabbed a robe and pulled it on quickly as she hurried to the living room. It was ten minutes before eight in the morning, and if she'd had her wits about her, she wouldn't even have bothered to go to the door. It was too darned early for visitors.

She peered through the peephole, then stifled a gasp. It was Wilson, and he didn't look happy. She opened the door without hesitation.

"What's wrong?"

Good morning had been on the tip of Wilson's tongue until he'd seen what she was wearing, or lack thereof.

"Uh…"

Cat rolled her eyes and pulled him into her apartment.

"For Pete's sake, come in. It's freezing out there in the hall, and I'm still wet."

Lord... I can see that, Wilson thought, then managed to pull himself together and close the door behind him.

"Do you have any coffee?" he asked, as he tossed his overcoat on the sofa.

"In the kitchen," Cat said. "Why are you here?"

"It couldn't possibly be because I missed your sweet disposition," he drawled.

She had the grace to blush. She was being rude.

"I'm sorry. Really. You just took me by surprise. Help yourself to the coffee. I'm going to get dressed."

"Okay," he said, and forced himself not to watch the way the fabric clung to her still damp body as she left the room.

He was in the kitchen, standing over the sink with a doughnut in one hand and his coffee in the other, when Cat came back.

"Wilson, those doughnuts are at least a week old," she said, as she poured herself a cup of coffee.

"They're fine," he said, and dunked the end of the doughnut before taking another bite.

Cat eyed him nervously. Their last words to each other hadn't exactly been comforting. Now he'd shown up at this ridiculous hour of the day and made himself at home as if nothing had happened.

"Wilson?"

He looked at her then, his mouth too full to

answer, and arched his eyebrows questioningly instead.

She bit the inside of her lip to keep from cursing. It was hard to be mad at someone so damned good looking. Between those dark eyes and that little gold hoop in his ear, he was fascinating. Still, this was her home. She should have the privilege of being in charge.

"I know you didn't come here to eat stale dough-nuts."

He chewed and swallowed the last bite quickly, then washed it down with a gulp of coffee.

"There's been a change of plans," he said.

Cat frowned. She didn't want a change of plans. She wanted Mark Presley's head on a platter and his balls hanging from the highest limb of a tree.

"How so?" she asked.

He wasn't going to tell her that Flannery had called him yesterday and then again this morning, because then she would think he was messing in her business. He just started talking.

"Homicide got a phone call from Mark Presley's wife this morning saying he wouldn't be able to come in as promised."

Cat bristled. "Why didn't someone call me like they called you, and why the hell isn't he coming?"

Wilson pointed to the red blinking light on her answering machine.

"Maybe they did and you didn't answer."

That took the indignation out of her disposition.

"I guess I was in the shower."

"So…you weren't left out of the loop after all," he said. "And, as I was about to say, Presley won't be coming in because he supposedly had some kind of seizure last night. Don't know whether it was a physical or mental thing, but at any rate, he isn't talking. In fact, they're not sure he even knows who he is anymore."

"Son of a bitch," Cat said, and sat down in disbelief. "He's going to get away with it."

Wilson frowned. "I wouldn't call becoming what amounts to a vegetable getting away with anything."

Cat turned on him in frustration. "Then you tell me how this is going to work? If he can't talk, he won't ever be charged."

"They say he's in pretty bad shape," Wilson said. "It's not like he's going to live the good life."

Cat's fingers curled into fists. "But he's alive," she muttered. "He's alive, and Mimi's not, and it's his fault."

"That hasn't been proven yet."

"It won't be, either. Not now," she said, then stared down at the floor. "I can't believe it. The sorry bastard is going to get away with murder."

"Maybe not," Wilson said. "They're obviously still going ahead with the investigation. They'll still compare his DNA to the baby Marsha was carrying. If he gets to a point where he can stand trial, they'll have the evidence."

Cat couldn't look at Wilson, though she heard

him just fine. A part of her even understood what he was trying to say. But she couldn't get past the fact that she was going to have to bury Mimi and the baby, while Presley was going to some fancy nursing home where someone else would wipe his face and his butt. It didn't matter to her that his quality of life would be next to nothing. He didn't deserve to live, no matter what.

"I don't suppose what I say is going to make a damn bit of difference," she muttered.

He wanted to put his arms around her, but the cold tone of her voice was warning enough to stay back.

"On the contrary," he said. "This is still an open case."

"Open case my ass," she insisted. "Then the cops better not stand in the draft of it, because they'll freeze to death before anyone ever knows the truth of how Mimi died."

"I'm sorry," Wilson said.

"It's not your fault," she said.

"Then don't treat me like it is," he said.

His accusation shredded her composure. Her eyes suddenly brimmed with tears. She looked away before he saw them.

Wilson saw the tears anyway. Damn the woman. He couldn't be mad at her if his life depended on it. "I'm not mad at you. If anything, I'm just mad at myself. I'm sorry I snapped, and I'm sorry as hell this has happened."

She raised her chin, unwilling to admit that she'd shown weakness, and poured herself a cup of coffee.

"They don't have any other suspects, do they?" she asked, as she stirred sugar and cream into the cup.

"They don't have anything but what you gave them. They wouldn't even know that Marsha Benton was missing if you hadn't turned in the report. All of this is because of you. The fact that her body was found somewhere other than Dallas doesn't change the fact that she went missing from here. Dallas P.D. will be involved in the case in whatever capacity they need to be."

Cat was silent, absorbing the information. "So…how long do you think it will be before they release her?"

"You mean her body?"

"Yes."

"Not sure, and for all I know, it's still back in Tyler. However, you know they'll only release her to family."

"I'm her only family," Cat said.

"I know," he said softly, and laid his hand on the back of her head. "But it will have to be after the autopsy, and we have no way of knowing how backed up they are at the coroner's office."

"My God," she said. "Imagine a job where everything you do depends on someone dying."

"I couldn't do it," he said.

"Me either," she said, then stepped back and wiped her face with the palms of her hands, trying not to think about the brutality of an autopsy. "When they finally release her, it will have to be to me."

"I'll tell Flannery to make a note of that," Wilson said.

Cat looked up at him then, unaware that every ounce of heartbreak was there on her face for the world to see.

"I also know I'm a hard-ass and stubborn and rude…but thank you for taking the time to come tell me this."

"I don't need an apology."

"Okay, fine."

"Fine then," he muttered. "I've got to be going."

Cat walked him to the door. "Have a nice day."

Have a nice day? She had to be kidding.

He glared at her, then strode out of the apartment without looking back, slamming the door behind him.

Penny Presley was perfect in the part of devastated wife. No one had ever witnessed them having a disagreement, let alone making threats to end their marriage, so her distraught behavior seemed right in line with what anyone would have expected.

When they'd admitted Mark to ICU, a huge weight had disappeared from her shoulders. Marsha Benton was dead, and she really was sorry about that. She'd liked Marsha tremendously and never would have wished that anything bad would befall her.

However, if she *had* been pregnant with Mark's child and Mark had truly killed her, then what had happened to both of them was of their own doing.

Penny had a broken nose but was free of any responsibility. After all, she was the injured party here in more ways than one. She'd been cheated on and suffered unexpected abuse at the hands of the man who'd promised to love her forever. It was obvious that Mark had chosen to ignore the meaning of his vows—or, at the least, had been manipulating them to suit his own needs.

The company had already issued a press release regarding his condition, with absolutely no mention of his possible involvement in the murder of an ex-employee.

Mark was in ICU, which meant Penny's visits were extremely limited. She'd spent the night and part of the next morning at the hospital and been allowed to see him a total of four times. Each time she'd talked to him—even prayed over him—and gotten no response for her trouble.

On her fourth visit, the doctors had assured her that Mark most likely knew she was there but just couldn't communicate. Penny had wept at the news and kissed him gently. Then, once the doctors were gone, she'd leaned over and whispered the truth of her feelings into his ear.

"If you fathered Marsha Benton's child, you are a true son-of-a-bitch."

The fact that the heart monitor hooked up to Mark's body didn't register any kind of fluctuation was not lost on Penny.

"And if you had anything to do with her murder, I will help them convict your sorry ass."

The heart monitor registered a small spike, then suddenly flat-lined.

Penny stared at the machine for a second, then turned around and screamed.

"Nurse! Nurse!"

She was ushered out of ICU as a crash cart and extra medical personnel headed for his bed.

Penny stared at the door they'd closed in her face. For a moment the enormity of what was happening hit her. Had she just killed him? Had her threat been the last straw, breaking the tie holding him to this earth? She thought of all the wonderful times they'd shared and of the perfect life they'd had, and actually worked up some real tears.

A reporter who'd snuck into the hospital snapped a picture of her, black eyes and broken nose in plain sight as she turned from the doorway.

Momentarily blinded by the camera flash, she held up her hands as if warding off a blow. By the time she could see clearly, he was gone.

It was night. Mark knew it because the shift had changed again. He pretended not to know anything or see anything, but he knew what was happening, right down to the fact that the DNA test they'd run on the fetus in Marsha Benton's body had shown that the child was his. He knew it because Penny had hissed the news in his ear on one of her visits to the ICU.

At the time, he'd wanted to grab her by the throat and squeeze until that whining voice was silenced forever. But at this point, revealing his resurrection wasn't in his best interests. As long as the police thought he was comatose, they were going to leave him alone.

He'd heard them talking to Penny earlier about moving him out of ICU to a private room. He prayed that they would. It had to happen, or he wouldn't be able to make his escape. He'd never seen or heard so much action in his life as went on in the ICU.

Someone was moaning in the opposite corner of the room, and whoever was in the bed next to him was dying.

Poor bastard. Mark could hear it in every strangled breath that he took.

His nose itched. He wanted to scratch it in the very worst way, but any movement from him and someone was bound to see it.

As he lay there, he heard the doors open near the nurses' desk, signifying visiting hours, which lasted for five minutes on the hour with no exceptions.

Penny wouldn't be back. She'd told him as much when she'd left earlier, so he thought nothing of the footsteps coming toward his end of the room. To his surprise, they stopped right beside his bed. He figured it was a nurse, but he wanted to open his eyes, just to see who was there. He waited, although there was no sign of movement. He knew it was a woman, because he could smell the lighter scent of a feminine shampoo and some sort of bath powder.

The sounds of her breathing seemed a little erratic, as if she'd climbed the stairs rather than taking the elevator. He didn't know a woman who was willing to break a sweat that way and decided that his instincts for guessing gender might not be so sharp after all.

Then she spoke.

Her voice was low and husky—like someone coming down with laryngitis—and he came so close to opening his eyes that he heard the heart monitor skip a beat as he remembered to practice restraint.

Cat had moved back into the stream of living with all the reluctance that came from overwhelming grief—angry when her stomach growled for food, ashamed when something made her laugh unexpectedly, crying over a tiny paper cut while opening her mail. She was a wreck with not a lot of hope for rebuilding. The authorities in Tyler had released Marsha Benton's body to the Dallas P.D. The medical examiner's report stated that she had suffered a cracked skull but had died from a multitude of internal injuries. It hurt Cat's heart to learn that there were no wounds on Marsha's hands to indicate she'd had time to fight back. She was guessing that Mark had rendered her unconscious, then flown out to the Presley oil lease and finished her off there.

Cat Dupree's vehemence kept them from assuming that Marsha would have gone willingly with Presley, thus providing an explanation for the head injury and how she'd gotten from Dallas to the bottom of a ravine outside Tyler without a fight.

Oddly enough, in searching the surrounding area, the sheriff's deputies had found a large sheet of blue plastic floating in the water of an abandoned rock quarry nearby.

It was uncertain whether it could be tied to the murder, but Sam Lohman had theorized that it would be one way to move a bloody body without leaving evidence behind and ordered divers to the quarry. After a half-day's work dragging the water, they'd found a pair of coveralls, a cap and a large mechanic's wrench, all rolled and tied up together. The DNA evidence that might have been left on the objects had, of course, been ruined by the water, but the coveralls were like the ones worn by the mechanics at the private airstrip belonging to the Presley corporation, and there was a wrench missing from a set at the airstrip just like the one found in the quarry.

Adding that to the fetus's DNA match to Mark Presley and having Marsha's body turning up on Presley property, and they had enough circumstantial evidence to arrest the man for murder.

What they didn't have was the man in any kind of condition to be interrogated, let alone be arrested or stand trial.

They were at an impasse, and Cat was making herself physically ill by dwelling on it. It had occurred to her that maybe, if she saw the condition Mark Presley was in, she would stop thinking that he'd escaped justice. If she could see him now and accept his loss of function as the punishment it was meant to be, then maybe she could get past her rage enough to bury her friend and get on with her life. But she didn't know, and wouldn't know for sure, until she saw him for herself.

It was with that purpose in mind that she'd dressed in what could only be construed as a disguise and headed for Dallas Memorial.

She had arrived with her shoulders slumped to the point that the dress and coat she was wearing appeared not to fit her body. She wore tennis shoes instead of heels, and had braided her hair, then fastened it at the back of her neck. With overdone makeup and a pair of out-of-style glasses, she looked like a caricature of herself. She sat quietly and motionless in the waiting room until she was completely certain that no one else was there to visit Presley, then, when the time came, moved with the others in the room to go into ICU.

She'd had to sign in, and had no qualms about using a fake ID and name. Presley had dark hair. So did she. It stood to reason that they could be related. And with that in mind, Laura Presley Conti signed in to visit her cousin Mark.

Luckily for Cat, the beds were far enough apart from each other that there was some measure of privacy, because there were things she intended to say to him, whether he could hear her or not, that she didn't intend to share with anyone else. By the time she arrived at his bedside, her hands were damp with perspiration and her heart was pounding so loudly against her chest that she feared it was going to explode.

She paused at the end of the bed, then, without looking around, moved quickly to his bedside. Her fingers were less than a foot from the back of his hand where the IV needle had been inserted. She glanced at it once, then let her gaze move upward until she found herself staring at the face of Marsha's killer.

He was good-looking. She had to give Mimi credit for going for looks, but it was unfortunate that she hadn't been able to see past the surface to the rot beneath. His skin was pale, and she could see a pulse at the base of his throat that matched the steady beep of the monitor measuring his heartbeat.

She glanced over her shoulder once, just to make sure they were still alone; then she leaned just the slightest bit forward, giving anyone who might be looking the impression that she was speaking tenderly to the man.

"You think you got away with it, don't you?"

Mark felt a heat flowing up his body from his feet to his head. He didn't recognize the voice, but he didn't dare look. Then the woman spoke again.

"I know what you did," she said. "You killed Marsha Benton. You killed your unborn child. If you don't die in this bed, I will find you and kill you myself."

Mark hiccupped in fear, then caught himself. It was the only outward sign he'd given that he'd heard every word she said.

Even though he was still immobile, Cat had seen his reaction. She'd heard the catch in his breath and knew that at least on some level, he could hear and understand her. She straightened up and turned around, walking with purpose, but without haste, and exited ICU without looking back.

If she had, she would have seen the nurse hurrying to Mark Presley's bedside in response to the sudden and frantic irregularity of his heartbeat.

By the time she got outside, she had a working plan that needed to be set in place. There was no doubt in her mind that Presley would wake up and that, when he did, he would run. She'd left him with no choice.

Fifteen

Cat came out of Dallas Memorial so furious she could hardly breathe. All the way home she had visions of him getting out of his bed, sneaking out of the hospital and disappearing before the authorities could arrest him. He had millions of dollars at his disposal, which meant he could buy anything he needed to create a new identity. It would be far too easy for him to escape, especially since he had yet to be questioned by the police or charged with anything.

By the time she pulled into the parking lot of her apartment building, it was after midnight. But she had a plan. If Presley tried to pull anything, she was going to know it.

The night was cold, and the wind blowing through the streets made it colder. She ran toward the front door with her head down and her hands in her pockets. The warmth inside the lobby was at once welcoming and familiar. Her steps were light as she hurried toward the elevator.

She rode it up anxiously, then hurried into her apartment, locking the door behind her. Normally, at night, she would wait until she got into a room to turn on lights, but not tonight. She turned on lights as she went from room to room until the whole place was blazing.

Changing from street clothes to an old pair of sweats was first on her agenda; then she hurried to the kitchen and made a cup of hot chocolate. That visit to the ICU had given her the creeps. Even though she knew it was just her imagination, she couldn't help but feel as if she'd spent time with the devil. She wanted something warm and sweet and comforting to take the chill out of her soul.

Once the cocoa was ready, she carried her cup into the office and sat down behind the desk. The mug shots pinned to the wall in front of her would have been daunting to a lesser person. To her, they were just reminders of what she'd survived and of the justice yet to be meted out.

She took a quick sip of the cocoa, just to prove to herself that it was still too hot to drink, then grabbed her Rolodex and began flipping through. She needed help in implementing her plan, and she knew just the man to help her do it. Despite the lateness of the hour, Pete Yokum would not be asleep. His friends called him the Count. Not because he was particularly regal in bearing or stature, but because, ever since his retirement, like the fictional vampire Count Dracula, Pete only came out after dark.

The cockroach running up the wall was already dead but didn't know it. Pete hated cockroaches with a passion, even though he'd spent the better part of his life co-habiting with them. With one eye on the eggs frying in the skillet, he picked up the spatula from the counter and used it to flatten the roach in mid-stride.

"Got you, you sombitch," Pete muttered, knocked the roach from the back of the spatula into the trash, then wiped the spatula on the leg of his jeans and flipped his eggs. The way he figured it, whatever germs had been left behind on the spatula were bound to perish in the hot grease.

He liked his eggs over easy, so by the time he reached for a plate, they were ready. His belly growled in hungry anticipation as he scooped them from the skillet onto his plate. He turned off the burner, grabbed his toast from the toaster, slathered it with butter and jelly, chose a fork from the drawer and headed for the couch.

His one-room apartment was small and a bit sordid, but it served his purposes. No one would ever have guessed that Pete had upwards of a half-million dollars in the bank. There were very few things he wanted, and none of them could be bought with money, so he just kept on banking it.

All his life he'd wanted a wife but had never found who he considered 'the right one.' He also wanted to meet Oprah Winfrey, but there wasn't a snowball's chance in hell that their paths would ever cross. He did, however, continue to admire her stand on most issues, even though he thought she got a little radical about her book club choices. Pete had tried a couple, but it was his opinion that you just couldn't beat a good paperback western.

He sat down on the sofa, pulled up his footstool and laid his plate in his lap. His coffee was already on the side table, right where he'd left it cooling. The aroma of hot fried eggs and toast and jelly made his mouth water, and he dug into his food with relish.

Right in the middle of his last bite of toast, the telephone rang. He didn't think it strange to be getting phone calls in the middle of the night. Despite the fact that it was after one in the morning, everyone knew if they intended to talk to him, it had to be after dark.

Quickly he washed down the toast with a sip of coffee and then picked up the receiver.

"You're too late for supper but just in time for dessert. Bring it over when you come," he said.

Cat grinned. Pete had answered the phone like that for as long as she'd known him.

"Hey, Pete, it's me, Cat Dupree."

Pete slid the plate from his lap to the coffee table. He was already grinning as he settled back for a visit.

"Catherine, it's been a while. How you been doin', honey?"

Cat felt even easier about calling. Pete had been one of her father's best friends. He'd taken it upon himself to check in on her from time to time, especially after she'd been old enough to be on her own.

"I'm all right," she said. "Have you been staying busy and out of trouble?"

Pete laughed out loud. "Now, darlin', you know I haven't. I spend most of my days layin' around the house or spendin' my Social Security check on booze and women."

"You lie," Cat said. Pete was what her father had called tight with money and picky about women.

"Maybe so," he said, and realized how good it was to hear from Cat. "Have you been takin' care of yourself?"

"I'm okay, but Mimi's not," she said, and then choked up a little, unable to continue.

Pete heard the emotion in her voice and frowned. Cat and Marsha had been best friends for years.

"What happened to Shortcake? Got the flu or somethin'?" he asked.

Cat knew that Mimi would have loved to hear Pete calling her that. It was because she was so little.

It made her feel special to be singled out in such an odd but familiar way.

"Or something. Oh, Pete...she was murdered. Haven't you been reading the papers?"

"No. Nothin' in 'em but bad news," Pete muttered. "I'm so sorry to hear that. Have they caught the bastard who did it?"

"Not yet," Cat said, and then quickly explained what she knew. By the time she had finished, Pete was livid.

"What can I do?" he asked.

"I'm ashamed to say that's why I called."

Pete's frown deepened. "It don't matter why you called. You know I'll help. What do you want me to do?"

"You know what I told you about Mark Presley being in the hospital after suffering some kind of breakdown?"

"Yeah?"

"Well, I saw him tonight. I disguised myself and went to visit him in ICU, and I gave him a little message he didn't like. His reaction was not that of a man in a coma. I can't prove it, but I know he's faking or, at the least, recuperating faster than anyone knows. I'm scared to death that he'll just walk out of the hospital when no one's looking and disappear, in which case, he'll have gotten away with murder."

"Damn, honey, that's bad, but I don't see any way of proving it, unless—"

"I don't intend to try and prove anything about his condition. But I do want something done that will keep him from getting away from me."

"Name it," Pete said.

"I want everything he might drive as a getaway vehicle bugged. I want tracking devices in his shoes. In his watch. Up his butt, if possible. In other words, I need to be tied to him electronically. I bought the equipment, but I don't have the skills to install it."

Pete grinned. Every penny he'd ever made had come from being an electrician, then, in his later years, installing security devices in people's homes. It was part of why, when he'd decided to retire, he'd turned his life upside down. He'd gotten up with the chickens every day of his working life, so he thought he'd try it the other way around for a while. Finally it had become a lifestyle that suited him. Still, he would do anything for Marcus Dupree's little girl.

When he didn't immediately comment, Cat figured she'd overstepped the bounds of their friendship.

"I'm sorry. I don't know what I was thinking by calling you. What I'm asking could get you in trouble, and—"

"No way, honey," he said. "I wasn't hesitating, I was thinking. And the answer is definitely yes. I'll enjoy doing my part to stick it to such a bastard. I was just a little sad that this is what's happening in your life.

You've had some rough times. I'm sure sorry about this, and sorry that Shortcake's life ended like this."

"Me too," she said, and swallowed back tears. Pete couldn't handle crying women. She needed to keep it together.

"So when do you want to do this?" he asked.

"I'll give you Mark Presley's home address, as well as the room he's in at Dallas Memorial and the address of his office. I hate to tell you, but I need it done as soon as possible. I'm afraid that whenever he gets the chance, he'll bolt. How can I get the surveillance equipment to you?"

Pete glanced at the clock. He'd been going to watch an old John Wayne movie tonight, but this took precedence.

"I have plenty of stuff around here to do the job. I'll scope out the premises. If everything looks all right, I'll have it done before morning. If there are complications, it might take a little longer."

Now that she'd asked and he'd agreed, Cat felt not just guilty but also nervous.

"Please be careful," she said. "Whatever you do, don't take chances that will get you caught, and send me the bill when you're done."

"There won't be any bill," he insisted. "Consider this my contribution toward finding Shortcake's killer."

The line went dead in Cat's ear, but she felt a deep sense of satisfaction as she hung up the phone.

"Ready or not, Mark Presley, your ass is mine."

* * *

As Mark had hoped, they'd moved him into a private room. He didn't know what Penny had asked of the doctor, but he thought it telling that she hadn't asked for a private nurse, as well. So much for the "for better or for worse" part of their marriage vows. When he thought about it, though, he knew it was all for the best. It made it easier to leave her behind.

Although he was playing this by ear, there was more than two million dollars in cash in his office. Where he was going, he was going to need it.

The stash he had in a bank account in the Cayman Islands was under another name. It would help him start a new life overseas, but he had to get there first. Once he got out of here, he would change his hairstyle, grow a neat little beard, maybe even gain some weight. Nothing like putting on a few pounds to change the contours of a face.

The wild card in this plan was whether or not he could walk. Something had happened to him after that nightmare. They hadn't called it a stroke, but he hadn't been on his feet once since they'd brought him in. Still, he could definitely feel his feet and legs, which said a lot. He had vague memories of drinking too much and passing out in bed.

But he couldn't take a chance on getting away with this much longer, especially after the visitor he'd had earlier tonight. He couldn't imagine who the hell the woman had been, but she knew too damn much about his business. The only thing he could figure was that she was some friend of Marsha's. Marsha must have spilled her guts about what was going on between them. He could only imagine what she would have said about him after he'd fired her.

He lay there contemplating a half-dozen scenarios that could get him out of this place unseen. It wouldn't be easy. He knew from previous trips to the hospital to visit acquaintances that there were video cameras on every floor, as well as in the elevators. So whatever he did, he had to do it in disguise.

Having satisfied himself of what had to be done, he began eyeing the clock on the wall against the times that the nurses would come in. They did little but check his IV, then take his pulse and blood pressure. Once in a while a nurse would come in with a needle full of something and shoot it into the IV. It always made him sleepy, so he had to make sure that when he made his break, it was before that was administered.

And there was always the possibility that once he got out, he would still need assistance, but he would cross that bridge when and if he came to it.

Wilson McKay was on a stakeout in a less than desirable part of the city, waiting for a man who called himself Two-bit to come home. Two-bit, whose legal name was Morris Sanders, had skipped out on bail to the tune of one hundred thousand dollars. Wilson had refused to bond him out through his business, although he had known Two-bit for several years. In fact, this would be the third time in as many years that Wilson had to go after Sanders. He didn't like the man, and liked this part of the city even less. Still, a job was a job, and he was helping a buddy out. Rufus Carter, of Carter Bonding, had taken a chance on Two-bit and was about to get burned. The skip tracer Rufus normally used was in the hospital, recovering from a broken leg suffered during the ice storm. And since Rufus was a paraplegic, he wasn't going after his bail jumpers himself. Wilson had offered his services, for which Rufus Carter was extremely grateful.

So Wilson was biding his time, parked across the street from the seedy hotel that was supposed to be Two-bit's place of residence. He had a free view of the front door, which was more than sufficient, since he'd already checked and found out that, while it was illegal, the back door to the place was chained and padlocked from the inside.

He was on his second cup of coffee in three hours when he saw a cab pull up to the curb across the street. He put the cup down and picked up his binoculars, adjusting the night-vision lenses for a clearer view, then began to grin.

Two-bit had finally come home.

Wilson waited until Sanders entered the building, then got out of his truck and started toward the door.

The night was bitterly cold, but at least the streets were clear. After the weather they'd had recently, he wasn't going to complain.

The latch was broken on the entrance to the hotel. The chair that had been put in front of the door to hold it shut slid across the old linoleum, squeaking loudly as it went. Intentional, or not, it was a fairly decent warning system for this part of the city.

Wilson cursed beneath his breath as he paused in the shadows, waiting to see if anyone came out and challenged him. When he realized that everyone who came and went had to make the same sound, he figured the occupants were used to it.

Just to be on the safe side, he pushed the door shut, then set the chair back in place. Now all he had to do was find out which room belonged to Two-bit and pay him a visit.

A quick look at the book behind the desk showed that Morris Sanders was occupying room 400.

Great. Only four flights. At least this time the place wouldn't be on fire.

Wilson stayed in the shadows for just a few seconds longer, making sure that he was still unobserved, then started up the stairs. He was still breathing easily by the time he reached the fourth floor and gave himself credit for his repeated trips to the gym.

Only once before he knocked on the door to room 400 did he think of Cat, and then he made himself focus. It was stuff like that, that could get a person killed. He felt in his pocket for his gun, then re-checked the back of his belt for his handcuffs. Once he was satisfied that all was as it should be, he gave the door a thump with a doubled-up fist, then began mumbling loudly while stumbling and staggering around, giving the impression that he was just a drunk in the hallway.

Two-bit was popping the cap from a long-neck beer when he heard the thump against his door. Then, when he heard the mumbling and cursing and the shuffling feet, he took a quick swig before heading to the door.

Stupid bastard was going to wake up that Latino woman's baby across the hall, and if it woke up, he would never get any sleep. The brat was always crying, and the last thing he wanted was to finish out the night listening to it again.

He yanked the door inward with a curse on his lips just as Wilson stepped out of the shadows.

"What the—?"

Wilson popped Two-bit in the nose with his fist, then followed him inside as he staggered backward.

"Gotdabbit!" Two-bit shrieked. "Ju boke by nodes."

"It's what you get for jumping bail again," Wilson said calmly as he handcuffed Two-bit.

"I'b bleeding," Two-bit whined.

Wilson looked around, saw a box of tissues and grabbed a handful. To Two-bit's horror, Wilson rolled the corners into a point and stuffed them up one side of Two-bit's nostril, then did the same thing with two more tissues, stuffing the other side, as well. He looked like a walrus until the tissue quickly turned to red.

"Hold your head back," Wilson said, as he grabbed Two-bit's coat, draped it around his shoulders and headed him out the door.

"By door! By door! Bull it jut or dey'll rob be blind."

Wilson shut the door behind them as they went, then aimed for the stairwell.

"Maybe next time you'll choose a better place to live," Wilson said, as they started down the stairs.

"I can't breed," Two-bit muttered.

Wilson smirked. "That's probably for the best," he said, even though he knew that wasn't what Sanders was trying to say. "Just stop talking and breathe out of your mouth, and you'll be fine," he added.

By the time they got out of the hotel, across the street and into Wilson's SUV, Morris Sanders was a subdued man. Wilson buckled him into the back seat, then shoved his head backwards until it was leaning against the head rest.

"Don't you, by God, bleed on my seats. Keep your head back. Do you hear me?"

"Jess, I hear ju," Two-bit mumbled, and fixed his gaze up and out the back window. He could barely see the night sky for the street lights, but he looked long and hard, because it would be a long damned time before he saw it again.

* * *

Pete Yokum was on a high. It had been a while since he'd been this excited about anything, and he wondered if he'd been wasting his time being retired when there was this whole world of crime just waiting for him.

There was a rational side of him that knew he would never partake of that lifestyle, but just this once, he had the opportunity to prove to himself how good he would have been.

It was easy to get onto the Presley property. Their security system was at least fifteen years old and in serious need of an update. He was on the grounds and in the garage within five minutes of trespass.

A quick sweep of the vehicles inside led him straight to the cars that were obviously driven by a female and the ones that were not.

Just to be on the safe side, he bugged all but the powder blue Jaguar, certain that it belonged to Mrs. Presley because of the way it smelled inside, and the bits and pieces of jewelry and makeup he'd found in the glove box.

Once he'd finished there, he found a window in the basement that was missing a small pane of glass. He opened the window and entered the house, then did a quick walk-through of the downstairs. He found the security system, but it was armed only for doors and the windows on the ground floor. It did have motion detectors, and he wondered why Mrs.

Presley wouldn't activate them, since she was sleeping here all alone. Within moments, a large, long-haired cat with a bored attitude wandered into the foyer where Pete was standing and gave him the answer.

Because of the cat, they couldn't arm the motion detectors without guaranteeing that they would be going off all night.

He grinned. This kept getting better and better.

He began going through the downstairs rooms, eliminating possibilities for bugging as he went. When he came to the library, he found a cell phone in the drawer and quickly bugged it.

When he walked back into the foyer, he stood at the foot of the stairs, gazing up. The bedroom was bound to be up there, and it couldn't be overlooked.

It was when he started up that he began to get nervous. He had no way of knowing if Mrs. Presley was here, or if she was a light sleeper. He already had a mental plan for escape, should he get caught, so he was treading lightly by the time he reached the top.

He paused at the head of the stairwell as the cat suddenly darted past his feet. It was all he could do not to panic as the cat scampered down the hall and then disappeared into a room two doors down.

It occurred to him then that that was probably where Mrs. Presley was sleeping. A quick check assured him that he was right, only the room didn't appear to be a master bedroom. Just to be on the safe side, he quietly shut the door before moving back toward the stairs. The first door on the right was closed. If the pair were sleeping in separate rooms and if he was the man of the house, it was the room he would choose.

When he entered, he knew he'd been right. The closet was full of men's clothing. The drawers in the dressers were full of men's socks, underwear and handkerchiefs. He began going through the stuff with swift precision, bugging what he thought Presley might take with him, including a duffel bag on the floor of the closet and several pairs of shoes.

There was a money clip on the dresser but no way to conceal a bug, so he reluctantly left it alone. By the time he was finished, he was shaking. He hurried back into the hallway, standing quietly just outside the door to make sure everyone was still asleep, reopened Mrs. Presley's door so she wouldn't suspect anything, then bolted for the stairs. He made it through the rooms and into the kitchen, then down into the cellar in record time. When he finally crawled out through the open window, he was breathing easier.

After a quick glance around the grounds, he left the same way he'd come in and made a run for his car. He was laughing from the adrenaline rush as he drove away.

It would be more difficult to bug Presley's office. Not only was it inside a twenty-story company building, but the building had a security guard in the lobby. He decided to wait until daylight and go in as a repairman.

As he drove home, he stopped at an all-night diner, and picked up a slab of ribs and some coleslaw and fries. After all the work he'd done tonight, he was starving. By the time he locked himself inside his apartment again, it was nearly morning. He ate what he called his evening dinner with relish, then brushed his teeth, stripped buck naked, set the alarm and crawled between the covers. All he needed was a few hours of sleep, and then he would get up and finish the job before the sun set on Dallas again.

As he drifted off to sleep, his thoughts were of the Presleys' fuzzy-faced cat and of Mrs. Presley, who'd slept through his breaking and entering, completely unaware of the intruder in her house.

He didn't know if what he'd done would help, but if Catherine asked, he would do it again, and gladly.

Sixteen

It was twenty minutes before four a.m. when Mark Presley woke up. At first he was confused as to where he was; then he remembered that they'd moved him from the ICU the evening before, right after he'd had that visitor.

He could see the clock on the wall in a shaft of light from the bathroom. The shift wouldn't change for another three hours, and the hall was quiet. Although he hadn't been here long, he already had a feel for the floor. They'd checked him every hour on the hour since he'd been moved, so he had no reason to assume they wouldn't be back again, but there was something he wanted to try.

He was impatient to know if his mobility was impaired. The problem was that if he began to move around, would the machines record it in any way?

Would they give away the little secret he'd been keeping? He couldn't go far, tethered as he was by tubes and leads, but he could try. With one last glance at the clock, he gripped the bed rails with both hands. He didn't know what would happen, but he was about to find out.

He pulled himself up, then sat for a moment, shocked at how light-headed he felt. But the longer he sat, the less dizzy he became. He reached down and ran his hands along the length of his legs, careful not to disturb the IV. Everything felt normal. He scratched an itch on his knee and then scratched himself beneath the hospital gown. It felt good to know that sensation seemed intact.

Now that he'd accomplished that much, he wanted down from the bed. But that presented a problem. The bed rails were up on both sides, and he wasn't sure how to lower them. And if he did, would he be able to get them back up undetected?

Caution suggested he wait, but he hadn't gotten where he was in this world by being cautious. He felt along the bed rail until something gave and the rail began to move. When it came to a stop just below the level of the mattress, he swung his legs off the side of the bed and let them dangle.

His heart was pounding so loudly that he felt dizzy. As he sat, he broke out in a cold sweat, fearing that if he stood up, he would go crashing to the floor.

It was ten minutes to four in the morning.

Suddenly a voice came over the intercom and into every room. Someone was calling for a nurse to Room 206. It sounded serious. He heard a shuffling of chairs and feet, and realized he wasn't far from the nurses' desk. Since he didn't know what room he was in, he panicked. What if his heart monitor had registered some huge spike? What if they had seen him? He hadn't thought about the room being monitored by a camera. What if he was about to be debunked?

He sat motionless, waiting for them to come bursting into his room, but no one came. Instead, he heard footsteps running to the other end of the hallway and decided that luck was on his side after all.

Confident that whatever was going on in 206 would keep the nurses busy for a time, he grabbed the head of his bed with one hand, then slid sideways, letting the toes of his right foot touch the floor.

Nothing happened. There were no sharp pains. No feelings of weakness. He could feel the cold floor against the bottom of his foot. It was the best thing he could remember feeling in a long, long time.

His confidence grew as he slid the rest of the way off the bed and then stood, testing how it felt to be upright. There was no dizziness, no feeling of an impending blackout. His legs didn't feel rubbery or weak, and there was sensation in all his limbs.

He would have tested his mobility a little better, but there was the heart monitor, a catheter up his penis, and the IV needle in the back of his left hand. Still, he considered his experiment successful.

He knew something about himself that no one else knew.

He could walk.

The seizure or the breakdown or whatever they chose to call what had happened to him hadn't paralyzed him. And, not that it mattered, he'd been so drunk when he'd gone to bed that he had no memory of the hours afterward or what had caused his seizure. All he needed now was to find a way out of the hospital and this mess he was in.

As reluctant as he was to lie back down, he knew he was pushing his luck. He scooted back up on the bed, positioned himself much the same as he'd been and pulled up the guard rail. Satisfied that it was safely locked into place, he lay back down, dragged the covers up to his chest, then shifted them around a bit so they wouldn't look too neat. When his bedclothes looked properly messy, he closed his eyes, willing his heart rate to settle. His mind was still racing when he heard the door to his room open. Before he could prepare himself not to react, the light came on. He flinched.

He heard a nurse gasp, then hurry to his bedside. She grabbed his wrist and began to take his pulse. He knew his heart rate was too rapid for someone who was supposed to be comatose, but he'd had no time to relax and let it slow down.

"Mr. Presley? Mr. Presley? Can you hear me?"

He didn't answer.

The nurse reached above his head and hit the intercom. A few moments later, he heard another nurse answer the call.

"Yes?"

"I need help in 220."

There was a brief moment of silence and then an answer.

"On my way."

Seconds later, another set of footsteps entered the room and he heard a second woman's voice.

"What's wrong?"

"You take his pulse."

"Why?"

"I want to make sure I'm not imagining things."

"Is there a change?"

"Yes."

"For the better?"

"Look at the monitor."

"Oh my."

"Go ahead...take his pulse, then tell me what you think."

Mark felt fingers moving along his other wrist. When they stopped, he knew the nurse was counting heartbeats. He'd been made, and all because he'd been impatient to see if he could get out of bed.

"You're right! I'll call the doctor while you get the rest of his vitals."

Damn it, Mark thought. *I've got to figure a way out of this without alerting the police that I've regained consciousness.*

"Mr. Presley? Can you hear me? Open your eyes."

He wanted to curse. Of course he heard her. She was yelling in his ear. It was all he could do not to slap her face.

He felt a blood pressure cuff going around his arm, then heard the machine humming as it automatically tightened. Just when he thought the damned thing was going to pop, it began to go back down.

He heard water running. Before he knew what was happening, there was a wet wash cloth on his face.

What the hell is she doing? Does she think just because I'm waking up I need my face washed?

Not since the night his father died had he felt so helpless. Everything was out of control. If only he could go back and relive the last six months of his life.

Penny Presley was dreaming about needing to go to the bathroom when the telephone beside her bed began to ring. Her arm slid out from under the covers before she opened her eyes. Her voice was shaking as she answered the call. At this time of night, it could only be bad news.

"Hello, Presley residence."

"Mrs. Presley, this is Dallas Memorial. I have—"

Penny started to weep. "Oh my God, he's dead, isn't he?"

"No, no, Mrs. Presley. Quite the contrary. The doctor wanted you to know that we think your husband is waking up."

Penny's emotions shuddered to a stop. *Not dead? Not dead after all? Waking up? What the hell was all this about?*

"You say he's waking up?"

"Yes, ma'am. The doctor wanted you notified immediately."

"Yes, well, that's wonderful news, I'm sure. Is he speaking?"

"No, ma'am. That's a little premature. But he's exhibiting all the signs of coming out of his coma. We knew you'd want to be here when he woke up."

That's what you think. But Penny couldn't voice her true feelings.

"Are you saying I should come right now?"

"I'm just delivering the message, Mrs. Presley."

"Of course," Penny muttered. "I'll be there as soon as I can get dressed and drive over."

"All right. Oh…sorry, but you'll have to come through the Emergency Room doors. The front door doesn't open until seven a.m."

Penny stifled a sigh. "Thank you for reminding me," she said, and hung up the phone.

She sat on the side of the bed with her bare feet

firmly on the thick Berber carpeting and tried to maintain a sense of calm. No need to let her emotions get the best of her. It wasn't as if this was a disappointment, exactly. Still, as she got up to get dressed, she couldn't help but think how much simpler this all would be if he'd gone ahead and died. Now the police would get involved, and there was nothing she could do to separate herself from the mess that was bound to come.

Joe Flannery was sleeping like a baby, dreaming of the tall blonde cheerleader for the Dallas Cowboys football team, the one who usually stood in the middle of the front row. It wasn't like he was committing adultery, even though he was married. A man couldn't control his dreams, so there was no need to feel guilty.

Still, when the telephone suddenly rang at the side of the bed, he reacted by raising his arm over his head, as if to protect himself from an oncoming blow.

When the phone rang a second time and his wife elbowed him, he began to come to.

"Joe! Phone! And you may as well get it, because we both know it's not for me. Not at this God-awful time of the night…or morning…or whatever the hell it is."

Joe rolled over, then reached across her to pick up the receiver. In all their married life, the phone had been on her side of the bed, although he was always the one to answer. Someday maybe he would mention the oversight and rectify the situation. In the meantime, he put the phone to his ear.

"Flannery."

"Flannery, this is Captain Henry. We just got a phone call from Mrs. Presley. Mark Presley is waking up. I need you to get over there as soon as possible and get a statement from him."

Flannery groaned beneath his breath as he sat up on the side of the bed, trying to collect his thoughts. Damn this phone call. He'd been about to nail the cheerleader. So close and yet so far away.

"Now, sir? It's just past four in the morning."

Henry cursed. "I know what time it is. They woke me up, too, remember? And yes, now. We got word the DNA from Marsha Benton's fetus matches Mark Presley's DNA."

"Damn. So Catherine Dupree was right about that."

"That's why I want you taking Presley's statement. She might be right about the whole damn thing. He'll lawyer up soon enough, but for the hell of it, see what he comes up with before that happens."

"Yes, sir. I'm on my way."

Flannery hung up the phone and hurried to get dressed. It was still dark by the time he got to the hospital, but it wouldn't be long. Already he could see a change in the night sky on the eastern horizon.

* * *

Cat woke before daybreak and couldn't go back to sleep. Even though it was so comfortable and warm beneath the covers, she had the feeling that everything was about to change. She didn't know whether it would be for the bad or the good, but she knew she needed to be prepared.

Reluctantly, she got up and made a quick trip to the bathroom, turning on lights as she went, so she wouldn't be tempted to lie back down when she came out. A short while later she emerged, showered, hair shampooed and dried, and feeling a strong need for caffeine.

She dressed without thought, choosing clothes that were warm and comfortable, and headed for the kitchen. As she was making coffee, the telephone rang. Somehow she knew as she went to answer it that it was connected to what she'd been feeling.

"Hello?"

Wilson momentarily closed his eyes, letting that whiskey voice wash over his senses.

"Cat, it's me. Wilson. I'm sorry to be calling so early, but—"

"It's okay. I was up. What's wrong?"

"It's all in how you look at the news, but I doubt you're going to call it wrong."

Cat's focus shifted from thinking about how it felt when they had sex to what he was saying.

"Mark Presley! Something's happened to Mark Presley."

"You could say that," Wilson said.

"What? Did he die?"

"No. He's waking up."

Although Cat was unaware of it, her grip tightened on the phone. "You're sure?"

"Absolutely."

"How did you find out?" she asked.

"I know one of the nurses who works night shift in the ICU. I asked her days ago if she would let me know if there was a change in Presley's condition. Although it's against the rules, she agreed, but only if I keep her name out of it."

"So she called and—"

"She called to tell me that they'd moved him to a private room on the second floor. Then, just as she was getting ready to go off shift, she called again to say she'd heard that Presley was waking up."

"Oh my God! You're kidding," Cat mumbled, remembering what she'd thought as she was leaving the ICU. She'd been right about him all along, and she would bet anything that someone, either a nurse or a doctor, had seen through his masquerade, too.

"Maybe we'll see justice yet," he said.

Wilson knew Cat well enough by now to know she wasn't the type to sit and wait and hope someone made all the right moves.

"Cat, I want you to promise me something, okay?"

Her eyes narrowed. "Like what?"

"Don't go and do something stupid. Let the police do their job."

Cat bristled. "There are two things you need to know about me."

Wilson frowned. He could tell he'd made her mad, even though it wasn't his intention.

"And those two things would be…?"

"I don't like to be told what to do."

"That's one," he counted.

Cat turned abruptly to stare out her kitchen window, as if trying to focus on something besides the condescending tone of his voice.

"I don't do stupid. And that's two. Thank you for letting me know about Presley."

She hung up in his ear before he could accept her thanks or offer an apology.

He replaced the receiver with a sigh and then crawled back between the covers. He'd been up most of the night and was too tired to care if he'd ticked her off. Either she would get over it or she wouldn't. Right now, he was going back to sleep.

Cat called Pete Yokum from the car as she was driving to the hospital. He answered on the first ring.

"Pete, it's Cat. This is a heads up for you. I heard Presley is waking up. I'm on the way to the hospital to find out the truth for myself."

"Stay cool, honey. Don't alert anyone that you're on to him in any way. I still have the office to do, and then we're good to go."

"You be careful, too," she said, then disconnected.

It did occur to her that Pete had offered almost the same advice that Wilson had, but Wilson's had made her mad. It was, she supposed, all in the delivery. She took the next exit off the freeway, straight to the hospital.

Joe Flannery showed up at Presley's hospital room about thirty minutes after Penny Presley's arrival. After finding out that Presley still wasn't talking, he left his name at the desk, asking to be notified when he could see the man, and moved to a small waiting room on the same floor.

Within fifteen minutes, Mrs. Presley came to meet him.

Flannery saw the attractive young woman entering the waiting room, then frowned as he saw the black eyes and bandaged nose. When he realized it was Penny Presley, he stood up.

"Mrs. Presley, I'm Detective Flannery. Captain Henry said you called."

Penny's hair was less than perfect, and her clothing was slightly awry, as if she'd dressed in the dark. She hadn't, but choosing an outfit at four o'clock in the morning wasn't something she'd done before, and she would be the first to admit she had failed.

"Yes. Thank you for coming, Detective. As you can imagine, I am extremely upset about this entire affair. I would like to feel confident enough in my husband's faithfulness to our marriage vows to vehemently deny these claims against him, but I fear I cannot. I've known for years about his…dalliances, but to my knowledge, this is the first time there has been a child involved."

"And that child is dead…murdered along with the mother," Flannery said.

Penny's expression stilled as her face turned pale.

"Yes. I'm also aware of that."

"So what's your take on all this?" Flannery asked. "Do you think your husband is capable of murder?"

Without thinking, Penny put a hand to her throat, remembering the sensation of not being able to breathe.

"I don't know what to think," she said, and looked away.

Flannery frowned. She knew more than she was letting on.

"You do realize that if you're covering up for your husband, you can be charged as an accessory to murder?"

Penny gasped.

"Good Lord! I am most certainly *not* covering up anything. I've been more than courteous to your department. I didn't have to call you about anything, and yet I've volunteered DNA from his hairbrush and toothbrush, as well as given my permission for blood to be taken for testing. How dare you accuse me?"

Flannery backtracked. He didn't want to piss off his only witness to Presley's whereabouts.

"I'm sorry. I didn't intend to insult you, but I felt it was my duty to make sure you understood the consequences of withholding evidence."

Penny's chin went up as her eyes flashed angrily.

"Well, you did insult me. As for consequences, as you put it, I'm well aware of my legal standing, including the fact that you can't *make* me testify against my husband, although if I knew for a fact that he'd committed such a horrible crime, I would most certainly do so…and by my own choice."

Flannery decided to go straight to the heart of the matter. "Has your husband truly come out of his coma?"

"The doctor says he has, although he has yet to open his eyes and speak to me."

"Do you think he's been faking?" Flannery asked.

Penny's eyes narrowed angrily. "I'm not a doctor. I don't know what to think!"

"Do you have a problem with me asking him some questions?"

"Not if I can be a witness to your interrogation."

Flannery frowned. He knew for a fact that Presley might tell him something that he wouldn't want his wife to hear. Still, she'd said he wasn't talking, so it might all be moot.

"I don't have a problem with that, but I would

ask you not to let on that you're in the room," Flannery said.

Penny nodded. "Yes. I understand."

"Can I see him now?"

She shrugged. "I don't see why not. Follow me."

Mark was sick to his stomach with fear. The doctor had as good as told Penny that he was awake. He didn't know what to do now except open his eyes. But what then? He needed time to make his getaway, time to delay the police from questioning or filing charges against him. If that happened, it would be twice as difficult to escape.

He knew that a nurse was still in the room. He could hear her walking around with her rubber-soled shoes, and once in a while heard the scratching of her pen on paper as she made notes.

Penny had been here, too, but he'd heard her walk out when the doctor left. They'd talked about him as if he wasn't even there, which was a little disconcerting. Still, he'd had no choice but to remain silent.

The tape holding his IV in place was itching. He wanted to scratch it in the very worst way, but didn't dare move. Then he heard voices out in the hallway and willed himself to be still. Soon he heard more than one set of footsteps coming into his room.

Penny nodded her okay at Flannery, who promptly moved to the side of the bed. He stood without talking, watching the monitors registering Presley's blood pressure and heart rate, as well as the steady rise and fall of his chest. His breathing was steady and deep, and there was the slightest flutter to his eyelids, which Flannery knew didn't necessarily signify cognizance. Still, there was something about Presley that seemed off. Flannery couldn't quite put his finger on what was bothering him. Maybe it would come to him later. Now it was time to see what reaction he got from identifying himself.

"Mr. Presley, I'm Detective Flannery from the Homicide Division. I have a few questions I want to ask you."

Shit. Shit. Shit. The cops? They shouldn't be here already. Who the hell had tipped them off that he was waking up?

Flannery thought he saw a muscle jerk near Presley's mouth, which gave him the impetus to continue.

"A few days ago, some detectives from Missing Persons interviewed you regarding an ex-employee of yours… Marsha Benton? I believe she was, at one time, your personal assistant. At any rate, she's been found. She was murdered. Do you know anything about that?"

Presley's stomach was in knots. If there was a God in heaven, he would surely put him out of his misery and just take him now. He didn't think he was going to be able to bear this inquisition.

When Flannery saw Presley's fingers trembling, he

knew the bastard could hear, but how could he break down the wall of silence behind which the man was hiding and drag his sorry ass out into the truth?

"I believe that would constitute a 'no comment,' right? Well, I have another little fact you can't deny. The baby that Miss Benton was carrying, the one that was murdered along with her, was yours. It's an undeniable fact. Do you have anything to say to that?"

Presley felt the contents of his stomach coming up and could do nothing to stop it. He wanted to cry out. He wanted to scream at the world to get out and leave him alone, but all he did was choke and then gag. Before Flannery could step back, Presley had thrown up all over the front of his sport coat and slacks.

"Oh crap!" Flannery yelled, as he stared down at himself in disbelief.

The nurse in the room hit the call button and then ran to Presley's side as Flannery moved toward the bathroom in the corner of the room.

"I'm so sorry," Penny said, as she grabbed a handful of paper towels and handed them to the detective.

Flannery took them without comment and began wiping himself off as best he could. But the scent was with him, no matter how much he tried to clean up.

"Obviously this wasn't a good time," he said. "I'll be back."

Without waiting for anyone to say otherwise, he stalked out of the room and down the hall to the elevator. Because of the hour, he rode it down alone and made it across the parking lot to his car without being noticed.

All the way home, he cursed Presley and his captain for sending him out on this wild goose chase in the middle of the night. His wife was in the bathroom getting ready for work by the time he strode into the house. He was taking off his clothes as he went through the house. By the time he got to the bathroom, intending to clean up, he found her in the act of getting out of the shower.

Mistaking his nudity for something else, his wife took one look at her naked husband as he entered the bathroom and then wrinkled her nose.

"Oh, for God's sake, Joe. Not now. I'm going to be late for work."

As she swept past him with her nose in the air, she paused long enough to offer a comment.

"You need to shower. You stink!"

"Do you think?" he asked sarcastically, and turned loose of the last bit of guilt for leaving a trail of tainted clothes all through the house.

By the time she figured out that she'd misread the situation, he was in a fresh set of clothes and on his way out the door.

Seventeen

It was fifteen minutes after nine in the morning. Presley's corporate offices were just opening up when Pete Yokum walked into the lobby and presented himself at the front desk.

He had dusted off one of his uniforms from when he was still on the job and written out a fake work order to replace some electrical outlets in Mark Presley's private office from 110 voltage to 220. He carried his work bag in one hand and a cup of coffee in the other.

"Texas Electric," Pete said, and flashed the work order to the guard as he calmly took a sip of coffee.

"Just a minute," the guard said, and picked up a phone, then punched in a couple of numbers. "This is Warren. I have a man from Texas Electric with a work order to do some repair in Mr. Presley's office."

Pete watched the guard frown and knew he was going to have to play it cool to get by.

The guard looked up at him, still frowning.

"They say they don't know anything about this."

Pete shrugged. "That's not my problem," he said. "If you don't want me to do it, then I'm outta here. However, keep in mind that it's taken more than three weeks to get to this work order, and with the holidays and all, I'm backed up even more, which means if somebody gets their head out of their ass and realizes I came and went without doing the work, it's gonna be your problem, not mine. I showed up like I told them I would."

The guard looked a little nervous.

"Wait a minute," he said, then spoke into the phone again, relaying Pete's message without mincing words. "What? Yeah…oh, okay," the guard said. "Just a minute. I'll ask him."

"So…when did you get the call to come do this?" the guard asked.

Pete pulled a notebook out of his pocket and pretended to leaf through the pages.

"Oh. Yeah, here it is. It was the first Monday in December. A real nice lady called me. Said her name was Benton."

The guard was well aware that Marsha Benton would have been the one to make this kind of appointment for the boss, and even though she was no longer here, that didn't mean Presley's plans for his office would change. He relayed that information to whoever he was talking to, then nodded when he got a reply.

"Will do," he said, then hung up the phone before looking back at Pete. "Okay, buddy. You can go on up. Take the elevator to the top floor. Someone will be there to show you to the right office."

"Thanks," Pete said, then drained the last of his coffee and tossed the cup in the trash as he headed for the elevator.

He had already located all the video cameras in place around the lobby, so he kept the bill of his cap pulled low across his face and pretended to check out the lace on a shoe as he rode the elevator up. At no time did he allow a full view of his face to appear on camera.

As promised, there was a woman waiting for him at the elevator. He showed her the work order. She eyed it briefly, then told him to follow her and led him straight into Mark Presley's inner sanctum.

"How long do you think this will take?" she asked.

Pete shrugged. "I don't know, lady. Is it comin' out of your pocket?"

The woman frowned, eyed the stains on Pete's coveralls and sniffed disapprovingly.

"Of course not. Just don't make a mess in here," she said. "Mr. Presley wouldn't like it."

"I always clean up after myself," Pete muttered, then set down his bag and turned his back on her.

She was gone before he had it unzipped.

He straightened up, then quickly checked out the room for hidden cameras. There were none, which didn't surprise him. A man like Mark Presley would have to have a place where he could be certain he was unobserved. Where better than his office?

He began looking through the desk and the closets, as well as a small dressing area off an elegant bathroom. There were a weight machine and an exercise bike in another alcove, and several changes of clothes in the closet, as well as a half dozen pairs of shoes. Several of the outfits were gym clothes, and there was a large gym bag in the back of the closet, which Pete promptly bugged, along with all the shoes.

With a quick glance toward the door, he began a thorough check of the desk, and as he was running his fingers along the bottom of each drawer, he felt a piece of paper that had been taped to one. When he checked it out, he saw an odd set of numbers and realized it was most likely the combination to a safe.

He hadn't see a safe anywhere in the room, though. He made quick note of the numbers and then stood. Just because he hadn't seen a safe, that didn't mean there wasn't one.

He started to search seriously and within a minute found it behind a painting of a farmer plowing around a field of pump jacks. The safe was unusually large for a wall safe, and using the numbers that he'd found, he quickly opened it.

He'd expected money, but not such a staggering amount.

Without taking time to count, he would venture a wild guess as to more than a million. The bills were all hundreds, and there were stacks and stacks of them. Almost immediately, he realized that if Presley *was* going to make a run for it, he wouldn't leave this behind.

Afraid that he would be caught, he quickly pushed a chair in front of the door and then dumped all of his tools right beneath an electrical outlet nearby. If anyone tried to come in, the chair would stop their immediate entry, giving him time to get back in place.

Once that was done, he grabbed a couple of the small electronic bugs and slipped them into bundles of bills he pulled from the middle of the stack. As soon as he'd finished, he quickly shut the door and spun the lock, then put the painting back in place.

He was down on his knees with the electrical socket out of the wall when the door swung inward. It did, as he'd expected, thump loudly against the chair.

"What the hell?" he yelped, then pulled the chair aside.

The woman who'd led him into the room entered with an accusing look on her face.

"Why did you block this door?" she snapped.

Pete frowned. "Dang, lady. You scared the shit out of me. And I didn't block the door...at least not intentionally. I just moved that chair to get to this outlet here."

The woman glanced down, saw the tools on the floor and the wires dangling from the wall and relaxed.

"Oh. Well. I'm sorry I startled you. I was just checking on your progress."

"I'm about done. This is my last one," he said. "If you want to wait around a bit, you can walk me back to the elevator. I wouldn't mind some pretty company."

To add insult to injury, Pete winked at her.

The young woman, properly horrified at being hit on by a man older than her father, quickly disappeared.

Pete chuckled as he screwed the plate back into the wall, then left the same way he'd come in. He nodded to the guard, who was talking to a FedEx delivery man, and disappeared out to the street.

As soon as he got in his van, he gave Cat a call.

"Hey, honey, it's me. I've got you taken care of."

"Any problems?" she asked.

"Not a one."

She sighed. "I hope this works."

Pete chuckled, thinking of all that money in the safe. "If he's a runner, we've got him nailed," Pete said.

"I hope so." Cat said.

"Trust me," Pete said. "Are you home?"

"No. I'm lurking around the hospital, trying to get some updates without outing myself."

"Do you know how to run the tracking programs on these bugs?" he asked.

"Do they register on a laptop?"

"Yes. I have one programmed to the stuff I used, and I'll lend it to you. I'll write up the instructions. If you have any problems, you know my number."

"Where should I meet you to pick it up?"

"I'll bring it over and get the manager to let me into your apartment."

"I'll call her right now and tell her that I sent my laptop out for repair and it's going to be delivered today. I'll tell her to let you in."

"That'll do it," Pete said.

"Thank you so much," Cat said.

"You're welcome, honey," he said softly. "And once again, I'm real sorry about Shortcake. I'll be missin' her, too."

Cat lurked around the waiting room on the second floor of the hospital long enough to see Detective Flannery leave. From what she'd learned, he'd been in and out, then back in again, since early this morning. A short while later Presley's wife also exited his room and took the elevator down. A nurse went into his room with a tray of medicines, then came out. Cat knew she needed to get out of there, too, before someone accused her of stalking, but she wanted to look at Presley one more time, just to reassure herself that she hadn't misread the situation.

She sat in the waiting room until it became obvious the shift was changing. There would be some confusion with all the coming and going, which should provide her with a fair chance of getting into his room unobserved. Still, she knew there were surveillance cameras in every hall and she knew where they were located. She took down her hair, shaking it out until it was hanging around her face, buttoned up her long coat in order to disguise her shape as best she could, and started down the hall.

Her shoulders were hunched a bit, as if from the cold outside, and she kept her gaze down just enough that her hair automatically fell forward. When she got to Presley's room, she paused as if checking room numbers, then very quietly slipped inside. There was no sound from her entrance, or from the door slowly swinging shut.

Then it was only Cat and the killer, alone in the dark.

She stood there until her eyes adjusted to the lack of artificial light and slowed her breathing to the point that she could barely hear herself. As she waited for him to make a move, her skin grew clammy with anticipation. A trickle of sweat ran down the middle of her back from the weight of the heavy coat she was wearing, but still she didn't move.

Mark knew Penny was gone, as was the detective. Even his nurse had left. Only then was he able to relax. He kept his eyes shut and his breathing steady, not wanting another incident with the doctors like before. Sounds came and went in the hall. He heard a call over the hospital intercom for a Dr. Fraser to call ICU.

The quiet in the room seemed to swell around him until every sound he heard was magnified to absurdity. He hiccupped once, and the sound was startling. There was a spot on the back of his neck that was itching, but he didn't dare scratch. The minutes passed as he continued his charade. Finally, when he was absolutely certain he was alone and there were no sounds of activity anywhere near his door, he dared a small peek, and saw nothing but the darkened room and the shades that had been pulled over the windows. Without thinking, he took a slow, deep breath and let himself relax. As he did, he passed gas and thought nothing of it. No one was there, and anyway, it was a natural body function. A nurse would have thought nothing of it.

He rolled his neck just the least little bit, and started to raise up and plump his pillow. As he did, he turned his head toward the door.

She stepped out of the shadows without warning and moved three steps toward his bed.

"Jesus," he said weakly, then shrank back against the pillows, his eyes wide with shock.

He tried to see past the long thick mane of hair hanging around her face but could make out only shadowy features. When her shoulders squared up and her hands doubled into fists, he flinched. He didn't know who she was, but she was damn sure the enemy.

For several long, silent seconds she stood motionless, her gaze fixed and staring at him. Then he saw her lips part, and he found himself holding his breath for a hint of her voice.

"Know this, you double-crossing, lying, son-of-a-bitch. You will never be able to run far enough or hide well enough to get away from me. Before this is over, I will watch you die."

The soft, raspy voice seemed like a whisper from hell. He felt sick from his head to his toes. He'd battled plenty of powerful people in his time, even bankrupting several, and always without a sliver of conscience complaining. But this was different. He didn't know who she was or why she kept showing up like this, but he knew there was a connection between her and Marsha Benton.

"Who are you?"

Suddenly he knew she was smiling, because he could see the white of her teeth.

"Your worst nightmare," she said softly, and without waiting for him to answer, she turned around and slipped out the door.

He wanted to ring for a nurse—or for security. But doing that meant he would have to admit that he'd not only seen someone come into his room, but he'd heard and understood her threat. Cursing the mess he was caught up in, he leaned back and closed his eyes, willing his heart rate to a calm rhythm he didn't feel.

As he lay there, it became apparent that he had no time left to waste. He had to get out of here—and fast—but how? For now, there was nothing to do but lie and wait for the opportune moment to present itself.

It was three a.m. when a nurse came into Mark Presley's room to check his vitals and change the IV bag on the pole. Mark had been dozing, but he woke almost immediately as the lights came on. He stayed motionless as she puttered around, resetting machines and checking hookups on the monitors that continued to register his vital signs. As best as he could judge, she was almost finished when there was a loud crash out in the hall.

Startled, she turned abruptly, and in doing so, knocked over a large bouquet of flowers that were sitting on a small table by the bed.

"Well, shit," the nurse muttered softly. The vase had shattered, sending water and cut flowers everywhere.

She buzzed the nurses' desk and was rewarded with a prompt answer. "How can I help you?"

"I don't know what spilled out in the hall, but when the orderly is through cleaning it up, send him in here. I knocked over a vase of flowers. There's broken glass, water and flowers all over."

"He'll be right there," the nurse replied.

Mark heard her leave, but within a couple of minutes, the door opened again. Mark could tell from the weight of the footsteps and the length of the stride that a man had entered. He heard the sound of squeaky wheels and guessed it was a mop bucket.

Obviously the orderly.

Unlike the nurse, the orderly made no attempt to hide his disgust and cursed intermittently as he picked up the flowers and broken glass while dragging the squeaky bucket around.

As the orderly worked, Mark lay in wait, like a lion waiting for the kill, and when he sensed the orderly was on the other side of the room, he ventured a quick look.

He saw a man in his late thirties with his back to the bed, slowly cleaning up the mess the nurse had made. Mark noted the man's neatly clipped dark hair and slim build, and when he suddenly stood up, Mark could tell he was similar to his own height.

Suddenly a wild plan began to take shape. It might take more strength than he had—and an inordinate amount of good luck that he didn't have—but if everything worked, it could prove to be his ticket out.

He watched the man use a large mop to sop up the water in which he was standing, and suddenly Mark's decision was made.

Within a few seconds, the orderly, still with his back to Mark, had mopped himself all the way to the guardrails of the bed. Mark rose up, grabbed the man around the neck and gave him a hard backward yank. The unexpected blow combined with the wet floor, and the orderly dropped as if he'd been pole-axed. He hit the floor flat on his back with a sickening thud. His head bounced once and made a sound not unlike that of a ripe melon being dropped.

Mark refused to feel guilty. At this point in his life, it was every man for himself. He pulled the oxygen tubing from around his ears, then unplugged the monitors and began unhooking himself from them by grabbing fistfuls of the wires connected to his body and giving them a yank. He pulled the IV out of his hand, wincing as blood began to spurt, then grabbed a washcloth lying nearby and wrapped it around his hand as tightly as he could. But it was the catheter up his penis that gave him pause. Finally he gritted his teeth and pulled, again, then again, until the tubing suddenly came free, spilling urine out onto the floor.

Pain shot through his body so fast that he doubled over, but he didn't have time to suffer. At any moment some nurse could come into the room and that would spell the end.

He felt shaky when his feet hit the floor, but there was no time to waste. Without hesitation, he grabbed the orderly's feet, yanking first at the shoes, then the pants. He was shaking so badly he could barely breathe when he began to put them on.

I can do this, he thought, as he tugged on the orderly's shirt until he managed to pull it over his head. There was blood all over the back of it from the orderly's head wound, and it was wet from the spilled water and urine, but it was something better than a hospital gown.

Mark shook out the shirt, then pulled it over his head, finding it a looser fit on him than it had been on the orderly. Now there was nothing left for him to do but get out undetected.

As he turned, his gaze jumping wildly from bed to table to window, he tried to think of how to make this happen. Then he realized he was looking at a cigarette lighter on the floor near the orderly's hand. It must have been in the man's shirt pocket and had fallen out when Mark undressed the orderly.

He looked at the lighter again, then at the oxygen tube lying in the middle of the bed where he'd discarded it. In that moment, his last bit of empathy for his fellow man flickered and died. He had his means of escape.

Carefully he stepped over the orderly, dropping his hospital gown on the body as he upped the flow of oxygen still coming through the tube. He stood, listening to the hiss until he was satisfied there was a noticeable amount pouring into the room.

Pure oxygen, the life-giving, body enriching—highly flammable—gas.

He moved toward the door. Then, with his hand

on the knob, he flipped open the lighter, opened the door, then looked back.

At that point, everything seemed to happen in slow motion.

He flicked the lighter.

It lit on the first try.

As he tossed it, it flew in a perfect arc toward the middle of his bed.

He was already into the hall and running when the oxygen caught. He didn't see the deadly tongue of blue flame as it appeared out of nowhere, but he, along with everyone else on the floor, felt the explosion.

It knocked him to his hands and knees, but he didn't look back. Sprinklers came on overhead, but the flames in his room were still being fed and were too intense to be put out so easily.

People were screaming.

Nurses were shouting orders and running in every direction.

A nurse raced past him to a fire alarm on the wall up ahead, broke the glass and pulled the lever. He knocked her aside on his way to the exit and took the stairs two at a time. His legs felt like rubber as he went stumbling, falling, then got up and did it all over again.

Suddenly he was running through the hallways on the main floor, along with dozens of others who were also on the move. He ran past a door marked employee lounge. Without hesitating, he ducked inside.

Rows of lockers lined the side of one wall. There was a winter parka hanging over the back of a chair. He grabbed it, and as he put it on, he found a set of car keys in the pocket.

Bingo.

The wheels he needed to escape.

The jacket was at least two sizes too large, and he had no idea what vehicle the car keys would fit. All he could do was punch the car alarm on the security key ring and hope he got a quick hit before the guards got suspicious.

The moment the cold air in the parking lot hit his face, he pressed his thumb on the alarm button and held it down as he ran, aiming it wildly from one vehicle to another. Suddenly a horn began to honk—repeatedly and in a frenzied monotone—leading him straight to a mid-sized Chevrolet.

Still in full stride, he silenced the alarm and hit the Unlock button.

It was only after he slipped behind the wheel and tried to put the key in the ignition that he realized how badly he was shaking. He took a slow breath, trying to calm down. It would be the final straw if he got this far, then passed out from exertion and missed his chance to escape.

Finally the key slid into the ignition. The engine started on the first turn, and he thought, as he put the car into gear, that he'd never heard a more beautiful sound.

The way he figured it, even if there was enough left of the orderly to pick up, it would take them days, maybe longer, to realize that it wasn't Mark Presley who'd died in that room.

By then, he would be gone.

As he turned a corner, he paused and looked back. Flames were shooting out of three windows on the second floor. Fire trucks and police cars with lights flashing and sirens screaming were turning into the hospital parking lot as he drove away.

He shuddered.

It was the only physical reaction he could muster to what he'd done. Above all else, he needed clothes and money. Going home to get clothes and a car was too risky, and he couldn't use an ATM without alerting everyone to the fact that he was alive and running.

But he did have a plan.

He had clothes and money at the office, and a set of keys to a company car that was parked in the adjoining garage. All he had to do was get inside without being seen. He couldn't go through the lobby and maintain the deception that he was dead, but there was his personal elevator down on the freight docks that led straight to his office. Normally he used the key on his key ring, but that was at the house. However, he was a man who was always prepared. There was another key hidden on the docks for emergencies. And if ever there was an emergency, this was it.

Eighteen

Cat was physically exhausted by the time she got home. There was another message from Al, who wanted her to call him back, but it was too late to return the call.

The laptop that Pete had promised was on the kitchen counter, along with a sealed envelope. She opened it, read the brief instructions and then booted up the machine. With a couple of key strokes, a map of Dallas appeared on the screen. Another couple of key strokes and a pattern of tiny lights came up, superimposed on the map.

Cat's eyes narrowed in satisfaction as she realized she was looking at the bugs Pete had left behind. For the moment, none of them were moving, which, if she understood Pete's instructions, meant they were still right where he'd left them.

The instructions also said that if anything started moving, the map would automatically change to accommodate the movement.

Now that the program was up and running, she was nervous about walking away. What if, while she was taking a bath, something started to happen and she didn't see it? Still, it was better than nothing, which was exactly what she would have had if not for Pete.

Satisfied that for the time being she had as much control of the situation as she could, she moved around the kitchen, turning up the thermostat in the apartment as she made herself a sandwich. She heated up some leftover coffee, but it tasted bitter, so she poured it down the drain and settled for a can of pop.

Too antsy to relax while she ate, she stood at the kitchen counter to eat her meal while keeping an eye on the computer screen.

Her telephone rang as she was downing her last bite. As soon as she saw caller ID, she answered.

"Hey you."

Wilson McKay stifled a soft groan. Just the sound of her voice turned him on.

"Hey yourself," he said. "How are you doing?"

Cat sat down on a nearby barstool and began fiddling with the ends of her hair.

"I'm okay. How about you?"

"That's part of why I'm calling," Wilson said. "I wanted to come by and see you tonight, but I'm on a stakeout."

"Is it a bad one?" she asked.

He knew what she was asking. Sometimes the people who jumped bail were scary.

"Nah…this guy's a toker. He probably got himself a bag of weed and forgot he was supposed to show up in court. I've got a line on his girlfriend, who swears that when the dude's smoking, he always comes to her place to crash. So here I am. You know how it goes."

"You don't think she'll warn him off?" Cat asked.

Wilson chuckled. "No. She's pretty pissed at him. Says he owes her money, and that when he's not smoking weed, he has a tendency to smack her around. She wants him off her back."

"Sounds like a real sweetheart," Cat said.

"Yeah. At any rate, I just wanted to check in with you."

"I'm fine," Cat said.

"Glad one of us is," he said.

She frowned. "What do you mean?"

"Nothing," he said shortly. "Ignore me. That doesn't require an answer. It's just an update on my state of mind."

Surprised by the unexpected humor, Cat laughed.

The sound curled around Wilson's heart and squeezed just tightly enough to make him feel short of breath.

"Have a good evening."

"You too."

"Okay, Miss Independent, I see a little movement down the street, which means I've got to go."

Even as she was hanging up the receiver, she felt as if she were floating off into space without a tether to anything stable.

Disgusted with herself for feeling something close to needy, she carried her dirty dishes to the sink. With one backward glance at the laptop, she headed for the shower.

A short time later, she moved the laptop into her bedroom and then crawled into bed, intent on watching the late news. She was asleep before it ever came on.

Pete Yokum stood at the window of his apartment overlooking the streets below and thought about the job he'd just done for Cat Dupree. It had felt good to get back in the swing of things. Maybe he would do a little something now and then, like installing security systems—or maybe troubleshooting for the ones he'd already installed.

As he stood there, he began to realize he was hearing sirens—a lot of sirens—and that he'd been hearing them for some time. It wasn't an unusual sound, not in a city the size of Dallas. But this wasn't the normal pattern. Curious, he turned around and picked up the television remote, turned on his set and then clicked on a local news channel.

The screen was alive with what he could only

describe as chaos. Fire trucks and firemen were everywhere. Water from the hoses was freezing on the parking lot where the trucks were parked, making the men's job even more hazardous than usual. Police cars could be seen in the distance, blocking off streets and redirecting traffic. Curious, Pete sat down on the sofa and turned up the volume, catching a live report of what was happening.

…been burning for more than thirty minutes now. They've managed to contain the fire to the floor on which it started but are having to evacuate patients in immediate danger. The weather and a shortage of available ambulances due to a bus wreck on the Fort Worth bypass are making it more difficult.

"What's on fire?" Pete muttered, willing them to mention the address, then leaning forward as the reporter continued his broadcast.

At this point, all they know for sure is that there was an explosion on the second floor and the fire spread from there. Unconfirmed reports are coming in that there could be as many as four to six dead. Not once in the history of this city has there been an incident of this magnitude at any hospital. Unidentified sources are even talking terrorism, although at this point, that seems a bit far-fetched.

A hospital? Pete's heart dropped as he frantically scanned the screen, looking for anything that would tell him the location.

He continued to watch as a camera began to sweep across the parking lot, giving an overview of what was happening to go with what the on-site reporter was saying, and as it did, he saw a sign in the background.

Dallas Memorial.

The fire was at Dallas Memorial!

What had that journalist said? It had started on the second floor?

Wasn't Mark Presley on the second floor of Dallas Memorial?

He began scrambling for his laptop, plugging it in, then quickly turning it on. He had a program on his that was the twin of the one he'd given to Cat. His hands were shaking as he waited for it to load. Typing quickly, he soon had the map up, highlighting the bugs he'd planted. Almost immediately, he saw movement.

It didn't take long for him to figure out what he was seeing. Someone was at Presley's office, taking clothes, shoes, the large duffel bag and the money that had been in the safe.

He stared back at the television, seeing the fire and imagining the horror of what must be happening inside. He didn't know how it had happened, but he was about to bet Cat Dupree's life that she'd been right. He grabbed his phone and punched in her number.

Cat was so deeply asleep that when the phone first rang, she thought it was part of her dream. It rang twice more before she woke up enough to realize that someone was calling her. She rolled over on her side without opening her eyes, grabbed the receiver, then put it to her ear.

"Hello?"

"Cat! It's Pete! Wake up and listen!"

It was the panic in his voice that made her sit up on the side of the bed.

"I'm awake," she muttered. "What's wrong?"

"Turn on the television."

Cat reached for the remote and aimed it.

"Which station?"

"Doesn't matter. Any local one," he said.

Cat leaned forward, staring in disbelief as the picture appeared on the screen.

"My God! What's on fire?"

"Dallas Memorial."

Her next heartbeat was so hard and irregular as it slammed against the inside of her chest that she almost lost her breath.

"What the hell are you saying?"

"The fire—they're saying it started on the second floor. But that's not all. Check your computer.

Someone's made a move on Presley's office. I bugged clothes, shoes and a butt load of money while I was there, and it's all on the move and going in the same direction!"

"Oh dear God," Cat muttered as her mind began to race. When she looked at the laptop on the other side of the room, she saw the moving blip. "How did he do this? How *could* he do this?"

"You don't know for sure that Presley was responsible for what happened," Pete said. "And you can't be certain that it's Presley who's at the office. For all we know, he fried in that fire."

Cat's voice was shaking as she began grabbing at her clothes.

"No, he's not dead. Evil like that isn't going to die that easy. I don't know how he did it, but I would bet money he caused the fire and used it to make an escape, without caring who else might be harmed. Thanks for calling me."

"Wait! What are you going to do?"

"I'm going after him."

Pete frowned. "No. What you need to do is call the police. Let them chase—"

"He'd be gone before I could convince anyone to go check out his office. I'm not going to let the bastard get away."

"Damn it, Cat. You can't go after someone like that without—"

The line went dead in Pete's ear. He returned his

attention to the computer screen and tried not to let his imagination go crazy. Still, there was no denying the fact that someone was on the move. When he saw the glowing blip on his screen hit I-35 and head south, he grabbed the phone, started to dial the police, then hung up. How was he going to explain what he knew without implicating himself into a jail cell?

"Damn it to hell."

He was caught between a rock and a hard place, forced to trust the fact that Cat was calling the shots.

Cat's hands were shaking as she plugged a battery charger into the cigarette lighter in her car, then plugged the other end into her laptop.

Immediately the tracking program reappeared.

She sat there long enough to watch the underlying map as it began to change with the route of the moving blip. When she saw the blip begin to move south down I-35, she drove out of the parking lot, heading for a drive-through ATM. Without knowing how long she would be gone, she figured she had better get some cash.

As she neared the ATM, she remembered her promise to Wilson, and grabbed her cell phone and made the call. It rang until his voice mail came on. She had no option but to leave him a message.

"Wilson? This is Cat. I had a friend bug some stuff belonging to Mark Presley. He just called to tell me that the tracking devices have been activated and are on the move south down I-35. Not only that, but Dallas Memorial is on fire. It started on the second floor. Presley was on the second floor. I can't prove it, but I think Presley started that fire to cover his escape. He had clothes and money at his office, which is where movement first showed up. I don't know why he didn't head for his airport, unless he wants everyone to believe he died in that fire. I'm about an hour behind him, following the blip on my laptop. I don't know what he's driving, so there's no need to notify the highway patrol. Maybe if I get closer... Anyway, just letting you know what's going on."

She disconnected as she pulled into the bank lot, then got out her ATM card and withdrew the limit, which was three hundred dollars. She hoped she wouldn't need more too soon, because it would be twenty-four hours before she could make another withdrawal. A short while later, she was heading south on I-35 herself.

Penny Presley was hysterical. A friend had called and awakened her to tell her that the second floor of Dallas Memorial was on fire. She'd been trying to call the hospital for more than fifteen minutes, but to no avail. Rationally, she understood why she couldn't get through, but the part of her that was trying to come to grips with the possibility that Mark had burned to death was coming undone. Despite her anger at the way things were turning out between them, she would never have wished such a horrible death on anyone—even him.

Joe Flannery hadn't been in bed for more than a couple of hours when he was jarred from sleep by the persistent ringing of the phone. He rolled over far enough to reach over his wife's sleeping body and grabbed the receiver. In the process, he managed to mash the shit out of her left breast.

She came awake screaming in pain.

All he'd tried to do was get the phone before it woke her, and instead, he'd managed to almost take out her left boob. He would never hear the end of it.

"Flannery," he said shortly, as he crawled out of bed and moved into the hallway so that he could hear what was being said above his wife's complaining.

"Flannery, we might have a problem."

"Captain?"

"Yeah. Turn on your television."

Joe staggered into the living room, turned on a light so he could find the remote, and then aimed it toward the TV.

"What channel?" he asked.

"Anything local," the captain said.

When the image on the screen emerged, Joe whistled beneath his breath. "God Almighty, Captain. What's burning?"

"Dallas Memorial. They're reporting an explosion on the second floor started the fire."

"An explosion on the—" Suddenly it hit him. "Oh shit. Presley."

"Exactly. Get over there and make sure the sorry bastard burned. I don't want to hear that he's missing and have to explain that we hadn't brought him in for questioning because we thought he was in a fucking coma, all right?"

"Yes, sir, but surely you don't think—"

"What I think is that if Catherine Dupree turns out to have been right on all counts, I don't want the Dallas Police Department to be the last to know."

"Yes, sir. I'll see what I can find out," Joe said.

"Do better than that. And call me," his boss said, then hung up.

Joe disconnected as he hurried back into the bedroom. His wife was sitting on the side of the bed with her nightgown off, inspecting her breast.

"I'm really sorry, honey," he said, and paused by the bed long enough to stroke her hair and give her a quick kiss. "That was the captain. Dallas Memorial is on fire. I've got to get over there now."

For once his wife was sympathetic.

"Dear lord," she said, and turned on the television in their bedroom. Her eyes welled with tears as she took in the scene—fire trucks and firemen everywhere, water spewing from hoses up to the second floor, and patients being wheeled out of the hospital in wheelchairs and on gurneys. "How terrible! Those poor, poor people."

Joe came out of the dressing room on the run, pulling a turtleneck sweater over his head and carrying his sport coat. He pocketed his badge, holstered his handgun, then slipped into the shoulder holster before putting on the coat.

"I don't know when I'll be back," he said.

"Just be careful," his wife said.

He blew her a kiss as he ran out of the room.

Wilson had his bail jumper and was at the precinct turning him over to the desk sergeant when the call went out about the fire. Policemen who'd been going off duty, as well as those coming on, were returned to their commanding officers for orders. It was an "all available patrol cars proceed to the location," which meant that, until they knew the magnitude of the problem, no one was going home.

He, along with a half dozen other people, looked up at the television screen behind the desk as the sergeant turned it on. They watched in horror as the media played and replayed the most sensational footage they'd shot so far.

As soon as he had finished signing papers, he took off for the parking lot. It was too late to go by Cat's apartment, and he had no excuse to wake her up that wouldn't tick her off. Besides that, he was tired and aching for a good night's sleep. He unlocked the car door and started to get in when he saw his cell phone on the floor. He frowned, guessing it must have fallen out of his pocket earlier. He dusted it off and dropped it in his jacket pocket.

The drive home seemed endless, and he resisted the urge to drive by the hospital, knowing there would be far too many sight-seers already on the street. Finally he pulled into the parking lot of his apartment building. His steps were dragging as he entered, then rode the elevator up.

He'd left a lamp on in the living room by mistake, but the circle of illumination was welcoming as he opened the door and went in. He locked the door, then glanced at his answering machine on the way through the room and noted there were no new calls. Thankful for the respite, he went through the kitchen on his way to bed, drank a full glass of milk and ate the last of some Chinese stir fry, then moved down the hall to his bedroom.

He undressed slowly, putting his gun in a drawer and his wallet and change on the dresser. He dropped his dirty clothes into a pile near the door to be carried to the utility room later, and hung his sport coat on the back of a chair. As he did, he heard a slight thump.

The cell phone.

He hadn't taken it out of his pocket.

He tossed it on the bed as he headed for the shower.

A short while later he was back, showered and shaved and all but walking in his sleep.

He started to turn back the covers, and as he pulled them aside, the cell phone slid to the floor with a thump.

"Well, hell," he muttered, and picked it up, checking to make sure that he hadn't damaged it in the process.

As he did, he finally realized someone had left him a message. When he checked Caller ID and saw Cat's name and cell phone number come up, he frowned.

He'd just talked to her earlier. She knew he was on a stakeout. Why would she be calling so late?

Quickly, he retrieved the message, and when he heard her voice, he froze, then slapped the wall with the flat of his hand. For all intents and purposes, she was chasing a killer on her own.

He knew she was capable of handling herself. He'd witnessed it firsthand more than once. But this was personal, and emotions could get in the way of good sense.

His heart was hammering as he sat down on the side of the bed and returned the call.

The first ring came and went.

Then the second.

Then the third.

Just when he was at the point of panic, he heard her answer.

"Wilson?"

He exhaled. "Yeah, it's me. I just got your message. Where are you?"

She frowned, trying to read a roadside marker without any success.

"I'm not sure. Maybe about halfway to San Antonio."

"Have you seen anything of the car you're following?"

"No. There's at least an hour and a half between us."

"You think it's Presley, don't you?"

Cat's voice hardened. "I know it's him. No one else would have the combination to his safe or a way to get into his office unseen, but someone did just that. And no one else has as much to lose."

"If this is Presley, why didn't he just take one of his airplanes...or that chopper? Why make his getaway slower by driving somewhere?"

"Pete asked me the same thing earlier."

"Who's Pete?"

"The friend who bugged Presley's stuff for me. Here's what I think. Somehow Presley started the fire that covered his escape. He wants everyone to believe that he died, which, if there's a body in his room, will be the assumption for some time. However, if an airplane or a chopper suddenly goes missing from his personal airport, then that's going to screw up his cover."

"He could take public transportation."

"And take a chance on being recognized? I don't think so. Also, you're at the mercy of someone else's timetables when you take that route. No control of when you leave, no way to change your mind in the middle of the trip and go somewhere else without a lot of hassle."

"Yeah, I see what you mean."

Cat shifted the phone to her other ear. "What have you heard about the fire? Is it out?"

"I don't know. Let me check." He turned on the television and upped the volume. It didn't take long to get an update.

"Cat."

"Yes?"

"They're saying that for all intents and purposes, it's out. They're still going through the building checking for hot spots."

"Any details on how it started?"

"They're saying there was an explosion on the second floor. But Presley was in ICU, not on two."

"No, they moved him down."

"Shit," Wilson said, then paused. "You know I'm coming after you."

The warning in his voice should have been unsettling, but instead, it gave her a feeling of security. At least someone else in the world knew where she was and what she was doing. Not that it would keep her alive, but if she disappeared, they would know where to start looking.

"I can't wait for you," she said.

"I know. Just stay in touch. Where do you think he's going?"

"Who knows? So far, he's staying southbound."

"Did you call the cops?"

"No, but feel free. I had no time to waste trying to make them believe Presley hadn't gone up in smoke."

"That wasn't smart."

"So sue me. I'll be fine. Besides, I've been taking care of myself for years."

"Maybe so," Wilson said. "But I didn't know you then."

"How does that change anything?" she asked.

"Hell if I know. I just don't like it, all right?"

Cat's fingers tightened on the steering wheel. She glanced at the speedometer. She was doing eighty and still not gaining on the sorry bastard, and Wilson wanted something from her she wasn't ready to give.

"Wilson?"

"Yeah?"

"Just don't lose me…okay?"

A knot of fear formed in the pit of his belly.

"I'll do my level best."

Then the line went dead in his ear.

Nineteen

Mark's elation at getting out of Dallas had faded to a sick, nervous feeling that he was being followed. Rationally, he knew it was far too early for anyone to know he hadn't died in that fire. He also knew there was the possibility that it would never be discovered, because the explosion and the fire that came after had been so intense that they should have destroyed every vestige of the orderly and his DNA. He knew that yet he couldn't get past his unease.

He attributed part of his anxiety to the fact that he'd been in a bed for so long. Driving was more difficult than he had expected. From time to time he felt weak and light-headed, and he was afraid that, in a moment of disorientation, he might drive off the side of the road.

The other part of his underlying panic involved

that strange woman who kept threatening him. For all he knew, she was just guessing about her accusations, although he had to admit that if she was, she was damned good at it.

Marsha's body being found so quickly was unexpected. He would have bet everything he owned that it would never have been found—at least not for years. The land where the wells had been drilled was not only isolated but heavily wooded, as well. No one lived close, no one hunted on the property, and the ravine where he'd dumped her body was about as far off the beaten path as it got. There was that damn fire, but he was certain that had in no way contributed to finding her, yet it had still surfaced in less than two weeks.

Normally Mark made it a habit to know everything there was to know about his adversaries, which was what Marsha had become after she'd announced her pregnancy. But he had come to realize that he knew nothing about her life beyond the workplace other than that she was an orphan—a fact that should have worked in his favor. It seemed, however, that Marsha had friends he knew nothing about, one being a tall dark-haired woman who wouldn't go away.

It was unnerving to know that if the woman walked up beside him and looked him in the face, unless she spoke, he wouldn't even recognize her. That, low, raspy voice, which in any other situation he would have considered sexy, came across as scary in the current circumstances.

As he was driving, that uneasy feeling came over him again, and he glanced up in his rearview mirror, half expecting to see the husky-voiced woman staring at him from the back seat. It was with relief that all he could see were a few lights in the distance. There were also three or four cars up ahead, but nothing to suggest he was being followed.

At that point his attention moved from the rearview mirror to the gauges on the dashboard. He'd known for a while now that he was going to have to stop at the next truck stop and get gas. It wasn't all that far to San Antonio. Showing his face without some kind of disguise wasn't ideal, but even if he'd had his wallet, he couldn't pay with a credit card without leaving a paper trail. No matter how he worked it, he was going to have to go inside the station to pay in cash and show his face.

Tears suddenly blurred his vision.

Before this was over, his entire identity would be permanently changed. Everything he'd worked and sacrificed for was lost. He didn't have a home anymore. He was no longer the power behind the Presley Corporation. He had nothing but the clothes in the back seat and a bag full of money in the trunk. His fingers tightened on the steering wheel as he blinked away the tears.

Fuck them all.

He could buy more clothes and he could buy a home—hell, he could buy a castle, with the money he had stashed away in a bank in the Cayman Islands. He'd been whipped before, and he hadn't let it get him down. At least this time he had plenty of money to buy a whole new dream.

But he had to be careful. Eventually, someone in the head office was going to realize this car was missing from the parking garage, which meant he couldn't take it across the border into Mexico. The way his luck was running, it could already have been reported stolen. Getting caught trying to cross the border in a stolen car would set off a whole mess of red flags. If he was going to do that, he might as well stick an "I'm a killer, come and get me" sign on the back of the car and just wait to be arrested.

No, he would park this car somewhere out of sight and wipe it down for prints before he left. Even if the authorities found it, they couldn't be sure he'd been the last one driving it. As far as he was concerned, it could go the way of Marsha's Lexus—chopped up for parts, or repainted and sold. It didn't matter, as long as it was gone.

An eighteen wheeler came up behind him in the dark. When the lights suddenly ricocheted from the rearview mirror into his eyes, he swerved and almost ran off the road. He cursed out loud as the truck went flying past, but it was a weak complaint. The trucker couldn't hear him, and it was too dark for the driver to see Presley flip him off.

Mark's belly rolled as a wave of nausea came and

went. He needed help. He needed a driver and started to reach for his cell phone when he remembered he didn't have one with him. He cursed again. He would just have to make his calls when he stopped to get gas.

As he was thinking it, he saw a cluster of lights on the horizon. He was coming up on an exit, and just in time. The warning light on the gas gauge had just started blinking.

With renewed belief in his ability to get away with murder, he pulled into the truck stop, parked at the pumps and got out, stretching wearily as he went inside to pay. He came back shortly and reached for the hose. His hands were trembling as he unscrewed the gas cap. When he was finished, he went back inside to make his calls.

Solomon Tutuola missed his bank shot and, in a fit of rage, broke the pool cue in half and then shoved the splintered end into his opponent's belly. The man screamed as blood spewed from the wound onto the pool table and Solomon's boots.

Two men leaped from the corner of the Nuevo Laredo cantina, tackling Tutuola in mid-air. He threw both of them off as if they weighed nothing, then pulled a switchblade from inside his boot. With one flick of the wrist, the blade was between them, gleaming like the fangs of a wolf.

Tutuola grinned at the pair, then taunted them in

Spanish. Despite the epithets he flung at them and their female ancestors, they weren't willing to try a second attack. They knew Tutuola for what he was: crazy, both in spirit and in appearance. Why else would a man look as Tutuola did if he wasn't insane?

Although his body was a light café au lait, he wasn't of Mexican descent. He was covered in crazy geometric tattoos all over his face and upper body— some in a zig-zag pattern like oversized rick-rack, some ovals within ovals or squares within squares— different, yet still connecting to each other like a black and tan crazy quilt.

When he got drunk, which was often, he talked in some crazy language the locals couldn't understand, nor would they ever, Solomon knew, unless, like him, they'd been born half a world away, in a country called New Zealand, to a race of people known as the Maori. Although he was a long way from home, Solomon still considered himself a throwback—a warrior. He used his size as power and a way to get easy money. He might have the blood of warriors in his veins, but he was a chicken-shit in every other way that counted.

Solomon stared at the duo as a big grin spread across his blood-splattered face. When his adversaries saw that smile, they panicked. The two men picked up their bleeding friend and carried him out of the cantina as fast as they could go.

Solomon tossed the knife from hand to hand for

a few moments; then, with another flick of the wrist, the blade disappeared back into the shaft. He dropped it inside his boot, then eyed the bartender, pointing at the bottles behind the bar.

"Tequila!" he demanded.

The bartender set an unopened bottle and a clean glass in front of him, then moved to the other end of the bar.

Solomon was downing his third straight shot when his cell phone rang. He pulled it out of his belt, eyed the Caller ID and shrugged. It was a number he didn't know, and he was in no mood to visit, but it continued to ring until finally, in a fit of pique, he growled an answer into the phone.

"*Hola.*"

"Diego gave me your number."

Solomon frowned. It was a code phrase that he used in his business, but he didn't recognize the voice speaking in English.

"How do you know Diego?" he asked, which was the proper answer to that phrase.

"He's a cousin."

"Ah," Solomon said, then grabbed the tequila bottle and strode outside, swigging it as he went. When he was outside and alone, he disposed of his cordial demeanor.

"Who the fuck is this, and what do you want?"

Mark shuddered, wondering what this man looked like.

A couple of years ago, he'd been in a hot tub with a hooker who called herself Satin when a man he knew slightly had staggered out of the shadows. He was drunk and crying, and he gave Mark some sob story about being down on his luck. He'd asked for a thousand dollars to get out of town, and in return, he'd offered Mark his little black book for collateral.

Money was no object, but Mark wasn't in the habit of doling it out—not even for friends. However, he'd been curious about the contents of the little black book, and thinking it contained names of hot women, he'd readily done the trade.

The next day, he'd learned that the man had been found dead in his hotel room. Mark felt sorry for him but glad he hadn't been somehow involved. He had, by right of possession, become the owner of the book. On going through it, he had deduced that the names in the book weren't hot women. They were names of men for hire who asked no questions, with instructions for contacting them.

He'd never believed in a million years that he would have need of it, and yet when he'd run across it in the safe, he'd brought it along. Now he was using it and wondering if he'd just made another in a long line of mistakes.

"It doesn't matter who I am," he said shortly. "I need a driver to get me from San Antonio into Mexico."

"I'm no fucking cabbie," Solomon growled, and

started to hang up. Then he heard the magic word: money.

"It's worth ten thousand dollars to me."

Solomon frowned, which made the tattoos between his eyebrows look like an upside down arrowhead. Then he smiled, and as he did, his teeth, filed to tiny, needle-sharp points, gave him the appearance of an animal and not a man.

"So if I give you this ten-thousand-dollar ride, where are we going?"

"I need a place to hide out…just until I can make arrangements to fly…elsewhere."

Solomon ran his tongue lightly over the points of his teeth. "There is an abandoned hacienda about fifteen miles south of Nuevo Laredo. It would serve your purposes." His grin widened. Whoever this American was, he was obviously in trouble, and in that case, ten thousand dollars was a pittance. "I will come get you and bring you across the border for fifty thousand American dollars."

"Fifty thousand!"

"That or nothing," Solomon said.

"Fine," Mark muttered. "Fifty it is. But you screw with me and I'll splatter your brains all over the windshield of your car and walk the rest of the way by myself."

Solomon's smile disappeared. Nobody threatened him, no matter who they were, but he could deal with that later.

"When and where do I pick you up?" he asked.

"Just get yourself to San Antonio. I'll be there in another hour or so. When I arrive, I'll call you. For now, that's all you need to know."

"Money up front," Solomon said.

Mark snorted and made no bones about trying to hide it. "Make no mistake about me. I am not a fool. You don't get a dime until you deliver me to the hacienda. It's that or nothing."

"Half when we meet. Half when I deliver you."

"Goddamn it! I have other names on this list I was given. Just because your name was first, that doesn't mean you're all I've got. If you want the fucking job, you will get paid when I get to my destination and not before. Is that understood?"

Solomon reconsidered. Just because the man was an American didn't necessarily mean he was a fool. He knew a good deal when he heard it, and decided that if he argued, he would still be bored and out fifty thousand dollars.

"Yes. It is understood."

"Fine. I'll call you when I get into San Antonio. If you're not available when I get there, I'll find another way to cross the border."

"I'll be there," Soloman said.

The line went dead in his ear.

He dropped the phone back in his pocket, eyed the bottle of tequila he was holding, then turned and dropped it into a trash can. Fifty thousand for one night's work was worth missing a good high.

He shoved his hands through his long curly hair, then took an elastic hair band from his pocket and pulled it into a ponytail at the nape of his neck. It was time to get down to business.

Cat was so tired she could hardly keep her eyes open, but every time she felt the need to sleep, the image of Mimi's battered and broken body would dance before her eyes. It was more than enough to keep her going. The laptop was in the seat beside her—her only connection to her prey. Despite her weariness, it was the rage inside her that kept her foot on the gas and her gaze darting between the laptop and the road.

There was a part of her that actually feared the confrontation when she and Presley came face to face again. She wasn't sure if she would be able to maintain control. In her estimation, what he was capable of doing made him highly expendable. She had no problem facing the fact that it might come down to him or her.

Somewhere along the way, she became aware that her fuel was running low. Despite her reluctance to stop, she was going to have to get gas before she could continue. About ten minutes later, she passed a roadside sign indicating she was approaching an exit. When she saw the large, well-lit truck stop just off the highway, she turned off the road and pulled up to the pumps. She got out, tried to use her credit card and after four tries, gave up and went inside to pay cash.

When she came back out the pump turned on as sweetly as a cheerleader in the back seat of a car with the quarterback of the high school football team. Within minutes, her fuel tank was full. She replaced the hose. Her cell phone, which she normally kept clipped to the waistband of her jeans, was lying on the passenger side of the seat. She didn't bother with it as she hurried back inside to make a quick trip to the bathroom.

Wilson kept glancing at his watch, then the mile markers on the side of the interstate, wishing there was a quicker way to get where he was going. He was thinking about Cat chasing a killer on her own, fully aware that she would ignore her own safety in order to catch Presley.

He'd been on the road for the better part of three and a half hours, having already stopped once for fuel and some coffee to keep him awake. He was exhausted physically, but the adrenaline rush he was riding kept him from a mental shutdown. He kept remembering what Presley had done to Marsha Benton.

After he'd finally downed the last of a cup of coffee that had gone cold, he picked up his cell phone. He needed to check in with Cat, to make sure she was all right and that he was still on course.

He dialed the number, then counted the rings.

When her voice mail came on, he got a sick, empty feeling in the pit of his stomach.

Where in hell was she? She had to be all right.

He left a message, then pressed down on the accelerator. He was already doing eighty. Another five miles over the speed limit wasn't going to change the fact that, if he drove up on the highway patrol, he would be getting one hell of a fine. But they were going to have to catch him first.

Cat came out of the truck stop with a bottle of pop and a package of Twinkies. Pure sugar and some caffeine were the next best things to drugs for staying awake. It wasn't hard to notice the difference in temperature the farther south she went. It had been in the thirties when she left Dallas and now, according to the thermometer that registered on the rearview mirror of her SUV, it was in the fifties.

She jumped in her car and buckled up, put the pop in a holder built into the dash, opened the Twinkies and started the engine. The laptop was still in the seat beside her, still registering movement down I-35. It appeared that he might be heading into Mexico, but no matter. As long as he kept moving, he was hers.

She drove back onto the interstate. She knew that Laredo, which was on the Texas side of the border, had an international airport and, remembering that he'd flown himself to Tyler to dump Mimi's body, knew there was a chance that he would fly himself out of the country from there. She had to catch up with him before that happened.

As she drove, she wondered why she hadn't heard any more from Wilson, then discarded the thought as being weak. She'd been on plenty of chases before, and she always caught her man. She didn't need anyone to take care of her—even though the notion of seeing Wilson McKay's familiar face was more appealing by the hour. The scent of the Twinkies beckoned, so she ate them in three bites apiece, washing them down with Pepsi.

She was licking the white fluffy filling from the tips of her fingers when her cell phone rang. She wiped her hands on the legs of her jeans, then dug around in the seat for the phone, which had slipped beneath the laptop. It was on the fifth ring before she got it to her ear.

"Hello?"

"Thank God," Wilson muttered. "Are you all right?"

"Yes. Why wouldn't I be?" Cat snapped.

"Oh, hell, Catherine… I don't know. For starters, maybe because you're trailing a killer by yourself?"

"I'm not by myself," she snapped back. "You're here."

Wilson stifled the urge to shout but was unable to mask his sarcasm.

"Excuse the hell out of me, Miss Dupree, but I am nowhere near you, which continues to cause me concern."

"You know what I mean," she snapped.

"Yes. And you, by God, know what *I* mean, too, so don't play dumb with me, okay?"

She didn't respond, so he changed the subject.

"Where are you?"

"Somewhere between Austin and San Antonio. Closer to the latter, I think."

"Is the blip still tracking southbound on I-35?"

"Yes. I'm pretty sure he's heading for the border, although there's an international airport in Laredo."

Wilson frowned. "Damn, you're right…but why go so far to catch a plane?"

"I don't know. I'm just guessing and driving. Where are you?"

"I'm just now on the south edge of Austin. Probably at least an hour behind you."

"Are you driving too fast?"

"Hell yes."

Cat grinned. "If you find any highway patrol, bring them with you."

"They have no authority across the border. For that matter, neither do you."

"Authority isn't all it's cracked up to be over there anyway," Cat said. "I'll be fine. I've done this before."

"But not with this much at stake."

She got quiet.

Wilson sighed. "Just promise to call and keep me updated on everything."

"Yes. I will."

"Drive safe," Wilson said. He heard the line go

dead, then the dial tone. "Witch," he muttered, and tossed his cell phone on the seat.

Mark was shaking as he drove past the city limit sign on the north side of San Antonio. He needed some food, and he needed some sleep, but he wasn't likely to get the latter for some time to come. Still, he could get a hamburger while he was waiting for his driver to show up—if he came. From their conversation, he wasn't all that convinced it was going to happen. However, when he saw a sign up ahead advertising fuel and food, he took the exit.

There was a gas station on the corner, with a fast food place across the street. He got the fuel first, then headed for a pay phone.

He called Solomon Tutuola again, thinking to himself as the phone began to ring that he was thoroughly fucked if the man didn't answer. There was no time to locate another driver. However, to his relief, the call was answered on the third ring.

"*Hola.*"

"Tutuola?"

"Yes."

"Are you in San Antonio?"

"Yes."

Mark breathed a sigh of relief.

"I'm at a burger joint called The Beef and Bean. It's on the north side of the city, just off I-35."

Tutuola wrote down the info as quickly as possible.

"How long do you think it will take you to get here?" Mark asked.

"I'm on the south side of the city. Traffic is pretty thick. Maybe as long as thirty minutes."

"That's fine," Mark said. "It will give me time to eat. Come into the burger joint when you get here."

"All right," Tutuola said.

"What are you driving? How will I know you?" Mark asked.

"When you see my face…you will know that it is me."

Mark frowned. At this point, he wasn't into riddles. "What the hell does that mean?" he asked.

"Think of your worst nightmare come to life," Solomon said, then disconnected.

Mark's frown deepened as he headed across the street. Once he pulled into the parking lot, he could see the place was doing a good business. The lot was nearly full, and, through the windows, he could see people eating.

Once inside, he was promptly seated in a corner at the back of the room. He wanted to be near an exit, and still be able to see who was coming and going. Satisfied with where he was, he ordered a burger and fries, and a large glass of iced tea.

The tea came first, and he downed it as the waitress looked on, then pushed it toward her for a refill, which she calmly provided. When he was finally alone, he leaned his head against the back of the booth and quietly closed his eyes.

God, he was tired. If he could just stretch out and sleep, he would be grateful. At this point, however, it wasn't a luxury he could afford.

He waited impatiently for his food to come, and when it finally did, he lit into it as if he'd been starving. A few bites into the meal, he realized that if he didn't slow down, he was going to be sick. He hadn't had solid food in days, and this basket of beef and grease was a poor choice to have made.

He slowed his chewing, drinking more tea than eating, and was glancing at his watch when he saw a set of headlights turn off the highway and into the parking lot. The time was about right. He frowned, wondering if this was his ride.

He saw the car door open, but just as the dome light came on, a truck pulled between the café and the car, blocking his view. By the time the truck passed, the driver was out of sight. Mark found himself staring at the front door. Just as he saw the door being opened from the outside, a group of customers got up from the table in front of him and sauntered toward the front, arguing about who was going to pay the bill as they went. Again he was forced into a wait-and-see situation.

The group of men paused up front by the cash register, teasing the hostess who was taking their money, and then suddenly everyone got quiet at the same time.

Mark caught himself holding his breath, watching as the men standing there began to move aside, as if making sure they were out of the way.

And then Mark saw him, standing in the front of the room, searching the tables for a man on the run. It took a few moments for everything to register. There was the extreme height of the man, who appeared to be seven or eight inches over six feet. And then there was the pulled-back mane of long black curly hair, framing a face straight out of a bad dream. A geometric maze had been tattooed on his face and arms, and although he couldn't see them, Mark suspected the tattoos were all over his body, as well.

Then the stranger looked straight at Mark, and without pause, came toward him. He stopped at Mark's booth, then smiled.

When Mark saw the perfectly filed teeth, he shuddered.

"Are you ready to go?" Solomon asked.

Mark took a quick drink of his tea, then asked, "How did you know it was me?"

"Who else but a man on the run would hide in the shadows in the back of the room?"

Mark frowned, tossed a handful of bills on the table, then slid out of the booth, only to find himself staring at the third button on the man's shirt. It was to that button, that he gave his first order.

"Follow me."

To his relief, the demon who would be driving him to hell followed without a word.

Twenty

Cat was caught between desperation and panic. When the blip she'd been following had suddenly come to a stop about half an hour ago, her heart had stopped with it.

All she could think was that she was going to lose him. There was an airport in San Antonio. What if he got on a plane before she got to the city? Why hadn't she called the police? They might have given her the benefit of the doubt. Why was she such a hard-headed, do-it-by-herself woman? Hadn't she already learned the hard way that didn't always work?

But true panic didn't set in until she realized she was no longer following the blip. At that point she hit the brakes and pulled over to the side of the interstate, then quickly scanned the screen on the laptop, making sure she wasn't misreading it.

"Oh crap," she muttered, as she began to reassess her position in accordance with the city map of San Antonio that was on the screen.

Somewhere within the last few miles, Presley had stopped and she'd passed him. But where?

She turned in her seat, looking back at the buildings and exits, then comparing them with the map on the laptop. Cars were flying past her, blinding her with their headlights to the point that she couldn't tell where she was at. Finally, not knowing what else to do, she pulled back into traffic and took the next off ramp. She began to backtrack, using the side streets and access roads until she came to an intersection. According to the map, she should be able to see the car. And she probably could. She just didn't know what the bastard was driving.

A car behind her honked, telling her to move on or get out of the way, and out of frustration, she pulled into the parking lot of a small burger joint. Now that she was here, she glanced at the map again. By all indications, she was right on top of him.

Desperate not to miss him again, she took her foot off the brake and continued driving between the lanes of parked cars, searching the faces of the customers who were coming and going. None of them was Presley.

As she turned to circle the lot again, two men walked out from between a row of parked cars and stepped directly in front of her. She hit the brake at the same time that she recognized Mark Presley.

He looked far different from the man who'd been supposedly comatose in that hospital bed. When she saw that the blip on the screen continued to move although they were on foot, she remembered Pete had bugged more than Presley's cars. The motion had to come from something he was carrying, or something that was on him. He was carrying an oversized duffel bag, as well as an armful of clothes. The bug could have been anywhere.

She was so focused on watching where Presley went that she almost didn't see the man he was with until they stopped beneath a security light, their backs to her. She first noticed the other man then, and was shocked at his size. Then her gaze moved to the thick bush of curly hair pulled into a pony tail at the back of his neck, and she wondered how he ever got something that unruly washed and dried. It wasn't until he turned sideways that she got a momentary glimpse of his profile.

As she did, a strange, anxious feeling skittered through her belly, then quickly disappeared. The stranger didn't matter. He couldn't matter. It was time to make her move. She had to stop Presley now, before he went any farther. She reached toward the glove box for her handgun and taser, slipped the taser in her pocket and was reaching for the door latch when the big man turned and faced her.

For a full fifteen or twenty seconds, Cat had a clear and unfettered view of his face, and in those seconds, the world fell out from under her.

She didn't know that she started moaning, or that she'd broken out in a cold sweat. All she knew was that she was no longer in her car in a San Antonio parking lot but back in her childhood home, trying to run from the intruder who'd come out of their bathroom.

She was screaming for her father when the intruder's arm slid around her chest and lifted her off her feet. She saw the strange geometric designs on his arm, then on the side of his face, as the cold slash of steel from his knife suddenly slid against her throat. The coppery scent of her own blood was thick in her nose as he dropped her to the floor, leaving her to watch as he slammed the same knife into her father over and over again. She tried to scream, but the sounds wouldn't come. The last things she saw before everything went black were the look of sorrow on her father's face and the demon who'd killed them running out the front door.

Suddenly someone was honking at Cat to move on. She came to with a gasp, much as she had in the emergency room when they'd finally closed the gash in her throat and given her back her life. Her gaze was frantic as she searched the parking lot for the two men, but they were nowhere in sight. She glanced at the clock on the dash and realized she'd been sitting there for at least ten minutes. Ten long minutes in which she'd given Presley a second chance to escape.

"Oh God, oh God, oh God."

The car behind her honked again. Too rattled to think what to do first, she finally took her foot of the brake and pulled out of the lane of traffic, parked, got out and threw up—over and over, until there was nothing left in her stomach to come up. At the point of hysteria, she fell to her knees.

"Hey, lady, are you all right?"

The stranger's voice was startling. Cat's hand went to her belt, but the gun was in the car. It took her a few moments to realize it was neither Mark nor the demon who was talking to her.

"Yes…yes…I'm fine," she finally answered, then got back in the car and locked the doors.

She was shaking so hard she had to hold onto the steering wheel to steady herself. She could feel the cold plastic against the palms of her hands and was cognizant of the way her fingers curled as she struggled to hang on. Even then, with a street light in her face and the scent of cooking burgers up her nose, she felt as if she were coming undone.

She rocked where she sat in an odd, repetitive motion, trying to think what to do next. She could see that the blip on the screen was once again, moving, but she couldn't quit shaking enough to drive. If she didn't pull herself together, she was going to lose the man who'd killed Mimi, as well as the man who'd ended her father's life.

Wilson. She needed to call Wilson.

She reached for her phone, but dropped it twice before getting the call to go through.

Wilson was less than half an hour from San Antonio when his cell phone began to ring. He glanced at caller ID. Cat. Since they'd just talked a short while ago, he was guessing that something was going down. He answered quickly.

"Hello, honey. What's—"

She was mumbling and groaning and basically making no sense. The sounds scared him to death.

"What the hell's wrong? Are you all right?"

"He was here! He was here, and I couldn't—it was too fast and I—ah, Jesus, Wilson…Jesus…"

Wilson felt sick to his stomach. He'd never heard her in this kind of shape. She sounded like she was having a breakdown.

"Catherine…take a deep breath and then talk to me. You're not making any sense. Did you find Presley?"

"Yes…but he wasn't… I let him…not sure how to—"

"Are you in your car?"

"Yes, but I—"

"Are you driving? Catherine…are you driving?"

"No…no, in the parking lot."

"What parking lot?"

"They were under the security light, and then he turned around and—"

"Who turned? Was it Presley? Did he see you? Did he hurt you?"

"No. No. He didn't see me. He didn't hurt me. It was the other man…the one who killed Daddy."

Wilson was so shocked by what she'd just said that he swerved and almost ran off the road.

"What the hell are you saying? I thought you were after Presley?"

She started to cry—quiet, almost silent sobs that tore straight through him.

"I am…was…didn't expect to see—"

She hiccupped on a sob.

Wilson cursed.

"Don't move. Tell me exactly where you are, and I'll come and get you. I can't be more than half an hour from where—"

Cat blinked as reality began to surface.

Half an hour?

She'd already wasted time having this…this…fit. She didn't have the luxury of waiting. Waiting another half hour on top of the time she'd already lost could mean losing Presley altogether. She took a deep breath, making herself focus when she wanted to crawl into some dark corner and never come out.

"No. No. It might be too late," she mumbled, and then grabbed a handful of tissues from a box on the floor of her car and blew her nose.

"But you…"

Cat shuddered, then dug the heels of her hands against her eyes.

"I'm okay…or at least I will be," she said. "I'm pulling out of the parking lot now. They're still heading south on I-35. Unless they pull off the road somewhere I don't know about, they appear to be heading to Laredo."

"Cat, please, wait for me."

"I can't. I'll be all right. It was just the shock that rattled me."

"Look! If you're right, then you're no longer following one killer, you're following two. You're going to fool around and get yourself killed. Please don't go."

"Just keep driving. If things change, I'll let you know."

"Don't hang up, Catherine. God damn it, don't hang up!"

The line went dead in his ear.

"Christ Almighty," he muttered, and grabbed his cell phone.

He didn't know what was going to happen, but he wasn't letting her call the shots any longer. He dialed the number Joe Flannery had given him.

"Homicide," a woman answered.

"I need to talk to Detective Flannery. Tell him it's Wilson McKay."

"I'm sorry, but Detective Flannery doesn't come on duty until—"

"Find him!" Wilson said. "Tell him it's about Marsha Benton's murder."

"Please hold," the woman said.

Wilson saw the lights of San Antonio in the distance. If only Cat had waited. He was trying not to panic when Flannery came on the line.

"This is Flannery."

"Sorry to be calling at this time of the morning, but we've got a situation," Wilson said.

"I'm already dealing with a situation," Deaver said. "I'm at Dallas Memorial trying to figure out what caused the fire that—"

"It was Presley," Wilson said.

Flannery almost dropped the phone.

"What the hell do you mean, it was Presley? Whatever you think you're about to tell me, just stop it right there. As best we can tell, Mark Presley is dead, along with at least a half-dozen other patients."

"No. He's not dead. He's the one who caused the fire," Wilson said. "At least, we think he did."

Flannery's stomach rolled.

"Talk to me, and it better make sense," he said.

"Here's what I know. Catherine Dupree suspected Presley was faking his condition. She had someone bug some of his things. She had the tracking program on a laptop. She said that within an hour of the explosion at Dallas Memorial, there was movement at his office. She's been following him south on I-35 ever since midnight. I just talked to her again. They're both south of San Antonio. She thinks he's heading for the border, or maybe the international airport in Laredo. I begged her to wait for me to catch up, but she wouldn't. I don't know how to make you believe me, but I'm telling you, this is on the up and up."

"Jesus Christ," Flannery muttered. "Do you know how far-fetched all this sounds?"

"Hell yes. That's why she didn't call you before she left Dallas. But she was right about Marsha Benton, wasn't she? She found her body when no one else would believe that Benton was even dead. She said that Benton was pregnant with Presley's baby. That's already been proved, too, right? So why are you hedging now?"

Flannery turned around, staring at the black smoke and flames still coming from parts of the hospital, then dropped his head and scrubbed a hand across his face. It was too early in the morning and too damned cold for all this crap.

"Okay. Say I believe you. Say I notify the Texas Highway Patrol. Say I give them a description and tag number for Dupree's vehicle."

"Do it," Wilson begged. "Tell them to assist her in following and catching Presley."

"What proof do we have that it's Presley? What if it's someone else entirely who's got the stuff?"

"Well, hell," Wilson muttered. "Then you've still

caught a thief, haven't you, because the bugs she's tracking were planted at Presley's private office. So it's either Presley on the run or a thief who's stolen his clothes and money."

"You better be right," Flannery said.

"Take down my cell phone number. Let me know if there's a problem."

"I'll see what I can do," Flannery said, wrote down the number, then disconnected.

Wilson gritted his teeth and pushed the accelerator all the way to the floor. He was doing ninety when he hit the city limits of San Antonio. The lights on the streets were little more than a blur, as were the head and tail lights of the cars he continued to pass.

Where was a cop when you needed one?

Before he knew it, the lights of the city were fading in the distance behind him. He picked up the phone and dialed Cat's number.

The ringing phone was startling. Cat had been so focused on making up for lost time that she jumped before she realized what she was hearing, then reached for it quickly, unwilling to pull over to talk.

"Hello?"

"It's me," Wilson said. "I just talked to Flannery. He's going to notify the highway patrol. If they try to stop you, let them. They're going to help."

Frustration shattered her concentration.

"Damn it, Wilson. I don't have time to stop and chit chat with them. Presley and his hired gun are less than an hour from the border and even closer to the Laredo airport. For all I know, he's got a plane waiting."

"Just do what I say…please," Wilson said. "And, Cat…don't disconnect this call, okay? If something starts to go down or they change direction, you can tell me where you are and what's happening, so I don't lose you."

Cat cursed beneath her breath before finally agreeing.

"All right, but I can't talk to you and drive. I'm going too fast."

"All I'm asking is that you don't hang up."

"I won't," Cat said. "I'm laying it down now."

Cat's voice was gone, but he could still hear the sound of her car engine and the occasional honk of a car horn. It wasn't the best situation, but it made him feel better, knowing they had a connection now, no matter how tenuous.

Mark Presley was sitting in the back seat of Tutuola's big Lincoln, congratulating himself for co-ordinating the rest of his escape with such ease. He had to admit that Tutuola was not only huge but intimidating. The tattoos had been distracting in their own right until Tutuola had smiled. The sight of those razor-sharp teeth was daunting. Was this really a man, or an animal? Either way, as long as he was on Presley's side, it didn't matter.

Tutuola had read Mark Presley in one glance. He didn't know what the man had done, but it was obvious he believed he had nothing to lose. The wild, almost vacant, look in his eyes had given Solomon a slight pause for concern, especially after Presley had refused to sit in the front seat with him.

Despite the fact that Solomon was armed, he couldn't help but think how easy it would be for the man behind him to go into some kind of fit and put a bullet through the back of his head. He had to be careful and not set the fool off until he'd gotten his money. After that, he didn't care what happened to him. He could shoot himself, for all he cared.

On the heels of that thought, Presley leaned forward and tapped Tutuola on the back of the shoulder. Solomon's heart skipped a beat. Was that a gun?

"How long to Laredo?" Presley asked.

Tutuola let out a slow, easy breath. "About a half hour," he said.

"All right," Mark said, and leaned back in the seat.

Tutuola eyed him nervously, then turned his attention back to the road. He couldn't help but notice that the man kept turning around and looking out the back window. Who was after him and—not that it mattered—but what the hell had he done?

* * *

It was daybreak.

The sky was just visible, and from the looks of it, it was going to be another dismal day. Although it wasn't nearly as cold here in Laredo as it had been in Dallas, it was still winter. The digital clock on one of the banks was registering seven o'clock in the morning and thirty-six degrees. It would, most likely be in the fifties before the day was over, but right now, Mark was cold. He stared at the back of Solomon Tutuola's head, as he'd done ever since they'd left San Antonio. As he thought back, he didn't know what had possessed him to hire someone like this. It would have been easier to hire some cab driver out of San Antonio to drive him to Laredo. He could have walked across the border into Nuevo Laredo and hired another car to take him wherever he wanted. Now he was stuck with a man he was afraid to turn his back on. He blamed it all on the panic. There had been a time in his life when he wouldn't have made mistakes like this. He used to be able to read people like a map. But that was before he'd made such a monumental mistake with Marsha Benton. He didn't know how he could have been so wrong, but he'd been wrong with a capital W and was paying for it now.

While Presley was ruminating about the error of his ways, his driver was contemplating a fifty-thousand dollar paycheck. They'd been in Laredo for all of fifteen minutes. The fuel gauge was rocking on empty—as empty as Tutuola's belly. He glanced up in the rearview mirror and caught Presley looking at him. It was instinct that made him scowl, but it was the wild-eyed look in Presley's eyes that cautioned him to keep his mouth shut.

"What's that dinging sound?" Presley asked.

"Need to fill up with gas," Tutuola said.

"Well…do it, for God's sake. I don't have time to run out of gas in the middle of the street."

Solomon's lips curled in what was supposed to pass for a grin, but he was pissed. Usually, he was the one giving orders.

He aimed for the nearest gas station and pulled up to the pumps.

Presley threw a handful of twenties over the seat. "Pay in cash."

Solomon pocketed the money and got out, went inside to pay then quickly returned. He started pumping and rolled his head from one side to the other, grunting softly as his neck popped both times. The morning air was chilly, but it felt good to stretch his legs.

Within minutes, the pump kicked off. He replaced the nozzle and then the gas cap, eyed the man in the back seat through the window, making sure he wasn't going to do something stupid, like try to steal his car, and then headed for the station to get some food.

He paid for two cups of coffee and a half-dozen sweet rolls from the deli inside. He was walking back to the car when he saw a tall, dark-haired woman get out of an SUV and start toward his car.

Her gaze was fixed on the man in the back seat, but when he saw the gun in her hand, he tossed the coffee and rolls and began to run.

Cat saw the killer putting fuel in his car. The sight rattled her so much that she drove right past before she thought to hit the brakes. Now she was forced to backtrack again as she took the next turn and drove back the way she'd just come. At that point, it occurred to her to tell Wilson.

"Wilson!"

He was so startled to hear Cat's voice that he jumped.

"What?"

"I'm in Laredo, and so are they. They've stopped at a station called Come and Get It. The big man's getting gas. Presley is in the back seat. I'm going after him now."

Wilson stifled a groan. Damn it all to hell, he was still at least fifteen minutes behind her.

"I don't suppose asking you to wait is going to work," he said.

"No."

"Then for the love of God, be careful. I'm calling the Laredo police for backup."

"Tell them to hurry," she said. "I've arrived at the station, and I'm going to get out now."

She laid down the phone without giving him time to argue any more and pulled up to the pumps. She parked behind the car she'd been following and slammed the gearshift into park. She got out with the gun in one hand and her handcuffs tucked loosely in the waistband of her pants. Even though it was cold, she left her coat in the SUV, unwilling to be hampered by the weight. When she saw the back of Mark Presley's head, she felt a huge sense of relief. She'd lost him once, but she wouldn't let it happen again.

"Come to Mama, you son-of-a-bitch," she muttered, and then grabbed the handle of the back door and yanked it open.

To say Presley was shocked would have been putting it mildly, but it was the gun in his face that left him speechless.

"Get out," Cat said, as she pushed the gun barrel into his left ear. "Don't make a scene, or it will be my pleasure to put a bullet right through that evil brain of yours."

"Jesus, God," Presley muttered, while looking wildly toward the station for Tutuola.

"Now!" Cat said, and shoved the barrel hard enough into his ear that she made it pop.

"No! Wait!" Presley begged. "I'm getting out. I'm getting out. Just don't pull the trigger."

Cat glanced around once, and as she did, saw the driver coming out of the station at the same time he saw her. She saw him toss his purchases and start running. In a panic, she grabbed Presley by the wrist and popped one handcuff around it, then pulled.

"Get out! Get out, or I swear to God I'll break it off!" she screamed.

Presley was moving as fast as he could, and still her strength was greater. She pulled so hard he came stumbling out and went down. She was on his back and grabbing his other wrist when she went flying through the air.

She hit feet first, then stumbled backward and sat down hard as her gun went sliding across the concrete. Ignoring the pain, she jumped to her feet, scrambling for the gun as she saw the tattooed man shove Presley back into the car and take off.

"No!" she screamed, and fired two shots at the car as it sped away.

The sound of gunfire sent everyone around into hiding as she ran for her car. Seconds later, she was right behind them, speeding through the streets.

"They made me!" she yelled, knowing that Wilson was undoubtedly still listening. "I'm right behind them. I think we're heading to the border."

The big Lincoln moved faster than she would have imagined, and since Laredo was unfamiliar to her, and despite the bug, she quickly lost them in a maze of side streets. She had to find out where the border crossing was and intercept them, so she rolled down a window as she came to a stop sign. There was a homeless man standing on the corner with a rolled up newspaper under his arm. She leaned out, waved a twenty at him and yelled, "Where's the border crossing?"

He grabbed the twenty and pointed.

She sped away with her heart in her throat as the sound of police sirens rose in the distance behind her.

"You fucking get me across the border or you don't get a dime!" Presley yelled.

Tutuola didn't answer. He was too busy taking the back streets to make sure the cops didn't follow. It was going to be hard enough to get this fool and his gun past the guards.

"When we get there, you fucking keep your mouth closed or I'll throw you out on your ass and leave you on the American side for that bitch to pick up," Tutuola said.

It was the calm, unemotional tone of his voice that shut Presley down.

"Who is she?" Tutuola asked.

"Hell if I know," Presley said. "She just keeps dogging my steps. She's into my business, and I don't know why."

Tutuola glanced up into the rearview mirror, meeting Presley's gaze.

"I think you lie," he said softly, then took the next right and drove south.

* * *

They were at the crossing talking to the guards when Cat finally drove up. She counted twelve cars in front of her and jumped out on the run. Just as she passed the first car, Presley's car moved forward.

Her heart sank. They were across the border.

She ran back to her car and got in. Now she needed to hide the gun and taser and calm herself down, or she would never be allowed to follow.

She lifted the lid of the console between the bucket seats, yanked out the CDs, pushed on the bottom until it gave and popped up, then dropped both weapons into a little compartment she'd had made after she bought the car.

Her hands were shaking when she put the CDs back into place, then shut the lid.

The cars moved up.

She moved with them.

She was almost at the gate when she remembered the program was still running on the laptop. She shut it down as fast as she could with one hand and then closed it. It wasn't against the law to take a laptop into Mexico, but she didn't want to have to try to explain why she was using it as a tracking device.

By the time she got to the guards, she was chewing gum like she'd been working on it all night, had a Willie Nelson CD blasting in the stereo, her hair was hanging wild and loose around her face and neck, and she'd unbuttoned the three top buttons on her shirt, leaving very little of her shapely bust to the imagination.

"Good morning, *señorita*," the first guard said.

"Hi, ya'll," she said softly, and then blessed him with a smile that changed her from pretty to stunning.

The second guard saw her, puffed up like a penguin and joined the first one at her window.

"Why are you entering our fair city?" the first guard asked.

"I'm meeting my boyfriend for a little…party," she said, and then tossed her head, well aware that it gave her a just-been-fucked look.

Both guards reacted just the way she'd hoped. They were so busy trying to look down her shirt that they waved her on before they thought.

She wiggled her fingers at them in a silly, sexy wave of goodbye, then, just for good measure, blew them a kiss.

The moment she was past, she booted up the laptop and checked the map. The blip was still moving, but in a new direction. All she could do was follow.

Twenty-One

Wilson was cursing the police in several languages by the time he reached Laredo. Despite his story and the back-up from Detective Flannery, not one Texas highway patrolman had been able to find Catherine Dupree or her car. Unfortunately, that wasn't the case for him. He was stopped for speeding about ten miles outside Laredo. By the time he got through explaining and the patrolman had talked to Joe Flannery, fifteen minutes had gone by. He was sick to his stomach with worry and fear when the patrolman finally let him go.

"Drive safe now, ya' hear?" the patrolman said, as he waved Wilson on.

Wilson glared at him without speaking and took off in a flurry of flying gravel and squealing tires. He laid down a trail of rubber on the highway for a good thirty feet before the car quit fish-tailing, and he didn't look back. He figured the cop was pissed, but it couldn't be helped. He'd promised Cat that he wouldn't lose her, and now that he knew she was physically in pursuit, it was not the time to break his word.

He'd no more than gotten back on I-35 when he heard Cat's voice over his phone, only she wasn't talking to him. From what he could tell, she was blowing smoke up some border guard's ass. A short while later he heard her muttering to herself, and knew that she'd crossed the border. He could do nothing but follow, and pray that she had the good sense to talk to him and lead him in the right direction.

Mark was rattled as hell and pissed about the handcuff on his wrist. No matter how hard he tried, he couldn't get it off. He was going to have to wait until they were at the hacienda to do something about it. Every time he banged it against something, the jingle and clank reminded him of how close he'd come to failure.

And that woman… Damn, but she was a bulldog. She'd taken a bite of his ass and wouldn't let go. Next time they came face to face—and he knew there would be a next time—he was going to find out who the hell she was, and then he was going to kill her.

He fidgeted angrily with the loose handcuff, then

glanced out the window and groaned in disgust as a woman standing in the alley between two houses efficiently wrung the neck of a rooster. Blood spurted all over her legs and the side of the building as the bird was parted from his head. Mark watched the headless bird as it flopped about in the throes of death and tried not to think of his secretary's face as he'd tossed her over the rim of the ravine. By the time they'd passed the scene of the rooster's death, he was on to another subject.

"How much farther to the hacienda?" he asked.

Solomon Tutuola glanced up in the rearview mirror, then back to the road.

"Only a few minutes now," he said softly.

Mark nodded, then looked at the huge fists of his driver. He remembered how relieved he'd been when Tutuola had pulled the woman off him.

"Say...thanks for what you did back there in San Antonio."

"I didn't do it for you, *señor*."

Mark frowned. "If not me, then why?"

"For the money, of course," Solomon answered, and stepped on the gas.

Now that Presley had brought it up, Solomon had to admit he was anxious to be done with this man and the task that he'd agreed to perform.

Mark's eyes narrowed angrily; then he shrugged it off. At least the bastard was honest. If it had been him, he might have felt the same.

He took a deep breath, then exhaled slowly, allowing himself a few moments to shut his eyes. He was exhausted, but no sooner had he closed his eyes than he had an epiphany. Just because he was across the border, that didn't mean he was safe. There was no reason to assume the woman wouldn't continue to follow them. What puzzled him most was how she managed to keep finding him. Hell, even *he* hadn't known for sure where he was going when he'd first left Dallas, yet she must have been right behind him all the way, waiting for the best time to strike.

The gray sky continued to lighten as the morning grew older, but Mark's view of it was somewhat distorted by the billowing dust stirred up by their car.

Just when he thought they would never arrive, the driver began slowing down. Mark shifted slightly in the seat so he could see around Tutuola's wide shoulders and realized they were there.

The hacienda was huge and sprawling and sorely in need of restoration. Some of the red Spanish tiles on the roof were broken; a few others had fallen off. The windows were shuttered, but he could tell by the clutter that from time to time squatters had been using it for shelter. He saw empty soda cans, scraps of packaging from food and crushed boxes, and wrinkled his nose, hoping the inside wasn't worse. Tumbleweeds had blown into the yard before coming to rest against a cactus. Another had come to rest at the base of a Joshua tree.

Mark kept reminding himself that it didn't matter what it looked like inside. All he needed was a place to hide until he had time to get a new set of identification papers. Once that was done, he would be on the first plane out of here and on his way to the Cayman Islands.

"Once I'm inside, pull around to the back so no one can see your car," Mark said.

Tutuola shook his head. "I have no plans to stay beyond the time it takes you to pay me."

Presley frowned. "But you can't just—"

"You hired me to drive you, not baby-sit you," Tutuola said. "If I stay, the price goes up."

Mark cursed beneath his breath. Tutuola had him in a bind, and he knew it. If he sent him on his way, he would have no way of getting around to procure papers, and there was the problem of no power and no food inside the house. This was definitely not one of the best laid plans he'd ever made. Still, he was, for the moment, out of reach of the Texas authorities, which had been the first course of business.

"Drive around back and park the damned car!" Mark said sharply.

Solomon shrugged. If the man pissed him off, he could always break his stupid neck and leave him for the vultures to devour. He glanced up in the rearview mirror without revealing his emotions, then back to the driveway as he began to circle the house. He would wait a bit to see which way the wind blew, and if he didn't like the weather, he would be gone.

Cat was about five miles behind the two men when the blip on her screen finally stopped moving. Her heart was beating rapidly, and although it was still a cool morning, there was a sheen of nervous perspiration on her skin.

She pulled over to the side of the road and then picked up the cell phone.

"Wilson?"

He breathed a quick sigh of relief. He'd never been so glad to hear someone say his name.

"I'm here."

"How far are you from the border?" she asked.

"I'm there, but waiting in a line about fifteen cars long."

"The men have stopped. I'm about five miles from their location and may have to go in on foot to keep the element of surprise."

"Tell me how to get where you are," Wilson said.

Cat rattled off the directions.

"Are you all right?" he asked.

Cat sighed. She knew what he was asking. Had she pulled herself together from the breakdown she'd so obviously had in San Antonio?

"Yes."

"Will you wait for me now?"

"Yes."

Wilson was so startled by her sudden acquiescence that he stuttered on the continuation of what was to have been further argument.

"Thank God," he said softly. "It won't take me much longer to get through the gate. I should be there soon. If something changes, please let me know."

"I will."

Wilson started to lay the phone back down, then changed his mind.

"Catherine?"

"What?"

He heard the tremble in her voice and knew that she was still rattled by the sight of her father's killer.

"Don't do anything stupid."

He heard a quick intake of breath and then a brief laugh.

The first time he'd told her that, she'd given him hell. This time she remembered and had gotten the joke.

He laid the phone back down in the seat and within ten minutes was at the front of the line. His handgun was under the truck bed, in the wheel well above the spare tire. The guards would have to lie down and remove the spare to find the gun. He was taking a chance that wouldn't happen.

He rolled down his window and nodded at the first guard who approached him.

"Morning," he said, and then rolled his head and popped the knuckles on both hands as the guard walked up beside him, running a mirror attached to a long rod all around the truck, giving him a fairly good view of the underside.

A second guard approached. "Why are you coming into Nuevo Laredo?" he asked.

Wilson grinned what he hoped was a fairly lustful grin.

"I'm meeting my girlfriend. We're gonna party a little down here. Maybe you saw her? Her hair is long and black and curls down around her back. Her eyes are so blue they put the sky to shame and her body…lord, but she's built. Legs all the way up to here. She drives a dark blue SUV."

The description sent a jolt of recognition through both of the guards. They started talking to each other in Spanish, gesticulating with their hands as they measured off her shape and the size of her breasts.

Wilson felt like punching them both in the face, but he'd started the story. It was his fault that they were playing into it.

"Ah…sounds like you've already met her," Wilson said, and pretended to frown. "You can look…but you don't touch," he added.

Both guards grinned, then waved him on. One of them called out to have a good day.

Wilson waved and grinned like a fool, but the moment he was on the Mexican side of the border, he drove through town as fast as he dared, following the directions Cat had given him earlier.

He was topping a hill with a flurry of dust behind him when he saw her SUV parked off to the side at the bottom. The relief that went through him was like nothing he'd ever known. He thanked God and every angel that had kept her in one piece as he pulled up behind her and stopped. He was out of the truck and on his way to her when he saw the door open.

As she got out, he saw that her jaw was set and her eyes were glittering, although her expression was blank.

He eyed her briefly, and while the urge to hug her was strong, he knew better than to break her concentration.

"I guess you know you've aged me a good ten years," he grumbled as he got up to her.

Cat allowed herself the luxury of giving him the once-over.

He was wearing what appeared to be a three-day growth of dark whiskers, a pair of dusty boots and a pair of well-fitting jeans. Like her, he'd abandoned his heavy winter coat for a jacket. His hair was growing out. There were changes since she'd seen him last, but nothing that mattered. He was still wearing that gold loop earring and a "don't piss me off" look in his eyes.

"You need to know what we're up against," she said.

"Talk to me," Wilson said.

"Presley is walking and talking just fine. I almost had him back in San Antonio. Got one handcuff on him before the devil pulled me free."

"The devil…you mean the man you believe is the one who attacked you and your father?"

"Oh…it's him," Cat said. A muscle was jerking at the side of her mouth, but her voice was clear and calm. "You have no idea how long I've been looking for him. I got into this business because of him. Ever since I saw him with Presley in San Antonio, I've been trying to figure out why God is playing this joke on me. I promised myself that I would not let Presley get away with what he did, just like I promised my daddy the last time I visited his grave that I would find the man who killed him and bring him to justice. But to have them somehow wind up together, with me walking on their heels, is a joke. I don't know what to do first. Who to focus on. How to begin."

"We'll take it one step at a time," Wilson said.

"I can't let them get away."

"So…let's go catch some bad guys," Wilson muttered. "Just wait a sec. I need to get some stuff."

Cat watched as he lay down on his back, then scooted underneath his truck. When he emerged, he was carrying a gun. He got a couple of boxes of ammunition from behind the seat, then put it all in the seat of Cat's SUV.

"Get in," he said. "I'll drive. You navigate."

She started to argue, then wisely shut her mouth. It was past time to admit that this was one instance where she needed all the help she could get.

They got in. Cat held the laptop as Wilson put the car in gear. Within five minutes, they were at their destination, hidden only by a small stand of mesquite and a shallow indentation in the lay of the land.

Cat frowned. "I don't see a car."

"It's probably around back," Wilson said.

"Drive all the way up to the front of the house like we own the place," Cat said.

Wilson arched an eyebrow. "Don't believe in sneaking up on them, huh?"

She waved a hand toward the property. "Look at this place. It's flat as my Sunday pancakes, and there's nothing to hide behind except my gun."

Wilson grinned. "So you're admitting your cooking leaves something to be desired?"

"I admit to nothing, especially my cooking skills. Let's get this over with, okay?"

"We could call for the Mexican police," he suggested.

She rolled her eyes. "You've got to be kidding."

He agreed with her wisdom, then curled his fingers a little tighter around the steering wheel.

"Okay, here goes nothing," he said. "Hang on, and if they start shooting, get down."

Cat nodded, then pulled out her gun as Wilson hit the gas and headed for the hacienda.

The interior of the hacienda had been destroyed. The once-beautiful adobe walls were marked with all sorts of graffiti, and the storage areas were full of trash. Someone had even set up what appeared to have been a mobile meth lab in the room that had once been a library. There were burn marks on the floor where cooking fires had been started, and, to Mark's dismay, what smelled like some kind of fuel oil in a barrel in the middle of the room. He kicked it and heard liquid slosh, then frowned.

He continued through the rooms and was trying to find a place clean enough in which to sleep when he heard Tutuola yell. He ran out into the hallway just in time to see the big man disappear around a corner.

"What's happening?" he called out, and when he got no answer, ran toward the front of the house.

As he entered the living room, he saw Solomon crouched behind some drapes, peering out a window.

"What the hell are you—"

Solomon gestured wildly for Mark to shut up, then pointed.

Presley saw a dusty, dark blue SUV slide to a stop. It was when he saw the woman getting out from the passenger side that he started to curse.

"It's her! It's that fucking woman! How in hell does she keep doing this?"

"They're coming in! Get down," Solomon ordered, and pulled a 9 mm handgun from inside his jacket and aimed it toward the door.

Before Mark could move, the front doorknob was

turning. Suddenly the door was pushed inward, hitting the wall with a solid thud.

Solomon aimed toward the opening, expecting one or both of the intruders to come running in. Instead, from the corner of his eye, he saw one of them running toward the back of the house. It distracted him enough that when the man came through the front door in a rolling dive, shooting as he went, he was forced to take evasive action.

Standing in plain sight with no cover behind which to hide, Solomon went into a sudden crouch just as the first shot splintered the window frame beside his head. He crawled on his hands and knees behind the sofa, then rose up and emptied a clip into the room, aiming in every direction.

Wilson was face down on the floor without cover, cursing with every breath. When it dawned on him that the man's gun was empty, he rolled behind a pile of boxes and began to fire at the old sofa, well aware that every shot was going through and into the floor or the wall behind it. If the bastard was still there, he was dead.

When the shots began, Presley was on the floor, crawling toward the hall on his belly. When he made it all the way out of the room without being shot, he headed for the back of the house.

The car keys were still in the car, along with his other belongings. It didn't bother him to leave

Tutuola alone to his own defenses. After all, it wasn't as if *he* had any means of protection. It was every man for himself.

Cat was crouched next to an outer door at the back of the house when the gunfire began. At that point her heart sank. If anything happened to Wilson McKay, she would never forgive herself. Before she could react, she heard running footsteps coming toward the door and tensed.

Just as she heard the hinges beginning to squeak, there was another round of gunfire. Then something exploded inside the house, followed by an orange ball of flame. She thought of Wilson and said a quick prayer.

It was all the time she had as the door swung inward. Smoke billowed out. Presley emerged on the run without looking behind him.

Cat tackled him from the back, hitting him waist high and sending him to the flagstones with a deadening jolt.

He tried to scream, but there was no breath left in his body, and the pain in his back was so sharp, he thought he'd been cut in half. He'd landed elbows down as his chin cracked on the flagstones. Blood began oozing from the various points of contact. While he was still trying to catch his breath, someone yanked on his hands and pulled them behind his back. He heard a distinct click, and when he tried to get up, realized he'd finally been hand-cuffed.

As he was rolled from his belly to his back, he had a skewed view of the smoke billowing from the house. Then he saw her.

When he opened his mouth to beg, she stabbed a boot against his neck and pushed just hard enough for him to gag.

"Don't talk to me, you sorry bastard. You don't have anything to say that I want to hear."

To his dismay, she dragged him up from the ground as if he weighed nothing and began hauling him around the house. When she got to the car, she opened the back hatch and pointed.

"Get in," she said.

He hesitated, which was a shame, because Cat's patience was gone. Presley never saw it coming. One minute he was upright and then he was not. She cold-cocked him with her fist and shoved him in the back of the SUV. He never knew when she grabbed a length of rope and tied his feet, then bent his knees until she had tied his bound feet to the handcuffs on his hands,

Cat was shaking as she turned toward the house. Smoke was coming out from under the eaves of the roof as well as from the front door. She didn't know what had happened, but she knew Wilson was still inside. Sudden fear that she would lose him, too, sent her running toward the house.

She reloaded as she ran and met Wilson coming out. He staggered straight into her arms, and when he realized who he was holding, began shaking with relief.

"Get in the car!" he shouted. "We've got to get out of here."

But Cat didn't move. She kept looking over his shoulder into the smoke.

"The other one! Where is he?"

"I don't know," he said. "Maybe dead in the fire. We were shooting the hell out of the place, and when we got into the second room, everything went up. I don't know what was in that barrel, but when a bullet hit it, it blew."

He grabbed Cat by the arm and started dragging her toward the car.

"Wait!" she begged, and pulled free from his grasp, only to have him catch her again before she could get away. "I can't let him go. I have to know. Don't you understand? Damn it, Wilson, I have to know for sure that he's dead."

"Like hell," he muttered, then grabbed Cat off her feet, threw her over his shoulder and started to run.

He threw her into the passenger seat, then slammed the door in her face. She was screaming his name and arguing with him as he slid behind the wheel. She reached for the door latch as Wilson started the car. Before she could open the door, he grabbed her by the arm and slammed the SUV into reverse. She was yelling and screaming as he began backing out of the yard. They were halfway down the drive when the second explosion occurred, shattering what was left of the sprawling hacienda and sending a shower of burning refuse up into the air.

"Get down!" Wilson yelled, and swerved as a ball of fire dropped right beside the front wheel of her car.

They were already past it before Cat realized it was what was left of a burning sofa. She was shaking so hard that she couldn't catch her breath. The last glimpse she had of the inferno was in the side-view mirror on the outside of the car.

She tried to focus. She needed to give Wilson what for because he'd taken away her choices, but for the life of her, she couldn't find the words to berate him when she knew that he'd just saved their lives.

There was nothing left to do now but get Mark Presley into the hands of the Texas law. She knew what they did to killers in her state, and she intended to watch every last second of his life, right up to the moment when they executed his ass.

When they finally returned to the place where Wilson had left his own truck, he pulled the SUV over and stopped.

"Are you all right?" he asked, as he ran his fingers all over her body, checking her arms and torso for signs of gunshot wounds.

"Yes. Presley wasn't armed."

Wilson's eyes widened. Suddenly he turned around and looked over the seats to the back. He could just see the top of a man's shoulder.

"You got him?"

Cat nodded.

"Way to go!" he said, and reached for her, but he felt her tense and stopped.

"You know I couldn't let you go back in that house," he said after a long moment.

"I needed to know he was dead."

"Yeah, well, I needed to know you weren't."

She wouldn't be swayed, and he couldn't change what he'd done. Finally he shook his head.

"I'm beginning to understand how you tick," he muttered, and then reached for her phone. "In the meantime, we need to call Detective Flannery."

"Why?"

"Because I don't think we're going to be able to get this sorry bastard across the border without some help. I don't want to take the chance of having the Mexican police take him away from us, do you?"

"Make the call."

The sandwich shop where Joe Flannery was having lunch was at maximum capacity. All the booths and tables were packed, as were the six stools at the counter. It was standing room only as customers waited in line to pick up their to-go orders. The sounds of so many people talking all at once was somewhat muted by the piped-in music, but the din inside was just below a dull roar, making it impossible to understand the person seated next to you. This was definitely not the place for a social lunch.

There were two other detectives at the table with him. One had gotten up to refill his drink at the self-help bar, while the other was smearing mustard on the top of his roast beef sandwich. Flannery was eyeing his buddy's roast beef and wishing he'd chosen the same instead of the pastrami on rye. For some reason, it just didn't suit his taste buds today. Still, he'd been raised by one of those "clean your plate" mothers, and habit ran deep. So he was chewing and swallowing his food without thought.

Then his cell phone rang. He glanced at the caller ID and frowned. "Flannery."

"Detective…this is Wilson McKay. Catherine Dupree and I have a situation we need help with."

Flannery frowned, not bothering to hide the frustration he was feeling. "What now?"

"Cat caught Mark Presley."

The entire Dallas Police Department—Joe Flannery included—had still been operating on the theory that Mark Presley was dead, so when Flannery heard that, he almost dropped his phone.

"The hell you say. Are you sure?"

"Yeah. I'm looking at his sorry-ass self right now,

tied up like a pig for roasting in the back seat of her car. Trouble is, we're in Mexico and not so sure we can get him across the border without your help."

"Hang on," Flannery said, and dropped his sandwich on the table while motioning for the other two detectives to join him outside. They scrambled for last bites and one more swallow of their drinks as Flannery walked out ahead of them. Once he was out on the street, it was easier to hear.

"Sorry about that," he said. "Now…tell me again. You two crossed the border and—"

"No. Cat followed Presley and a hired gun across the border. I met up with her just outside Nuevo Laredo. She knew where they were hiding. We went in after them together. They started shooting. The place went up in flames."

"Hell of a lot of things catching fire around this Presley character," Flannery muttered.

"Yes, well, at any rate, Presley went one direction and his hired gun another. Cat caught Presley, and we think the hired gun burned with the house, although at this point, we can't be sure. However, it's Presley she was after, and she got him."

"And you say he's with you right now?"

"Yeah. Tied up and unconscious in the back of her SUV."

Flannery whistled softly beneath his breath. This changed everything. Once the hospital fire had been put out, the firemen had found what was left of a body in Presley's room. First assumptions had been that it was Presley, but if he was in Mexico, then who had died in his room? Now they had an unexplained death to lay at Presley's feet, as well as several patients who'd succumbed to smoke and flames.

"Exactly where did you cross the border?"

"Laredo. We're about fifteen miles outside of Nuevo Laredo now. We need to get Presley back across the border, but neither one of us has any authority here."

"You don't make this easy," Flannery muttered.

"On the contrary, Detective. Cat Dupree made this easy as hell for you. Presley is the one who's been leaving bodies in his wake. She's been doing clean-up for you all the way."

Flannery winced. The police department had been a little hard on Cat Dupree, and yet, despite her far-fetched story, it appeared that she'd been right.

"Yeah, yeah, I read you," he said. "Here's what I want you to do. Give me about fifteen minutes to make some calls, then head back to the border crossing. I'll have police on the US side waiting to take Presley into custody. Whatever the hangups might be with red tape, we'll handle."

"All right," Wilson said.

"When you get back to Dallas, I would appreciate it if you and Miss Dupree came in and gave us a full report."

Wilson glanced at Cat, who appeared to be operating on little else but sheer will and determination.

"After she gets some rest."

"Yeah, all right," Flannery said, and then added, "Hey...McKay."

"What?"

"Tell her she did a damn good job."

Wilson eyed the tic at the side of Cat's mouth and frowned. "I will."

"See you soon," Flannery said, and disconnected.

Wilson laid the phone back on the console. "Flannery said to tell you that you did a damn good job."

Cat shuddered. The adrenaline rush that had carried her from one end of the state to the other was crashing and taking her with it. She felt as if she could sleep for a week.

"I did it for Mimi," she said, then exhaled slowly. "What did Flannery say?" she asked.

"We get to the border. They'll take it from there."

"Fine," she said, as she glanced back at Presley, who was still unconscious. "I hate to think I would have to ride all the way back home with that piece of shit in the back of my car."

Wilson tilted her chin up just as he leaned toward her.

"Come here, Catherine. You might not need this, but I damn sure do."

He kissed her. Once because he just needed to feel

her breath against his face, then again because he'd been so afraid he wouldn't get there in time to find her alive.

"I'll have to drive my truck back to the border. Are you okay to drive on your own?"

Cat frowned. "Of course I'm all right. You can't believe I'd wimp out at this point?"

He grinned. "On the contrary, Miss Dupree. I don't think you know the meaning of the word, okay?"

Wilson kissed her once more for good luck, then got out of her car and headed for his own.

"I'll follow you," he called.

She watched, waiting until he was inside and turning around, then she drove north. She'd gone several miles and was just coming up on the outskirts of Nuevo Laredo when she saw what she could only call a parade of Mexican police cars awaiting them at the edge of town. She didn't stop, and they didn't try to stop her, but by the time she got to the border, it was evident that Flannery's phone calls had been fruitful. Not only were the Mexican police behind them, but others were awaiting them at the gates. Besides them, she saw officers from the Laredo Police Department, as well as a Texas Ranger who'd just pulled up on the U.S. side of the gates. Wilson parked beside her and was heading toward the lawmen as she walked to the back of her car and opened the hatch.

Presley was awake. "Get out!" she said sharply.

He moaned. "My head hurts, these cuffs are too tight, and my feet are still tied."

Cat grabbed him, cutting the rope as she pulled. Presley came halfway out, then tried to sit up, at which point he bumped his forehead on the hatch.

"Ooww. Damn it, woman. What are you trying to do? Kill me?"

It was a poor choice of words.

Cat leaned forward, grabbed him by the collar and whispered, "If that was an invitation, I would be happy to oblige."

Presley paled but went mute as she dragged him the rest of the way out. He started to complain when she took him by the back of his belt.

"Walk, damn it," Cat said. "Walk, or I'll end your misery right where you stand and let someone else worry about feeding your sorry ass to the worms."

Presley's belly rolled. This woman was scary— almost as scary as that crazy Tutuola.

"Answer me one thing," he said, as they walked toward the waiting officers.

"Like what?" Cat asked.

"Who are you?"

"Catherine Dupree."

"I never heard of you."

Her eyes narrowed as she yanked at his handcuffs.

"I would have thought you were a smart enough man to know your enemies."

Presley paused, then looked over his shoulder, staring at her in frustration.

"But how did you become my enemy? I would swear I've never met you."

"You lied to my friend, got her pregnant, fired her, then killed her and your child. You're lucky I wasn't alone today. If I had been, I would have shot you dead right there on the patio and left you to roast in that fire."

"Marsha Benson? This is all because of her?"

"Yeah, smart man. It's all because of her."

At that point she looked around for Wilson. When he motioned her over, she shoved Presley in the small of the back.

"Move," she said.

He did.

Epilogue

Wilson rolled over in the bed and became aware of the empty space within his arms. He felt for Cat, then pulled her close against his chest before settling back into a deep, dreamless sleep.

Cat sighed as she spooned against Wilson's warmth and strength, and then, once more, let herself relax.

For the time being, she'd quit fighting herself about Wilson. He'd gotten her through the last three days of coping with the police reports while living with the satisfaction that Mark Presley was no longer a free man. Despite her fears that he would find a way to get out of this, given his power and money, she'd been proven wrong.

She'd heard through the courthouse grapevine that Presley's lawyer was trying to make a deal that would keep his client off death row. Personally, Cat wanted to see him executed, but she knew it would be years before that ever came about. She was at the point of accepting that making a man like Mark Presley live out a long life behind bars just might be a worse punishment than a swift death.

At least he was in prison, which was the justice she'd wanted for Mimi all along.

From time to time, she couldn't help but think of the tattooed man who'd burned up in that fire. There was a part of her that wished she'd been given the chance to watch him die, just as she'd had to watch her father die. Obviously it wasn't meant to be.

She settled into the warmth of Wilson's chest and started to go back to sleep. There was plenty of time to call Art and let him know she was available again. For now, she felt as if she could sleep for a week.

Pete Yokum was fiddling with one of his laptops and realized it was the one that had the duplicate tracking program on it.

He had just finished booting it up when the screen suddenly came alive with a map of Northern Mexico and a slow-moving blip on a westward track.

He frowned, trying to figure out what was happening. He knew all about Cat's big capture. It had been in all the papers and all over the news for the past three days. He also knew that Presley was safely behind bars.

But that didn't explain the activity on the map.

He glanced at the clock. It was fifteen after three in the morning. Too early to call Cat. He figured she would have an explanation and decided to leave it until later. He would call her right before he went to bed for the day.

Having made up his mind, he got up and made himself a sandwich, then settled down to watch a rerun of an old John Wayne movie. The way he figured it, nobody beat The Duke when it came to a story with lots of action.

"I've got to go by my apartment," Wilson said, as he paused at the front door to kiss Cat goodbye. "There was a message from my receptionist, wanting to know why the hell I don't answer my phone anymore."

"Did you tell her it was because you were in bed with a witch."

He frowned.

"I only called you that once, and it was in self-defense."

Their sexual sparring was uncomfortable for Cat. It smacked of intimacy, of a relationship—which, as far as she was concerned, wasn't about to happen.

"I'll probably check in with Art myself," she said.

He swept her hair away from her face with both hands, then ran a thumb along the curve of her cheek.

"Ease back into it slowly. This took a lot out of you."

Every time Cat looked in the mirror, she knew the truth of his words.

"I'll call you," Wilson said.

She ignored the slight leap of her heartbeat.

"Leave a message if I'm not around."

Wilson frowned. She wasn't going to let him get under her skin. Damn it.

"Later," he said.

"Yeah," Cat said, and then locked the door after he left.

She was standing at the window, watching for him to emerge from the building and drive away, when her telephone rang. Reluctant to give up her spot, she let it ring a couple more times; then the answering machine came on. It wasn't until she heard Pete Yokum's voice that she ran to answer.

"Hello," she said breathlessly.

"Hello yourself," he said.

"You sound sleepy. I can't believe you're still up," Cat said.

Pete yawned. "I won't be long. Just had a quick question to ask you."

"Ask away," Cat said.

"You know that program on that computer I gave you…the tracking one?"

Cat frowned. "Yes. What about it?"

"Have you looked at it lately?"

Cat suddenly shivered, almost afraid to ask.

"No. Why?"

"Well, last night I was fooling with one of my laptops and forgot that I had a duplicate program on it."

"So?"

"So can you tell my why the tracking system would still be active? In Mexico?"

Cat felt as if all the air had been kicked out of her lungs.

She leaned against the wall and then slowly slid downward until she was sitting on the floor with her knees beneath her chin.

"What are you talking about?"

"You know…I bugged a lot of Presley's property. I just wondered what you might have left behind down in Mexico that would be on the move. Maybe someone found his clothes or is wearing a pair of his shoes, something like that."

Cat was starting to shake. She thought of all the stuff that was supposed to have burned up in the fire.

"You said Mexico?"

"Yep."

"Are you sure?"

Pete frowned. "Well hell, girl, of course I'm sure. I'm looking at the map right now. So is there something still down there that could account for this?"

"Wait a second while I go get my laptop," she said, and raced for her office.

She hadn't touched it since the day they'd come home. Now she was frantic to bring the program back up. It didn't take long for it to load, and when it did, she saw it, just like Pete claimed.

"Yes. I see it, too," she said.

"What do you think?" he asked.

She thought of the car Presley and the tattooed man had driven across the border, and the money Pete had bugged that had been taken from Presley's office. Although she'd never seen it, she had assumed that it had burned up in the fire. However, the car had been at the back of the house, a distance away from the fire. What if it hadn't burned up? What if Presley's stuff had still been inside? What if they only thought Tutuola had died? She had a very sick feeling in the pit of her stomach that she should have overridden Wilson's urgency to get away and gone back to search the ruins for a body.

Pete frowned. She wasn't answering, which didn't bode well.

"Cat?"

"What?"

"What do you suppose we're seeing?"

She knew the man's name now. Mark Presley had given that up along with everything else when his lawyer had bartered for his life.

Solomon Tutuola had killed her father. He was supposed to be dead. But what if he wasn't?

She rubbed a finger along the scar on her neck and had to clear her throat twice before she could speak. Even then, her voice cracked when she answered.

"I'm not sure, but it just might be a ghost."

The third novel in a sensational new series from
the bestselling author of *Intern* and *Killer Body*

BONNIE HEARN HILL

OFF THE RECORD

The perfect story comes to journalist Geri LaRue when successful
businesswoman Kathleen Fowler is found dead—her battered
body dropped from the balcony of her home to the cliffs
below. But Geri doesn't have to chase this story: she inherits
it. Somehow she's been named the murdered woman's sole
beneficiary, despite never having met her.

As Geri sets out to discover why the estate has been left to her,
everything leads back to her own, troubled childhood. And when
another person is brutally murdered, Geri realizes that the key to
finding a killer may be hidden in her own mind.

"…a real page-turner. Hill gets the reader's attention with a
contemporary issue…intriguing characters and clever plotting."
—*Publishers Weekly* on *Killer Body*

MIRA®

*Available the first week of November 2006
wherever paperbacks are sold!*

REQUEST YOUR
FREE BOOKS!

2 FREE NOVELS
FROM THE ROMANCE/SUSPENSE
COLLECTION PLUS 2 FREE GIFTS!

YES! Please send me 2 FREE novels from the Romance/Suspense Collection and my 2 FREE gifts. After receiving them, if I don't wish to receive any more books, I can return the shipping statement marked "cancel." If I don't cancel, I will receive 4 brand-new novels every month and be billed just $5.24 per book in the U.S., or $5.74 per book in Canada, plus 25¢ shipping and handling per book plus applicable taxes, if any*. That's a savings of at least 10% off the cover price! I understand that accepting the 2 free books and gifts places me under no obligation to buy anything. I can always return a shipment and cancel at any time. Even if I never buy another book from the Reader Service, the two free books and gifts are mine to keep forever.

185 MDN EF3H   385 MDN EF3J

Name	(PLEASE PRINT)	
Address		Apt. #
City	State/Prov.	Zip/Postal Code

Signature (if under 18, a parent or guardian must sign)

Mail to The Reader Service:

IN U.S.A.	IN CANADA
P.O. Box 1867	P.O. Box 609
Buffalo, NY	Fort Erie, Ontario
14240-1867	L2A 5X3

Not valid to current subscribers to the Romance Collection,
the Suspense Collection or the Romance/Suspense Collection.

Want to try two free books from another line?
Call 1-800-873-8635 or visit www.morefreebooks.com.

* Terms and prices subject to change without notice. NY residents add applicable sales tax. Canadian residents will be charged applicable provincial taxes and GST. This offer is limited to one order per household. All orders subject to approval. Credit or debit balances in a customer's account(s) may be offset by any other outstanding balance owed by or to the customer. Please allow 4 to 6 weeks for delivery.

BOB206

SHARON
SALA

MIRA®

www.MIRABooks.com

MSS1106BL